U0051555

NEW TOEIC 新制多益

閱讀 5 回

全真模擬試題 ＋ 詳盡解析

RC

笛藤出版

NEW 新制多益

TOEIC

閱讀5回

全真模擬試題 ＋ 詳盡解析

NEW TOEIC新制多益：閱讀五回 全真模擬試題＋詳盡解析 /
Michael A. Putlack等合著；陳怡臻譯.
-- 初版. -- 臺北市：笛藤, 2020.04
　　面；　公分
ISBN 978-957-710-783-1 (平裝)
1.多益測驗
805.1895　　　　　　　　　　　　　　　　　109004601

2023年8月10日　初版第3刷　定價 430 元

作者	Michael A. Putlack、Stephen Poirier Tony Covello、多樂院多益研究所
譯者	陳怡臻
編輯	江品萱
封面設計	王舒玕
總編輯	洪季楨
編輯企劃	笛藤出版
發行所	八方出版股份有限公司
發行人	林建仲
地址	台北市中山區長安東路二段171號3樓3室
電話	(02) 2777-3682
傳真	(02) 2777-3672
總經銷	聯合發行股份有限公司
地址	新北市新店區寶橋路235巷6弄6號2樓
電話	(02)2917-8022・(02)2917-8042
製版廠	造極彩色印刷製版股份有限公司
地址	新北市中和區中山路2段380巷7號
電話	(02)2240-0333・(02)2248-3904
印刷廠	皇甫彩藝印刷股份有限公司
地址	新北市中和區中正路988巷10號
電話	(02) 3234-5871
郵撥帳戶	八方出版股份有限公司
郵撥帳號	19809050

●本書經合法授權，請勿翻印●
(本書裝訂如有漏印、缺頁、破損，請寄回更換。)

Original Korean language edition was first published in September of 2018 under the title of 500 문제로 끝내는 실전 토익 RC by Darakwon, Inc.
Written by Michael A. Putlack, Stephen Poirier, Tony Covello & Darakwon TOEIC Research Team Copyright ⓒ 2018 by Michael A. Putlack.
All rights reserved.Traditional Chinese translation copyright ⓒ 2020 Ba fun Publishing Co., Ltd.(DEE TEN)
This edition is arranged with Darakwon, Inc. through Pauline Kim Agency, Seoul, Korea. No part of this publication may be reproduced,
stored in a retrieval system or transmitted in any form or by any means, mechanical, photocopying,
recording,or otherwise without a prior written permission of the Proprietor or Copyright holder.

前言

多益在全世界中是具權威的公認英語考試之一。也因為如此，在學校或是職場上判斷一個人的英語實力時，多以多益分數作為標準，但是想要得到期望的分數卻並不容易。

若是想在多益考試中取得理想成績，首先必須要有基本英語實力作為基礎，但即使已經具備基本實力，卻無法瞭解考試的特點或是對考試沒有充分準備的話，在考場上是絕對無法發揮出自己真正的實力。

〈用500個問題完成的多益實戰〉系列是透過針對不同的領域分成的五次模擬考試幫助考生能夠在實際考試中充分地發揮出自己的實力。在這本書中收錄的所有試題都反映出了多益的最新方向，其試題難度也與實際試題難度相同。因此，透過本系列學習的考生們能夠在較短的時間內培養出對於實際面對考試的適應能力。

我們多樂院多益研究所肩負著驕傲及使命感開發了和實際多益試題最為接近的模擬試題，而本系列就是其成果之一。真心地希望透過此書讓所有考生們都能得到自己期望的多益分數。

多樂院多益研究所

目錄

多益是什麼

多益(TOEIC)是Test of English for International Communication的縮寫，這是用來測試非英語系國家的人在國際環境中生活或執行業務時所需要的實用英語能力考試。目前不只是韓國和日本，全世界約有60個國家每年會有400萬名以上的考生報考多益，而其考試結果也會在招聘及晉升、海外派遣工作人員的選拔等多種領域上作為選擇的依據之一。

考試題型

類別	PART	題型內容		題數	作答時間	配分
Listening Comprehension	1	照片描述		6	45分	495分
	2	應答問題		25		
	3	簡短對話		39		
	4	簡短文章		30		
Reading Comprehension	5	句子填空		30	75分	495分
	6	段落填空		16		
	7	閱讀理解	多篇閱讀	29		
			單篇閱讀	28		
TOTAL				200	120分	990分

出題內容

多益考試的目的是為了測試日常生活和執行業務所需要的英語能力，所以出題內容也不會脫離這個範圍。即使是在涉及商務相關主題的情況下，也不會要求具備有專門知識，並且也不會要求瞭解特定國家或文化。具體的出題內容如下。

一般商務（General Business）	契約、協商、行銷、營業、策劃、會議相關
辦公室（Office）	公司內部規定、辦公室流程、辦公室器材及傢俱相關
人事（Personal）	求職、招聘、晉升、退休、工資、獎勵相關
財務（Finance and Budgeting）	投資、稅務、會計、銀行業務相關
製造（Manufacturing）	製造、全套整組設備經營、品質管理相關
開發（Corporate Development）	研究、調查、實驗、新產品研發相關
採購（Purchasing）	購物、訂貨、裝貨、結算相關
外食（Dining Out）	午餐、晚餐、聚餐、招待會相關
保健（Health）	醫院預約、看醫生、醫療保險業務相關
旅遊（Travel）	交通方式、住宿、機票預訂及取消相關
娛樂（Entertainment）	觀看電影及戲劇、欣賞演出、參觀展示會相關
房屋／公司地產（Housing / Corporate Property）	不動產買賣及租賃、電力及瓦斯服務相關

● 考試當天流程

應考生需攜帶身分證（或有個人大頭照之有效證件）及文具(2B鉛筆、橡皮擦)，於考前三十分鐘抵達考場，並依工作人員指示進入考場就座。

時間	行程
9:20 - 9:40	**考場就座** 依准考證號碼依序入座，非考試相關物品須放置於工作人員指定位置。
9:40 - 9:50	**注意事項說明** 在答案卡上寫好姓名、准考證號碼等，並回答有關職業或是應考次數等相關問券調查。
9:50	**測驗時間開始，禁止進入考場** 測驗開始時便禁止出入，遲到者便視同放棄考試資格。
9:50 - 10:05	**核對身分證** 在聽力測驗開始之前，監考人員會核對身分並在答案卡上簽名。 閱讀測驗時，監考人員會再次進行核對並簽名。
10:08 - 10:10	**破損檢查** 確認拿到的試題本有無破損，確認後在試題本上填寫准考證號碼，在答案卡上填寫試題本編號。即使發現試題本有破損，若考試開始的話則不會給予更換試題本，此時重要的是應當要迅速地再檢查過一遍。
10:10 - 10:55	**聽力測驗作答** 45分鐘的時間作答聽力測驗的問題。
10:55 - 12:10	**閱讀測驗作答** 75分鐘的時間作答閱讀測驗的問題。

● 成績查詢

可從台灣區多益官方網站（http://www.toeic.com.tw）查詢成績。
成績單發放則是依照應試者報考時選擇的方式選擇郵寄或是網路發放。

模擬考試分數計算方法

多益分數是以5分為一單位來計分，每領域的滿分都為495分。總分(Total Score)則是會落在10分到990分之間，兩領域都獲得滿分的話則會拿到990分，但是實際成績是根據多益特有的統計處理方式計算，因此不能單純地以正確答案個數或是錯誤答案個數來計算多益成績。但模擬考試通常可以透過下列兩種方法來估算自己的分數。

● 單純利用換算法的情況：以每題5分來計算

聽力測驗答對75題，閱讀測驗答對69題的情況→(375)+(345)=720分

● 利用分數換算表的情況

Listening Comprehension		Reading Comprehension	
答對題數	換算分數	答對題數	換算分數
96-100	475-495	96-100	460-495
91-95	435-495	91-95	425-490
86-90	405-475	86-90	395-465
81-85	370-450	81-85	370-440
76-80	345-420	76-80	335-415
71-75	320-390	71-75	310-390
66-70	290-360	66-70	280-365
61-65	265-335	61-65	250-335
56-60	235-310	56-60	220-305
51-55	210-280	51-55	195-270
46-50	180-255	46-50	165-240
41-45	155-230	41-45	140-215
36-40	125-205	36-40	115-180
31-35	105-175	31-35	95-145
26-30	85-145	26-30	75-120
21-25	60-115	21-25	60-95
16-20	30-90	16-20	45-75
11-15	5-70	11-15	30-55
6-10	5-60	6-10	10-40
1-5	5-50	1-5	5-30
0	5-35	0	5-15

聽力測驗答對90題，閱讀測驗答對76題的情況→(405～475)+(335～415)=740～890分

Actual Test RC

1

READING TEST

In the Reading test, you will read a variety of texts and answer several different types of reading comprehension questions. The entire Reading test will last 75 minutes. There are three parts, and directions are given for each part. You are encouraged to answer as many questions as possible within the time allowed.

You must mark your answers on the separate answer sheet. Do not write your answers in your test book.

PART 5

Directions: A word or phrase is missing in each of the sentences below. Four answer choices are given below each sentence. Select the best answer to complete the sentence. Then mark the letter (A), (B), (C), or (D) on your answer sheet.

101. TR Partners, a consulting firm, ------- to sign contracts with several companies in the next few days.

(A) expecting
(B) expected
(C) expectation
(D) expects

102. The software proved to be unreliable, so the buyer ------- it for another product that worked better.

(A) considered
(B) repaired
(C) uploaded
(D) exchanged

103. Mr. Bender ------- a table for eight at a restaurant, where he intends to entertain some foreign clients.

(A) will book
(B) was booked
(C) will booking
(D) has been booked

104. The Tomato Garden is such a popular restaurant that diners must sometimes wait an hour to be -------.

(A) seats
(B) seating
(C) seated
(D) seat

105. ------- fulfill the order, the assembly line will be kept running for the entire week.

(A) In order to
(B) As a result of
(C) In addition to
(D) In spite of

106. The ------- menu at Pier 88 gives the chef the opportunity to vary the dishes he cooks all year long.

(A) seasoned
(B) seasonal
(C) seasoning
(D) seasons

107. Despite receiving more than fifty applications, only three people were ------- qualified for the position.

(A) carefully
(B) patiently
(C) fully
(D) purposely

108. ------- for the project was given to Angela Turner, who will be assisted by Frank Grant.

(A) Response
(B) Responsiveness
(C) Responsibility
(D) Responding

109. The Lexington Zoo is looking for individuals interested in volunteering ------- and help take care of its animals.

(A) to feed
(B) feeding
(C) will feed
(D) feed

110. Each volunteer will be given a voucher that can be ------- for a free meal at Sal's Deli.

(A) approved
(B) converted
(C) purchased
(D) redeemed

111. ------- Ms. Winters is retiring from the company, there will not be a farewell party held for her.

(A) Moreover
(B) Although
(C) Because
(D) For

112. Accountants are urged to ------- themselves with the software once it is installed.

(A) familiarize
(B) research
(C) utilize
(D) calculate

113. The company directory is updated on a ------- basis since correcting information online is simple.

(A) temporary
(B) standard
(C) continual
(D) reported

114. Management ------- employees to leave work early if they arrive before the start of the workday.

(A) permits
(B) grants
(C) lets
(D) consents

115. Ravenwood Manufacturing recently acquired Davis, Inc., one of its ------- in the Providence area.

(A) competitions
(B) competitors
(C) competitive
(D) competitively

116. According to reports, the deal with Duncan Electronics could be worth ------- seven million dollars.

(A) most of
(B) up to
(C) as of
(D) in with

117. More than half of the members of the focus group ------- the advertisement for the utility vehicle which they saw.

(A) disliked
(B) were disliked
(C) will be disliked
(D) had been disliked

118. Funds are to be ------- only when a supervisor has authorized the purchase the worker wishes to make.

(A) spend
(B) spending
(C) spends
(D) spent

119. Employees who recommend ------- for a position will receive a $200 bonus should that individual be hired.

(A) something
(B) someone
(C) somewhere
(D) somehow

120. All interactions with clients are ------- unless permission to share information is granted.

(A) confidence
(B) confidential
(C) confiding
(D) confidentiality

GO ON TO THE NEXT PAGE

121. Thus far, little ------- has been made on the blueprints for the building by the lead architect.
(A) design
(B) announcement
(C) progress
(D) proposal

122. Customers have ------- options to choose from when trying to decide which wallpaper to purchase.
(A) such
(B) many
(C) little
(D) any

123. The box was sealed with a lock, and nobody was aware of the combination to open -------.
(A) it
(B) them
(C) those
(D) its

124. Ms. Carter is in line for a promotion if she ------- the merger with Dexter Associates well.
(A) handling
(B) handles
(C) handled
(D) has handled

125. Please ------- to the user's manual if you experience any problems with your newly purchased toaster.
(A) refer
(B) request
(C) renew
(D) revise

126. The building at 49 Cross Street was ------- a theater but has been converted into a department store.
(A) original
(B) originally
(C) origin
(D) originated

127. ------- planning to attend a meeting scheduled for later in the day should cancel it at once.
(A) Each
(B) Another
(C) Anyone
(D) Few

128. Mr. Roberts believes the investors are ------- regarding the viability of the Anderson project.
(A) accused
(B) regarded
(C) involved
(D) mistaken

129. The brochure is extremely -------, so it has been praised by many of the store's customers.
(A) informed
(B) information
(C) informative
(D) informs

130. Even though the furniture requires -------, doing so takes little time or effort.
(A) assembly
(B) purchase
(C) connection
(D) placement

PART 6

Directions: Read the texts that follow. A word, phrase, or sentence is missing in parts of each text. Four answer choices for each question are given below the text. Select the best answer to complete the text. Then mark the letter (A), (B), (C), or (D) on your answer sheet.

Questions 131-134 refer to the following letter.

November 12

Dear Mr. Sullivan,

This is to inform you that payment of the bill dated October 3 has yet -------. The amount
                                                                              131.
on your bill was $894.23, and the minimum monthly payment was $75.00. Payment was

due on October 31. As such, a late ------- of $30 has been applied to your account, and the
                                      132.
entire balance owed is being charged interest at a rate of 17.9%. We encourage you to make

a payment at once. If you are currently ------- financial hardship, please call us at 1-800-
                                          133.
945-9484. -------. Should you have any questions regarding your bill, you can contact us at
           134.
1-800-847-1739.

Sincerely,

Desmond Watts
Customer Service Representative
Silvan Card

---

131. (A) been received
   (B) will receive
   (C) be receiving
   (D) to be received

132. (A) fee
   (B) rate
   (C) salary
   (D) refund

133. (A) experience
   (B) experiencing
   (C) have experienced
   (D) be experienced

134. (A) As a result, your card will be canceled by the end of the month.
   (B) The address you should send the payment to is listed at the bottom of the page.
   (C) You can speak to one of our representatives to work out a repayment plan.
   (D) Instructions on how to get to our main office will be given to you.

GO ON TO THE NEXT PAGE ➡

Questions 135-138 refer to the following e-mail.

To: <undisclosed-recipients@ferris.com>
From: <johnharper@ferris.com>
Subject: Overtime Work
Date: April 19

To all employees,

We have secured several new contracts which will require us to keep the factory open for at least 20 hours a day for the next 2 months. At this time, we have no ------- of hiring new
135.
employees. Instead, we would prefer ------- our current employees work extra hours.
136.

If you are interested in working overtime, particularly on the night shift or on the weekend, please speak with your immediate supervisor at once. -------. You are permitted to work up
137.
to 15 hours of overtime ------- week. You will be compensated at 1.5 times your normal pay
138.
rate. Supervisors will allot hours on a first-come, first-served basis.

Regards,

John Harper
Factory Supervisor
Ferris, Inc.

135. (A) reasons
(B) announcements
(C) intentions
(D) plans

136. (A) that
(B) how
(C) why
(D) which

137. (A) You may also respond to this e-mail.
(B) Your resignation will then be accepted.
(C) This will let you reduce your working hours.
(D) That will begin the process of applying for a transfer.

138. (A) few
(B) many
(C) some
(D) each

Questions 139-142 refer to the following article.

Repair Work at Fullerton Library

Fullerton (March 18) – Last night, the city council voted in ------- of providing enough funds
139.

to repair the parking lot at the Fullerton Library. Library patrons have complained for years

about the potholes and other problems there. -------.
140.

However, the city recently received a grant of one million dollars from the state government.

The money is supposed to be used to improve the city's -------. The library's request of
141.

$60,000 was approved by a vote of 4 to 1. The work is scheduled to begin on March 23 and

should conclude in 5 days. The parking lot will be closed ------- that entire time.
142.

---

139. (A) lieu
(B) favor
(C) appearance
(D) state

140. (A) The city has frequently promised to
improve the library's collection.
(B) This will enable the library to provide
more services for its users.
(C) Yet the city has always claimed it lacked
the money needed for repairs.
(D) As a result, usage of the library has
been higher than ever this year.

141. (A) infrastructure
(B) budget
(C) schools
(D) roads

142. (A) within
(B) during
(C) about
(D) since

GO ON TO THE NEXT PAGE

To: All Managers

From: Jessica Blanco

Subject: Training

Date: August 6

-------. It will instead be held on August 9. In addition, the -------- has been moved. It will
143.   144.

start at 10 in the morning and conclude at noon. Finally, the instructor will not be Timothy

Warden but has been changed to Simon Palmer. Mr. Warden has to visit the home office on

an important project all week, which is -------- the session has been delayed.
                                        145.

Please inform any employees of yours who are scheduled to attend the session. If you are

-------- who should be there, call me at extension 46, and I can inform you of that.
146.

143. (A) We are pleased to announce that Mr.
        Palmer will be handling your training.
    (B) This is a reminder that the training
        session is taking place this afternoon.
    (C) The training session set to be held
        tomorrow has been postponed.
    (D) All employees need to report for their
        training three days from now.

144. (A) day
    (B) instructor
    (C) room
    (D) time

145. (A) how
    (B) why
    (C) where
    (D) what

146. (A) unsure
    (B) pleased
    (C) reported
    (D) aware

PART 7

Directions: In this part you will read a selection of texts, such as magazine and newspaper articles, e-mails, and instant messages. Each text or set of texts is followed by several questions. Select the best answer for each question and mark the letter (A), (B), (C), or (D) on your answer sheet.

Questions 147-148 refer to the following letter.

December 16

Dear Sir/Madam,

Last night, I visited your store, Deacon's Clothing Store, at the Cloverdale Mall to do some shopping for the upcoming holiday. I found several items I was interested in purchasing yet was unable to acquire them. There were just too many people waiting in line at the checkout counter.

I understand more shoppers than usual are visiting your store these days. However, there were more than twenty people standing in line, but only a single cash register was open. In addition, I saw at least two employees who weren't doing anything at that time. I wonder why they didn't open a second register. As I was in a hurry, I departed the store without buying anything and instead shopped at one of your competitors on the other side of the mall.

Regretfully,

Cynthia Harris

147. What problem does Ms. Harris mention?

(A) Some items were unavailable.
(B) An employee was rude to her.
(C) She could not try any clothes on.
(D) The waiting time was too long.

148. What did Ms. Harris do after leaving Deacon's Clothing Store?

(A) She visited another store.
(B) She went to a different shopping center.
(C) She ordered some items online.
(D) She called the store to complain.

GO ON TO THE NEXT PAGE

Questions 149-150 refer to the following text message chain.

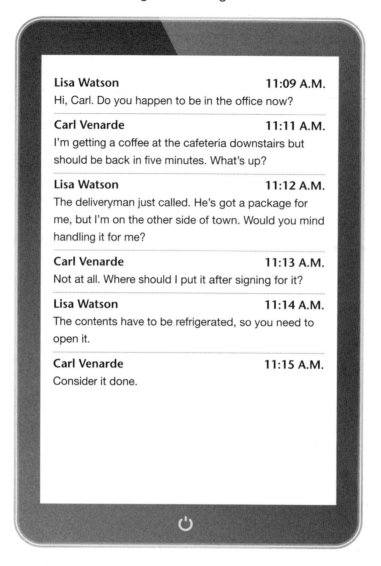

Lisa Watson	11:09 A.M.

Hi, Carl. Do you happen to be in the office now?

Carl Venarde	11:11 A.M.

I'm getting a coffee at the cafeteria downstairs but should be back in five minutes. What's up?

Lisa Watson	11:12 A.M.

The deliveryman just called. He's got a package for me, but I'm on the other side of town. Would you mind handling it for me?

Carl Venarde	11:13 A.M.

Not at all. Where should I put it after signing for it?

Lisa Watson	11:14 A.M.

The contents have to be refrigerated, so you need to open it.

Carl Venarde	11:15 A.M.

Consider it done.

149. Why did Ms. Watson write to Mr. Venarde?

(A) To have him contact a deliveryman
(B) To ask him to do a favor for her
(C) To inquire about an item he ordered
(D) To tell him to mail a package at the post office

150. At 11:15 A.M., what does Mr. Venarde mean when he writes, "Consider it done"?

(A) He already signed for the package.
(B) He just returned to the office.
(C) He will put some items in a refrigerator.
(D) He will pay the delivery fee.

Questions 151-152 refer to the following receipt.

Medford Deli
42 Anchor Street
Medford, IL

Item	Quantity	Price
Ham & Cheese Sandwich	1	$ 5.99
Pasta Salad	2	$13.98
Turkey Breast	1	$ 7.99
Eggplant Parmesan	1	$ 8.49
	Subtotal	**$36.45**
	Tax	**$ 1.82**
	Delivery	**$ 7.00**
	Total	**$45.27**

Your order was paid for with the credit card ending in 8944. Thank you for your business.

151. What is indicated on the receipt?

(A) The customer paid cash for the items.
(B) The customer bought one of each item.
(C) The customer received a discount.
(D) The customer paid to have the order delivered.

152. According to the receipt, which item is the most expensive?

(A) Eggplant parmesan
(B) Pasta salad
(C) Ham and cheese sandwich
(D) Turkey breast

GO ON TO THE NEXT PAGE

Questions 153-154 refer to the following announcement.

 Book Giveaway

This Saturday, August 10, the Midtown Library will be holding its annual book giveaway. The library will give away many of its older, unread books to make room for new arrivals. The event will take place in the library's main lobby from 12 P.M. to 3 P.M. Each person is permitted to take no more than five books for as long as supplies last. Included in the event will be books for people of all ages. Many science-fiction books, fantasy novels, and romance books will be given away, and there are an especially large number of children's books that must be disposed of. No reservations are necessary, but only residents of Midtown may participate in this event.

153. What is NOT mentioned about the event?

(A) There is a limit on the number of books people can acquire.

(B) Only people from a specific area may take books.

(C) Books in several different genres will be included in it.

(D) It is scheduled to take place over the entire weekend.

154. What is suggested about the books at the event?

(A) Some of them can be acquired for a small fee.

(B) Visitors may not take them until they pay their library fines.

(C) There are more children's books than other genres.

(D) Many of them will be recently released books.

Questions 155-157 refer to the following e-mail.

To: customerservice@kerrigans.com
From: geraldlong@mymail.comm
Subject: Easy Reader
Date: April 21

To Whom It May Concern,

My name is Gerald Long, and my membership number is 3840-939348. I have been a longtime customer of yours and have never had any problems with my purchases until now. —[1]–. However, on April 10, I bought an Easy Reader from your Web site. I was very excited to start reading e-books, so I ordered five e-books as soon as my Easy Reader arrived the following day. —[2]–. Unfortunately, last night, my Easy Reader suddenly turned off and wouldn't turn back on again. —[3]–. I know that it's not a battery problem because I recharged it immediately prior to using it.

I tried operating it again this morning, but it still wouldn't operate properly. —[4]–. I'd like to get my Easy Reader fixed without having to return it to you by mail. Is it possible for me to have it fixed at my local Kerrigan's?

I would appreciate a prompt response to my inquiry.

Regards,

Gerald Long

---

155. What happened on April 10?

(A) An order was received.
(B) An item stopped working.
(C) A purchase was made.
(D) A battery malfunctioned.

156. What would Mr. Long prefer to do?

(A) Have his Easy Reader repaired at a store
(B) Receive a refund on his Easy Reader
(C) Get instructions on how to repair his Easy Reader
(D) Request a repairperson visit his home

157. In which of the positions marked [1], [2], [3], and [4] does the following sentence best belong?

"I have no idea what I should do now."

(A) [1]
(B) [2]
(C) [3]
(D) [4]

GO ON TO THE NEXT PAGE

Questions 158-161 refer to the following memo.

MEMO

To: All Employees
From: Nancy Clark, HR Department
Re: Intranet System
Date: October 9

Please be aware that the IT team has just completed the installation of the new companywide intranet system. Before you will be given an ID and a password, you must take a training course to learn to how utilize the system properly.

Starting tonight, we will be providing training sessions each evening for the rest of the week. The sessions will start at 6 P.M. and will last until 8 P.M. There will be two simultaneous sessions in rooms 304 and 305. A maximum of 20 individuals can take a session at the same time. Each employee must undergo the training at least once.

Your department heads will provide you with the schedule. You are free to switch days with another employee if the day assigned to you does not fit your schedule. However, both employees changing days must confirm this with their managers. Should you be unable to be trained at any time this week, speak with your supervisor at once.

As the sessions will take place outside normal working hours, you will receive two hours of overtime, which will be reflected in your next paycheck.

158. Why was the memo sent?
(A) To provide information on an educational course
(B) To request feedback on the training sessions
(C) To encourage managers to speak with their workers
(D) To confirm that employees will be paid for the training

159. What will each employee receive after completing the training?
(A) A promotion
(B) A certificate
(C) A user ID and a password
(D) A manual for the intranet

160. What is NOT true about the training?
(A) It will last until the end of the week.
(B) The classes will last for two hours.
(C) There will be two classes each day.
(D) At least 20 students must take each class.

161. What should employees switching schedules do?
(A) Contact the trainer
(B) Talk to their bosses
(C) Get permission in writing
(D) Check the schedule

Questions 162-164 refer to the following advertisement.

Introducing the New Waycool Refrigerator

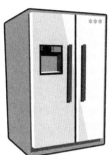

The Belmont Corporation is proud to introduce the perfect refrigerator for the twenty-first century: the Waycool. It has everything you could possibly need in a refrigerator and more. This refrigerator-freezer has plenty of space for fresh fruits and vegetables, meats, beverages, and frozen foods. You'll love the individual compartments that permit you to separate foods from one another to keep your refrigerator well organized.

The Waycool comes with the world's fastest-filling ice maker, which is capable of producing one liter of ice cubes every five minutes. The thru-the-door ice and water dispensers provide convenient access for drinks and also contain child locks to avoid nasty mishaps. Internally, the water is filtered before it gets to the dispenser, ensuring you get the cleanest and freshest water possible. Inside the Waycool, you can control the precise temperature by using the digital control, or you can download the voice-controlled app. The app also runs the child lock and ice and water dispensers.

The Waycool comes in four separate models in three colors and is sold at prices starting at $899. Visit www.belmont.com/waycool to learn more about the Waycool.

---

162. According to the advertisement, what will customers like about the Waycool?

(A) Its unique design
(B) Its multiple colors
(C) Its various sections
(D) Its large size

163. What is NOT mentioned as a feature of the Waycool?

(A) The ability to lock parts of it
(B) An internal light
(C) A fast ice maker
(D) Temperature controls

164. What is indicated about the Waycool?

(A) It has been on the market for years.
(B) The refrigerator comes in four colors.
(C) The newest version does not have a freezer.
(D) Some models may cost more than $899.

GO ON TO THE NEXT PAGE

Questions 165-168 refer to the following article.

www.prwmanufacturing.com

| HOME | ABOUT US | OUR PRODUCTS | NEWSLETTER | CONTACT US |

Health at PRW Manufacturing
by Oriana Verducci

Last year, more employees than ever before took time off due to sickness. Others reported health issues which resulted in lower productivity. As such, the company has determined that it must make employee health a primary focus during the next twelve months.

Yesterday, Vice President of Personnel Daniel Herbst announced that the company is taking several steps toward improving the health of everyone at the firm. He started by discussing the food at the company cafeteria. —[1]—. This weekend, a salad bar will be installed at the cafeteria to provide more green vegetables for employees. In addition, the cafeteria will serve fewer fried foods and will instead offer healthier and more nutritious options. —[2]—. Vending machines will no longer sell chocolate, chips, and other junk food but will instead contain fresh fruit such as oranges, apples, and bananas.

The firm has also taken out a group membership for all employees at the Silver Star Health Club located at 129 Hampton Lane, a mere two-minute walk from the front gate. —[3]—. All employees need to do is show their company ID to be able to work out there for free.

Finally, the company will be conducting health screenings for all employees during the month of April. These checkups will test employees' physical condition and check for any major diseases or health issues. —[4]—. Mr. Herbst stated that the schedule would be posted sometime in the middle of March.

---

165. What is suggested about PRW Manufacturing?

(A) It is charging employees more for health insurance.
(B) It was negatively affected by sick employees last year.
(C) It will give bonuses to employees who get in good shape.
(D) It has installed a health clinic in its facility.

166. What is NOT mentioned about the changes in food service?

(A) Certain foods will no longer be available.
(B) Many new foods will be nutritious.
(C) Fried foods will not be sold anymore.
(D) Employees will be able to eat salads.

167. How can employees gain access to the Silver Star Health Club?

(A) By registering online
(B) By paying a monthly fee
(C) By contacting a supervisor
(D) By bringing a work ID

168. In which of the positions marked [1], [2], [3], and [4] does the following sentence best belong?

"There will be no noticeable difference in the prices of the dishes either."

(A) [1]
(B) [2]
(C) [3]
(D) [4]

Questions 169-171 refer to the following e-mail.

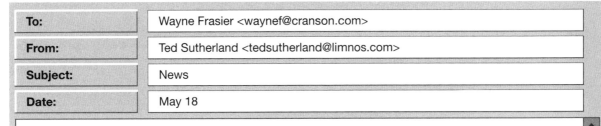

To:	Wayne Frasier <waynef@cranson.com>
From:	Ted Sutherland <tedsutherland@limnos.com>
Subject:	News
Date:	May 18

Dear Mr. Frasier,

I need to inform you of something which has just come up. While I was looking forward to attending the conference in Dallas five days from now, it appears that I must alter my plans. There is a major problem at my firm's factory in Berlin, and the CEO has decided to send me there to deal with it. I'm scheduled to fly there tonight.

I have no idea when I am going to be back in the country, but I was told to expect to be there for at least one week. As a result, it appears as though I will not be able to attend the conference.

I regret doing this since I was scheduled to be the keynote speaker. Fortunately, I know someone who would be an ideal replacement. His name is Fred Peterson, and he is a researcher in my laboratory. He knows a great deal about robot technology and is also an accomplished speaker. He indicated to me that he is willing to speak in my place and doesn't mind giving the speech I had already prepared. I have given him your e-mail address so that the two of you can discuss the matter. I hope this works out to your advantage.

Sincerely,

Ted Sutherland

169. What is the purpose of the e-mail?

(A) To make a reservation
(B) To confirm an agreement
(C) To discuss an upcoming talk
(D) To cancel a scheduled appearance

170. Why will Mr. Sutherland go to Berlin?

(A) To give a speech
(B) To attend a conference
(C) To visit a company facility
(D) To interview for a position

171. What does Mr. Sutherland suggest about Mr. Peterson?

(A) He intends to write his own speech.
(B) He will contact Mr. Frasier soon.
(C) He will be promoted to manager.
(D) He already registered for the conference.

GO ON TO THE NEXT PAGE

Brenda Long [1:11 P.M.]		The meeting regarding sales last quarter has just been scheduled. It's set to take place this Friday morning right after the weekly staff meeting.
Harold Pruitt [1:13 P.M.]		Who's giving the presentation for our team? I haven't seen any of the details yet.
Brenda Long [1:15 P.M.]		Me neither. Frederick, do you happen to have the sales figures and other information we need?
Frederick Patton [1:16 P.M.]		Yes, I just got everything ten minutes ago. I'll send it to both of you now.
Harold Pruitt [1:17 P.M.]		How did we do? Was our performance as good as we had expected it to be?
Frederick Patton [1:19 P.M.]		Open your e-mail and take a look for yourself. Then tell me what you think.
Brenda Long [1:23 P.M.]		Wow. It looks like we're in line for bonuses.
Harold Pruitt [1:24 P.M.]		You can say that again. Anyway, which of us should give the presentation?
Frederick Patton [1:25 P.M.]		Brenda, you've been here the longest. It will look better if you do it.
Brenda Long [1:26 P.M.]		That sounds reasonable.

Send

172. What is supposed to happen on Friday?

(A) Bonuses will be awarded.
(B) An agenda will be released.
(C) A presentation will be rehearsed.
(D) A sales meeting will be held.

173. How does Mr. Patton give the agenda to Mr. Pruitt and Ms. Long?

(A) By presenting it in person
(B) By sending it by fax
(C) By sending it via e-mail
(D) By having an intern deliver it

174. At 1:23 P.M., what does Ms. Long imply when she writes, "It looks like we're in line for bonuses"?

(A) She expects to receive more than last year.
(B) She is satisfied with her bonus.
(C) She just looked at the sales figures.
(D) She has already passed her sales quota.

175. What does Ms. Long agree to do?

(A) Speak at an upcoming meeting
(B) Lead an orientation session
(C) Give some advice to Mr. Pruitt
(D) Help Mr. Patton with the agenda

GO ON TO THE NEXT PAGE

Open Position at PTR, Inc.

PTR, Inc. is a manufacturer of high-end electronics which currently has an opening for an assembly line manager at its newest facility. The ideal candidate should have a minimum of seven years of management experience. A college degree is not required but is desired. The person selected for the job needs the ability to get along well with others and also possess outstanding time-management and communication skills. This is a full-time position that will require working overtime on occasion, but extra work will be paid at overtime rates. The starting salary is $62,000, and benefits will be provided. They include a pension and medical insurance. Send your application to Henry Coburn at henry_c@ptr.com by August 10. Only qualified individuals will receive responses, and those who are selected for an interview will be required to complete a test of their skills and abilities.

To:	henry_c@ptr.com
From:	mauricedavidson@mymail.com
Subject:	Open Position
Date:	August 4

Dear Mr. Coburn,

My name is Maurice Davidson, and I am interested in the assembly line manager position at your company. I have attached my résumé and application form to this e-mail so that you can take a look at my qualifications.

I am presently employed at Kendrick Motors, where I manage the assembly line at its Scottsdale plant. I have worked here for the past five years, and I get along well with both management and my employees. There have never been any injuries in the factory while I have been working. I really enjoy my job and would prefer to remain here, but I will be moving to Richmond because my wife accepted a job there.

I am able to interview by phone or in person, but should you need me to be there in person, I will have to make travel arrangements, which could take some time. Please contact me with any questions. I look forward to hearing from you soon.

Sincerely,

Maurice Davidson

176. What is NOT indicated about the assembly line manager position?

(A) It may require a person to work long hours.
(B) The person who does it must have prior experience.
(C) A college degree is necessary for it.
(D) The ability to speak well to others is important.

177. According to the advertisement, what will people being interviewed have to do?

(A) Prove their knowledge
(B) Meet with the CEO
(C) Negotiate their salary
(D) Show their leadership skills

178. Why did Mr. Davidson send the e-mail?

(A) To accept an offer of employment
(B) To schedule an interview
(C) To inquire about the requirements of a job
(D) To express interest in a position

179. What does Mr. Davidson mention about his work at Kendrick Motors?

(A) He has been there for more than a decade.
(B) It involves him working with upper management.
(C) It has resulted in increased efficiency.
(D) He has kept his employees safe.

180. What is suggested about PTR, Inc.?

(A) It is expanding into foreign markets.
(B) It opened a new building in Richmond.
(C) It expects to make a profit this year.
(D) It has several positions that are open.

GO ON TO THE NEXT PAGE

Questions 181-185 refer to the following order form and e-mail.

Florence Catering Services

1010 Lincoln Ave.
Tulsa, OK 74108
(539) 830-9101

Customer Name	Tom Snyder	Company Name	Harrison Manufacturing
Phone Number	(539) 239-8347	E-Mail Address	t_snyder@hm.com
Address	483 Main Street, Tulsa, OK 74111		
Deliver To	Main Entrance, Forest Park, Tulsa, OK 74109		
Order Date	June 28	Delivery Date	July 15

Product Number	Description	Quantity	Price
4830	Sandwich Platter (Large)	3	$210.00
1012	Salad Platter (Large)	2	$ 80.00
3829	Italian Sampler Platter (Medium)	2	$130.00
8393	Dessert Tray (Large)	3	$120.00
7331	Assorted Beverages (Large)	4	$200.00
		Subtotal	$ 740.00
		Delivery	$ 0.00
		Tax	$ 37.00
		Total	$ 777.00

Thank you doing business with us. Your order has been paid for using the credit card ending in 7484. If you have any questions or requests, please contact us at orders@florencecatering.com, and we will do our best to accommodate you.

To: t_snyder@hm.com
From: orders@florencecatering.com
Re: Your Order
Date: June 30

Dear Mr. Snyder,

We received the online order form you submitted as well as the questions you contacted us with yesterday. First, I would like to confirm your order. A representative from Florence Catering Services will arrive with the items at 11:00 A.M. on July 15 and will assist you in setting up everything.

To answer the inquiry that you were the most concerned about, one of the dessert items has peanuts in it. It is clearly labeled, so your employee with a peanut allergy has no need to worry. In addition, I regret to inform you that we do not sell salmon this time of year. However, we could easily provide you with plenty of hamburger patties, hotdogs, and buns to have a cookout. We can even bring a couple of grills if you are interested. This will require the payment of a fee to rent the grills, and you will be charged for any propane gas you use.

Please let me know if there is anything else I can do for you.

Regards,

Melanie Jackson
Florence Catering Services

181. What information is NOT included on the order form?

    (A) How many people the food is for
    (B) Who made the order
    (C) What the total price is
    (D) Where the items will be sent

182. On the order form, the word "accommodate" paragraph 1, line 3, is closest in meaning to

    (A) house
    (B) assist
    (C) lend
    (D) update

183. According to Ms. Jackson, what will happen on July 15?

    (A) Food will be delivered.
    (B) A bill will be paid.
    (C) An order will be confirmed.
    (D) New foods will arrive.

184. Which item contains something one of Mr. Snyder's employees cannot eat?

    (A) Product number 4830
    (B) Product number 1012
    (C) Product number 3829
    (D) Product number 8393

185. Why did Ms. Jackson suggest Mr. Snyder have a cookout?

    (A) To respond positively to Mr. Snyder's question
    (B) To propose some alternative foods
    (C) To encourage Mr. Snyder to rent some grills
    (D) To mention a special offer that is available

GO ON TO THE NEXT PAGE

Questions 186-190 refer to the following online order form and e-mails.

◀ ▶   www.westendstyle.com

Customer Name   Heidi Mann
E-Mail Address   hmann@homemail.com
Mailing Address   483 Beaumont Avenue, Las Alamos, NM
Membership Number   859403
Total Number of Orders   9
Order Date   May 12

Item Number	Description	Quantity	Price
340834	High-Heeled Shoes (Black Leather)	1	$120.00
923409	Blouse (Small, Blue)	2	$ 40.00
812374	Sweater (Small, White)	1	$ 35.00
238433	T-Shirt (Small, Red)	1	$ 25.00
		Subtotal	$220.00
		Delivery	$ 00.00
		Total	$220.00

* Your order has been paid for with the credit card ending in 8433.
* All orders totaling $200 or more receive free overnight shipping.
* Click here to learn about our special sales this month.

Thank you for shopping at West End Style.

To:	hmann@homemail.com
From:	customerservice@westendstyle.com
Subject:	Your Order
Date:	May 12

Dear Ms. Mann,

We received the order you made last night and are currently processing it. While we are pleased to inform you that three of the items you ordered are available, the sweater which you requested is currently out of stock. According to our records, this item will not be available until later this fall when we start selling sweaters again. We can either refund the money you paid for the item or replace it with another one. In the meantime, we have mailed the other items you ordered so that you can receive them by tomorrow. Should you decide to order an additional item, we will send it by regular mail for no charge.

Sincerely,

Russell Washington
West End Style

To:	hmann@homemail.com
From:	customerservice@westendstyle.com
Subject:	Your Order
Date:	May 13

Dear Ms. Mann,

This is notification that your replacement order has been processed and is being mailed at once. The item you purchased cost $30, so an extra $5 has been credited to your account. In addition, we apologize that the item you initially ordered was not available. Please download the attached coupon. You can use it to get 50% off any one item of your choice the next time you order with us. There is no expiration date for this coupon. Please be aware that upon making your next order, you will become a VIP shopper at West End Style, which comes with a variety of privileges. If you have any questions in the future, please call our toll-free hotline at 1-888-394-8333.

Sincerely,

Ashley Harper
Customer Service Representative
West End Style

186. Why did Ms. Mann receive free shipping?

(A) She is a VIP shopper.
(B) She spent more than $200.
(C) She belongs to a shopping club.
(D) She used a coupon.

187. What item is currently unavailable?

(A) Item number 340834
(B) Item number 923409
(C) Item number 812374
(D) Item number 238433

188. What does Mr. Washington indicate about Ms. Mann's order?

(A) Part of it is being shipped.
(B) It is eligible for a bulk discount.
(C) The price of one item has been reduced.
(D) It was placed over the telephone.

189. What does Ms. Harper give Ms. Mann?

(A) A full refund
(B) A new password
(C) A buy-one, get-one-free coupon
(D) Store credit

190. What is suggested about VIP shoppers at West End Style?

(A) They spend an average of $100 per order.
(B) They have made at least ten orders.
(C) They make a purchase once a month.
(D) They receive discounts of up to 50%.

GO ON TO THE NEXT PAGE

ISA

February 26

Dear Ms. Sullivan,

The International Society of Architects (ISA) is meeting this summer in London, England from July 9-12. As a member of the ISA, you are invited to attend. The theme of this year's event is "new technology in architectural designs." The keynote speaker is Mr. William Forsythe, a world-famous architect and the owner of Croswell Architecture. There will be numerous seminars as well as presentations, conferences, and workshops. The daily topics are the following:

July 9	current technology in architecture
July 10	future technology in architecture
July 11	international trends in architecture
July 12	the overall state of architecture

We have enclosed a registration form. If you wish to attend, please complete it and return it by June 30. You may also register online. The registration fee for members is $90.

Sincerely,

Cindy Nguyen

Cindy Nguyen
Vice President
International Society of Architects

To: Tracy Perry, Gordon Scott, Alexis Montgomery, Sabrina Murray
From: Cynthia Sullivan
Date: March 10
Subject: ISA Meeting

I have been informed that you are eligible to attend the ISA meeting in London. If you're interested in going, the firm will pay for a round-trip economy-class ticket to London, hotel accommodations, and the registration fee. There's only enough money in the budget for two hotel rooms, so you'll have to share the rooms. You'll also receive $60 a day for meals. Please let me know by the end of the month if you'll be attending. I'll then instruct our travel agent to make the necessary arrangements. I'll do my best to get you on the same flight as Mr. Forsythe so that you can travel with the boss.

To: Cindy Nguyen
From: Cynthia Sullivan
Subject: Registration
Date: June 29

Dear Mr. Nguyen,

Hello. My name is Cynthia Sullivan. I am a member of the ISA (membership number 1934129). I registered four employees at my firm for the meeting in March, but I would like to sign up an additional person. Unfortunately, when I tried registering her on the ISA Web site, I was unable to complete the process. When I did the same thing in March, I had no problems, but the Web site simply didn't work this time.

There is not enough time to send a paper application form, so I wonder if you can assist me. Could you please let me know what I should do?

Regards,

Cynthia Sullivan

---

191. What is true about the ISA meeting?

(A) It will have a keynote speech every day.
(B) It charges a higher rate for nonmembers.
(C) It is only taking place on the weekend.
(D) It requires advance registration.

192. When would an attendee learn about architecture in different countries?

(A) On July 9
(B) On July 10
(C) On July 11
(D) On July 12

193. What is indicated about Ms. Sullivan?

(A) She works at Croswell Architecture.
(B) She frequently visits London.
(C) She will attend the meeting in London.
(D) She does not belong to the ISA.

194. What did Ms. Sullivan do for Mr. Scott in March?

(A) Signed him up for a meeting
(B) Reserved his plane ticket
(C) Introduced him to Mr. Forsythe
(D) Permitted him to attend a special event

195. What does Ms. Sullivan request Ms. Nguyen do?

(A) Call her at her office
(B) Help her register a colleague
(C) Cancel a registration
(D) Assist with booking accommodations

GO ON TO THE NEXT PAGE

Special Event

After thirty-two years here, Erica Yang is resigning from Cross Airlines to enjoy some time with her family. To honor her service, there will be a party for Erica in the grand ballroom of the Madison Hotel on Friday, November 6. The party will start at 6:30 in the evening and will end around 9:00. All employees are invited. If you plan to be there, please let Kelly Arbor in HR know by 6:00 P.M. on Monday, November 2. We intend to purchase a gift for Erica, so please feel free to give Kelly whatever you can afford.

Madison Hotel

Special Events Reservation Form

Company	Cross Airlines
Address	829 Airport Boulevard, Springfield, IL
Contact	Kelly Arbor
Phone Number	854-3029
E-Mail Address	karbor@crossair.com
Room Rented	Grand Ballroom
Date	Saturday, November 7
Time	6:30 P.M. - 9:00 P.M.
Number of Expected Guests	120
Catering Service	[✓] Yes [ ] No
Number of Meals	120

Special Requests: The room should have a stage with a microphone and a/v equipment. We need 20 vegetarian meals. We will order the other 100 meals from the regular menu.

Customer's Signature:	Manager's Signature:
Kelly Arbor	*Dave Fleming*
Date: *October 31*	Date: *October 31*

To: Teresa St. Clair
From: Brian Crosby
Subject: Erica's Party
Date: November 3

Teresa,

I wonder if you can give me a hand with something. It looks like I'll be able to attend Erica's party after all. My business trip is going extremely well. I had been expecting to stay in Buenos Aires until the weekend, but it appears as though we'll be signing a contract tomorrow. That means I'll be flying home two days from now. I don't know the contact person's e-mail address or phone number, so I'd appreciate your letting her know I'm planning to be there. And if you would contribute $30 for a gift for me, that would be great. I'll pay you back when I return to the office.

Thanks a lot.

Brian

196. Why is the party being held?

(A) To celebrate a retirement
(B) To hand out awards
(C) To introduce a new employee
(D) To honor the CEO

197. According to the form, what information in the notice is incorrect?

(A) The number of attendees at the event
(B) The date of the event
(C) The time of the event
(D) The location of the event

198. What is NOT requested on the form?

(A) Meals with no meat
(B) A microphone
(C) Floral arrangements
(D) A stage

199. What does Mr. Crosby ask Ms. St. Clair to do?

(A) Sign a contract he will fax her
(B) Talk to Ms. Arbor about him
(C) Book a return flight for him
(D) Purchase a present for Ms. Yang

200. In the e-mail, the word "contribute" in paragraph 1, line 4, is closest in meaning to

(A) suggest
(B) offer
(C) donate
(D) lend

Stop! This is the end of the test. If you finish before time is called, you may go back to Parts 5, 6, and 7 and check your work.

Actual Test

Test

RC

2

READING TEST

In the Reading test, you will read a variety of texts and answer several different types of reading comprehension questions. The entire Reading test will last 75 minutes. There are three parts, and directions are given for each part. You are encouraged to answer as many questions as possible within the time allowed.

You must mark your answers on the separate answer sheet. Do not write your answers in your test book.

PART 5

Directions: A word or phrase is missing in each of the sentences below. Four answer choices are given below each sentence. Select the best answer to complete the sentence. Then mark the letter (A), (B), (C), or (D) on your answer sheet.

101. Ms. Shaw's ------- personality makes her an ideal mentor for many young employees.

(A) approaching
(B) approached
(C) approachable
(D) approachably

102. No orders have been received on the Web site ------- four o'clock in the afternoon.

(A) because
(B) when
(C) even
(D) since

103. The customer ------- that she had the right to return the item even though she lacked a receipt.

(A) insisted
(B) criticized
(C) talked
(D) resorted

104. Mr. Flanders made the decision to invest in the commodities market on -------.

(A) his
(B) him
(C) himself
(D) his own

105. Several celebrities ------- to attend the benefit in an attempt to raise a million dollars for charity.

(A) are agreed
(B) have agreed
(C) were agreed
(D) have been agreed

106. Profits rose an ------- amount during the past quarter thanks to the release of the new laptop.

(A) impressed
(B) impression
(C) impressive
(D) impresser

107. More than two million dollars has been ------- for the construction of a new warehouse.

(A) allocated
(B) determined
(C) restored
(D) purchased

108. Max Performance's online survey was completed by ------- 2,500 customers during the past three months.

(A) approximative
(B) approximation
(C) approximated
(D) approximately

109. The Lawrence Gardening Center ------- a variety of free instructional classes during the spring and summer months each year.

(A) offers
(B) is offered
(C) has offered
(D) will offer

110. Dr. Lambert promised to take the ------- train available so that he could arrive on time to give the keynote speech.

(A) early
(B) earlier
(C) earliest
(D) earlies

111. Companies that are ------- upon the weather for business often suffer slowdowns during the winter months.

(A) resilient
(B) considerate
(C) dependent
(D) apparent

112. Outstanding leadership skills and prior experience are ------- necessary for individuals interested in the job.

(A) both
(B) some
(C) much
(D) none

113. Only Cathy Vanderbilt, who is out of the country, is ------- from attending the planning committee's meeting tomorrow.

(A) exemption
(B) exempt
(C) exempting
(D) exemptible

114. The Golden Travel Agency agreed to change the dates of Mr. West's flight without ------- a fee.

(A) considering
(B) approving
(C) charging
(D) verifying

115. ------- having ordered the products three weeks ago, Mr. Roswell has yet to receive any of them.

(A) Despite
(B) However
(C) Since
(D) Moreover

116. Fans around the world are ------- anticipating the release of the next novel by Martin Stewart.

(A) eager
(B) eagerness
(C) eagerly
(D) eagers

117. Customers are permitted to pay their bills in monthly ------- over the course of a year.

(A) issues
(B) units
(C) installments
(D) appropriations

118. According to the company's guidelines, it is suggested ------- employees take one break between the hours of two and six.

(A) what
(B) that
(C) how
(D) when

119. Guests at the facility ------- an escort at all times to ensure they do not visit an off-limits area.

(A) required
(B) are required
(C) require
(D) will be required

120. Until every sales report is submitted, no decisions regarding the company's ------- can be made.

(A) financial
(B) financed
(C) financeable
(D) finances

GO ON TO THE NEXT PAGE

121. Since the patient ------- by health insurance, the cost to him was minimal.

(A) covers
(B) will be covering
(C) was covered
(D) has covered

122. The hiring committee is considering ------- to offer the position to Ms. Medina or Mr. Schultz.

(A) if
(B) what
(C) which
(D) whether

123. The merger between the two groups is still ------- because the lawyers have not yet agreed on some issues.

(A) pending
(B) considering
(C) negotiating
(D) discussing

124. The applicants being considered for the position ------- no later than this Friday.

(A) have interviewed
(B) will be interviewed
(C) are interviewed
(D) have been interviewed

125. Members of the shoppers' club can have their online purchases gift-wrapped at ------- charge.

(A) nothing
(B) not
(C) no
(D) none

126. At a press conference, a spokeswoman issued a ------- about the upcoming acquisition of the construction firm.

(A) statement
(B) release
(C) contract
(D) promise

127. Please look at the attached file to read the ------- for the furniture desired by the client.

(A) specific
(B) specifically
(C) specified
(D) specifications

128. The terms of the contract called for the payment to be made in full ------- the next two months.

(A) for
(B) during
(C) within
(D) since

129. Ms. Grande is aware of what to say at the presentation to get the most ------- response.

(A) considered
(B) positive
(C) convinced
(D) alert

130. Mr. Richardson wrote a ------- report on the possible benefits of opening a branch in Mexico.

(A) comprehended
(B) comprehensive
(C) comprehension
(D) comprehensively

PART 6

Directions: Read the texts that follow. A word, phrase, or sentence is missing in parts of each text. Four answer choices for each question are given below the text. Select the best answer to complete the text. Then mark the letter (A), (B), (C), or (D) on your answer sheet.

Questions 131-134 refer to the following e-mail.

To: jnightingale@homecafe.com
From: sdavidson@andersonfestival.org
Subject: Anderson Festival
Date: August 28

Dear Ms. Nightingale,

Congratulations. You have been selected to be one of the ------- at the Anderson Festival.
131.
You may set up a food truck every day of the festival from September 12 to 15. -------. It
132.
shows where you are permitted to park your truck.

Please be advised that you must be on the festival grounds at least one hour before the

event begins on each day. You are also ------- for keeping the area around your food truck
133.
clean. Failure to do so will result in a warning for the first violation. The second one will result

in your privileges being -------.
134.

Please contact me if you have any questions.

Regards,

Sam Davidson
Organizer, Anderson Festival

---

131. (A) organizers
(B) vendors
(C) sponsors
(D) guests

132. (A) Please refer to the file attached with this e-mail.
(B) You must send a check to cover the deposit by September 4.
(C) This year's festival should be bigger and better than ever.
(D) Several other food trucks will be located near you.

133. (A) responsible
(B) necessary
(C) considerable
(D) accurate

134. (A) suspension
(B) suspense
(C) suspended
(D) suspensive

GO ON TO THE NEXT PAGE

Call for Papers

The International Association of Geologists (IAG) is holding its fifteenth annual conference on March 10-12. The event will take place at the Hampton Conference Center in London, England. Those individuals wishing to present papers at the festival should submit them no later ------- January 10. Submissions must be made over the Internet by sending ------- to
   135.   **136.**
submissions@iag.org. Individuals will be notified by January 31 if their submissions -------.
                                                                          137.
All presenters are responsible for paying for their own transportation and accommodations.
-------. IAG members must pay £60 to attend whereas nonmembers must pay £85.
138.

---

135. (A) when
(B) for
(C) than
(D) as

136. (A) it
(B) him
(C) her
(D) them

137. (A) are accepting
(B) have been accepted
(C) will be accepting
(D) being accepted

138. (A) No more applications are being considered at this time.
(B) The paper you present must be at least ten pages long.
(C) You can apply for a small grant if you require assistance.
(D) However, the registration fee will be waived for them.

Questions 139-142 refer to the following letter.

October 3

Dear Ms. Lambert,

We received your request about altering the date of the flight you're scheduled to go on with your family on December 11. Unfortunately, the airline does not fly to Cairo on the date you requested your flight be changed to. -------. There are still open seats available on the 3:30
139.
P.M. flight on both days. If ------- date fits your new schedule, you are permitted to cancel
140.
your entire tour package. However, there will be a ------- fee of 15% of the value of your
141.
entire group tour. Please call me at 803-8547 during regular business hours so that we can

discuss the ------- in more detail.
142.

Regards,

David Smiley
Papyrus Tours

---

139. (A) Are you considering vacation in a different city?
(B) Would you like to fly on a different airline?
(C) How about flying there on December 9 or 12?
(D) Do you need me to change your hotel as well?

140. (A) neither
(B) both
(C) each
(D) some

141. (A) canceled
(B) canceling
(C) cancelation
(D) cancels

142. (A) refund
(B) matter
(C) offer
(D) response

GO ON TO THE NEXT PAGE

Questions 143-146 refer to the following review.

A New Place to Try Out
by Elena Carter, Staff Reporter

Augusta (October 11) – After undergoing ------- renovations, the Alderson Hotel recently
                                        143.

reopened. One of the numerous changes was the addition of a buffet restaurant, which the

hotel has been ------- as the best in the city. Let me assure you that the statement is correct.
                144.

The selection includes beef, pork, chicken, lamb, fish, and seafood dishes. There are also

numerous side dishes, salad options, and desserts. The food is fresh, and the platters are

------- refilled, so there is no waiting for any food you desire. -------. But it's worth the cost
145.   **146.**

due to the quality of the food. Reservations are recommended, especially for weekends.

---

143. (A) extent
(B) extending
(C) extensive
(D) extendable

144. (A) promoting
(B) requesting
(C) sponsoring
(D) considering

145. (A) fairly
(B) continually
(C) exclusively
(D) variously

146. (A) The price is a bit steep at $95 per
person.
(B) Three banquet rooms are also available
to rent.
(C) You can tell the chefs how to cook your
meat as well.
(D) The waitstaff is highly attentive and
professional.

PART 7

Directions: In this part you will read a selection of texts, such as magazine and newspaper articles, e-mails, and instant messages. Each text or set of texts is followed by several questions. Select the best answer for each question and mark the letter (A), (B), (C), or (D) on your answer sheet.

Questions 147-148 refer to the following announcement.

Summer Picnic

Harris Manufacturing will once again be holding a summer picnic, the most popular event of the year. This year's event promises to be even bigger and better than last year's. It will take place in Forest Park from noon to six in the evening on Saturday, July 28. All employees and their immediate family members are invited. This year, the food we are serving will be the same as we had last year, but to celebrate our recent financial successes, we'll also be grilling steaks and salmon. We'll be playing all sorts of games, so it will be a fun-filled afternoon. Please let Tom Snyder (ext. 91) in HR know if you intend to be there and how many people will be accompanying you. We look forward to seeing you there.

---

147. What is NOT true about the summer picnic?

(A) Steak and salmon will be among the food served.

(B) It is scheduled to take place on the weekend.

(C) There will be games for the attendees to play.

(D) This is the first year that it is being held.

148. What are company employees advised to do?

(A) Tell a colleague they will be attending the event

(B) Purchase tickets for the picnic in advance

(C) Inform Mr. Snyder they need transportation to the event

(D) Let someone know which food they will be bringing

GO ON TO THE NEXT PAGE

Steve Lewis   2:25 P.M.

Hello, Jennifer. There's a man named Percy Sinclair here at the office looking for you.

Jennifer Kelvin   2:26 P.M.

He's already here? Our meeting isn't until an hour from now.

Steve Lewis   2:28 P.M.

He said the roads were clearer than normal, so he didn't get caught in traffic.

Jennifer Kelvin   2:30 P.M.

That explains it. Why don't you ask him to visit the coffee shop downstairs? Tell him I'll be there as soon as I can.

Steve Lewis   2:31 P.M.

He said he'll be there waiting for you when you arrive.

149. At 2:26 P.M., why does Ms. Kelvin write, "He's already here"?

(A) To confirm her response
(B) To express her surprise
(C) To ask for an opinion
(D) To respond to a question

150. What is suggested about Ms. Kelvin?

(A) She will visit a coffee shop before going to the office.
(B) She frequently leaves the office on business.
(C) She has not met Mr. Sinclair in person before.
(D) She gave Mr. Sinclair directions to the office.

Stetson's is here to help you remodel your home or office. We will help you make the most out of the space you have available to create the ideal home or office space.

We'll talk to you to figure out what you want. And then we'll design everything just the way you like it. We purchase directly from major furniture dealers. So you'll always get the lowest prices.

We can provide you with the accessories you need, including lamps, rugs, and artwork. We will provide you with the blinds, curtains, wallpaper, and paint work you want.

Call 980-1823 to request a free estimate now.

151. What most likely is Stetson's?

(A) A furniture store
(B) An architectural firm
(C) An interior designer
(D) A landscaping company

152. What is mentioned about Stetson's?

(A) It does work at residences and businesses.
(B) It provides a money-back guarantee on its work.
(C) It charges clients for providing an estimate.
(D) It has a warehouse full of accessories for clients.

GO ON TO THE NEXT PAGE

Questions 153-154 refer to the following product review.

I can't say enough about the Burger Master Grill made by the Pacific Corporation. The Burger Master is easy to use and cooks food evenly without burning anything. It runs on propane gas, and you can easily control the temperature at which the food cooks. Every spring and summer, I barbecue food with it at least three times a week. The grill is also easy to clean thanks to the fact that the grill grates have no-stick coating on them. The only complaint I have is that the wheels don't rotate well, which makes moving the Burger Master difficult at times. I would love to see this aspect of it changed. Nevertheless, the grill is excellent, and the price can't be beat.

David Carter

153. What is suggested about Mr. Carter?

(A) He uses his grill to cook meat and vegetables.
(B) He enjoys cooking outdoors.
(C) He recently bought a Burger Master Grill.
(D) He is a professional chef.

154. How would Mr. Carter like to see the Burger Master Grill improved?

(A) By adding wheels to it
(B) By changing its appearance
(C) By making it more mobile
(D) By lowering the price

April 28

Dear Mr. Spencer,

I'm sure you have been eagerly awaiting the results of your application. It is my great pleasure to inform you that you have been approved as a member of the Center City Business Association. —[1]—. We're looking forward to the positive contributions we expect you will make to our organization.

Before you can receive your membership card and gain full access to the association, there are a few things you must do. —[2]—. First, a one-time fee of $300 must be paid in addition to the annual membership fee. Afterward, you will only have to pay the regular dues of $100 on an annual basis. —[3]—. Thus, we require a payment of $400 before the association's next meeting. Second, you must attend that meeting, which will be held on Saturday, May 6. —[4]—. You will meet the other new members and then be officially enrolled in the association.

Please contact me at 908-3842 if you require any assistance.

Sincerely,

Stanley Harper
President, Center City Business Association

155. Why did Mr. Harper send the letter?

(A) To request that Mr. Spencer pay a late fee
(B) To provide a status report on an application
(C) To note that all required materials have been submitted
(D) To approve a suggestion made by Mr. Spencer

156. What must Mr. Spencer do by May 6?

(A) Meet the other members of the association
(B) Pick up his membership card
(C) Make a payment of $400
(D) Speak with Mr. Harper in person

157. In which of the positions marked [1], [2], [3], and [4] does the following sentence best belong?

"Congratulations on this achievement."

(A) [1]
(B) [2]
(C) [3]
(D) [4]

GO ON TO THE NEXT PAGE

Cardiff Ski Resort Set to Reopen
by Roger McCabe

Florence (November 10) – Florence's only place for skiing, the Cardiff Ski Resort, is planning to reopen on December 1 this year. This should come as a welcome surprise to many eager skiers who were concerned the resort might not open until January.

Janet Marston has spent the last five months overseeing the renovating of the place. Among the improvements ordered by the owner were an addition to the main ski lodge, the installation of a new ski lift system, and the construction of two new ski slopes. A new kitchen and ten bedrooms were built in the main ski lodge, so there are now thirty rooms available for rent. There is also a new lounge with an enormous fireplace for skiers to gather around to warm themselves up after coming in from off the slopes. The entire interior has been redone in wood paneling with a wilderness motif.

"I decided to improve the way the resort looks," remarked Ms. Marston. "And I'm incredibly pleased with the results." As for the ski lift, it uses the latest technology to provide users with a smooth, safe, and swift trip to the top of Cardiff Mountain, where they can easily reach all of the slopes on the mountain. The two new slopes include one exclusively for snowboarders, who now comprise around 30% of all visitors to the resort.

158. What is the article mainly about?

(A) Winter sports on Cardiff Mountain
(B) The changes made to a ski resort
(C) Activities that can be done near Florence
(D) The increase in the popularity of skiing

159. What is suggested about the Cardiff Ski Resort?

(A) It opened several decades ago.
(B) It was built halfway up Cardiff Mountain.
(C) It provides special rates for groups.
(D) It is located near Florence.

160. Who is Ms. Marston?

(A) The owner of a resort
(B) A ski instructor
(C) A resident of Florence
(D) A resort employee

161. What is mentioned about the new slopes on Cardiff Mountain?

(A) They are both only for snowboarders.
(B) They are considered advanced courses.
(C) They are not yet ready for skiers.
(D) They are located close to the ski lift.

Questions 162-164 refer to the following memo.

To: All Department Heads, Susan Rogers, Joseph Roth, Erica Dane
From: Aaron Hoyle, Vice President
Subject: Meeting
Date: September 21

Several departments are on pace to surpass their annual budgets while three have already spent their entire allotment for the year. This type of overspending has gotten out of control and must be halted.

CFO David Winter is displeased with the amount of spending going on and intends to address this issue immediately. Tomorrow at one, he will lead a meeting in the large conference room on the fifth floor. All department heads and upper-level accountants are required to attend. This meeting will last the entire afternoon, so cancel any other plans you have scheduled. No absences will be permitted unless you are already out of town.

Please come prepared with your department's annual budget as well as documentation of all the spending done in your department for the entire year. Be prepared to share this information with your colleagues. We will also be discussing potential avenues for reducing spending as well as the implementation of various policies regarding spending procedures.

Each attendee may bring one assistant to help with documents and notetaking.

162. What problem does Mr. Hoyle mention?

(A) Departments are spending too much money.
(B) The company's budget is being reduced.
(C) Spending procedures are difficult to understand.
(D) Departments are keeping poor records.

163. Who is NOT expected to be in attendance at the meeting?

(A) Some accountants
(B) The company's CEO
(C) Mr. Winter
(D) The heads of all departments

164. What are attendees instructed to bring to the meeting?

(A) Suggestions for increasing individual budgets
(B) Information on this year's expenditures
(C) Documents on spending from the past three years
(D) Copies of budget proposals for the coming year

GO ON TO THE NEXT PAGE ▶

Questions 165-168 refer to the following e-mail.

To: undisclosed_recipients
From: tinakline@museumofscience.org
Subject: New Exhibit
Date: September 10

Greetings, everyone.

We are pleased to announce we're nearly ready to unveil our much-hyped exhibit for the coming fall. Our newest display, entitled "The Science of the Nineteenth Century," is set to open to the public on the first day of October. —[1]—.

The display is located in the east wing on the first floor, and those visiting it will have the opportunity to view some of the most important inventions of the 1800s. Take a look at early prototypes of Edison's lightbulb. —[2]—. We'll have one of Bell's first telephones on display as well. You'll get a chance to view some early internal combustion engines as well as some telegraphs. Even better, this is an interactive exhibit, so you will have the opportunity to handle some machines to see how they actually worked. —[3]—.

We already know you're wondering how you can wait until the beginning of the month to see the exhibit. As current financial backers of the museum, you're welcome to visit the museum on September 29 and 30 to get in before the crowds. —[4]—. The museum will be open at its regular hours but will only permit those with cards to enter on those two days.

Regards,

Tina Kline
Curator

---

165. Who most likely are the recipients of the e-mail?

(A) Students at local schools
(B) Collectors of special items
(C) Museum donors
(D) Previous museum visitors

166. What is indicated about the exhibit?

(A) It will be on display until the end of the year.
(B) Visitors can use the items on display.
(C) The items shown are on loan to the museum.
(D) It will require an extra fee to visit.

167. When will the exhibit open to the public?

(A) On September 29
(B) On September 30
(C) On October 1
(D) On October 2

168. In which of the positions marked [1], [2], [3], and [4] does the following sentence best belong?

"Just bring your museum-issued card with you when you visit on either day."

(A) [1]
(B) [2]
(C) [3]
(D) [4]

Questions 169-171 refer to the following notice.

Fifth Street Bridge Notice

Notice is hereby given that the toll for the Fifth Street Bridge will increase from eighty cents to one dollar for all noncommercial vehicles starting on May 15. This increase was passed by the city commission on transportation by a vote of 3-2 at its last meeting on May 4. The extra money collected from the tolls will be used to assist the city in developing its biking infrastructure. Construction of bicycle lanes on some of the city's busiest streets will begin on June 10. This is being done to promote the usage of bicycles over motor vehicles such as automobiles and trucks. This should also serve to decrease traffic congestion in the downtown area and to reduce the amount of air pollution in the city.

169. For whom is the notice intended?

(A) City employees
(B) Local residents
(C) Construction companies
(D) The city council

170. What happened on May 4?

(A) Bicycle lanes were opened.
(B) Construction of a bridge was finished.
(C) The city's public transportation was improved.
(D) A price increase was voted on.

171. What is suggested about the bicycle lanes?

(A) They will be added to most of the city's roads.
(B) They should help make the city cleaner.
(C) They were requested by local residents.
(D) They are already being constructed.

GO ON TO THE NEXT PAGE

Questions 172-175 refer to the following online chat discussion.

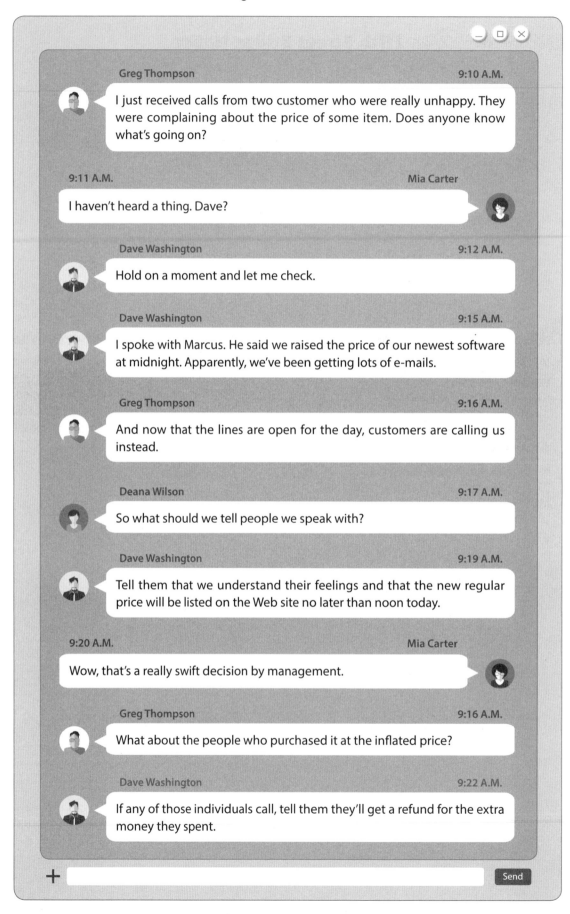

Greg Thompson   9:10 A.M.

I just received calls from two customer who were really unhappy. They were complaining about the price of some item. Does anyone know what's going on?

9:11 A.M.   **Mia Carter**

I haven't heard a thing. Dave?

Dave Washington   9:12 A.M.

Hold on a moment and let me check.

Dave Washington   9:15 A.M.

I spoke with Marcus. He said we raised the price of our newest software at midnight. Apparently, we've been getting lots of e-mails.

Greg Thompson   9:16 A.M.

And now that the lines are open for the day, customers are calling us instead.

Deana Wilson   9:17 A.M.

So what should we tell people we speak with?

Dave Washington   9:19 A.M.

Tell them that we understand their feelings and that the new regular price will be listed on the Web site no later than noon today.

9:20 A.M.   **Mia Carter**

Wow, that's a really swift decision by management.

Greg Thompson   9:16 A.M.

What about the people who purchased it at the inflated price?

Dave Washington   9:22 A.M.

If any of those individuals call, tell them they'll get a refund for the extra money they spent.

Send

56

172. What is the online chat discussion mainly about?

(A) Some money that must be refunded
(B) The uses of the company's newest software
(C) The prices of the company's products
(D) A recent decision by the company

173. At 9:15 A.M., what does Mr. Washington imply when he writes, "We've been getting lots of e-mails"?

(A) Many customers are making complaints.
(B) He recently checked his e-mail inbox.
(C) Users are reporting a bug in the software.
(D) Some customers are returning their purchases.

174. What is suggested about the software?

(A) Several problems with it have been found.
(B) It is not compatible with some computers.
(C) The first time it was sold was last night.
(D) The company lowered the price of it.

175. What does Mr. Thompson inquire about?

(A) How to respond to customers
(B) Why a price was changed
(C) When to expect more calls
(D) Who to blame a mistake on

GO ON TO THE NEXT PAGE

New Vacation Policy

The Azuma Corporation is instituting a new vacation policy. Employees must request time off one week prior to going on vacation. The only exceptions are for medical issues and family emergencies. In addition, employees must receive written permission to take time off from work. Supervisors can provide that for vacations lasting between one and five days. For vacations of six days or longer, department heads must grant permission. Employees taking vacations of more than five days are also required to indicate the reason why they need so much time off in writing. Supervisors will approve or deny requests within twenty-four hours of receiving them. This policy will go into effect on June 1.

To:	a_yeager@azumacorp.com
From:	peter-matthews@azumacorp.com
Subject:	Vacation
Date:	June 20

Dear Ms. Yeager,

I would like to inform you that I should be finished with the two projects I am presently working on by June 28. Please find attached to this e-mail a file describing the work I have completed and which is yet to be done on both assignments.

As I will no longer have any major tasks to do starting on June 29, I would like to formally request time off from work. I will be gone from June 30 to July 14 and will miss a total of 11 workdays. In case you are curious, my wife and I will be traveling to Australia during this time. I believe you are aware that we go on one long trip each summer. Last year, we visited Italy, and we have toured Russia and gone to South Africa on a safari in the past as well.

This year, my wife took advantage of an outstanding offer, so we bought tickets for a flight to Sydney. We have relatives in Melbourne, so we intend to go there, too. I have arranged for Phil Jenkins and Denise Kennedy to handle my individual clients while I am away. I hope you see fit to approve my request.

Regards,

Peter Matthews

176. How should a person request time off for three days?

(A) By completing an online form
(B) By contacting the department head
(C) By speaking to a supervisor
(D) By getting in touch with Human Resources

177. According to the notice, what must supervisors do regarding vacation requests?

(A) Speak with employees making them in person
(B) Respond to them quickly
(C) Give written permission for all of them
(D) Provide answers by e-mail

178. What did Mr. Matthews send with the e-mail?

(A) An update on his work
(B) A copy of his itinerary
(C) A form for Ms. Yeager to sign
(D) A request for reimbursement

179. What is suggested about Ms. Yeager?

(A) She is out of the country at the moment.
(B) She is the head of a department.
(C) She has several individual clients.
(D) She will give Mr. Matthews a new project soon.

180. What does Mr. Matthews imply about his tickets?

(A) They are nonrefundable.
(B) They were reserved with a travel agency.
(C) They are unable to be changed.
(D) They were purchased for a low price.

GO ON TO THE NEXT PAGE

Rockport Festival to Start in One Week

by staff reporter Kendra Ellington

Rockport (May 21) – The annual Rockport Spring Festival is set to begin next Tuesday. It will open on May 29 and conclude on June 3. This spring's festival has expanded, so it will be taking place in two locations. The first is Liberty Park, the traditional venue, while the second is Shell Beach.

"We're expecting more than 35,000 people at the festival this year," said organizer Donovan West. "There will be all kinds of events, including music concerts, a farmers' market, an international food fair, and amusement park rides." There will also be a fishing contest, which will be held at the beach, along with a fireworks show to be held every night.

The city is currently looking for volunteers for the festival to ensure that everything runs smoothly. Interested individuals are urged to contact city hall at 849-9382.

Rockport Festival Ends on a High Note

by staff reporter Craig Sinclair

Rockport (June 4) – The Rockport Spring Festival came to a conclusion last night. 20,000 people were in attendance on the last day, and organizers estimate that more than 70,000 people attended the festival during the entire time it was open. Mayor George Allard commented, "Our volunteers were amazing. Thanks to them, this was the city's best festival ever."

A large number of festival attendees remarked that they had come to see Shell Beach. The beach had been polluted for years, but during winter, the garbage was removed and the beach restored over the course of a couple of months. Now, the beach is among the most beautiful ones in the state.

"I'm planning to return later in the summer," said Julie Smith. The resident of Haverford said, "I can't believe how great the beach looks. I'm going to tell everyone I know back home all about it."

181. What is suggested about the fishing contest?

(A) It was held for the first time.
(B) It took place at Liberty Park.
(C) Hundreds of people participated in it.
(D) There was an entry fee for it.

182. Why would a person call city hall?

(A) To reserve tickets for the festival
(B) To register for some festival events
(C) To offer to help at the festival
(D) To make a donation for the festival

183. What is indicated about the Rockport Spring Festival?

(A) There were more attendees than expected.
(B) Most of its events were popular with attendees.
(C) It averaged 20,000 visitors each day.
(D) The scheduled parade had to be canceled.

184. What is mentioned about Shell Beach?

(A) It has gotten visitors from out of state.
(B) It reopened to the public in June.
(C) Its appearance has been improved.
(D) Its facilities are still being repaired.

185. Who most likely is Ms. Smith?

(A) A festival organizer
(B) A festival attendee
(C) A festival volunteer
(D) A festival vendor

GO ON TO THE NEXT PAGE

March 11

Dear Mr. Andre,

The hiring committee was impressed with you at our meeting on March 8. We liked your outgoing attitude, prior work experience, and fluent command of English, French, and Spanish. As such, we would like to extend an offer of employment to you to work at our office in Nantes, France. As a sales manager, you'll be responsible for sales in the western region of France as well as all of Spain, so you'll be on the road constantly.

The position comes with an annual salary of $95,000, and you can earn quarterly bonuses based on sales. As you're presently based in Athens, Greece, we'll pay for you to move and will also provide a three-bedroom apartment in downtown Nantes. Finally, you'll receive two weeks of paid vacation and full benefits, including medical insurance and a pension.

Please call me at 749-3844 to inform me of your decision.

Regards,

Javier Solas
Hardaway International

To: Lucia Bouchard
From: Javier Solas
Subject: David Andre
Date: March 18

I received confirmation from Mr. Andre that he has accepted our offer. He'll be paid $110,000 annually plus the other benefits we discussed previously. Mr. Andre's first day of work will be on April 10. I've given him your number, so expect a call from him. In addition, I provided him with Rene Faucher's e-mail address since he'll require assistance with the transition to life in France. Please inform Rene that he should be hearing from Mr. Andre within the next day or so.

David Andre Makes Positive Impression

by Kate Jung

(July 11) – David Andre has only been working with us for three months, but he's already made quite an impression. Thanks to him, the number of customers we have in France and Spain has doubled to 38 since April. "I really enjoy working here," said Mr. Andre. "I spent time in France during my youth, and my job has taken me all around the country. Being able to relive my past while I work has been delightful."

Mr. Andre started in April and has quickly gained the confidence of country manager Lucia Bouchard. "I knew he'd be a good employee, but I wasn't expecting this," she remarked. "I'm going to keep giving him more assignments to see how he handles them."

186. In the letter, what is NOT mentioned about Mr. Andre?

(A) He will be involved in sales.
(B) He is currently in another country.
(C) He has a friendly personality.
(D) He has worked in Spain before.

187. What is a requirement of the sales manager position?

(A) Having a marketing degree
(B) Working outside the office
(C) Speaking foreign languages
(D) Entertaining clients

188. What is the purpose of the memo?

(A) To request information on an employee
(B) To schedule a job interview
(C) To provide some contact numbers
(D) To inform a person of a new hire

189. What did Mr. Andre most likely do?

(A) Transferred to the Paris office
(B) Rejected the initial salary offer
(C) Met Mr. Faucher in person in March
(D) Kept his home in Athens

190. What is suggested about Ms. Bouchard?

(A) She will be transferring to Spain soon.
(B) She writes for the company newsletter.
(C) She accompanies Mr. Andre on his business trips.
(D) She increased Mr. Andre's responsibilities.

GO ON TO THE NEXT PAGE

Barton's Office Supplies

Do you need office supplies? Whenever you run out of items, give Barton's a call. We have the best selection of items in town. We also have the lowest prices.

This week, we're having a special sale:

pens and pencils: 30% off

office furniture: 20% off

white and colored paper: 35% off

printer ink: 10%

Visit our Web site at www.bartons.com or call us at 749-0493 to make an order.

Spend more than $80, and we will deliver your order within the city limits for no extra charge.

Barton's Office Supplies
384 Broadway Avenue
Ashland, VA
749-0493

Customer Name Leslie Devers
Company Parker International
Address 48 Cumberland Drive, Ashland, VA
Telephone Number 473-2984
E-Mail Address lesliedevers@parkerint.com
Customer Account Number 3847302
Order Date August 18
Delivery Date August 18

Item Number	Description	Quantity	Price
584-393	Copy Paper (White)	5 Boxes (1,500 Sheets/Box)	$48.75
202-192	Ballpoint Pen (Black)	3 Boxes (20 Pens/Box)	$11.50
943-293	Printer Ink (Blue)	2 Cartridges	$28.80
331-004	Spiral Notebook	10 (100 Pages/Notebook)	$20.00
		Subtotal	$109.05
		Delivery	$5.45
		Total	$114.50

Your order has been charged to the credit card ending in 4980. We appreciate your doing business with us at Barton's Office Supplies.

To: customerservice@bartons.com
From: lesliedevers@parkerint.com
Subject: Order
Date: August 19

To Whom It May Concern,

This is Leslie Devers from Parker International. My company purchased some supplies from your online store yesterday. The items arrived early this morning, which impressed us. This is the first time for us to deal with a store that provides such quick delivery service before.

However, when I looked at the invoice which accompanied the items, I noticed that no discount had been applied to the ink cartridges we purchased. I'm sure this was just a simple oversight on your part, but if you would credit the money to our company account, we would appreciate it.

We look forward to doing business with you in the future.

Regards,

Leslie Devers

Parker International

---

191. According to the advertisement, how long will the sale last?

(A) One day
(B) Two days
(C) One week
(D) One month

192. What is indicated about the order for Parker International?

(A) It was sent a day after being made.
(B) It was mailed in two boxes.
(C) It wasn't delivered for free.
(D) It was sent by courier.

193. In the e-mail, the phrase "deal with" in paragraph 1, line 2, is closest in meaning to

(A) do business with
(B) negotiate with
(C) approve of
(D) report to

194. What is suggested about Parker International?

(A) It has offices in several cities in the country.
(B) It is located across the street from Barton's.
(C) It made a purchase from Barton's for the first time.
(D) It deals with clients in the publishing industry.

195. How much of a discount does Ms. Devers want to receive?

(A) 10%
(B) 20%
(C) 30%
(D) 35%

GO ON TO THE NEXT PAGE

Software Training Seminar

Delta Consulting is presenting a one-day seminar on software training on Saturday, October 8, from 9 A.M. to 5 P.M. The following talks will be given:

★ 9 A.M. – 11 A.M.   The Internet of Things and Software Development (Rohit Patel)
★ 11 A.M. – 12 P.M.   The Effects of Artificial Intelligence on Software (Igor Rachmaninov)
★ 1 P.M. – 3 P.M.   Problems in Software Design (George Arnold)
★ 3 P.M. – 5 P.M.   New Coding Languages and Their Uses (Hans Dietrich)

All of the lecturers are experts in the fields they'll be discussing. Individual seats cost $250 per person, but discounts will be given to groups consisting of 5 or more people. Call 384-0938 to make the necessary arrangements. Same-day registration is permitted if seats are available.

To:	sbrandt@deltaconsulting.com
From:	awells@kaysoftware.com
Subject:	Request
Date:	October 10

Dear Ms. Brandt,

I represented my firm, Kay Software, at the training seminar your firm gave on Saturday and found it quite educational. Mr. Rachmaninov's lecture was of great interest to me because my company is currently experiencing problems regarding the topic of his talk. I wonder if he's available to visit my company to speak with our software engineers. They could surely benefit from his experience.

The following days and times are the best for us: October 19 at 3:00 P.M., October 21 at 1:00 P.M., November 3 at 9:00 A.M., and November 5 at 3:00 P.M. A talk and Q&A session lasting three hours should be sufficient.

I'm looking forward to receiving a response from you.

Best regards,

Alicia Wells
Kay Software

To:	awells@kaysoftware.com
From:	sbrandt@deltaconsulting.com
Subject:	[Re] Request
Date:	October 16

Good morning, Ms. Wells.

I'm very sorry for not responding to your request faster. I was in Brazil until the 15th and couldn't contact Mr. Rachmaninov until today. In fact, I just got off the phone with him a moment ago.

He indicated that his schedule is mostly full until December, but he can visit your firm on the second date you mentioned. In addition, Mr. Rachmaninov charges $1,000 per hour to visit companies. As he lives here in the city, he won't require the payment of any travel expenses.

Should this be acceptable to you, please call me at 584-3822, and we can finalize the details.

Sincerely,

Stacia Brandt
Destin Consulting

196. According to the flyer, what is true about the seminar?

(A) It is offered once a month.
(B) Groups can get lower prices.
(C) Tickets for it can be bought online.
(D) Participants in it receive certificates.

197. How did Ms. Wells feel about the seminar?

(A) She thought it was too expensive.
(B) She found it entertaining.
(C) She did not enjoy herself.
(D) She learned a great deal.

198. What do the software engineers at Kay Software most likely need help with?

(A) Coding languages
(B) The Internet of Things
(C) Software design
(D) Artificial intelligence

199. Why did Ms. Brandt apologize?

(A) She forgot to respond to a request.
(B) She missed a deadline Ms. Wells mentioned.
(C) She did not send an e-mail for several days.
(D) She could not find a speaker for Ms. Wells.

200. When can Mr. Rachmaninov visit Ms. Wells' company?

(A) On October 19
(B) On October 21
(C) On November 3
(D) On November 5

Stop! This is the end of the test. If you finish before time is called, you may go back to Parts 5, 6, and 7 and check your work.

Actual Test RC

3

READING TEST

In the Reading test, you will read a variety of texts and answer several different types of reading comprehension questions. The entire Reading test will last 75 minutes. There are three parts, and directions are given for each part. You are encouraged to answer as many questions as possible within the time allowed.

You must mark your answers on the separate answer sheet. Do not write your answers in your test book.

PART 5

Directions: A word or phrase is missing in each of the sentences below. Four answer choices are given below each sentence. Select the best answer to complete the sentence. Then mark the letter (A), (B), (C), or (D) on your answer sheet.

101. The workers will ------- the foundation of the building to ensure that it does not collapse.

(A) strong
(B) stronger
(C) strength
(D) strengthen

102. According to reports, Mr. Randolph ------- the offer and will make a decision on it within three days.

(A) will considered
(B) is considering
(C) has been considered
(D) considers

103. Several styles of sneakers are no longer in -------, so they must be delivered to the store from the warehouse.

(A) shelf
(B) amount
(C) stock
(D) order

104. Mr. Robinson was usually -------, which was something that his employees truly appreciated.

(A) decision
(B) decisive
(C) deciding
(D) decided

105. When the headquarters building was completed, ------- employees at the Delmont branch moved to it.

(A) most
(B) much
(C) every
(D) somebody

106. Unless the equipment is properly maintained by following the instructions in the manual, it is liable to break down with -------.

(A) regular
(B) regularity
(C) regulation
(D) regulatory

107. If Mr. Sheldon ------- for assistance, several people would have been willing to provide it.

(A) asks
(B) is asking
(C) will ask
(D) had asked

108. The easiest way ------- something from the company is to visit its online shopping mall.

(A) ordering
(B) ordered
(C) to order
(D) have ordered

109. We were ------- surprised by the decision to invest in the foreign commodities market.

(A) high
(B) highness
(C) higher
(D) highly

110. Ms. Breckinridge remarked that she had already visited the museum on a ------- visit to the city.

(A) previous
(B) probable
(C) practical
(D) positive

111. The researchers are ------- to conducting experiments and then writing reports on them.

(A) accustomed
(B) utilized
(C) comfortable
(D) approved

112. Unless the port is widened and deepened, large ships will be unable to dock at it, so they will sail ------- other locations.

(A) at
(B) over
(C) to
(D) in

113. According to the lease, the tenant is permitted to move out of the unit by giving one month's notice in -------.

(A) written
(B) writer
(C) write
(D) writing

114. ------- from vacation, Ms. Hollister discovered she had a large amount of work to complete.

(A) Be returned
(B) Returning
(C) Have returned
(D) Returns

115. Some customers are willing to pay a ------- to obtain better service and seats on their flights.

(A) scale
(B) discount
(C) premium
(D) wage

116. While the concert lasted longer than expected, it was not as ------- as the audience had hoped it would be.

(A) good
(B) well
(C) better
(D) best

117. Guests are expected to ------- with all rules and regulations, or they will be ordered to leave the premises.

(A) obey
(B) follow
(C) comply
(D) observe

118. Orders must be paid for in advance ------- the shipping process can be initiated.

(A) through what
(B) so that
(C) as such
(D) until then

119. It should take around a week for the market research firm to ------- the results of the recent survey it conducted.

(A) compile
(B) compiled
(C) compilation
(D) compiler

120. The orders, most ------- were from regular clients, were boxed and shipped out in the morning.

(A) by what
(B) of whom
(C) in that
(D) of which

GO ON TO THE NEXT PAGE

121. Individuals with a master's degree or higher ------- to apply for the supervisor's position being advertised.

(A) have encouraged
(B) will encourage
(C) are encouraging
(D) are encouraged

122. While Mr. Reynolds and Ms. Venters ------- their quotas for the month, Mr. Stark failed to do so.

(A) exceeded
(B) prepared
(C) indicated
(D) supported

123. Ms. Thompson requested that several documents be submitted for ------- presentation.

(A) she
(B) her
(C) hers
(D) herself

124. By the end of next week, Mr. Rogers ------- at Stevens Consulting for fifteen years.

(A) was employed
(B) is being employed
(C) will have been employed
(D) has been employed

125. The full ------- of the vehicle must be determined before it is released on the market.

(A) capacities
(B) capabilities
(C) capably
(D) capable

126. Purchases of office supplies may not be made ------- written permission from a supervisor.

(A) through
(B) among
(C) around
(D) without

127. All ------- expenses will be paid in full so long as receipts are submitted to the Personnel Department.

(A) mover
(B) moved
(C) moving
(D) movable

128. The complete failure of the new cosmetics line resulted in the ------- of the company's CEO.

(A) transition
(B) resignation
(C) retraction
(D) improvement

129. Those wishing to work abroad have to be willing to make a three-year ------- to the company.

(A) committing
(B) committee
(C) committed
(D) commitment

130. Not ------- on the agenda was discussed, so another meeting was scheduled to cover those topics.

(A) everything
(B) anyone
(C) another
(D) one

PART 6

Directions: Read the texts that follow. A word, phrase, or sentence is missing in parts of each text. Four answer choices for each question are given below the text. Select the best answer to complete the text. Then mark the letter (A), (B), (C), or (D) on your answer sheet.

Questions 131-134 refer to the following notice.

Notice for Tenants

Every spring, Bayside Apartments sends employees from the maintenance office to check each unit. We will be ------- inspections from April 2 to 12. They are typically completed in
        131.
around 30 to 45 minutes. Please visit www.baysideapartment.com/inspections ------- for an
                                                                              132.
inspection time. -------.
               133.

Our employees will be looking for problems such as faulty appliances, plumbing issues, and faded or worn carpeting and paint. ------- you need something replaced or repaired, the
                                                                     134.
employee will schedule a time for the work to be completed. Tenants who have not had their units painted in the past 4 years may request that work be done.

---

131. (A) replacing
        (B) approving
        (C) considering
        (D) conducting

132. (A) registering
        (B) be registered
        (C) to register
        (D) have registered

133. (A) We hope you are satisfied with the results of the inspection.
        (B) Thank you for letting us know when you will be available.
        (C) Be sure to fill out the survey to rate our inspectors when you sign up.
        (D) You must be in your apartment during the entire inspection.

134. (A) Because
        (B) However
        (C) If
        (D) Moreover

GO ON TO THE NEXT PAGE

December 11

To the Editor,

The article "Mulberry, Inc. to Close Factory Next Month," by Peter Chase in yesterday's *Daily Times* contained several factual -------. First, the factory in question is not being closed
                                            135.
down. In actuality, parts of it are being improved as state-of-the-art machinery will be added

to the third and fourth assembly lines. ------- will the company be laying off any workers.
                                         136.
-------. Finally, the company is not experiencing any financial issues. In fact, we set records
137.
for profits in the second and third quarters of the year, and we anticipate doing the same

thing this quarter. We would appreciate ------- being printed in your paper.
                                        138.

Regards,

Dean Morris
CEO, Mulberry, Inc.

---

135. (A) appearances
(B) data
(C) statements
(D) errors

136. (A) So
(B) But
(C) Nor
(D) And

137. (A) We intend to hire up to 30 new
employees in February.
(B) Several workers may receive
promotions in the next few months.
(C) They were given raises for their
outstanding performances.
(D) This is the reason we are no longer
hiring anyone.

138. (A) correctives
(B) corrections
(C) correctible
(D) correctly

The Employee of the Quarter Award

We are pleased to announce the employee of the quarter here at Drummond Technology. The winner for the second quarter of the year is Derrick Hutchinson from the Sales Department. During the months of April, May, and June, Derrick was responsible for signing contracts with a ------- value of more than $2.7 million. -------. There, he led several seminars and
139.   140.
workshops for the staff members to improve their sales -------. Derrick has been an
141.
employee at Drummond Technology ------- six years, and this is his third time to win the
142.
award. Be sure to congratulate him on his outstanding performance whenever you see him.

---

139. (A) combination
(B) combined
(C) combining
(D) combinate

140. (A) They were with two new companies.
(B) He also spent time at the Beijing office.
(C) The CEO personally congratulated him for that.
(D) This is the most anyone has ever sold in three months.

141. (A) contracts
(B) lessons
(C) skills
(D) deals

142. (A) for
(B) since
(C) during
(D) after

GO ON TO THE NEXT PAGE

Questions 143-146 refer to the following article.

Cumberland Parade Canceled

Cumberland (May 11) – The annual Cumberland Parade, which was scheduled for Saturday, May 12, has been canceled. The ------- was made at an emergency meeting involving the
143.
mayor and city council last night. Mayor David Cord stated, "The parade has been a tradition for 52 years, so we hated to cancel it. However, ------- the wildfires raging in the forests near
144.
the city, we felt that having a festive event wouldn't be appropriate. -------." Mayor Cord
145.
remarked that he hoped to reschedule the parade for some time in the summer. But he said the most ------- thing to do was to put out the fires.
146.

---

143. (A) election
(B) result
(C) promise
(D) decision

144. (A) in addition to
(B) on account of
(C) in spite of
(D) instead of

145. (A) Therefore, the parade will go on as initially planned.
(B) It will therefore be delayed until the following Saturday.
(C) Now that the fires are extinguished, we have lots of other work to do.
(D) After all, so many people are being evacuated from their homes.

146. (A) urgent
(B) urgently
(C) urgency
(D) urgencies

PART 7

Directions: In this part you will read a selection of texts, such as magazine and newspaper articles, e-mails, and instant messages. Each text or set of texts is followed by several questions. Select the best answer for each question and mark the letter (A), (B), (C), or (D) on your answer sheet.

Questions 147-148 refer to the following memo.

MEMO

To: All Staff Members
From: Kimberly Wingard
Date: October 22

Despite undergoing renovations during spring, sales at our grocery store have been declining in the past few months. In August, they dropped by 11%, and last month, they fell by 18%. If this trend continues, we may have to close down the store.

I would like for everyone to do some brainstorming. Come up with some ways you believe will improve our financial situation here. Think of what we can do to convince customers to come and spend more money here. Tomorrow, before you begin your work shift, I'd like for each of you to speak with your direct supervisor to share what you came up with. Don't be shy about sharing your thoughts. No idea is too silly. We are in serious trouble and need to make immediate changes.

147. What is the problem?

(A) There are not enough employees.
(B) Renovations are needed.
(C) Similar stores have opened nearby.
(D) Fewer sales are being made.

148. What does Ms. Wingard request the staff members do?

(A) Make changes in their schedules
(B) Work longer hours for the same pay
(C) Consider how to attract more shoppers
(D) Think of some special promotions to run

GO ON TO THE NEXT PAGE

Questions 149-150 refer to the following advertisement.

Wallace Department Store Giveaway Event

Wallace Department Store is having a special promotion for customers. The offer runs from July 1 to August 10.

Customers can get the following:

Spend $50 and get a free bottle of Watson hand lotion.
Spend $100 and get a free pair of Stetson sunglasses.
Spend $200 and get a free Verducci T-shirt.
Spend $400 and get two free movie tickets.

You can pick up your gift at the customer service center. Just bring your receipt with you. This offer is valid at all Wallace Department Stores except for the stores in Fairview and Wilmington.

---

149. What is NOT mentioned in the advertisement?

(A) The promotion will last for two months.
(B) A receipt is needed to get a complimentary item.
(C) Some stores are not participating in the event.
(D) Customers can receive different free items.

150. How can a shopper receive a free clothing item?

(A) By spending $50
(B) By spending $100
(C) By spending $200
(D) By spending $400

Questions 151-152 refer to the following text message chain.

Robert Harkness	**11:25 A.M.**
Good morning, Stephanie. Have you made any progress with Mr. Grimes yet?	
Stephanie Lowe	**11:27 A.M.**
Sorry, Robert. He has been in meetings in his office all morning, so I haven't had a chance to speak with him yet.	
Robert Harkness	**11:30 A.M.**
Talk to his secretary and make sure she knows how important it is for the deal to get done today. If he won't sign the contract, we'll lose the client.	
Stephanie Lowe	**11:31 AM.**
Okay. I'll give Tina a call.	
Robert Harkness	**11:33 A.M.**
Great. I'll be back after lunch. If you haven't talked to him by then, I'll visit his office myself.	
Stephanie Lowe	**11:35 A.M.**
All right. See you in a bit.	

151. What problem is mentioned?

(A) A client was lost.
(B) Mr. Grimes is not in his office.
(C) A document has not been signed.
(D) A lunch meeting was canceled.

152. At 11:31 A.M., what does Ms. Lowe imply when she writes, "I'll give Tina a call"?

(A) She will speak with a customer.
(B) She will telephone her supervisor.
(C) She will get in touch with her client.
(D) She will contact Mr. Grimes's secretary.

GO ON TO THE NEXT PAGE

Nominations Needed

It's time to submit nominations for the employee of the year award. All full-time employees are eligible to suggest a fellow worker. To nominate someone, visit www.fostertech.com/awards and complete the form. Be sure to write the employee's name and department and then write a short explanation describing why you feel this individual should win this year's award. All nominations must be submitted by December 15. The winner of the award will be announced at the year-end party on December 29. This year's winner will receive a $2,500 cash bonus, one extra week of vacation, and a promotion.

153. How should a nomination be submitted?

(A) By sending an e-mail
(B) By filling out an online form
(C) By speaking with a supervisor
(D) By submitting a handwritten form

154. What will the winner of the award NOT receive?

(A) Time off from work
(B) A monetary prize
(C) A complimentary trip
(D) A better position

Travel Industry Trade Show

The annual Travel Industry Trade Show will take place in Orlando, Florida, this year. The conference is scheduled to be held in the convention center at the Radcliffe Hotel from Friday, October 10, to Monday, October 14. Besides the usual industry trade booths, there will be several world-famous speakers discussing various issues concerning domestic and international travel. Of special note is the seminar on the new travel aide computer software system which many travel agencies and airlines are considering using. Advance reservations for it are highly recommended. Please check the convention Web site (www.travelindustrytradeshow.org) for the complete schedule. Those who wish to attend should pay the required fee of $75 before October 5. The conference is not responsible for booking hotel rooms for attendees, so please make sure you do so in advance.

155. What is true about trade show?

(A) The keynote speaker is a computer programmer.
(B) It is taking place for the first time.
(C) Advance registration is necessary.
(D) The only focus is international travel.

156. What is suggested about the seminar on the computer system?

(A) It will be led by the person who designed it.
(B) An extra fee is required to take part in it.
(C) There are only 75 spots available for it.
(D) Many people will be interested in attending it.

157. What are attendees advised to do?

(A) Reserve their own accommodations
(B) Become members of an organization
(C) Show up early for several events
(D) Pay the attendance fee by October 10

GO ON TO THE NEXT PAGE

Questions 158-161 refer to the following e-mail.

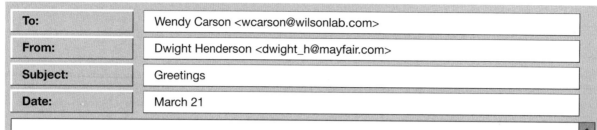

To:	Wendy Carson <wcarson@wilsonlab.com>
From:	Dwight Henderson <dwight_h@mayfair.com>
Subject:	Greetings
Date:	March 21

Dear Ms. Carson,

Greetings. This is Dwight Henderson from the Mayfair Company in Toronto. It was a real pleasure to talk to you at the Internet Designer Conference in Albany. As I hope you recall, we spoke for a while about my company's products last week. At the time, you appeared to be interested in our new wireless routers. Unfortunately, I couldn't talk with you for too long since I had to meet another client at that time.

Fortunately, it just so happens that I'll be stopping over in London on my way to Paris next week. I would love to visit you in your office to demonstrate some of my firm's newest products. I will be there for the entire day on Tuesday, March 27, and can arrange to go to your office on the 28th if that fits your schedule better.

My company has just developed a new wireless Internet system which can be used with no lag time or interruptions. It's not only better than anything else available on the market, but it's also 20% cheaper. I hope you take me up on my offer so that I can show you the latest in cutting-edge technology.

I look forward to hearing back from you soon.

Regards,

Dwight Henderson
Mayfair Company

158. According to the e-mail, how does Mr. Henderson know Ms. Carson?

(A) They work at the same company.
(B) She got in touch with him online.
(C) He met her at a professional meeting.
(D) They attended the same university.

159. Where does Mr. Henderson propose meeting Ms. Carson?

(A) In London
(B) In Albany
(C) In Paris
(D) In Toronto

160. What does Mr. Henderson want to do for Ms. Carson?

(A) Install a wireless router
(B) Give her some pamphlets
(C) Conduct a demonstration
(D) Renegotiate a contract

161. What is mentioned about the Mayfair Company's Internet system?

(A) It is not yet being sold.
(B) It costs less than similar products.
(C) It is being offered at a discounted price.
(D) It requires a technician to install.

Questions 162-164 refer to the following letter.

June 11

Dear Mr. Robinson,

I would like to inform you of a change that is occurring here at Whitson, Inc. The Personnel Department has instituted a new policy. –[1]–. Now, rather than outsourcing various activities to freelancers such as yourself, we instead desire employees who are fully committed to our company and vision.

According to these new guidelines, we will no longer be making offers to motivational speakers to have them give talks to our employees. We are, however, creating a full-time job for an employee motivation specialist. –[2]–.

Over the years, you have been a major contributor to Whitson's success as you have been our most effective speaker. –[3]–. We hope you see fit to apply for the position. We are currently accepting applications and will continue to do so until the position is filled. Applicants will be evaluated almost entirely on their body of work as well as how influential their talks have been. We consider you a prime candidate. –[4]–.

I look forward to hearing from you soon.

Sincerely,

Jason Daniels
Whitson, Inc.

162. Why did Mr. Daniels write to Mr. Robinson?

(A) To request that he speak at the company
(B) To confirm that he has been hired
(C) To inform him of an available job
(D) To let him know about an upcoming interview

163. What does Mr. Robinson indicate about the new position?

(A) It requires a college degree.
(B) It will be in the Personnel Department.
(C) It will involve a lot of traveling.
(D) It will be a full-time position.

164. In which of the positions marked [1], [2], [3], and [4] does the following sentence best belong?

"This will be an upper-management position."

(A) [1]
(B) [2]
(C) [3]
(D) [4]

GO ON TO THE NEXT PAGE ▶

Questions 165-168 refer to the following online chat discussion.

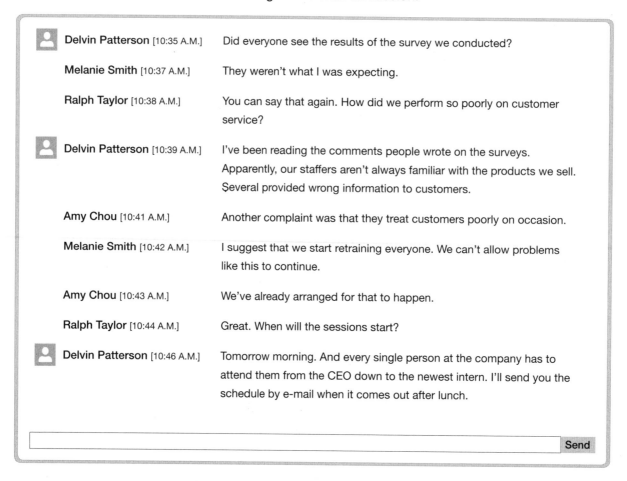

Delvin Patterson [10:35 A.M.]   Did everyone see the results of the survey we conducted?

Melanie Smith [10:37 A.M.]   They weren't what I was expecting.

Ralph Taylor [10:38 A.M.]   You can say that again. How did we perform so poorly on customer service?

Delvin Patterson [10:39 A.M.]   I've been reading the comments people wrote on the surveys. Apparently, our staffers aren't always familiar with the products we sell. Several provided wrong information to customers.

Amy Chou [10:41 A.M.]   Another complaint was that they treat customers poorly on occasion.

Melanie Smith [10:42 A.M.]   I suggest that we start retraining everyone. We can't allow problems like this to continue.

Amy Chou [10:43 A.M.]   We've already arranged for that to happen.

Ralph Taylor [10:44 A.M.]   Great. When will the sessions start?

Delvin Patterson [10:46 A.M.]   Tomorrow morning. And every single person at the company has to attend them from the CEO down to the newest intern. I'll send you the schedule by e-mail when it comes out after lunch.

Send

165. What is the problem?

(A) Revenues are down at the company.
(B) Employees are doing their jobs poorly.
(C) Too many employees are calling in sick.
(D) Prices have been rising quickly lately.

166. What type of industry do the writers most likely work in?

(A) Retail
(B) Consulting
(C) Manufacturing
(D) Travel

167. At 10:43 A.M., what does Ms. Chou mean when she writes, "We've already arranged for that to happen"?

(A) Several employees will be fired.
(B) A job advertisement will be posted.
(C) Apologies will be made.
(D) A training event will be held.

168. What will Mr. Patterson do in the afternoon?

(A) E-mail some information
(B) Attend a managers' meeting
(C) Schedule a seminar
(D) Speak with some salespeople

Questions 169-171 refer to the following information.

http://www.fairfaxmuseum.org

| HOME | HOURS | SPECIAL ACTIVITIES | NEWS | VISIT US |

The Fairfax Museum is proud to announce an exciting new exhibit featuring dinosaur fossils. Among the fossils to be displayed are a nearly complete Tyrannosaurus Rex and a velociraptor. There will be a total of 32 different types of dinosaur fossils on display. They range in size from tiny eggs to a partial skeleton of an enormous brontosaurus. These fossils are on loan from Central University as well as the separate private collections of Jarod Watson and Melanie Zhong.

The exhibit is scheduled to run from June 10 to June 30. It will be open during the museum's regular hours of operation, which are from Tuesday to Sunday from 9 A.M. to 6 P.M. There is a separate fee required to view the exhibit. Teens and adults will be charged $7 while senior citizens ages 60 or older must pay $5. Children 12 or under will be admitted for free. Please inquire about group rates (10 or more people) by calling 584-7212. Museum members will not be charged to see the exhibit.

For pictures of the exhibit and for more information about dinosaurs, click here.

169. Where most likely would this information be located?

(A) Home
(B) Special Activities
(C) News
(D) Visit Us

170. What is suggested about the fossils?

(A) They were found in the local area.
(B) They are not owned by the museum.
(C) They are mostly in poor condition.
(D) They were found by the same person.

171. What is NOT indicated about the exhibit?

(A) Children do not have to pay to attend it.
(B) People cannot view it on Mondays.
(C) It will be open for less than a month.
(D) Groups will be given a 10% discount.

GO ON TO THE NEXT PAGE

ACTUAL TEST 3

Upcoming Work

Tenants should be aware that the management at Harbor View Apartments has scheduled some repair work to be done in the coming week. Please take note of the following and make the necessary adjustments in your daily schedules.

Tuesday, May 12: The electricity in the entire complex will be shut down from 10 A.M. to noon. During that time, a new master control board will be installed for the complex's entire electric system. –[1]–. This means that the elevators in every building will be nonoperational. Computers and televisions will not work either. Nor will refrigerators, freezers, or washing machines.

Wednesday, May 13: The gas in Buildings 101 and 105 will not work from 2 P.M. to 5 P.M. During that time, some gas pipes will be replaced. –[2]–. Neither building will have hot water while the repairs are being made. In addition, gas stoves and ovens cannot be used.

Thursday, May 14: The swimming pool between Buildings 106 and 109 will be closed for cleaning. –[3]–. The pool will not be open the entire day.

Friday, May 15: The grass will be cut and other lawn maintenance will be done. Those with allergies should take precautions.

–[4]–. Should the work take longer than expected, various services will be unavailable for a longer period of time. We will keep everyone updated as the work progresses.

172. What is the purpose of the notice?

    (A) To advise tenants of some inspections

    (B) To inform people of upcoming work projects

    (C) To request that tenants help care for the complex

    (D) To announce some problems at the complex

173. According to the notice, what will NOT happen on May 12?

    (A) Individual units will be inspected.

    (B) Appliances will not work for some time.

    (C) The electric system will be worked on.

    (D) There will be no electricity for two hours.

174. When will landscaping work be done at the apartment complex?

    (A) On May 12

    (B) On May 13

    (C) On May 14

    (D) On May 15

175. In which of the positions marked [1], [2], [3], and [4] does the following sentence best belong?

"Be advised that the times are merely estimates."

    (A) [1]

    (B) [2]

    (C) [3]

    (D) [4]

GO ON TO THE NEXT PAGE

To: Angela Carpenter <angela_c@performancemail.com>
From: Robert Harper <robert@tourpro.com>
Subject: Itinerary
Date: May 12
Attachment: Carpenter_itinerary

Dear Ms. Carpenter,

Thank you for making the payment for your upcoming trip to Europe. I would like to confirm that your airline, railroad, and hotel reservations have all been made.

Attached, please find a complete itinerary of your trip. You will be departing from Boston's Logan Airport on June 20 and will arrive at Fiumicino Airport in Rome, Italy, on the same day. You can pick up your rental car there. You'll fly to Athens, Greece, on June 26 and will go to Munich, Germany, on June 30. At the conclusion of your trip, on July 5, you will fly from Kloten Airport in Zurich, Switzerland, back to Boston.

If you need to make any changes to your itinerary, please let me know no later than May 31. Changes made prior to then will be free of charge, but any changes made afterward will result in a charge of $50 for each alteration to the itinerary.

Sincerely,

Robert Harper

Tour Pro

To:	Robert Harper <robert@tourpro.com>
From:	Angela Carpenter <angela_c@performancemail.com>
Subject:	My Trip
Date:	July 6

Dear Mr. Harper,

My husband and I just returned from our trip to Europe. I want you to know that we had the trip of a lifetime, and we appreciate everything you did to make that possible.

We were both a bit skeptical about your claim that we would be staying at 4-star hotels everywhere we went. However, that was definitely the case. The Pallas Hotel in Athens was particularly memorable. Our guides everywhere were not only extremely knowledgeable but were also fluent in English and very helpful. The only negative experience we had was having our train from Rome to Venice depart late by a couple of hours. But that was merely a minor setback.

We'll be sure to inform our friends about your travel agency and the quality trips you provide. I'll also be in touch again later when we go on our next trip.

Regards,

Angela Carpenter

176. Which mode of transportation is NOT mentioned by Mr. Harper?

   (A) Airplane
   (B) Train
   (C) Car
   (D) Taxi

177. According to Mr. Harper, what will happen after May 31?

   (A) Refunds will not be offered.
   (B) A fee will be charged for changes.
   (C) Tickets will be unable to be canceled.
   (D) The prices of hotels will increase.

178. Why did Ms. Carpenter send the e-mail?

   (A) To express her thanks
   (B) To request a clarification
   (C) To make a new reservation
   (D) To criticize a service

179. When most likely did Ms. Carpenter check in to the Pallas Hotel?

   (A) On June 20
   (B) On June 26
   (C) On June 30
   (D) On July 5

180. In the second e-mail, the word "setback" in paragraph 2, line 6, is closest in meaning to

   (A) retreat
   (B) delay
   (C) penalty
   (D) cancelation

GO ON TO THE NEXT PAGE

Questions 181-185 refer to the following text message chain and itinerary.

Edward Halpern   9:32 A.M.
Good morning, Carla. We're still planning to meet for the product demonstration next Tuesday, aren't we?

Carla Welch   9:34 A.M.
That's correct, Ed. When will you be coming here? Have you already made your travel arrangements?

Edward Halpern   9:35 A.M.
I just received my itinerary from the travel agency. It looks like I'll be flying in next Monday night. I'll be arriving at 10:45 P.M. on Flight RE232.

Carla Welch   9:36 A.M.
Do you need someone to pick you up at the airport? I can arrange for a driver to meet you there to take you to your hotel.

Edward Halpern   9:37 A.M.
I really appreciate it, but I've decided to rent a car this time. If I get some free time, I'm going to try to do a bit of sightseeing.

Carla Welch   9:38 A.M.
That sounds good. I can point out some places you ought to visit. See you next week.

Schloss Travel Agency
Zurich, Switzerland

Itinerary for Edward Halpern

Phone Number: 493-1933
E-Mail Address: edhalpern@mmc.com
Prepared By: Edith Mann

Date	Flight Number	Departure Time	Departing From	Arriving At
April 12	RE232	9:25 P.M.	Zurich	Berlin
April 15	RE11	10:30 A.M.	Berlin	Warsaw
April 17	NM490	2:05 P.M.	Warsaw	Athens
April 21	RE98	12:15 P.M.	Athens	Zurich

All of your seats are confirmed for business class. You may visit the VIP lounge in each airport prior to your departure. You may check two bags weighing no more than a combined 40kg. Please arrive at the airport at least two hours before your flight takes off.

181. Why most likely did Mr. Halpern write to Ms. Welch?

(A) To discuss a demonstration
(B) To provide his arrival date
(C) To confirm a meeting
(D) To negotiate a contract

182. What does Ms. Welch offer to do?

(A) Reschedule her meeting with Mr. Halpern
(B) Give Mr. Halpern a tour of the city
(C) Arrange a rental car for Mr. Halpern
(D) Have Mr. Halpern met when he arrives

183. According to the itinerary, what is NOT true?

(A) Mr. Halpern will visit Athens on April 17.
(B) Mr. Halpern has a weight limit on his luggage.
(C) Mr. Halpern will be seated in first class.
(D) Mr. Halpern will take flight RE11 on April 15.

184. Where will Mr. Halpern meet Ms. Welch?

(A) In Zurich
(B) In Berlin
(C) In Warsaw
(D) In Athens

185. Who most likely is Ms. Mann?

(A) An airline employee
(B) Mr. Halpern's colleague
(C) A travel agent
(D) Ms. Welch's driver

GO ON TO THE NEXT PAGE

Questions 186-190 refer to the following memo, information, and e-mail.

To: All Cranston Burgers Franchise Owners

From: David Cotton

Subject: Revenues

Date: April 4

We have calculated the revenues from the first three months of the year, and the results are mostly positive. Revenues are generally up from the same time last year. However, one store is lagging behind the others. Tom Reynolds, I need to inspect your establishment in person to see if there are any obvious problems I can detect which will help you improve the situation at your franchise. It also appears as though our special promotion in March was successful as revenues were much higher than normal. Let's try to come up with some more ideas like the one Edith Thompson suggested so that we can keep customers coming to our stores.

After I inspect Tom's store, I'm going to call a meeting at my office. I expect to have it sometime in the week starting on April 16. I'll be in touch later.

Cranston Burgers Revenues

Franchise Location	January Revenues	February Revenues	March Revenues
Walden	$220,000	$240,000	$280,000
Edinburg	$310,000	$315,000	$350,000
Hampton	$175,000	$160,000	$180,000
Windsor	$255,000	$270,000	$305,000

To:	David Cotton
From:	Tom Reynolds
Subject:	Revenues
Date:	June 3

Dear Mr. Cotton,

Since you visited my restaurant in early April, my staff and I have been busy attempting to implement the suggestions you made. At first, I must admit that I was somewhat skeptical about how well some of them would work; however, I decided to give them a try since nothing else was working.

It took us two weeks for everything to go into effect, so revenues only improved moderately in April. It was in May that the effectiveness of the changes revealed themselves. Our revenues jumped a considerable amount. I don't have the exact numbers yet, but we brought in somewhere around the amount the Windsor franchise recorded in February. That's by far the most my restaurant has ever made. I'm looking forward to many more months of success in the future.

Sincerely,

Tom Reynolds

186. What does Mr. Cotton mention about Ms. Thompson?

(A) She had fewer customers in March.
(B) She calculated all of the revenues.
(C) She will have a sale at her establishment.
(D) She thought of a recent promotion.

187. What is suggested about Mr. Reynolds?

(A) He owns the Hampton franchise.
(B) He is the newest owner.
(C) He recently met with Mr. Cotton.
(D) He has previous restaurant experience.

188. Which franchise recorded the highest overall revenues?

(A) Walden
(B) Edinburg
(C) Hampton
(D) Windsor

189. Why did Mr. Reynolds send the e-mail?

(A) To ask for permission
(B) To provide an update
(C) To report a failure
(D) To make a suggestion

190. According to Mr. Reynolds, what were his franchise's approximate revenues in May?

(A) $240,000
(B) $255,000
(C) $270,000
(D) $280,000

GO ON TO THE NEXT PAGE

Questions 191-195 refer to the following advertisement, schedule, and e-mail.

ILLUSTRATOR NEEDED

Samson Publishing is seeking a full-time illustrator for its Saratoga office. The ideal candidate should have professional experience as an illustrator, preferably at a publisher, newspaper, or magazine. A college degree is not required, but a high school diploma is. The individual selected needs to be able to handle multiple projects and must be good at meeting deadlines and working in a fast-paced environment. Applicants must be proficient in software programs such as Art Decorator and Graphic Illustrator. The salary and benefits will be determined by the individual's experience. Interested applicants should send a résumé, a cover letter, and some samples of their work to illustratorjob@samsonpublishing.com. The final date applications will be accepted is August 1. Interviews will be scheduled for mid-August.

Interviews for the illustrator position have been scheduled. Please take note of the following:

Applicant	Interview Date	Interview Time	Room	Interviewer
Josh Sheldon	August 14	10:30 A.M.	103	Eric Martel
Rosie Rodriguez	August 14	1:00 P.M.	102	Jane Garbo
Lawrence Smith	August 15	1:00 P.M.	105	Ken Murray
Adison Mattayakhun	August 16	9:00 A.M.	108	Eric Martel
Lily Ngoc	August 17	2:30 P.M.	102	Tim Watson

Interviewers should take comprehensive notes. All relevant information along with the interviewer's recommendation should be forwarded to Sue Grossman at suegrossman@samsonpublishing.com. Second interviews will be scheduled for late August.

To: amattayakhun@wondermail.com
From: suegrossman@samsonpublishing.com
Subject: Illustrator Position
Date: August 19

Dear Mr. Mattayakhun,

My name is Sue Grossman. I work at Samson Publishing and am in charge of hiring at the company. Your interviewer was highly impressed with you, particularly your ability to utilize various computer programs. As such, he recommended that you be called in for a second interview.

We have scheduled you to be here on Saturday, August 25, at 9:00 in the morning. The interview will last several hours, so be prepared to stay here all day. During that time, you will meet several individuals and will also be asked to make some illustrations for us so that we can get a first-hand look at your skills. When you come, make sure you have your portfolio as several of the people you'll be meeting need to look at it.

We look forward to seeing you soon.

Regards,

Sue Grossman
Samson Publishing

191. What is mentioned about the position?

(A) It requires a college diploma.
(B) It starts on the first of August.
(C) It requires the use of a computer.
(D) It is for work at a newspaper.

192. What is NOT indicated in the advertisement?

(A) The salary depends on the person who gets hired.
(B) Interested individuals must apply in person.
(C) A person with experience is preferred.
(D) The deadline to apply is August 1.

193. What is suggested about Ms. Rodriguez?

(A) She is able to work well with others.
(B) She possesses multitasking skills.
(C) She majored in computer science.
(D) She has management experience.

194. Who recommended that Mr. Mattayakhun be interviewed again?

(A) Eric Martel
(B) Jane Garbo
(C) Ken Murray
(D) Tim Watson

195. What does Ms. Grossman request Mr. Mattayakhun do?

(A) Wear formal clothes to his interview
(B) Contact her to confirm his appearance
(C) Bring a collection of his work
(D) E-mail a copy of his résumé

GO ON TO THE NEXT PAGE

Questions 196-200 refer to the following announcement, article, and letter.

Annual Auction

The Paulson Group, a Westchester-based charity, is hosting an auction on Saturday, December 18, in the Gold Room at the Regina Hotel. The festivities will start with a five-course dinner at 6:00 in the evening. At 7:30 P.M., Paulson Group president and founder Laurie Mitchell will give a short speech. Then, at 8:00, a silent auction will take place. Among the items being auctioned are some artwork by local resident Ken Dellwood, autographed movie memorabilia, and a trip for two to Hawaii. The evening will end with bids on the top item, a brand-new Sidewinder sports car donated by local car dealer Varnum Cars. The Paulson Group hopes to raise $200,000. All proceeds from the event will be used to support good causes in the city. Call 383-9487 to purchase tickets for the dinner and auction.

A Night to Remember

by Anna Belinda, Staff Reporter

Westchester (December 19) – Last night was definitely a night to remember for the Paulson Group, which hosted its annual fundraiser. More than 450 people attended both the dinner and the silent auction held afterward at the Regina Hotel.

The highlight of the event was the sale of a sports car for $50,000, which was more than the $38,000 it was expected to fetch. Other items were sold for high prices as well, with the end result being that more than $270,000 was raised on the night. "I can't believe how successful this event was," said Laurie Mitchell, the president of the group. "We only raised $150,000 last year. I'd like to thank the residents of Westchester for making this event a total success. We couldn't have done this without them."

December 23

Dear Mr. Anderson,

This is a friendly reminder that you have not yet transferred the $50,000 you bid on Saturday night. While we normally insist that all bids be paid in full on the night of the auction, we gave you extra time since the amount you bid was so high.

However, several days have passed, and we haven't heard from you since the night of the auction. Would you please call me at 754-3722 to let me know how you intend to make the payment? I hope to hear from you soon.

Sincerely,

Laurie Mitchell

President, Paulson Group

196. Who is Mr. Dellwood?

(A) An auctioneer
(B) A donor
(C) An artist
(D) A Paulson Group employee

197. What should individuals do to attend the event on Saturday?

(A) Make a small donation
(B) Send an e-mail
(C) Acquire tickets
(D) Make a reservation

198. What is indicated about the auction?

(A) It started later than expected.
(B) It exceeded its organizers' goals.
(C) It was attended by the most people ever.
(D) It was free for people to attend.

199. Why did Ms. Mitchell send the letter to Mr. Anderson?

(A) To congratulate him on a winning bid
(B) To confirm that he received an item
(C) To request payment for an item
(D) To thank him for attending the auction

200. What did Mr. Anderson bid on?

(A) A vehicle
(B) A painting
(C) A trip
(D) An autographed item

Stop! This is the end of the test. If you finish before time is called, you may go back to Parts 5, 6, and 7 and check your work.

Actual Test RC

4

READING TEST

In the Reading test, you will read a variety of texts and answer several different types of reading comprehension questions. The entire Reading test will last 75 minutes. There are three parts, and directions are given for each part. You are encouraged to answer as many questions as possible within the time allowed.

You must mark your answers on the separate answer sheet. Do not write your answers in your test book.

PART 5

Directions: A word or phrase is missing in each of the sentences below. Four answer choices are given below each sentence. Select the best answer to complete the sentence. Then mark the letter (A), (B), (C), or (D) on your answer sheet.

101. Half of the relocation costs are to be paid by the company while Mr. Rosemont is expected to handle the -------.
    (A) rest
    (B) amount
    (C) salary
    (D) lease

102. Should there be delays or ------- problems, LRW Manufacturing may file a complaint against its supplier.
    (A) another
    (B) each other
    (C) any other
    (D) others

103. Employees are requested not to arrive ------- to the meeting since the CEO will be in attendance.
    (A) late
    (B) lately
    (C) lateness
    (D) latest

104. Mr. Chen reviewed the proposal and then asked that several sections of it be considered for -------.
    (A) revised
    (B) revision
    (C) revisor
    (D) revisable

105. Ms. Cartwright ------- the project now that Mr. Wilson has resigned from his position.
    (A) has overseen
    (B) overseeing
    (C) will oversee
    (D) was overseen

106. Mr. Davidson learned about the job ------- he read an advertisement for it on the Internet.
    (A) when
    (B) therefore
    (C) so
    (D) but

107. Every effort to repair the broken machinery -------, so a new piece of equipment was ordered.
    (A) failed
    (B) resisted
    (C) attempted
    (D) considered

108. Due to the security breach, ------- to the computer files has been denied to certain individuals.
    (A) access
    (B) accession
    (C) accessible
    (D) accessing

109. Mr. Cranston will be replacing Daniel Kim, who is departing ------- having worked in the R&D Department for ten years.

(A) because
(B) which
(C) after
(D) thereby

110. An attempt to ------- new subscribers resulted in 550 more people signing up online.

(A) purchase
(B) recruit
(C) announce
(D) suspend

111. The museum curator will announce the opening of a new exhibit ------- art from the Renaissance.

(A) features
(B) will feature
(C) to be featured
(D) featuring

112. Some people complained about the unfair ------- of work projects by the senior engineers.

(A) distributor
(B) distribution
(C) distributed
(D) distributive

113. The negotiations came to an end as soon ------- the lawyers for Culberson International increased their offer.

(A) if
(B) on
(C) as
(D) for

114. Thanks to the ------- of the spring sale, a decision was made to hold another one a month later.

(A) popular
(B) popularly
(C) popularity
(D) popularities

115. It is vital to ------- the number of profitable items which are sold by the company.

(A) involve
(B) produce
(C) maneuver
(D) increase

116. The ------- of the firm's stock is expected to rise once the market opens tomorrow morning.

(A) value
(B) asset
(C) sale
(D) movement

117. Mr. Sullivan asked several questions ------- the effectiveness of the medicine the researchers developed.

(A) on account of
(B) in response to
(C) with regard to
(D) on top of

118. If you want to learn how to sign up for the program, please ------- your contact information with Ms. Winger.

(A) leave
(B) be leaving
(C) will leave
(D) have left

119. Of all the people who requested -------, only Ms. Appleton was permitted to move elsewhere.

(A) transfers
(B) raises
(C) promotions
(D) positions

120. Mr. Richards ------- attends conferences, preferring instead to send other individuals in his department.

(A) always
(B) appropriately
(C) seldom
(D) eventually

ACTUAL TEST 4

GO ON TO THE NEXT PAGE ➤

121. Engineers ------- projects are about to conclude will receive new assignments from Ms. Ross on Thursday.

(A) whom
(B) whose
(C) which
(D) who

122. The museum will be hosting a ------- to celebrate the opening of its newest exhibit.

(A) receiver
(B) receptor
(C) reception
(D) receiving

123. Items must be returned in their ------- packaging to qualify for a full refund.

(A) origin
(B) original
(C) originally
(D) originality

124. ------- conference attendees are required to provide their estimated times of arrival to the organizers.

(A) Any
(B) Each
(C) All
(D) Much

125. Interns at Focus Machinery are typically assigned projects that ------- them with practical experience.

(A) provide
(B) provision
(C) provisional
(D) provided

126. The real estate agency agreed to give a tour of the facility in an effort to find a renter ------- it.

(A) with
(B) for
(C) by
(D) in

127. Mr. White suggested a ------- that would enable the tour group to avoid the heavy traffic downtown.

(A) form
(B) transportation
(C) concept
(D) detour

128. While the payment was being processed, the customer ------- on hold for a moment.

(A) puts
(B) will put
(C) was put
(D) is putting

129. The new apartment building has a recreation room, a laundry room, and other -------.

(A) facilities
(B) accommodations
(C) utilities
(D) functions

130. Managers are expected to meet with their employees at least ------- a quarter to give them a progress report.

(A) some
(B) once
(C) few
(D) any

PART 6

Directions: Read the texts that follow. A word, phrase, or sentence is missing in parts of each text. Four answer choices for each question are given below the text. Select the best answer to complete the text. Then mark the letter (A), (B), (C), or (D) on your answer sheet.

Questions 131-134 refer to the following memo.

To: Sandra Carter

From: Melissa Sanchez

Date: May 27

Subject: New Hires

Please be ------- that three new employees will be starting in your department tomorrow.
131.
Their names are Cleo White, Marcia Strong, and Xavier Thompson. Mr. White will be

working on Roland Porter's team while Ms. Strong and Mr. Thompson will be on Kendra

Murray's team. In the morning, all three will attend the orientation session we're holding

in the auditorium. -------, they'll have lunch at noon with the CEO and department heads
132.
in the cafeteria. -------. Once lunch ends, you'll ------- them back to your department and
133. **134.**
introduce them to everyone there. Please do everything you can to make their first week here

comfortable.

131. (A) advice
(B) advisory
(C) advised
(D) advisor

132. (A) Afterward
(B) However
(C) Beforehand
(D) Occasionally

133. (A) Your presence will not be necessary the entire day.
(B) That's when you'll get the opportunity to meet them.
(C) Someone from HR will lead them through the entire process.
(D) The orientation session will take place at that time.

134. (A) approach
(B) instruct
(C) leave
(D) escort

GO ON TO THE NEXT PAGE

ACTUAL TEST 4

March 8

Dear Mr. Grimes,

-------. She will be taking possession of the apartment on April 3. You must therefore
135.

------- the premises no later than April 2. Prior -------, please contact George Shultz, the
136. **137.**

building manager. He will conduct an inspection of the unit on your last day there. If there is

no damage to the apartment, your security deposit will be returned in -------. If he detects a
138.

problem, you may be required to pay to fix it. Please be sure to inform him when you will be

moving out. It has been a pleasure having you as a tenant at Griswold Apartments for the

past five years.

Regards,

Karen Lawson
Owner, Griswold Apartments

---

135. (A) We have decided to rent the apartment
you asked about to someone else.
(B) Your mortgage has been approved, so
you can move into the apartment.
(C) A replacement tenant has been found
for the unit you are moving out of.
(D) The rent on your apartment is being
raised by $50 a month.

136. (A) attempt
(B) move
(C) terminate
(D) vacate

137. (A) left
(B) leave
(C) to leaving
(D) will leave

138. (A) full
(B) complete
(C) amount
(D) entire

Questions 139-142 refer to the following announcement.

Munford Tunnel to Reopen Soon

The Munford Tunnel, which goes ------- through Sidewinder Mountain, will be reopening on
          139.

April 21. The tunnel had been closed for repairs to its ventilation system. ------- a failure with
          140.

the air conditioning, air was not being cycled in and out of the tunnel. That problem has since

been solved, so the tunnel is once again safe for traffic. The reopening of the tunnel should

------- traffic conditions in the local area. -------. For more information regarding the tunnel
  141.   **142.**

and the repair work done on it, please contact the mayor's office at 580-2948.

---

139. (A) direction
(B) directive
(C) directly
(D) directed

140. (A) In spite of
(B) In return for
(C) Due to
(D) Instead of

141. (A) ease
(B) approve
(C) involve
(D) remove

142. (A) More funding to complete the
necessary work is required.
(B) Local residents are pleased the tunnel
has finally been built.
(C) The first vehicles will be allowed
through the tunnel in May.
(D) It should also reduce commuting times
by a significant amount.

ACTUAL TEST 4

GO ON TO THE NEXT PAGE

Introducing the Chamberlain Café

The Chamberlain Café will be opening its doors ------- the first time on November 1.
143.
Located at the corner of Duncan Street and Lucent Avenue, it's on the first floor of the Maple

Building. All kinds of hot and cold beverages will be sold at the café. Visitors can also buy

pastries, sandwiches, and salads. On the café's opening day, all food and drinks will be

sold for half off. Free Wi-Fi is ------- with the purchase of any drink. We will provide takeout
144.
services and make ------- within a five-block area of our location. -------. Visit our Web site at
145.   **146.**
www.chamberlaincafe.com to learn more about us.

143. (A) at
(B) for
(C) on
(D) in

144. (A) available
(B) installed
(C) applied
(D) considered

145. (A) delivery
(B) deliverance
(C) deliveries
(D) delivered

146. (A) Ask a server about the types of drinks
we sell.
(B) This offer only applies to stores located
in the city limits.
(C) Our customers can't stop talking about
our service.
(D) A small fee will be applied to the total
charge.

PART 7

Directions: In this part you will read a selection of texts, such as magazine and newspaper articles, e-mails, and instant messages. Each text or set of texts is followed by several questions. Select the best answer for each question and mark the letter (A), (B), (C), or (D) on your answer sheet.

Questions 147-148 refer to the following notice.

Grayson Gym to Undergo Renovations

Grayson Gym will be closed for renovations from April 10 to April 16. During that time, the gym will increase in size by nearly 70%. This will provide more room for the gym's members to exercise. When the renovations are completed, there will be additional space for weightlifting, yoga, and aerobics. The men's and women's locker rooms will be enlarged, and two squash courts will be added. Most of the equipment will be replaced with newer and more modern machines. We regret to inform everyone that our doors will be closed during the renovation period

147. According to the notice, what is NOT true about the renovations?

(A) There will be more room for aerobics.
(B) Squash courts and a sauna will be made.
(C) Some new equipment will be added.
(D) They will make the gym become larger.

148. What is suggested about the gym's members?

(A) Their membership fees will increase in April.
(B) They requested that the renovations be done.
(C) Their class schedules will be altered by management.
(D) They will be unable to work out from April 10 to 16.

GO ON TO THE NEXT PAGE

ACTUAL TEST 4

Questions 149-150 refer to the following e-mail.

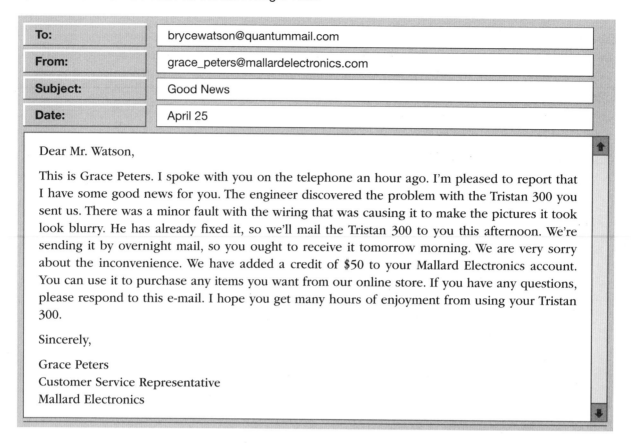

To:	brycewatson@quantummail.com
From:	grace_peters@mallardelectronics.com
Subject:	Good News
Date:	April 25

Dear Mr. Watson,

This is Grace Peters. I spoke with you on the telephone an hour ago. I'm pleased to report that I have some good news for you. The engineer discovered the problem with the Tristan 300 you sent us. There was a minor fault with the wiring that was causing it to make the pictures it took look blurry. He has already fixed it, so we'll mail the Tristan 300 to you this afternoon. We're sending it by overnight mail, so you ought to receive it tomorrow morning. We are very sorry about the inconvenience. We have added a credit of $50 to your Mallard Electronics account. You can use it to purchase any items you want from our online store. If you have any questions, please respond to this e-mail. I hope you get many hours of enjoyment from using your Tristan 300.

Sincerely,

Grace Peters
Customer Service Representative
Mallard Electronics

149. What most likely is the Tristan 300?

(A) A laptop computer
(B) A digital camera
(C) A laser printer
(D) A fax machine

150. What did Mr. Peters give to Mr. Watson?

(A) Credit to his store account
(B) A discount coupon
(C) A free user's manual
(D) Some complimentary accessories

Questions 151-152 refer to the following text message chain.

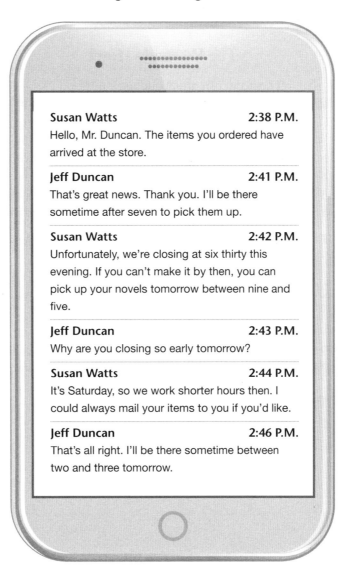

Susan Watts   2:38 P.M.
Hello, Mr. Duncan. The items you ordered have
arrived at the store.

Jeff Duncan   2:41 P.M.
That's great news. Thank you. I'll be there
sometime after seven to pick them up.

Susan Watts   2:42 P.M.
Unfortunately, we're closing at six thirty this
evening. If you can't make it by then, you can
pick up your novels tomorrow between nine and
five.

Jeff Duncan   2:43 P.M.
Why are you closing so early tomorrow?

Susan Watts   2:44 P.M.
It's Saturday, so we work shorter hours then. I
could always mail your items to you if you'd like.

Jeff Duncan   2:46 P.M.
That's all right. I'll be there sometime between
two and three tomorrow.

151. Where does Ms. Watts most likely work?

(A) At an electronics store
(B) At a clothing store
(C) At a shoe store
(D) At a bookstore

152. At 2:46 P.M., why does Mr. Duncan write, "That's all right"?

(A) To thank Ms. Watts for her assistance
(B) To indicate he will visit today
(C) To express his happiness
(D) To turn down a suggestion

GO ON TO THE NEXT PAGE

The Westside Hotel

The holder of this voucher is entitled to
a free stay in a junior suite for one week at the Westside Hotel.

- This offer is valid at all 153 Westside Hotel locations around the world.
- The holder must make a reservation at least two weeks in advance.
- This voucher has no expiration date and may be used at any time of the year.
- Call 1-888-403-3039 to make a booking or to ask questions.
- A booking request may be rejected if the hotel has no available rooms.

153. What is suggested about the Westside Hotel?

(A) Its best rooms are junior suites.
(B) It can be found in several countries.
(C) Its average rates are more than $150 a night.
(D) It gives coupons to all returning guests.

154. What is indicated about the coupon?

(A) It cannot be used during some months.
(B) It provides an upgrade to a better room.
(C) It is good for a stay lasting seven days.
(D) It is only valid for one year.

A New Start
by Rachel Weiss

Cooperstown (March 27) – In recent years, Cooperstown has been experiencing hard times. – [1] –. The population has declined, and several major employers have left. Many local residents have felt as if the town is in danger of dying.

Fortunately, one of Cooperstown's native sons has remembered his roots. Harold Williams moved away from Cooperstown when he was 18, but he never forgot the place where he grew up. – [2] –. Mr. Williams became a highly successful businessman and owned several sawmills throughout the country. Last month, Mr. Williams sold his properties so that he could retire.

He promptly contacted the Cooperstown City Council and asked what the town needed from him. – [3] –. Last night, it was revealed that the town's two schools will be completely renovated, and more teachers will be hired. Mr. Williams will be paying the bill for everything. "I want to make sure the children here get educated well," commented Mr. Williams. "I'm sure I'll do something else for the town in the near future. – [4] –. I'm open to suggestions."

---

155. What is the purpose of the article?

(A) To profile a local resident
(B) To describe ongoing renovations
(C) To advertise for some teaching positions
(D) To report on a donation to the city

156. What does the article indicate about Mr. Williams?

(A) He no longer works.
(B) He moved back to Cooperstown.
(C) He will become a teacher.
(D) He sold a property in Cooperstown.

157. In which of the positions marked [1], [2], [3], and [4] does the following sentence best belong?

"I'm just not sure what that will be."

(A) [1]
(B) [2]
(C) [3]
(D) [4]

GO ON TO THE NEXT PAGE

MEMO

To: All Managers

From: David Bowman

Subject: Directory

Date: December 18

The Personnel Department will be updating the employee directory, so we need recent pictures of every manager at the firm. You can either submit a picture yourself, or you can visit Room 182 on December 20 between the hours of 1 P.M. and 4 P.M. to have one taken for you.

Should you hand in your own picture, you should be dressed in formal wear, and there should be a white background behind you. If you elect to have your picture taken here, please be sure to dress accordingly on Friday. All pictures must be submitted before the end of the day on Monday, December 23.

Because the company has grown so much in recent years, the directory will no longer be printed but will instead be posted online. Short biographies of each manager will be posted in it, so please write around 150 words about yourself. Your education, work history, and interests should be included.

158. What does the memo explain?

(A) Where employees can upload the directory

(B) Why the directory is being updated

(C) Who is in charge of making the directory

(D) What is needed to put in the directory

159. What is mentioned about the pictures?

(A) They should be taken in black and white.

(B) They can be taken at the company.

(C) They can be taken in casual wear.

(D) They will be taken on December 23.

160. What is suggested about the directory?

(A) Employees must pay for it.

(B) It is too big to print.

(C) It has already been posted.

(D) It needs to be edited.

Questions 161-164 refer to the following e-mail.

To: Rachel Bellinger <rachelb@condortech.com>
From: Gerald Storm <g_storm@condortech.com>
Subject: This Friday
Date: September 8

Dear Ms. Bellinger,

I received the notice in my e-mail about the farewell party being held for Mr. Pike on his last day of work this coming Friday. I have had the pleasure of working alongside Mr. Pike for the past six years. He has served as a mentor to me, and I have learned a great deal from him about the technology industry.

I am truly sorry to hear that he is retiring and moving away after all these years. It's therefore with great regret that I must inform you that I will be unable to attend the party. I'm scheduled to lead a seminar in Dallas on that day, and there is no way I can alter my plans without causing problems for the seminar's organizers.

I wonder if I could send you a recorded message that you could play for Mr. Pike at the party. I think that would be a nice way to express my thanks and to let him know how much I will miss him. In addition, I'll drop by your office after lunch to contribute to the fund to purchase a gift for Mr. Pike.

Sincerely,

Gerald Storm

161. What is NOT indicated about Mr. Pike?

(A) He is resigning from his position.
(B) He was mentored by Mr. Storm.
(C) He will stop working this Friday.
(D) He will live in another city.

162. What is Mr. Storm scheduled to do on Friday?

(A) Conduct a professional event
(B) Travel to another country
(C) Meet some seminar organizers
(D) Interview some job applicants

163. What does Mr. Storm request he be allowed to do?

(A) Purchase his own going-away present
(B) Show up late for Mr. Pike's party
(C) Record a farewell for Mr. Pike to hear
(D) Thank everyone for attending the event

164. What will Mr. Storm probably do in the afternoon?

(A) Visit Mr. Pike
(B) Call Ms. Bellinger
(C) Send an e-mail
(D) Make a donation

GO ON TO THE NEXT PAGE ➡

Questions 165-168 refer to the following Web site.

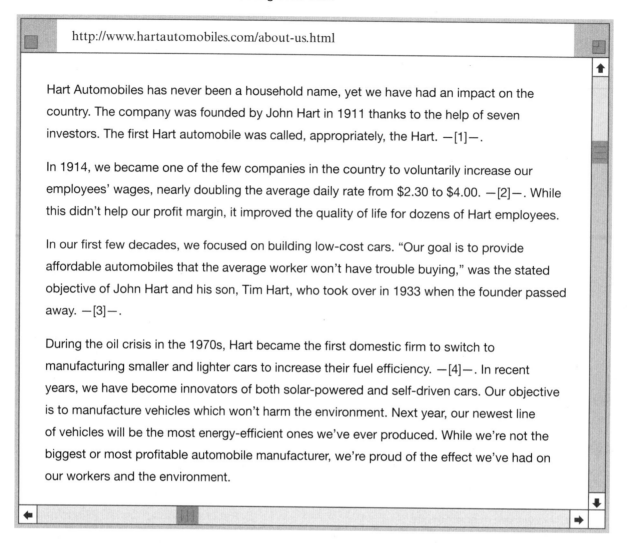

http://www.hartautomobiles.com/about-us.html

Hart Automobiles has never been a household name, yet we have had an impact on the country. The company was founded by John Hart in 1911 thanks to the help of seven investors. The first Hart automobile was called, appropriately, the Hart. —[1]—.

In 1914, we became one of the few companies in the country to voluntarily increase our employees' wages, nearly doubling the average daily rate from $2.30 to $4.00. —[2]—. While this didn't help our profit margin, it improved the quality of life for dozens of Hart employees.

In our first few decades, we focused on building low-cost cars. "Our goal is to provide affordable automobiles that the average worker won't have trouble buying," was the stated objective of John Hart and his son, Tim Hart, who took over in 1933 when the founder passed away. —[3]—.

During the oil crisis in the 1970s, Hart became the first domestic firm to switch to manufacturing smaller and lighter cars to increase their fuel efficiency. —[4]—. In recent years, we have become innovators of both solar-powered and self-driven cars. Our objective is to manufacture vehicles which won't harm the environment. Next year, our newest line of vehicles will be the most energy-efficient ones we've ever produced. While we're not the biggest or most profitable automobile manufacturer, we're proud of the effect we've had on our workers and the environment.

165. According to the information, what is true about Hart Automobiles?

(A) It has a line of solar-powered cars.
(B) It was established by Tim Hart.
(C) It is the country's largest car maker.
(D) It made vehicles that used less fuel.

166. When did Hart Automobiles pay its employees more?

(A) In 1911
(B) In 1914
(C) In 1933
(D) In 1970

167. What is the current goal of Hart Automobiles?

(A) To make the most affordable vehicles on the market
(B) To protect the environment with its vehicles
(C) To provide competitive salaries for its employees
(D) To increase the profits it earns each year

168. In which of the positions marked [1], [2], [3], and [4] does the following sentence best belong?

"It was praised for the quality of its workmanship."

(A) [1]
(B) [2]
(C) [3]
(D) [4]

Questions 169-171 refer to the following letter.

November 8

Dear Mr. Bell,

Thank you for your continued patronage at the Whistler Health Club. You have been a valued client for the past three years.

This notice is to remind you that you must make regular payments to utilize our services. According to our records, you opted to make monthly payments of $30. Perhaps you were busy last month and forgot, but we have not yet received the payment for October, which was due on the 31st of the month. Looking back at your history of payments, we see that you normally take care of your monthly bill between the 25th and 29th of each month.

Would you please submit your payment for October as soon as possible? You can do so with cash anytime you visit the gym, or you can send a check made out to Whistler Health Club to the following address: 4938 Grant Street, Madison, WI. You can also set up automatic payments through online banking. Visit www.whistlerhealthclub.com/payment to learn how to do that.

We look forward to receiving a positive response from you soon.

Regards,

Jeremy Gill

Whistler Health Club

169. Why did Mr. Gill send the letter?

(A) To request a membership renewal
(B) To provide an update on services
(C) To ask about a failure to pay
(D) To suspend a customer's membership

170. What is suggested about Mr. Bell?

(A) He has paid on time in the past.
(B) He works out at the gym daily.
(C) His home is located near the gym.
(D) His workplace pays for his membership.

171. According to the letter, which is NOT a way a customer can make a payment?

(A) By check
(B) By bank transfer
(C) By cash
(D) By credit card

GO ON TO THE NEXT PAGE ▶

Questions 172-175 refer to the following online chat discussion.

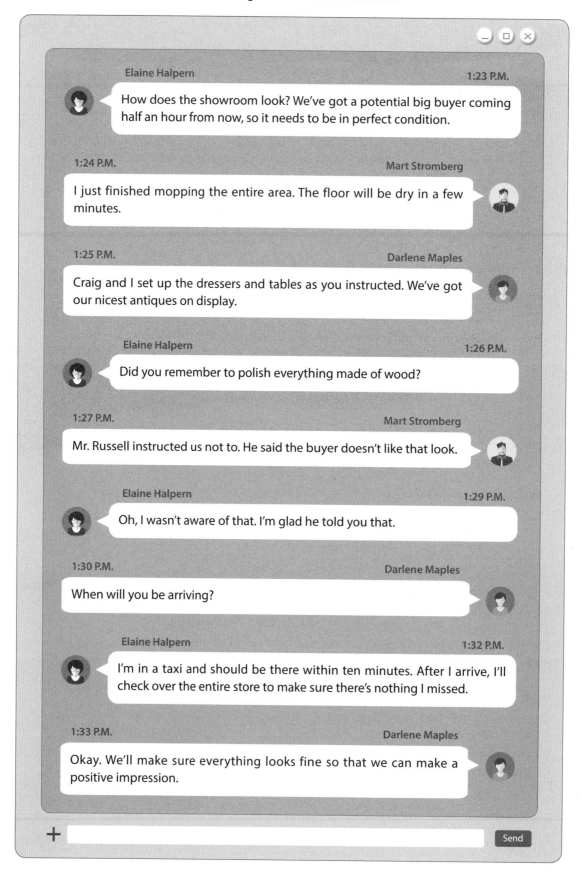

Elaine Halpern 1:23 P.M.

How does the showroom look? We've got a potential big buyer coming half an hour from now, so it needs to be in perfect condition.

1:24 P.M. Mart Stromberg

I just finished mopping the entire area. The floor will be dry in a few minutes.

1:25 P.M. Darlene Maples

Craig and I set up the dressers and tables as you instructed. We've got our nicest antiques on display.

Elaine Halpern 1:26 P.M.

Did you remember to polish everything made of wood?

1:27 P.M. Mart Stromberg

Mr. Russell instructed us not to. He said the buyer doesn't like that look.

Elaine Halpern 1:29 P.M.

Oh, I wasn't aware of that. I'm glad he told you that.

1:30 P.M. Darlene Maples

When will you be arriving?

Elaine Halpern 1:32 P.M.

I'm in a taxi and should be there within ten minutes. After I arrive, I'll check over the entire store to make sure there's nothing I missed.

1:33 P.M. Darlene Maples

Okay. We'll make sure everything looks fine so that we can make a positive impression.

Send

172. Where does Ms. Halpern most likely work?

(A) At a furniture store
(B) At an electronics shop
(C) At a car dealership
(D) At a grocery store

173. According to the writers, what did they NOT do?

(A) Arranged some items
(B) Did some mopping
(C) Removed price tags
(D) Displayed some items

174. At 1:27 P.M. what does Mr. Stromberg imply when he writes, "Mr. Russell instructed us not to"?

(A) He did not contact the customer.
(B) He is not working today.
(C) He is waiting for more instructions.
(D) He did not polish anything.

175. What will Ms. Maples do next?

(A) Call a taxi for Ms. Halpern
(B) Speak with a customer
(C) Look over the store
(D) Clean the showroom

GO ON TO THE NEXT PAGE

Questions 176-180 refer to the following notice and article.

Construction on Hampton Road

Construction crews will work on Hampton Road from Monday, June 10, to Wednesday, June 12. They will begin at 6 A.M. and finish at 9 P.M. every day. The five affected areas are located between Jackson Lane and Carpenter Avenue. The work is being done to repair the street after it suffered a large amount of damage due to the flashflood that happened during last month's thunderstorms. Motorists should avoid traveling on Hampton Road during this time. Only one lane will be open on Hampton Road in each direction during the construction period. Visit the city's Web site at www.oxford.gov/construction to see the precise locations of the work as well as alternative roads that can be taken.

City Apologizes for Long Construction

reported by Christine Lee

Oxford (June 17) – Work on Hampton Road ended on Saturday, June 15. For five days, people driving in the downtown area experienced severe delays. "My morning commute usually only lasts for around thirty-five minutes," said Oxford resident Dean Reynolds. "But it took me two hours to get to work every single day this week," he complained.

Many other commuters made similar complaints. Mayor Melissa Carmichael apologized for the problems at a press conference last night. "We regret the lengthy construction period, but the road was much more severely damaged than we had anticipated before work started. Fortunately, everything is fine now."

According to the mayor, traffic should improve this week now that every lane on Hampton Road has been reopened. If this doesn't, the mayor's office is sure to get many calls from upset residents.

176. According to the notice, what is NOT true about the work on Hampton Road?

(A) It shut down the entire road.
(B) It lasted from morning until night.
(C) It was shown on a map on the city's Web site.
(D) It was done in multiple places.

177. What was the cause of the damage to Hampton Road?

(A) Heavy snow
(B) A traffic accident
(C) Rising water levels
(D) A gas explosion

178. What is indicated about the construction work on Hampton Road?

(A) Two different companies did it.
(B) Traffic was not interfered with.
(C) The work has not been paid for yet.
(D) It took longer than expected.

179. What happened on June 16?

(A) Road construction was completed.
(B) A press conference was held.
(C) A road was closed to traffic.
(D) A street was inspected.

180. What is suggested about the residents of Oxford?

(A) They are unhappy with the roadwork.
(B) Many of them complained to the mayor.
(C) They objected to the work done on the road.
(D) Some of them arranged a meeting at city hall.

GO ON TO THE NEXT PAGE

Benjamin's Specials of the Day

All entrées come with a choice of soup or salad. Diners will also receive a free cold beverage of their choice. The specials of the day change on a daily basis. See the regular menu for all available appetizers and entrées.

Appetizers	Price	Entrées	Price
Fried Calamari	$4.99	Seafood Paella	$18.99
Ceviche	$6.99	Beef Lasagna	$15.99
Roasted Eggplant	$5.99	Lamb Kebabs	$19.99
Tuna Salad	$6.99	Shrimp Alfredo	$17.99

Customers with a Benjamin's Membership Card will not have any discounts applied to the above menu items.

To: benjamin@benjamins.com
From: lisajacobs@thismail.com
Subject: Lunch
Date: October 11
Attachment: receipt.jpg

Dear Mr. Morris,

My name is Lisa Jacobs. Yesterday, October 10, I had lunch at your dining establishment with one of my colleagues. I thoroughly enjoyed the meal that was prepared for me. The appetizer and the entrée were impressive, and the chocolate mousse which my waitress recommended to me for dessert was the best I've ever had. I definitely intend to return to your restaurant in the future.

However, as you can see from the picture of the receipt I am sending with this e-mail, I was charged too much for my meal. I paid $28.99 for my meal when I should have been charged only $18.99. I'm sure this was a simple mistake, but I would like to have the extra $10.00 refunded to my credit card.

Thank you.

Lisa Jacobs

181. What will individuals who order an entrée receive for free?

(A) A vegetable side dish
(B) A salad and coffee
(C) A cold drink
(D) A dessert

182. What is indicated about Benjamin's?

(A) It offers specials five days a week.
(B) It changes its menu every season.
(C) It is located inside a shopping center.
(D) It charges some customers lower prices.

183. What does Ms. Jacobs mention about the dessert she ate?

(A) She enjoyed it very much.
(B) She had ordered it on a previous visit.
(C) She requested the recipe for it.
(D) She thought it went well with her meal.

184. Why did Ms. Jacobs send the e-mail?

(A) To make a reservation
(B) To compliment the waitress
(C) To request some money back
(D) To ask about an upcoming special

185. What did Ms. Jacobs have for an entrée?

(A) Seafood paella
(B) Beef lasagna
(C) Lamb kebabs
(D) Shrimp alfredo

GO ON TO THE NEXT PAGE

ACTUAL TEST 4

Cumberland Clothes Survey

We value our customers at Cumberland Clothes. Please complete this survey and give it to any employee at the store to receive a coupon for $5. If you leave your name and contact information, we will enter you in a drawing. Ten winners will win special gifts.

How would you rate the following?

	Excellent	Good	Average	Poor	Terrible
Selection of Items			✓		
Prices of Items		✓			
Quality of Items				✓	
Style of Items					✓

Comments: *I used to shop here every month but rarely come anymore. The clothes are too old fashioned and get worn out quickly. I feel like I'm wasting my money by shopping here, so I doubt I'll come back again.*

Name: *Wilma Hamilton*

Contact Information: *whamilton@personalmail.com*

To: Daniel Marbut, Raisa Andropov, Jordan West, Elaine Nash
From: Craig Murphy
Subject: Survey Results
Date: August 21

In the past six week, we received more than 1,700 online and offline survey responses, and the overall results are disappointing. However, the responses clearly explain why we've been losing so many customers. Basically, our customers dislike the looks of our clothes, referring to them by words such as "ugly," "old fashioned," and "out of style." Many customers believe our clothes are poorly made. They complained about items ripping, tearing, and fading. They disliked the service we've been providing as well.

I took the liberty of speaking with every individual who left contact information on the survey and got in-depth responses from many of them. What we need to do is change the brands of the items we sell, or we'll go out of business soon.

BIG SALE

Visit every location of
Cumberland Clothes
for a sale lasting from
October 1-31.

We are introducing several new lines of clothes.

We now sell clothes made by:

Urias, Marconi, Andretti, and Christopher's.

You'll love the quality and the look of these clothes.

They are the most fashionable on the market.

And don't worry because the prices we're famous for will stay the same.

Visit the new Cumberland Clothes.

We provide the clothes our shoppers want.

186. What is indicated about Ms. Hamilton?

(A) She purchases items at Cumberland Clothes for their quality.
(B) She thinks the prices at Cumberland Clothes are high.
(C) She belongs to the Cumberland Shoppers Club.
(D) She received a coupon for Cumberland Clothes.

187. How did Ms. Hamilton feel about the items at Cumberland Clothes?

(A) She thought they were out of style.
(B) She thought they were overpriced.
(C) She thought they were well made.
(D) She thought they were colorful.

188. What is suggested about Mr. Murphy?

(A) He is the owner of Cumberland Clothes.
(B) He sent an e-mail to Ms. Hamilton.
(C) He works for a market research firm.
(D) He dislikes the selection at Cumberland Clothes.

189. What does Mr. Murphy recommend doing?

(A) Selling new brands
(B) Training workers better
(C) Lowering prices
(D) Conducting a new survey

190. Which complaint made by customers is NOT addressed in the advertisement?

(A) The styles of the clothes
(B) The customer service
(C) The clothing selections
(D) The appearances of the clothes

GO ON TO THE NEXT PAGE

Questions 191-195 refer to the following letter, order form, and schedule.

February 15

Dear Mr. Swanson,

Congratulations on being hired by the Greenbrier Hotel. Your first day of work will be March 10. You will be employed in the Room Service Department. At times, you will assist with food preparation like the type you're doing at your current job. At other times, you will deliver food to guests in their rooms or work as a member of the wait staff at Crawford's, our fine-dining establishment on the third floor.

Room Service Department employees must wear uniforms at all times. You have to wear white pants and a white shirt while in the kitchen or delivering food. You must wear black pants and a white button-down shirt when working at Crawford's. Please complete the order form included with the letter and return it at once. The Greenbrier Hotel will pay for two of each clothing item listed above. You must pay for anything else you purchase.

Sincerely,

Tabitha Lang

Supervisor, Room Service Department
Greenbrier Hotel

Imperial Fashions
874 Crossway Road
London, England
WP36 7TR

Order Form

Customer Name: Allan Swanson
Address: 39 Baker Street, London, England, OL43 2SE
Telephone Number: 954-3922
E-Mail Address: allanswanson@thamesmail.com

Item	Quantity	Unit Price	Total Price
Pants, Black (L)	2	£20	£40
Shirt, White (L)	1	£17	£17
Button-Down Shirt, White (L)	3	£25	£75
Pants, White (L)	2	£22	£44
		Total	£176

Bill To: Greenbrier Hotel, Room Service Department
Client Number: 9404392

Room Service Department Schedule
April 1-7

Employee: Allan Swanson

Day	Time	Location	Notes
April 1	9 A.M. – 6 P.M.	Kitchen	Delivery + Food Preparation
April 2	9 A.M. – 6 P.M.	Kitchen	Delivery
April 3	1 P.M. – 9 P.M.	Crawford's	Wait Staff
April 4	1 P.M. – 9 P.M.	Crawford's	Wait Staff + Food Preparation
April 5	6 P.M. – 2 A.M.	Kitchen	Delivery

Comments

April 6 and 7 are days off. However, this schedule is subject to change if another employee requests vacation time on either day. You will be informed no later than 6 P.M. on April 4 if your presence is required.

191. What is the purpose of the letter?

(A) To describe a process
(B) To give a schedule
(C) To make a request
(D) To provide instructions

192. What is Crawford's?

(A) A convenience store
(B) A restaurant
(C) A café
(D) A bakery

193. What is indicated about Mr. Swanson?

(A) He expected to work at the hotel's front desk.
(B) He will begin his new job in February.
(C) He has experience in the food service industry.
(D) He will be paid by the hour at his job.

194. How much money must Mr. Swanson reimburse the hotel?

(A) £17
(B) £20
(C) £22
(D) £25

195. According to the schedule, what is true about Mr. Swanson?

(A) He must wear black pants on April 3.
(B) He has three days off from April 1 to 7.
(C) He is working the night shift on April 2.
(D) He will cook food on April 5.

GO ON TO THE NEXT PAGE

Archer Grocery Store Coming to Haven

by Nabil Apu

Haven (January 4) – The CEO of Archer Grocery Store, a large national chain, stated he hopes to open a store in Haven this year. "Haven's downtown lacks supermarkets," commented David Leatherwood. "Local residents would benefit by having a store there," he added.

Archer is highly regarded for the wide selection of inexpensive fresh foods its sells. Every Archer features a deli and a bakery and is open 24 hours a day, 7 days a week, increasing the convenience for shoppers. Most Archers are located in so-called food deserts, where there is a relative lack of fresh food options. Thus local residents reacted positively upon hearing the news Archer may be moving there.

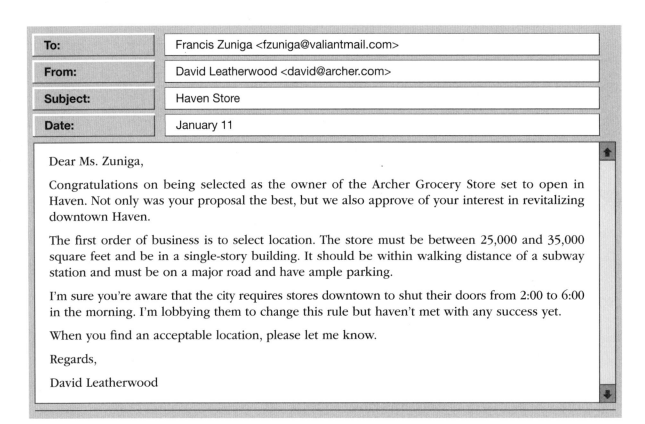

To:	Francis Zuniga <fzuniga@valiantmail.com>
From:	David Leatherwood <david@archer.com>
Subject:	Haven Store
Date:	January 11

Dear Ms. Zuniga,

Congratulations on being selected as the owner of the Archer Grocery Store set to open in Haven. Not only was your proposal the best, but we also approve of your interest in revitalizing downtown Haven.

The first order of business is to select location. The store must be between 25,000 and 35,000 square feet and be in a single-story building. It should be within walking distance of a subway station and must be on a major road and have ample parking.

I'm sure you're aware that the city requires stores downtown to shut their doors from 2:00 to 6:00 in the morning. I'm lobbying them to change this rule but haven't met with any success yet.

When you find an acceptable location, please let me know.

Regards,

David Leatherwood

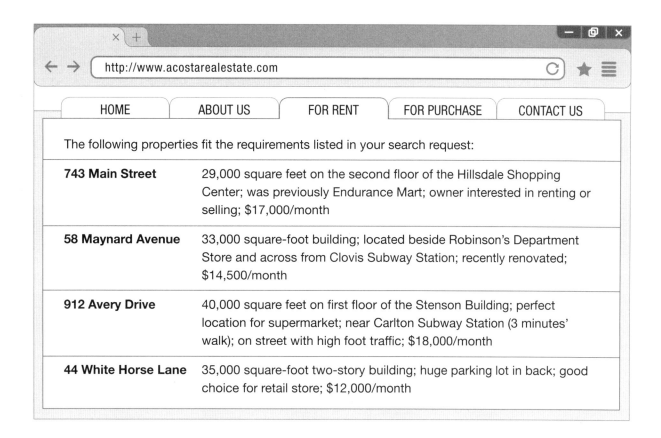

http://www.acostarealestate.com

| HOME | ABOUT US | FOR RENT | FOR PURCHASE | CONTACT US |

The following properties fit the requirements listed in your search request:

743 Main Street	29,000 square feet on the second floor of the Hillsdale Shopping Center; was previously Endurance Mart; owner interested in renting or selling; $17,000/month
58 Maynard Avenue	33,000 square-foot building; located beside Robinson's Department Store and across from Clovis Subway Station; recently renovated; $14,500/month
912 Avery Drive	40,000 square feet on first floor of the Stenson Building; perfect location for supermarket; near Carlton Subway Station (3 minutes' walk); on street with high foot traffic; $18,000/month
44 White Horse Lane	35,000 square-foot two-story building; huge parking lot in back; good choice for retail store; $12,000/month

196. Who is Mr. Leatherwood?

(A) A Haven resident
(B) An investor
(C) A shopper
(D) A company president

197. In the article, the word "relative" in paragraph 2, line 9, is closest in meaning to

(A) familial
(B) excessive
(C) unfortunate
(D) comparative

198. Why did Mr. Leatherwood send the e-mail?

(A) To describe some restrictions
(B) To offer a contract
(C) To negotiate a deal
(D) To respond to a suggestion

199. How will the Archer Grocery Store in Haven differ from other Archer Grocery Stores?

(A) It will not have a bakery.
(B) It will be on two floors.
(C) It will close each night.
(D) It will sell imported food.

200. Where is the place Ms. Zuniga will most likely recommend to Mr. Leatherwood?

(A) At 743 Main Street
(B) At 58 Maynard Avenue
(C) At 912 Avery Drive
(D) At 44 White Horse Lane

Stop! This is the end of the test. If you finish before time is called, you may go back to Parts 5, 6, and 7 and check your work.

Actual Test RC

5

READING TEST

In the Reading test, you will read a variety of texts and answer several different types of reading comprehension questions. The entire Reading test will last 75 minutes. There are three parts, and directions are given for each part. You are encouraged to answer as many questions as possible within the time allowed.

You must mark your answers on the separate answer sheet. Do not write your answers in your test book.

PART 5

Directions: A word or phrase is missing in each of the sentences below. Four answer choices are given below each sentence. Select the best answer to complete the sentence. Then mark the letter (A), (B), (C), or (D) on your answer sheet.

101. Ms. Collins cited several ------- of signing a contract with Delmont Shipping during the meeting.

(A) reasons
(B) opinions
(C) advantages
(D) considerations

102. New cutting machines were installed to increase the ------- of the workers on the factory floor.

(A) effective
(B) effecting
(C) effectiveness
(D) effectively

103. ------- options exist for individuals who are interested in changing the terms of their memberships.

(A) Several
(B) All
(C) Much
(D) Little

104. Tickets for the book signing ------- away on a first-come, first-served basis all week long.

(A) are giving
(B) are being given
(C) have been giving
(D) will give

105. The mayor hopes to ------- the plan to improve the city's infrastructure at the beginning of June.

(A) attract
(B) report
(C) approach
(D) implement

106. The unemployment rate in the region has improved ------- since several local manufacturers started hiring more workers.

(A) tremendously
(B) eventually
(C) responsibly
(D) quietly

107. Managers are investigating how ------- like the one that happened yesterday can be avoided.

(A) incidental
(B) incidents
(C) incidentally
(D) incident

108. Individuals who hope to take time off during the winter months need to clear it ------- a supervisor first.

(A) for
(B) with
(C) by
(D) on

109. As a general rule, the company selects the most ------- option when deciding on new suppliers.

(A) afford
(B) afforded
(C) affording
(D) affordable

110. The clerk ------- Ms. Carpenter to a suite as a way of apologizing for losing her reservation.

(A) awarded
(B) upgraded
(C) announced
(D) paid

111. While only three people applied for the position, ------- of them were highly qualified, which made selecting the ideal candidate difficult.

(A) each
(B) all
(C) both
(D) none

112. Several individuals had their schedules ------- since a new project was suddenly announced.

(A) changed
(B) been changing
(C) will change
(D) are changed

113. Once the contract is signed, ------- to pay for the raw materials must be sent within 48 hours.

(A) accounts
(B) intentions
(C) matter
(D) funds

114. The interns had lunch with the CEO ------- on their first day of work at the Ampere Company.

(A) him
(B) his own
(C) he
(D) himself

115. Ms. Kennedy will ------- up to six employees to attend this weekend's seminar in Des Moines.

(A) permit
(B) credit
(C) remit
(D) submit

116. The artist ------- to display more than 30 of her most recent works at an upcoming exhibition at the Furman Gallery.

(A) has been intended
(B) will have been intended
(C) intends
(D) is intended

117. All ------- must be interviewed before they complete the firm's competency test.

(A) applications
(B) applies
(C) applicants
(D) applicable

118. Ms. Thompson got in touch with the buyer ------- her meeting with Mr. Roberts concluded.

(A) instead of
(B) as a result of
(C) as soon as
(D) in spite of

119. ------- for the contractors to enter the warehouse was given by Ms. Hoskins, the supervisor on duty.

(A) Clear
(B) Clearance
(C) Clearly
(D) Cleared

120. Ever since last November, Fulton Research ------- scientists to work in several of its laboratories.

(A) will hire
(B) will be hiring
(C) has been hiring
(D) was hire

GO ON TO THE NEXT PAGE ▶

121. The demonstration at RC Technology was attended by a large number of ------- of the local media.

(A) members
(B) performers
(C) editors
(D) reporters

122. The company's new logo received widespread praise from both customers and industry -------.

(A) insides
(B) insiders
(C) inside
(D) insider

123. Once the ------- for proposals was made, several employees offered suggestions that were deemed interesting.

(A) admission
(B) submission
(C) request
(D) approval

124. Traffic had to be diverted while construction work was being done at the -------.

(A) intersect
(B) intersection
(C) intersective
(D) intersected

125. Lincoln Interior always provides a price ------- for customers before starting any work.

(A) endorsement
(B) warranty
(C) estimate
(D) support

126. ------- the article is rejected by the editor, another magazine might be interested in publishing it.

(A) Since
(B) However
(C) In addition
(D) Even if

127. The snowfall was ------- heavy that most vehicles in the downtown area could not move until snowplows were brought in.

(A) so
(B) very
(C) too
(D) most

128. The inspector hopes to ------- whether safety regulations are being followed.

(A) arrange
(B) determine
(C) clear
(D) approve

129. Unless the ID cards ------- soon, their holders will not be able to unlock any doors in the entire facility.

(A) fix
(B) will fix
(C) are fixed
(D) have fixed

130. The contract must be signed ------- Friday evening, or the agreement will be considered invalid.

(A) by
(B) within
(C) about
(D) in

PART 6

Directions: Read the texts that follow. A word, phrase, or sentence is missing in parts of each text. Four answer choices for each question are given below the text. Select the best answer to complete the text. Then mark the letter (A), (B), (C), or (D) on your answer sheet.

Questions 131-134 refer to the following e-mail.

To: rclark@betaengineering.com
From: lmarlowe@personalmail.com
Subject: Engineering Position
Date: September 28

Dear Mr. Clark,

I received your offer of employment by certified mail yesterday. After ------- the matter with
131.
my family, I have decided to accept your offer. I am looking forward to working at Beta

Engineering in the near future.

-------. I wonder if you would mind waiting until November 1. My current employer requires
132.
that I give 30 days' notice before resigning. I also need to move my family to a new city,

which will take ------- time.
133.

As for the financial ------- and benefits package you offered, I am fully satisfied. I will be
134.
signing the contract and returning it to you in the mail tomorrow.

Regards,

Lewis Marlowe

ACTUAL TEST 5

131. (A) discussed
(B) discussion
(C) discussing
(D) discusses

132. (A) Increasing my salary by $10,000 a year
would be ideal.
(B) I'm willing to start my tenure at the firm
as soon as possible.
(C) It is important for me to give this matter
a bit more consideration.
(D) Your letter mentioned that you would
like me to begin on October 15.

133. (A) some
(B) few
(C) many
(D) any

134. (A) compensate
(B) compensation
(C) compensated
(D) compensatory

GO ON TO THE NEXT PAGE

Questions 135-138 refer to the following memo.

To: All Department Heads
From: Jason Cheswick
Subject: Funds
Date: March 25

As you should be aware, departmental funds are distributed on a quarterly basis.

------. Any funds not spent by that time will be returned to the company's general fund
135.

unless you explain in writing ------ they should remain in your budget. In addition, please
136.

be aware that failure to spend all of the money ------ in your budget being decreased in the
137.

coming quarter. If you have already exceeded your quarterly budget, I need ------ explaining
138.

why no later than April 4. The amount of money you went over your budget will be extracted

from your funds for the second quarter unless I determine otherwise.

135. (A) We are giving consideration to changing this policy.
(B) The end of the first quarter of the year is on March 31.
(C) You may apply for extra funding if you need it at once.
(D) I do not have access to the funds that you were given.

136. (A) where
(B) when
(C) why
(D) how

137. (A) has resulted
(B) may result
(C) will have resulted
(D) is resulting

138. (A) document
(B) documented
(C) documentable
(D) documentation

Questions 139-142 refer to the following article.

Housing Prices in Benson Continue to Rise

Benson (August 19) – According to the latest statistics, the prices of individual houses in Benson have risen for the past fourteen months in a row. In July, the average price of a 3-bedroom home in the city was $147,400. -------.
139.

Benson is currently suffering a housing shortage as its ------- rises dramatically. This is
140.
happening because several companies in the local area have expanded and are therefore hiring large numbers of workers.

Construction companies in Benson are busy building dozens of new houses, ------- the first
141.
ones are not scheduled to be completed until November. When that happens, it is expected that housing prices will ------- to some extent.
142.

---

139. (A) This is an increase of 1.2% from the average price in June.
(B) Residents can sell their homes with various real estate agencies.
(C) June saw prices of homes go down by a slight amount.
(D) Apartment buildings are considered more convenient by some residents.

140. (A) unemployment
(B) income
(C) population
(D) taxation

141. (A) or
(B) when
(C) before
(D) but

142. (A) stabilize
(B) appear
(C) increase
(D) advertise

GO ON TO THE NEXT PAGE

ACTUAL TEST **5**

March 4

Dear Mr. Merriweather,

I am writing this letter to announce that ------- application to become a member of the Salem
                                            143.
Community Swimming Pool has been accepted. You requested a family membership, and it

has been granted. -------. However, your application fee of $150 will be ------- to the cost of
                   144.   **145.**
this year's membership. Please make the remaining $600 payment no later than March 31.

Otherwise, we will assume you are no longer interested in joining the swimming pool. For

more information about the pool, the hours, swimming lessons, and our swim team, please

call 843-9283 during ------- business hours.
                      146.

Sincerely,

Steve Atkins
Salem Community Swimming Pool

143. (A) my
     (B) his
     (C) their
     (D) your

144. (A) It was a pleasure meeting your family at
         the interview.
     (B) The total cost of membership per year
         is $750.
     (C) We hope you enjoy swimming at the
         pool.
     (D) You are now welcome to visit the pool
         at any time.

145. (A) deducted
     (B) applied
     (C) reduced
     (D) observed

146. (A) regular
     (B) regulated
     (C) regulation
     (D) regulatory

Directions: In this part you will read a selection of texts, such as magazine and newspaper articles, e-mails, and instant messages. Each text or set of texts is followed by several questions. Select the best answer for each question and mark the letter (A), (B), (C), or (D) on your answer sheet.

Questions 147-148 refer to the following announcement.

Employee Benefits

As previously announced, we are switching medical and dental insurance providers. The new providers are able to offer much more affordable insurance packages. These changes will not only guarantee that you get more money in your monthly paychecks but will also give you more comprehensive health care. According to the law, we need your permission to permit our new providers to access your personal information. Please log on to the computer system and update and confirm your family records, such as names and birthdates. In addition, check the box at the bottom of the screen stating "I agree" so we can guarantee that the transition goes smoothly. The deadline is this Friday at 6:00 P.M.

147. What is being announced?

(A) An increase in health insurance rates
(B) A new way to make insurance payments
(C) An alteration to employee benefits
(D) A date for annual employee checkups

148. What are employees asked to do?

(A) Complete a form
(B) Check some information
(C) Pay a fee
(D) Select a new provider

GO ON TO THE NEXT PAGE

Questions 149-150 refer to the following e-mail.

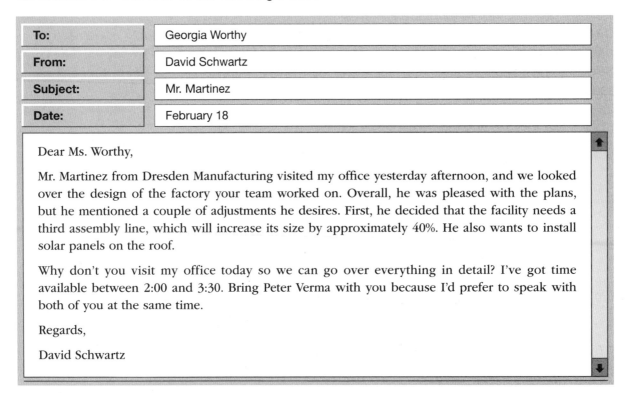

To:	Georgia Worthy
From:	David Schwartz
Subject:	Mr. Martinez
Date:	February 18

Dear Ms. Worthy,

Mr. Martinez from Dresden Manufacturing visited my office yesterday afternoon, and we looked over the design of the factory your team worked on. Overall, he was pleased with the plans, but he mentioned a couple of adjustments he desires. First, he decided that the facility needs a third assembly line, which will increase its size by approximately 40%. He also wants to install solar panels on the roof.

Why don't you visit my office today so we can go over everything in detail? I've got time available between 2:00 and 3:30. Bring Peter Verma with you because I'd prefer to speak with both of you at the same time.

Regards,

David Schwartz

149. Why did Mr. Schwartz send the e-mail?

(A) To ask for an opinion
(B) To request advice
(C) To provide an update
(D) To make an apology

150. What is suggested about Mr. Verma?

(A) He is involved with Mr. Martinez's project.
(B) He is an employee at Dresden Manufacturing.
(C) He has not met Mr. Schwartz in person.
(D) He is currently inspecting a facility.

Questions 151-152 refer to the following receipt.

```
                    Oceanside Resort
           488 Pacific Avenue, Honolulu, HI 96813
                 Telephone: (808) 371-8473
```

Receipt

Name: Caroline Mason
Address: 81 Liberty Road, Los Angeles, CA 90219
E-Mail Address: carolinemason@privatemail.com
Reservation Date: May 3
Reservation Number: OR847-944

Date	Description	Amount
May 5	Double Room	$75.00
May 6	Double Room	$75.00
May 6	Room Service	$22.00
May 7	Double Room	$75.00
May 7	Mini Bar	$34.00
	Subtotal	$281.00
	Tax	$16.86
	Total	$287.86

E-Mail Address: May 8
Credit Card Holder: Caroline Mason
Signature: *Caroline Mason*

ACTUAL TEST 5

151. When did Ms. Mason check in to the Oceanside Resort?

(A) On May 3
(B) On May 5
(C) On May 6
(D) On May 7

152. What is indicated about Ms. Mason?

(A) She stayed at the resort for four nights.
(B) She reserved her room online.
(C) She ate a meal in her room.
(D) She received a discounted rate.

GO ON TO THE NEXT PAGE

139

Questions 153-154 refer to the following text message chain.

Sylvia Hasselhoff   10:11 A.M.
Cliff, I'll be visiting Wilbur's in a few minutes.
Do you need me to pick up anything?

Cliff Mellon   10:12 A.M.
Thanks for asking. I've got a long list.

Sylvia Hasselhoff   10:13 A.M.
I don't know if I can carry everything by
myself.

Cliff Mellon   10:14 A.M.
Why don't I go with you then? Would you
mind waiting for half an hour? I have to meet
with Mr. Donovan about my project now.

Sylvia Hasselhoff   10:15 A.M.
That's fine with me. Just let me know when
you're ready to go. I'll be waiting in my office.

153. At 10:13 A.M., what does Ms. Hasselhoff mean when she writes, "I don't know if I can carry everything by myself"?

(A) She has not been going to the gym lately.
(B) She has decided to drive to the store instead.
(C) She will ask another employee to go with her.
(D) She cannot purchase everything Mr. Mellon wants.

154. What will Mr. Mellon probably do next?

(A) Talk to Mr. Donovan
(B) Visit Ms. Hasselhoff's office
(C) Drive to Wilbur's
(D) Make a telephone call

Questions 155-157 refer to the following e-mail.

To: customerservice@falconair.com
From: pedrodelgado@lombard.com
Subject: Flight FA34
Date: August 18

To Whom It May Concern,

My name is Pedro Delgado. I flew on Falcon Air Flight FA34 from Miami, Florida, to Panama City, Panama, this morning. My reservation number was GT8594AR, and I was seated in economy class in seat 45B. —[1]—.

Unfortunately, it appears as though I didn't take all of my possessions when I got off the plane. I was working the entire flight and placed some important papers in the pocket in the seat in front of me. —[2]—. When it was time to get off the plane, I forgot to recover those documents. —[3]—. I need them for a business meeting tomorrow.

I'm staying in room 283 at the Excelsior Hotel in downtown Panama City and can be reached anytime on my cellphone at (615) 398-9021.

Thank you very much. —[4]—.

Pedro Delgado

155. What problem does Mr. Delgado mention?

(A) He left something on the airplane.
(B) He missed his flight to Panama.
(C) He arrived late for a meeting.
(D) He failed to book a return flight.

156. What is suggested about Mr. Delgado?

(A) He has taken Flight FA34 in the past.
(B) He works at an office in Miami, Florida.
(C) He would prefer to be contacted by phone.
(D) His changed seats on his flight.

157. In which of the positions marked [1], [2], [3], and [4] does the following sentence best belong?

"Could you please see if anyone has found them?"

(A) [1]
(B) [2]
(C) [3]
(D) [4]

GO ON TO THE NEXT PAGE

Questions **158-161** refer to the following schedule.

MPT, Inc. Certification Seminars

MPT, Inc. will be holding certification seminars for its software in several cities throughout the country. The following is the schedule for June and July:

Date	Time (Seminar Only)	Location	Software	Instructor
June 14	9 A.M. – 12 P.M.	Los Angeles, CA	Art Pro	Darlene Campbell
June 28	1 P.M. – 4 P.M.	Houston, TX	Omega	Sophia Beam
July 12	11 A.M. – 2 P.M.	Chicago, IL	Art Pro	Rudolph Mudd
July 19	2 P.M. – 5 P.M.	Baltimore, MD	Diamond	Martin Croft
July 26	10 A.M. – 1 P.M.	Atlanta, GA	Vox	Sophia Beam

Each seminar will consist of a three-hour class providing instruction on the software in question. Then, following a one-hour break, a certification exam will be given. The length of the exam depends upon the software being tested.

All seminars cost $250 to attend. The registration period begins on June 1. Registration for each seminar will end the day before it is scheduled to take place. Those who intend to take the exam must pay a testing fee of $150. Anyone wishing to do both activities can pay a discounted rate of $350. Individuals can register by visiting www.mpt.com/seminarregistration. Test takers will be notified of their scores within 24 hours of taking the exam.

158. Where will the seminar on Diamond be held?

(A) In Chicago
(B) In Atlanta
(C) In Los Angeles
(D) In Baltimore

159. What is indicated about Ms. Beam?

(A) She works in the Houston office.
(B) She prefers afternoon seminars.
(C) She is an expert on Art Pro.
(D) Her job requires her to travel.

160. By when must a person taking the exam in Houston register?

(A) By June 25
(B) By June 26
(C) By June 27
(D) By June 28

161. What is suggested about people who take the exam on July 19?

(A) They will learn their scores on July 20.
(B) They will learn about some art software.
(C) They will take the exam in the morning.
(D) They will pay $400 for the seminar and exam.

A Festival Comes to Town

by staff reporter Brad Thompson

Bayside (October 2) – While Bayside has long been known for its beautiful beaches and outstanding seafood restaurants, another part of the city has been ignored in recent years. That's going to change thanks to the inaugural Bayside Festival.

The festival will last from Friday, October 5, to Sunday, October 7. The festival will focus on the historical aspects of the city, which was founded in 1753. The majority of the festival will be held at Harbor Park, but there will be places for visitors to go all around the city. Many of the city's 43 historical homes will be available for viewing, and the Bayside Museum will be hosting some special events to coincide with the festival.

The featured activity will be the historical reenactments set to take place. Among the events to be recreated will be the founding of the city, the battles that were fought here, and the rivalry between the Burns and Watsons, the two original founding families. These can be viewed at the park.

Numerous restaurants and stores will be taking part in the festival as well. For a full description of the events and locations, interested individuals can go to www.baysidefestival.org.

162. What is the article mainly about?

(A) The results of an event in a city
(B) The local history of Bayside
(C) The events at an upcoming festival
(D) The founding of Bayside

163. What is NOT mentioned about the festival?

(A) It will be held in many places.
(B) It is being sponsored by some restaurants.
(C) It is taking place for the first time.
(D) It will focus on the city's history.

164. Where should attendees go to see the historical reenactments?

(A) To the Bayside Museum
(B) To some historical homes
(C) To Harbor Park
(D) To the waterfront

GO ON TO THE NEXT PAGE

👤	Eric Inness [9:34 A.M.]	The workshop we're hosting is two weeks from now. We need to get together to practice the individual classes we're teaching. How does Wednesday morning sound?
	Jasmine Park [9:36 A.M.]	I'm scheduled to lead the new employee orientation then.
	Peter Welch [9:37 A.M.]	I'll be working with Jasmine as well.
	Henrietta Graves [9:39 A.M.]	What about Friday afternoon? After we finish, we could go out to dinner and discuss what we ought to improve upon.
👤	Eric Inness [9:41 A.M.]	I've got a meeting with Donald Radcliffe then, but I could ask him to meet me earlier in the day.
	Peter Welch [9:42 A.M.]	I don't have anything planned for the entire day. Count me in.
	Jasmine Park [9:43 A.M.]	I'll be there.
👤	Eric Inness [9:46 A.M.]	All right, I'll handle the arrangements with Ms. Landry in HR. Expect to be in one of the conference rooms from 2 to 6. I'll tell you the number once I find out. If I run into any problems, I'll let everybody know at once.

Send

165. Why did Mr. Inness start the online chat discussion?

(A) To discuss plans for a workshop
(B) To make a change in plans
(C) To schedule a meeting
(D) To ask for some opinions

166. At 9:37 A.M., what does Mr. Welch imply when he writes, "I'll be working with Jasmine as well"?

(A) He is busy on Wednesday morning.
(B) He shares an office with Ms. Park.
(C) He was recently hired.
(D) He will go on a business trip soon.

167. What does Ms. Graves suggest doing?

(A) Having a meal together
(B) Postponing the workshop
(C) Meeting with Mr. Radcliffe
(D) Talking in a conference room

168. What does Mr. Inness indicate he will do?

(A) E-mail Mr. Radcliffe
(B) Rehearse his lecture today
(C) Invite Ms. Landry to a meeting
(D) Reserve a room

You are invited to attend the world premiere of the play *Daylight*.

Daylight is the most recent play written by Jodie Camargo. It tells the story of the last day of a man's life and what he does during it.

The play will be performed for the first time at the Humboldt Theater in downtown Springfield at 7:00 P.M. on Friday, November 8. Following the performance, there will be a special Q&A session with Ms. Camargo and award-winning director Neil Peterson.

Tickets for the play cost $35 per person. They include the performance and the Q&A session. For those who wish to gain backstage access following the play, a ticket will cost $60. There are only 40 of these tickets available.

Tickets may be purchased at the theater's Web site at www.humboldttheater.com. They will also be sold at the theater's box office on the day of the performance starting at 5:00 P.M. The more expensive tickets may only be acquired online. Any questions regarding the performance may be addressed to Darlene Mercy at 854-1732.

169. What is being advertised?

(A) An autograph session with a writer
(B) The grand opening of a theater
(C) The first performance of a play
(D) The premiere of a film

170. What is mentioned about *Daylight*?

(A) There is only one performer in it.
(B) Audiences have enjoyed watching it.
(C) The setting for it is Springfield.
(D) It was composed by Ms. Camargo.

171. How can a person buy a ticket to go backstage?

(A) By visiting a Web page
(B) By contacting a ticket broker
(C) By visiting a theater
(D) By making a phone call

ACTUAL TEST 5

GO ON TO THE NEXT PAGE

To:	All Staff <undisclosed_recipients@belmontindustries.com>
From:	Brian Lockwood <blockwood@belmontiindustries.com>
Subject:	Trenton Fun Run
Date:	April 18

Everyone,

The Trenton Fun Run will be on Saturday, April 28, and we are once again going to be one of the sponsors of the event. In case you don't know, the race is held to help local elementary schools raise enough money to purchase materials they can use for their classes.

We encourage everyone at Belmont Industries to participate in the race. While the main race is ten kilometers, there are also a 5k race, a 3k race, and a 6k walk. The 10k race starts at 9:30 A.M. while the others begin a bit later in the morning. There is an entry fee of $15, and you will receive a free T-shirt and water bottle upon registering.

If running is not for you, the organizers would love for you to devote some time to volunteering. People are needed to help with registration, to give water to participants as they run, and to lend a hand at the finish line. You can speak with Jade Kennedy regarding this.

We hope to see you there next Saturday. A group from Belmont Industries will be running together. Let Maynard Williams know if you'd like to join them. They won't be trying to win any prizes but will be focused on enjoying the race.

Regards,

Brian Lockwood

172. What is the purpose of the e-mail?

(A) To request donations to charity
(B) To announce the winners of a race
(C) To encourage people to attend a picnic
(D) To promote a sporting event

173. How can a person get a T-shirt?

(A) By taking part in a running event
(B) By winning one of the races
(C) By working as a volunteer
(D) By making a monetary donation

174. What is NOT mentioned about the Trenton Fun Run?

(A) It utilizes the services of unpaid workers.
(B) There are walking and running events.
(C) It is scheduled to begin in the morning.
(D) People of all ages can register for it.

175. According to the e-mail, what is Ms. Kennedy in charge of?

(A) Handling people who want to help
(B) Organizing a group of runners
(C) Collecting registration forms
(D) Arranging transportation for volunteers

GO ON TO THE NEXT PAGE

Coldwater Academy
Registration Form

Please fill out the form in its entirety and submit it in person to the front office by August 30. Classes for the fall session will begin on August 31. Classes cost $200 per credit.

Name	Name	Address	930 W. Davidson Ave., Milton, OH
Telephone Number	857-4093	E-Mail Address	roger_dare@homemail.com

Class Number	Title	Day/Time	Credits
RJ54	Introduction to Robotics	Mon. 9:00 A.M. – 11:30 A.M.	3
AT22	Mechanical Engineering	Thurs. 1:00 P.M. – 3:00 P.M.	4
MM98	Advanced Calculus	Wed. 9:00 A.M. – 10:30 A.M.	2
XR31	Organic Physics w/ Lab	Fri. 2:00 P.M. – 5:00 P.M.	3

Are you a returning student?	[✓] Yes	[ ] No
Are you receiving financial assistance?	[ ] Yes	[✓] No
Payment Method	[✓] Credit Card [ ] Cash	[ ] Check [ ] Bank Transfer

Amount Owed: $2,400
Signature: Roger Dare
Date Submitted: August 27

To: roger_dare@homemail.com
From: registration@coldwateracademy.edu
Subject: Fall Semester
Date: August 29

Dear Mr. Dare,

We are looking forward once again to having you as a student at the Coldwater Academy. We received your registration form and would like to inform you that you have been successfully enrolled in three of the classes on your list.

Unfortunately, Professor Wilcox, whom you were scheduled to learn calculus with, will not be teaching here this fall because of a personal reason. His classes have therefore been canceled.

We have hired a replacement for him. Her name is Andrea Wang. If you are interested in learning with her, you can take her class on Monday afternoon from 2:00 to 3:30 P.M. We would appreciate your informing us of your intentions before 6:00 P.M. tomorrow, which is the day before the semester begins.

Best of luck in the coming semester.

Meredith Watson
Registration Office

176. What will happen on August 31?

(A) Orientation will take place.
(B) Registration will begin.
(C) A professor will be hired.
(D) Classes will be held.

177. What is indicated about Mr. Dare?

(A) He visited the academy on August 27.
(B) He is studying at the academy for the first time.
(C) He is primarily interested in studying business.
(D) He paid for his classes with a bank transfer.

178. Which class Mr. Dare registered for costs the most?

(A) Introduction to Robotics
(B) Mechanical Engineering
(C) Advanced Calculus
(D) Organic Physics w/Lab

179. Which class was canceled?

(A) RJ54
(B) AT22
(C) MM98
(D) XR31

180. What does Ms. Watson request Mr. Dare do?

(A) Attend class on the first day of the semester
(B) Respond to her question by the next day
(C) Give her a telephone call to discuss a class
(D) Make his final tuition payment

GO ON TO THE NEXT PAGE

Deerfield Branch Moving

Hobson, Inc., one of the largest manufacturers of high-end electronics in the country, will be moving its Deerfield branch. The Deerfield location, which employs 27 full-time and 12 part-time employees, is being relocated to Andover. The new branch will be at 982 Fulton Street and will be in a building owned by Hobson, Inc. and built specifically to house the new branch. The Deerfield branch will close on Friday, April 19, and the Andover branch will open the following Monday, April 22. The Andover branch will handle all matters in the tri-state area, so several new employees will be hired to work there. Any questions or comments regarding the Deerfield and Andover locations should be directed to Melvin Sullivan at 897-1902

To: Ken Worthy, Sue Parker, Elliot Jung, Rosemary Kline
From: Andrew Meade
Subject: Transfers
Date: April 4

We have made our decision regarding internal transfers at our domestic locations. Here is the list of the branch managers we are permitting to move. In all cases, they will retain the same titles and duties at their new locations:

Manager	Present Location	New Location	Transfer Date
Dina Smith	Biloxi	Harrisburg	April 10
Serina Chapman	Sweetwater	Baton Rouge	April 17
Lucas Bobo	Jacksonville	Andover	April 22
Tom Wright	Anniston	Athens	April 29
Peter Sullivan	Harrisburg	Gainesville	May 1

The list of regular workers who are transferring is much longer, so it will be sent through e-mail sometime after lunch. You can contact me at extension 58 anytime.

181. What is mentioned about the Deerfield branch?

(A) It will be shut down.
(B) It is run by Mr. Sullivan.
(C) It will get a new supervisor.
(D) It recently fired some workers.

182. In the announcement, the word "matters" in paragraph, line 9, is closest in meaning to

(A) associations
(B) comments
(C) buildings
(D) business

183. What is suggested about Mr. Sullivan?

(A) He requested a transfer to Athens.
(B) He recently started at Hobson, Inc.
(C) He will be replaced by Ms. Smith.
(D) He will move to another state.

184. What is indicated about the Andover branch?

(A) Its manager will be Mr. Bobo.
(B) It will be on one floor of a building.
(C) 50 full-time employees will work there.
(D) It will handle some international clients.

185. What will Mr. Meade probably do in the afternoon?

(A) Make some decisions about transfers
(B) E-mail a list to his colleagues
(C) Hold some employee interviews
(D) Schedule a meeting about transfers

GO ON TO THE NEXT PAGE

Questions 186–190 refer to the following notice, comment card, and article.

Calhoun Library Workshop

The Calhoun Library is holding a workshop for writers on Saturday, May 23. The following events will take place:

10:00 A.M. – 10:50 A.M.	Making Fictional Characters	Carlos Correia
11:00 A.M. – 11:50 A.M.	Creating New Worlds	Mei Johnson
1:00 P.M. – 2:50 P.M.	Editing Your Work	Xavier Mahler
3:00 P.M. – 3:50 P.M.	Publishing Your Manuscript	Belinda York

This event may be attended at no charge by all residents of Richmond, but seats are limited. Please call 482-8274 to reserve a seat.

The leaders of the individual sessions are locally based writers of fiction novels. Their works will be on sale at the library on the day of the workshop.

The workshop will take place on the second floor of the library in the Belmont Room. Light snacks and cold beverages will be made available for a small price.

Calhoun Library Comment Card

Guest: Carla Stewart
Date: May 23

Comments: I attend several workshops at the library each year, and this was easily the best I've been to. I didn't arrive until eleven but managed to stay until the end. I'm writing my own fiction novel now, so the advice I received at the workshop was invaluable. With luck, I'll be able to complete my work and become a published author by the end of the year.

Workshop Series Proves to Be Popular
by Jefferson Lee

The Calhoun Library started hosting workshops last year, and they've been the most popular activities there. Last weekend, a writers' workshop took place. Every seat was filled, and the library had so many requests for tickets from aspiring writers that it will be holding the same workshop again next month. Librarian Beth Robinson said every writer but one had committed to coming back. Xavier Mahler will be promoting his recent released novel *The Dark Side of the Moon*, so he'll be replaced by Melissa Gilbert.

Ms. Robinson said the library plans to have two workshops each month until the year concludes. If it can acquire more funding, then more will take place next year.

186. What is suggested about the Calhoun Library?

(A) It has three floors.
(B) It charges a fee for late books.
(C) It has a workshop each weekend.
(D) It is located in Richmond.

187. What is NOT true about the workshop?

(A) Anyone in the local area could attend.
(B) Refreshments were available.
(C) Novels were sold during it.
(D) There was a fee to attend it.

188. Whose session was Ms. Stewart unable to attend?

(A) Mr. Correia's
(B) Ms. Johnson's
(C) Mr. Mahler's
(D) Ms. York's

189. What is the article mainly about?

(A) The expansion of the library
(B) The success of a program
(C) The library's future activities
(D) The best way to write a book

190. What is most likely true about Ms. Gilbert?

(A) She is friends with Ms. Robinson.
(B) She has published a novel.
(C) She works at a publishing company.
(D) She knows Mr. Mahler.

GO ON TO THE NEXT PAGE

Memories of Georgia
by Richard Horner
Kirkwood Studios

Richard Horner is back after a four-year absence from recording and touring. The multimillion-selling folk singer/songwriter has just released a new album, entitled *Memories of Georgia*. The songs on this album are easily some of his best since his debut work, *My Life*, and his second album, *Heading out West*. It's a tremendous improvement over his last album, *What's Going On?* Fans will be pleased to know that Mr. Horner not only wrote all the lyrics to the songs on this album but also played every single musical instrument. This album is sure to be recognized for its outstanding music, and the first single, "Appalachian Home," is already getting plenty of airplay on radio stations around the country. Be sure to pick up a copy of this album and don't forget to see Mr. Horner if he visits your city on his upcoming tour.

Richard Horner

Richard Horner is coming back to the Rosemont Theater in Louisville after a four-year absence.

Mr. Horner will be performing live on the following nights:
Thursday, September 28
Friday, September 29
Saturday, September 30
Sunday, October 1

All concerts will start at 7:00 P.M. Call 849-2892 or visit www.rosemonttheater.com to make reservations. Tickets start at $30 per seat. Don't miss this opportunity to see a living legend up close and personal.

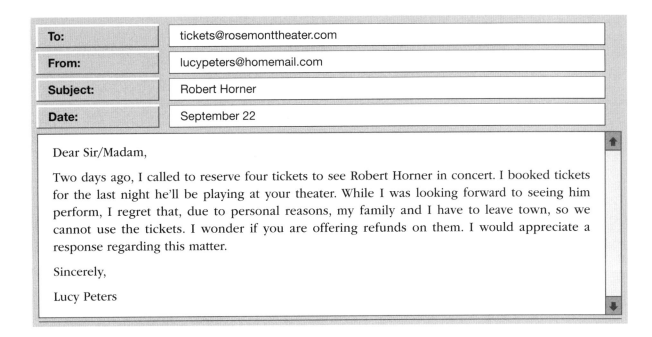

To:	tickets@rosemonttheater.com
From:	lucypeters@homemail.com
Subject:	Robert Horner
Date:	September 22

Dear Sir/Madam,

Two days ago, I called to reserve four tickets to see Robert Horner in concert. I booked tickets for the last night he'll be playing at your theater. While I was looking forward to seeing him perform, I regret that, due to personal reasons, my family and I have to leave town, so we cannot use the tickets. I wonder if you are offering refunds on them. I would appreciate a response regarding this matter.

Sincerely,

Lucy Peters

191. What is NOT indicated about Mr. Horner?

(A) His new album has not been released yet.
(B) He can play musical instruments.
(C) He writes lyrics to songs.
(D) His last album came out a few years ago.

192. In the review, the word "recognized" in paragraph 1, line 9, is closest in meaning to

(A) awarded
(B) greeted
(C) understood
(D) appreciated

193. Which album did Mr. Horner just release when he last appeared in Louisville?

(A) *Heading out West*
(B) *Memories of Georgia*
(C) *What's Going On?*
(D) *My Life*

194. Why did Ms. Peters send the e-mail?

(A) To make a booking for a concert
(B) To inquire bout getting her money back
(C) To find out where her seats are
(D) To ask about a method of payment

195. For which concert did Ms. Peters reserve tickets?

(A) September 28
(B) September 29
(C) September 30
(D) October 1

GO ON TO THE NEXT PAGE ▶

To:	Susan Wallace <susanwallace@caravanhotel.com>
From:	Cathy Wilde <cathy_w@honoria.com>
Subject:	Question
Date:	March 14

Dear Ms. Wallace,

This is Cathy Wilde from Honoria, Inc. We will be holding a special dinner for an employee who's leaving the firm after many years. We'd like to treat him to dinner at one of your restaurants. The event will take place on Friday, March 29, from approximately 6:30 to 9:00 P.M. There will be 40 people in attendance at the event.

We are hoping to spend between $60 and $75 per person for food. This price does not include any beverages but should be inclusive of appetizers and dessert. A buffet-style dinner would be ideal, but we would also be satisfied with a seafood or steak restaurant. We'd also prefer to have a private room. The last time we had an event there, we were told no restaurants had private rooms, but I believe you underwent some renovations recently, so I hope your response will be positive this time.

Sincerely,

Cathy Wilde
Honoria, Inc.

CARAVAN HOTEL RESTAURANTS

Company: Honoria, Inc.

Contact Person: Cathy Wilde

Number of Guests: 40

Restaurant	Type of Food	Price (Person/Total)	Private Room
The Grill	Steak/Barbecue	$62 / $2,480	Yes
Blue Rhapsody	Seafood	$85 / $3,400	No
The Washingtonian	Western/Asian Buffet	$80 / $3,200	Yes
Green Forest	Vegetarian	$50 / $2,000	Yes

A nonrefundable deposit amounting to half the total cost must be paid at least 3 days prior to the dinner. Food orders should be made 1 day before the dinner.

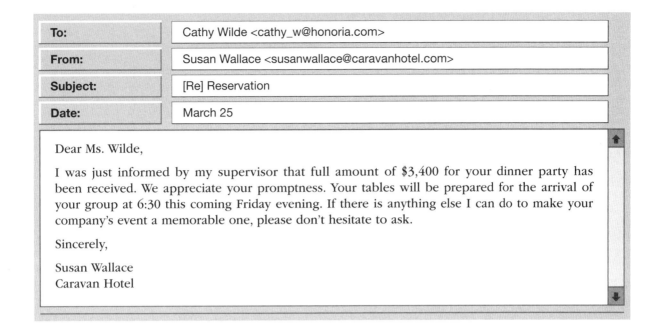

To:	Cathy Wilde <cathy_w@honoria.com>
From:	Susan Wallace <susanwallace@caravanhotel.com>
Subject:	[Re] Reservation
Date:	March 25

Dear Ms. Wilde,

I was just informed by my supervisor that full amount of $3,400 for your dinner party has been received. We appreciate your promptness. Your tables will be prepared for the arrival of your group at 6:30 this coming Friday evening. If there is anything else I can do to make your company's event a memorable one, please don't hesitate to ask.

Sincerely,

Susan Wallace
Caravan Hotel

196. According to the first e-mail, what type of event will be celebrated?

(A) A birthday party
(B) A contract signing
(C) An awards ceremony
(D) A farewell party

197. What does Ms. Wilde mention about the Caravan Hotel?

(A) The hotel's rates increased.
(B) She has never eaten there before.
(C) It has been improved recently.
(D) A new restaurant just opened there.

198. Which restaurant fits the budget mentioned by Ms. Wilde?

(A) The Grill
(B) Blue Rhapsody
(C) The Washingtonian
(D) Green Forest

199. Why did Ms. Wallace send the e-mail to Ms. Wilde?

(A) To ask about her reservation
(B) To list the dinner menu
(C) To confirm a payment
(D) To change the time of the dinner

200. What type of food will be served to the guest from Honoria, Inc.?

(A) Steak
(B) Seafood
(C) Western and Asian food
(D) Vegetarian

Stop! This is the end of the test. If you finish before time is called, you may go back to Parts 5, 6, and 7 and check your work.

ANSWER SHEET

TOEIC TOEIC 實戰測試

確認

准考證號碼

姓名

LISTENING COMPREHENSION (Part 1-4)

No.	ANSWER	No.	ANSWER	No.	ANSWER	No.	ANSWER	No.	ANSWER
1	Ⓐ Ⓑ Ⓒ Ⓓ	21	Ⓐ Ⓑ Ⓒ	41	Ⓐ Ⓑ Ⓒ Ⓓ	61	Ⓐ Ⓑ Ⓒ Ⓓ	81	Ⓐ Ⓑ Ⓒ Ⓓ
2	Ⓐ Ⓑ Ⓒ Ⓓ	22	Ⓐ Ⓑ Ⓒ	42	Ⓐ Ⓑ Ⓒ Ⓓ	62	Ⓐ Ⓑ Ⓒ Ⓓ	82	Ⓐ Ⓑ Ⓒ Ⓓ
3	Ⓐ Ⓑ Ⓒ Ⓓ	23	Ⓐ Ⓑ Ⓒ	43	Ⓐ Ⓑ Ⓒ Ⓓ	63	Ⓐ Ⓑ Ⓒ Ⓓ	83	Ⓐ Ⓑ Ⓒ Ⓓ
4	Ⓐ Ⓑ Ⓒ Ⓓ	24	Ⓐ Ⓑ Ⓒ	44	Ⓐ Ⓑ Ⓒ Ⓓ	64	Ⓐ Ⓑ Ⓒ Ⓓ	84	Ⓐ Ⓑ Ⓒ Ⓓ
5	Ⓐ Ⓑ Ⓒ Ⓓ	25	Ⓐ Ⓑ Ⓒ	45	Ⓐ Ⓑ Ⓒ Ⓓ	65	Ⓐ Ⓑ Ⓒ Ⓓ	85	Ⓐ Ⓑ Ⓒ Ⓓ
6	Ⓐ Ⓑ Ⓒ Ⓓ	26	Ⓐ Ⓑ Ⓒ	46	Ⓐ Ⓑ Ⓒ Ⓓ	66	Ⓐ Ⓑ Ⓒ Ⓓ	86	Ⓐ Ⓑ Ⓒ Ⓓ
7	Ⓐ Ⓑ Ⓒ Ⓓ	27	Ⓐ Ⓑ Ⓒ	47	Ⓐ Ⓑ Ⓒ Ⓓ	67	Ⓐ Ⓑ Ⓒ Ⓓ	87	Ⓐ Ⓑ Ⓒ Ⓓ
8	Ⓐ Ⓑ Ⓒ Ⓓ	28	Ⓐ Ⓑ Ⓒ	48	Ⓐ Ⓑ Ⓒ Ⓓ	68	Ⓐ Ⓑ Ⓒ Ⓓ	88	Ⓐ Ⓑ Ⓒ Ⓓ
9	Ⓐ Ⓑ Ⓒ Ⓓ	29	Ⓐ Ⓑ Ⓒ	49	Ⓐ Ⓑ Ⓒ Ⓓ	69	Ⓐ Ⓑ Ⓒ Ⓓ	89	Ⓐ Ⓑ Ⓒ Ⓓ
10	Ⓐ Ⓑ Ⓒ Ⓓ	30	Ⓐ Ⓑ Ⓒ	50	Ⓐ Ⓑ Ⓒ Ⓓ	70	Ⓐ Ⓑ Ⓒ Ⓓ	90	Ⓐ Ⓑ Ⓒ Ⓓ
11	Ⓐ Ⓑ Ⓒ Ⓓ	31	Ⓐ Ⓑ Ⓒ	51	Ⓐ Ⓑ Ⓒ Ⓓ	71	Ⓐ Ⓑ Ⓒ Ⓓ	91	Ⓐ Ⓑ Ⓒ Ⓓ
12	Ⓐ Ⓑ Ⓒ Ⓓ	32	Ⓐ Ⓑ Ⓒ	52	Ⓐ Ⓑ Ⓒ Ⓓ	72	Ⓐ Ⓑ Ⓒ Ⓓ	92	Ⓐ Ⓑ Ⓒ Ⓓ
13	Ⓐ Ⓑ Ⓒ Ⓓ	33	Ⓐ Ⓑ Ⓒ	53	Ⓐ Ⓑ Ⓒ Ⓓ	73	Ⓐ Ⓑ Ⓒ Ⓓ	93	Ⓐ Ⓑ Ⓒ Ⓓ
14	Ⓐ Ⓑ Ⓒ Ⓓ	34	Ⓐ Ⓑ Ⓒ	54	Ⓐ Ⓑ Ⓒ Ⓓ	74	Ⓐ Ⓑ Ⓒ Ⓓ	94	Ⓐ Ⓑ Ⓒ Ⓓ
15	Ⓐ Ⓑ Ⓒ Ⓓ	35	Ⓐ Ⓑ Ⓒ	55	Ⓐ Ⓑ Ⓒ Ⓓ	75	Ⓐ Ⓑ Ⓒ Ⓓ	95	Ⓐ Ⓑ Ⓒ Ⓓ
16	Ⓐ Ⓑ Ⓒ Ⓓ	36	Ⓐ Ⓑ Ⓒ	56	Ⓐ Ⓑ Ⓒ Ⓓ	76	Ⓐ Ⓑ Ⓒ Ⓓ	96	Ⓐ Ⓑ Ⓒ Ⓓ
17	Ⓐ Ⓑ Ⓒ Ⓓ	37	Ⓐ Ⓑ Ⓒ	57	Ⓐ Ⓑ Ⓒ Ⓓ	77	Ⓐ Ⓑ Ⓒ Ⓓ	97	Ⓐ Ⓑ Ⓒ Ⓓ
18	Ⓐ Ⓑ Ⓒ Ⓓ	38	Ⓐ Ⓑ Ⓒ	58	Ⓐ Ⓑ Ⓒ Ⓓ	78	Ⓐ Ⓑ Ⓒ Ⓓ	98	Ⓐ Ⓑ Ⓒ Ⓓ
19	Ⓐ Ⓑ Ⓒ Ⓓ	39	Ⓐ Ⓑ Ⓒ	59	Ⓐ Ⓑ Ⓒ Ⓓ	79	Ⓐ Ⓑ Ⓒ Ⓓ	99	Ⓐ Ⓑ Ⓒ Ⓓ
20	Ⓐ Ⓑ Ⓒ Ⓓ	40	Ⓐ Ⓑ Ⓒ	60	Ⓐ Ⓑ Ⓒ Ⓓ	80	Ⓐ Ⓑ Ⓒ Ⓓ	100	Ⓐ Ⓑ Ⓒ Ⓓ

READING COMPREHENSION (Part 5-7)

No.	ANSWER	No.	ANSWER	No.	ANSWER	No.	ANSWER	No.	ANSWER
101	Ⓐ Ⓑ Ⓒ Ⓓ	121	Ⓐ Ⓑ Ⓒ Ⓓ	141	Ⓐ Ⓑ Ⓒ Ⓓ	161	Ⓐ Ⓑ Ⓒ Ⓓ	181	Ⓐ Ⓑ Ⓒ Ⓓ
102	Ⓐ Ⓑ Ⓒ Ⓓ	122	Ⓐ Ⓑ Ⓒ Ⓓ	142	Ⓐ Ⓑ Ⓒ Ⓓ	162	Ⓐ Ⓑ Ⓒ Ⓓ	182	Ⓐ Ⓑ Ⓒ Ⓓ
103	Ⓐ Ⓑ Ⓒ Ⓓ	123	Ⓐ Ⓑ Ⓒ Ⓓ	143	Ⓐ Ⓑ Ⓒ Ⓓ	163	Ⓐ Ⓑ Ⓒ Ⓓ	183	Ⓐ Ⓑ Ⓒ Ⓓ
104	Ⓐ Ⓑ Ⓒ Ⓓ	124	Ⓐ Ⓑ Ⓒ Ⓓ	144	Ⓐ Ⓑ Ⓒ Ⓓ	164	Ⓐ Ⓑ Ⓒ Ⓓ	184	Ⓐ Ⓑ Ⓒ Ⓓ
105	Ⓐ Ⓑ Ⓒ Ⓓ	125	Ⓐ Ⓑ Ⓒ Ⓓ	145	Ⓐ Ⓑ Ⓒ Ⓓ	165	Ⓐ Ⓑ Ⓒ Ⓓ	185	Ⓐ Ⓑ Ⓒ Ⓓ
106	Ⓐ Ⓑ Ⓒ Ⓓ	126	Ⓐ Ⓑ Ⓒ Ⓓ	146	Ⓐ Ⓑ Ⓒ Ⓓ	166	Ⓐ Ⓑ Ⓒ Ⓓ	186	Ⓐ Ⓑ Ⓒ Ⓓ
107	Ⓐ Ⓑ Ⓒ Ⓓ	127	Ⓐ Ⓑ Ⓒ Ⓓ	147	Ⓐ Ⓑ Ⓒ Ⓓ	167	Ⓐ Ⓑ Ⓒ Ⓓ	187	Ⓐ Ⓑ Ⓒ Ⓓ
108	Ⓐ Ⓑ Ⓒ Ⓓ	128	Ⓐ Ⓑ Ⓒ Ⓓ	148	Ⓐ Ⓑ Ⓒ Ⓓ	168	Ⓐ Ⓑ Ⓒ Ⓓ	188	Ⓐ Ⓑ Ⓒ Ⓓ
109	Ⓐ Ⓑ Ⓒ Ⓓ	129	Ⓐ Ⓑ Ⓒ Ⓓ	149	Ⓐ Ⓑ Ⓒ Ⓓ	169	Ⓐ Ⓑ Ⓒ Ⓓ	189	Ⓐ Ⓑ Ⓒ Ⓓ
110	Ⓐ Ⓑ Ⓒ Ⓓ	130	Ⓐ Ⓑ Ⓒ Ⓓ	150	Ⓐ Ⓑ Ⓒ Ⓓ	170	Ⓐ Ⓑ Ⓒ Ⓓ	190	Ⓐ Ⓑ Ⓒ Ⓓ
111	Ⓐ Ⓑ Ⓒ Ⓓ	131	Ⓐ Ⓑ Ⓒ Ⓓ	151	Ⓐ Ⓑ Ⓒ Ⓓ	171	Ⓐ Ⓑ Ⓒ Ⓓ	191	Ⓐ Ⓑ Ⓒ Ⓓ
112	Ⓐ Ⓑ Ⓒ Ⓓ	132	Ⓐ Ⓑ Ⓒ Ⓓ	152	Ⓐ Ⓑ Ⓒ Ⓓ	172	Ⓐ Ⓑ Ⓒ Ⓓ	192	Ⓐ Ⓑ Ⓒ Ⓓ
113	Ⓐ Ⓑ Ⓒ Ⓓ	133	Ⓐ Ⓑ Ⓒ Ⓓ	153	Ⓐ Ⓑ Ⓒ Ⓓ	173	Ⓐ Ⓑ Ⓒ Ⓓ	193	Ⓐ Ⓑ Ⓒ Ⓓ
114	Ⓐ Ⓑ Ⓒ Ⓓ	134	Ⓐ Ⓑ Ⓒ Ⓓ	154	Ⓐ Ⓑ Ⓒ Ⓓ	174	Ⓐ Ⓑ Ⓒ Ⓓ	194	Ⓐ Ⓑ Ⓒ Ⓓ
115	Ⓐ Ⓑ Ⓒ Ⓓ	135	Ⓐ Ⓑ Ⓒ Ⓓ	155	Ⓐ Ⓑ Ⓒ Ⓓ	175	Ⓐ Ⓑ Ⓒ Ⓓ	195	Ⓐ Ⓑ Ⓒ Ⓓ
116	Ⓐ Ⓑ Ⓒ Ⓓ	136	Ⓐ Ⓑ Ⓒ Ⓓ	156	Ⓐ Ⓑ Ⓒ Ⓓ	176	Ⓐ Ⓑ Ⓒ Ⓓ	196	Ⓐ Ⓑ Ⓒ Ⓓ
117	Ⓐ Ⓑ Ⓒ Ⓓ	137	Ⓐ Ⓑ Ⓒ Ⓓ	157	Ⓐ Ⓑ Ⓒ Ⓓ	177	Ⓐ Ⓑ Ⓒ Ⓓ	197	Ⓐ Ⓑ Ⓒ Ⓓ
118	Ⓐ Ⓑ Ⓒ Ⓓ	138	Ⓐ Ⓑ Ⓒ Ⓓ	158	Ⓐ Ⓑ Ⓒ Ⓓ	178	Ⓐ Ⓑ Ⓒ Ⓓ	198	Ⓐ Ⓑ Ⓒ Ⓓ
119	Ⓐ Ⓑ Ⓒ Ⓓ	139	Ⓐ Ⓑ Ⓒ Ⓓ	159	Ⓐ Ⓑ Ⓒ Ⓓ	179	Ⓐ Ⓑ Ⓒ Ⓓ	199	Ⓐ Ⓑ Ⓒ Ⓓ
120	Ⓐ Ⓑ Ⓒ Ⓓ	140	Ⓐ Ⓑ Ⓒ Ⓓ	160	Ⓐ Ⓑ Ⓒ Ⓓ	180	Ⓐ Ⓑ Ⓒ Ⓓ	200	Ⓐ Ⓑ Ⓒ Ⓓ

TOEIC TOEIC實戰測試

准考證號碼　姓名

確認

LISTENING COMPREHENSION (Part 1-4)

No.	ANSWER	No.	ANSWER	No.	ANSWER	No.	ANSWER	No.	ANSWER
1	A B C	21	A B C D	41	A B C D	61	A B C D	81	A B C D
2	A B C	22	A B C D	42	A B C D	62	A B C D	82	A B C D
3	A B C	23	A B C D	43	A B C D	63	A B C D	83	A B C D
4	A B C D	24	A B C D	44	A B C D	64	A B C D	84	A B C D
5	A B C D	25	A B C D	45	A B C D	65	A B C D	85	A B C D
6	A B C D	26	A B C D	46	A B C D	66	A B C D	86	A B C D
7	A B C D	27	A B C D	47	A B C D	67	A B C D	87	A B C D
8	A B C D	28	A B C D	48	A B C D	68	A B C D	88	A B C D
9	A B C D	29	A B C D	49	A B C D	69	A B C D	89	A B C D
10	A B C D	30	A B C D	50	A B C D	70	A B C D	90	A B C D
11	A B C D	31	A B C D	51	A B C D	71	A B C D	91	A B C D
12	A B C D	32	A B C D	52	A B C D	72	A B C D	92	A B C D
13	A B C D	33	A B C D	53	A B C D	73	A B C D	93	A B C D
14	A B C D	34	A B C D	54	A B C D	74	A B C D	94	A B C D
15	A B C D	35	A B C D	55	A B C D	75	A B C D	95	A B C D
16	A B C D	36	A B C D	56	A B C D	76	A B C D	96	A B C D
17	A B C D	37	A B C D	57	A B C D	77	A B C D	97	A B C D
18	A B C D	38	A B C D	58	A B C D	78	A B C D	98	A B C D
19	A B C D	39	A B C D	59	A B C D	79	A B C D	99	A B C D
20	A B C D	40	A B C D	60	A B C D	80	A B C D	100	A B C D

READING COMPREHENSION (Part 5-7)

No.	ANSWER	No.	ANSWER	No.	ANSWER	No.	ANSWER	No.	ANSWER
101	A B C D	121	A B C D	141	A B C D	161	A B C D	181	A B C D
102	A B C D	122	A B C D	142	A B C D	162	A B C D	182	A B C D
103	A B C D	123	A B C D	143	A B C D	163	A B C D	183	A B C D
104	A B C D	124	A B C D	144	A B C D	164	A B C D	184	A B C D
105	A B C D	125	A B C D	145	A B C D	165	A B C D	185	A B C D
106	A B C D	126	A B C D	146	A B C D	166	A B C D	186	A B C D
107	A B C D	127	A B C D	147	A B C D	167	A B C D	187	A B C D
108	A B C D	128	A B C D	148	A B C D	168	A B C D	188	A B C D
109	A B C D	129	A B C D	149	A B C D	169	A B C D	189	A B C D
110	A B C D	130	A B C D	150	A B C D	170	A B C D	190	A B C D
111	A B C D	131	A B C D	151	A B C D	171	A B C D	191	A B C D
112	A B C D	132	A B C D	152	A B C D	172	A B C D	192	A B C D
113	A B C D	133	A B C D	153	A B C D	173	A B C D	193	A B C D
114	A B C D	134	A B C D	154	A B C D	174	A B C D	194	A B C D
115	A B C D	135	A B C D	155	A B C D	175	A B C D	195	A B C D
116	A B C D	136	A B C D	156	A B C D	176	A B C D	196	A B C D
117	A B C D	137	A B C D	157	A B C D	177	A B C D	197	A B C D
118	A B C D	138	A B C D	158	A B C D	178	A B C D	198	A B C D
119	A B C D	139	A B C D	159	A B C D	179	A B C D	199	A B C D
120	A B C D	140	A B C D	160	A B C D	180	A B C D	200	A B C D

裁切線

NEW TOEIC 新制多益

閱讀 **5** 回 解析本

全真模擬試題 ＋ 詳盡解析

RC

笛藤出版

PART 5				p.12
101. (D)	**102.** (D)	**103.** (A)	**104.** (C)	**105.** (A)
106. (B)	**107.** (C)	**108.** (C)	**109.** (A)	**110.** (D)
111. (B)	**112.** (A)	**113.** (C)	**114.** (A)	**115.** (B)
116. (B)	**117.** (A)	**118.** (D)	**119.** (B)	**120.** (B)
121. (C)	**122.** (B)	**123.** (A)	**124.** (B)	**125.** (A)
126. (B)	**127.** (C)	**128.** (D)	**129.** (C)	**130.** (A)

PART 6				p.15
131. (D)	**132.** (A)	**133.** (B)	**134.** (C)	**135.** (C)
136. (A)	**137.** (A)	**138.** (D)	**139.** (B)	**140.** (C)
141. (A)	**142.** (B)	**143.** (C)	**144.** (D)	**145.** (B)
146. (A)				

PART 7				p.19
147. (D)	**148.** (A)	**149.** (B)	**150.** (C)	**151.** (D)
152. (A)	**153.** (D)	**154.** (C)	**155.** (C)	**156.** (A)
157. (D)	**158.** (A)	**159.** (C)	**160.** (D)	**161.** (B)
162. (C)	**163.** (B)	**164.** (D)	**165.** (B)	**166.** (C)
167. (D)	**168.** (B)	**169.** (D)	**170.** (C)	**171.** (B)
172. (D)	**173.** (C)	**174.** (C)	**175.** (A)	**176.** (C)
177. (A)	**178.** (D)	**179.** (D)	**180.** (B)	**181.** (A)
182. (B)	**183.** (A)	**184.** (D)	**185.** (B)	**186.** (B)
187. (C)	**188.** (D)	**189.** (D)	**190.** (B)	**191.** (D)
192. (C)	**193.** (A)	**194.** (A)	**195.** (B)	**196.** (A)
197. (B)	**198.** (C)	**199.** (B)	**200.** (C)	

PART 1

101.

諮詢機構TR Partners期待幾天之後能與幾家企業簽約。

(A) expecting
(B) expected
(C) expectation
(D) expects

主語是TR Partners，而a consulting firm和TR Partners是相同的。在給予的句子中找不到動詞，所以正確答案是現在式動詞(D)。作為參考，因為TR Partners是公司名稱，應視其為單數。

詞彙 consulting firm 顧問公司

102.

因為那軟體被判定為是無法信賴的，所以消費者把它換成了更優質的產品。

(A) considered
(B) repaired
(C) uploaded
(D) exchanged

思考消費者對於「無法信賴的(unreliable)」產品會採取何種行動是最自然的，就可以很容易地找到正確答案。正確答案是(D)，exchange A for B表示「將A換成B」。

詞彙 prove 判定，證明　unreliable 無法信賴的　exchange A for B 將A換成B，替換　upload 上傳

103.

Bender先生將會在餐廳預訂8個位置，他打算在那裡接待外國客人。

(A) will book
(B) was booked
(C) will booking
(D) has been booked

空格中應該要加入以Mr. Bender為主book(預約)的適當形態。由於主語是人，使用被動態形式的(B)和(D)不能成為正確答案，(C)在語法上是不正確的。因此正確答案是單純未來時態的(A)。

詞彙 book a table 預訂位子　intend to 打算，準備　entertain 接待

104.

Tomato Garden是一間很受歡迎的餐廳，顧客想要入座有時需要等一個小時。

(A) seats
(B) seating
(C) seated
(D) seat

seat是「坐」的意思，所以應以被動語態表達。因此正確答案是(C)。

詞彙 diner 餐廳顧客　seat 坐下

105.

為了處理訂單，一整個星期間裝配線都會運作。

(A) In order to
(B) As a result of
(C) In addition to
(D) In spite of

從內容上來看，空格中應該加入表現出目的的詞語。選項中可以表現出「為了～」，帶有目的性詞語的是(A)。另外so as to等詞語也可以成為正確答案。

詞彙 fulfill 履行，實行　assembly line 裝配線　as a result of 結果是～　in addition to 除此之外　in spite of 儘管

106.

通過Pier 88的季節性菜單，廚師長一年四季都可以為自己的料理帶來變化。

(A) seasoned
(B) seasonal
(C) seasoning
(D) seasons

「季節性菜單」是以seasonal menu來表示的，所以正確答案是(B)。作為參考，season分別有「季節」和「調味」的意思，前者的形容詞是seasonal，後者的形容詞是seasoning或是seasoned。

詞彙 seasonal 季節性的，季節的 opportunity 機會 vary 不同；
做出變化 all year long 一整年 seasoned 調味的；經驗豐富的
season 季節；調味

107.

儘管有超過50名的應聘者，但只有3人滿足職位所需的要求。
(A) carefully
(B) patiently
(C) fully
(D) purposely

選項中最自然地修飾qualified(具備資格)的副詞只有(C)的fully(完
全，充分)。

詞彙 despite 儘管 be qualified for具備~的資格 patiently 有耐心
地 purposely 故意地

108.

那個項目交給Angela Turner負責，她將會得到Frank Grant的幫助。
(A) Response
(B) Responsiveness
(C) Responsibility
(D) Responding

找到能夠最自然地修飾for the project的名詞。正確答案是表示責
任之意的(C)。

詞彙 responsibility 責任，責任感 response 回答，回信
responsiveness 敏感性 respond 回答，反應

109.

Lexington動物園正在尋找對於餵食動物、照顧動物等志願服務感
興趣的人。
(A) to feed
(B) feeding
(C) will feed
(D) feed

Volunteer(自願，志願服務)是以to不定詞作為目的的動詞。因此(A)
是正確答案。

詞彙 look for 尋找 interested in 對~感興趣 take care of 照顧

110.

所有志願者都將得到一張抵用券以換取Sal's Deli的免費餐券。
(A) approved
(B) converted
(C) purchased
(D) redeemed

redeem表示「更換」或「交換」，特別是如果使用類似be
redeemed for的形式，則會表示「獲得~補償、以~交換」的意
思。如果留意到空格背後的for的話，正確答案是(D)。

詞彙 volunteer 志工 voucher 抵用券 be redeemed for 獲得～補
償 convert 轉換，改造

111.

Winters小姐打算從公司退休，但不會舉行送別會。
(A) Moreover
(B) Although
(C) Because
(D) For

「即將退休」和「不會舉行送別會」是相反的意義。因此在空格
中應加入表示反義的連接詞(B)的Although。

詞彙 retire 退休 farewell party 送別會 moreover 更加，再加上

112.

會計部的員工在安裝軟體後得要熟悉軟體。
(A) familiarize
(B) research
(C) utilize
(D) calculate

思考哪一個要求對於新安裝的軟體會是最為自然的。正確答案是
其意思為「使熟悉、使親近」的(A)。

詞彙 accountant 會計 urge 催促 familiarize 使熟悉，使親近
install 安裝 utilize 活用 calculate 計算

113.

因為在線上修改信息很簡單，所以公司目錄持續不斷地更新。
(A) temporary
(B) standard
(C) continual
(D) reported

Since所導向的條件句是正確答案的線索。因為修改信息非常簡
單，所以只要考慮更新會以何種方式進行就能輕易知道正確答案
是(C)的continual(不斷的，持續的)。

詞彙 directory 目錄 on a continual basis 連續的，持續的 correct
修改 temporary 一時的，臨時的 standard 標準的，一般的

114.

管理層允許員工在提早上班的情況下提前下班。
(A) permits
(B) grants
(C) lets
(D) consents

考慮到management(管理層)和employees(員工)的關係，空格中應
該加入表示「許可」或「允許」之意的(A)permits。Permit也可以
通過使用to副詞來確認正確答案。

詞彙 management 經營，管理層 workday 工作時間 grant 給予，
授予；同意 consent 同意

3

115.

Ravenwood Manufacturing最近收購了曾是普羅維登斯區域內競爭對手之一的Davis股份公司。

(A) competitions
(B) competitors
(C) competitive
(D) competitively

空格前面的its是指Ravenwood Manufacturing，因此只有表達出收購了一間競爭公司的意思，才能夠自然地完成句子，所以正確答案是(B)。

詞彙 acquire 得到，獲得　competition 競爭　competitor 競爭者　competitive 有競爭力的　competitively 競爭地

116.

根據報導，與Duncan Electronics的協商金額最多可能會高達7百萬美元。

(A) most of
(B) up to
(C) as of
(D) in with

尋找表示金額數值的seven million dollars(7百萬美元)最符合的表達方式。答案是(B)的up to，意思是「高達～」。

詞彙 worth 價值　up to 高達～　as of 自～起　in with 與～親近

117.

焦點團體的成員中有超過一半以上的人不喜歡自己看到的多用途汽車廣告。

(A) disliked
(B) were disliked
(C) will be disliked
(D) had been disliked

主語是人more than half of the members of the focus group，賓語是事物the advertisement。因此正確答案是(A)，被動形式的其他選項不能成為正確答案。

詞彙 focus group 焦點團體(為了調查廣告或是市場行銷，由代表各階層的人們聚集在一起的團體)　utility vehicle 多用途車輛，小型卡車

118.

只有在管理人批准了員工希望進行的購買時，資金才能夠被使用。

(A) spend
(B) spending
(C) spends
(D) spent

從進入空格的動詞的意義來看，主語是funds(資金)，所以正確答案是spend過去分詞型(D)的spent。作為參考，本文中「be + to不定詞」表示義務的意義。

詞彙 fund 資金，基金　authorize 給予權限

119.

在某職位上推薦某人的員工，如果他被錄用的話將會得到200美元的獎金。

(A) something
(B) someone
(C) somewhere
(D) somehow

在某個職位上(for a position)可以推薦(recommend)的對象應該是人。因此正確答案是指人的代名詞(B)。作為參考，"should that individual be hired"是省略if的條件句。

120.

資訊分享未經批准，與客戶溝通的內容都會是保密的。

(A) confidence
(B) confidential
(C) confiding
(D) confidentiality

如果留意空格前面的be動詞的話，就會知道空格應該要填入形容詞，如果注意到unless所引領的條件句的含義，可以知道空格中應該要填入帶有「信息不能洩漏」意義的(B)confidential(秘密的)。

詞彙 interaction 相互作用；交流　share 共享　grant 准許；授予　confidential 秘密的，機密的　confidence 自信感；信賴　confiding 信任的　confidentiality 秘密

121.

到目前為止，首席建築師在建築設計圖上進展甚微。

(A) design
(B) announcement
(C) progress
(D) proposal

將這句子換成主動語態來看的話找到正確答案並不困難。 即"The lead architect has made little _____ on the blueprints for the building."。重新寫一次句子的話，就會輕鬆地知道填入空格最合適的單字是(C)的progress(進步，發展)。

詞彙 thus far 現在為止，目前為止　make progress 發展，進步　blueprints 藍圖，設計圖　architect 建築師

122.

顧客在決定要購買哪種壁紙時，可以選擇的選項有很多。

(A) such
(B) many
(C) little
(D) any

(A)的such主要是使用在稱讚前面所指物品時使用，因此在內容上不適合在本句子中使用，(C)是在不可數名詞前使用，(D)主要在疑問句或否定句中使用。因此正確答案是(B)的many。

詞彙 option 選擇，選項　wallpaper 壁紙

123.

那個箱子被鎖著，沒有人知道能夠打開它的密碼。

(A) it
(B) them
(C) those
(D) its

考慮到空格前面的open，空格中應該加入代指the box的代名詞賓語。因此(A)是正確答案。

詞彙 seal 封印　lock 鎖　combination 組合，結合

124.

Carter先生如果處理好與Dexter Associates的合併問題，晉升的可能性很大。

(A) handling
(B) handles
(C) handled
(D) has handled

空格應該填入以if作為開頭的條件句動詞。因為句子的時態是現在式，所以選項中能夠進入空格的只有現在時態的 (B)handles。

詞彙 in line for ～的可能性很大　handle 對待，處理　merger 合併

125.

新購買的麵包機使用有問題時，請參考使用手冊。

(A) refer
(B) request
(C) renew
(D) revise

「參考」以refer to表示。答案是(A)。

詞彙 refer to 參考　manual 說明書，手冊　renew 更新　revise 修改，更正

126.

Cross街49號的建築原本是劇場，後來改為百貨公司。

(A) original
(B) originally
(C) origin
(D) originated

空格中應該要填入句子中漏掉的副詞部分。選項中的副詞只有(B)的originally(本來，原來)。

詞彙 convert 轉變，改建　department store 百貨公司　original 原始的；有獨創性的　origin 起源　originate 發源，來自

127.

今天晚一點要參加預定會議的人應該要立即取消。

(A) Each
(B) Another
(C) Anyone
(D) Few

空格中應該要填入能夠修飾planning to attend a meeting的單字。代名詞原則上不能用來修飾形容詞，但是像something或anyone的情況，接上-thing，-one的代名詞後面可以加上修飾詞。因此正確答案是(C)。

128.

Roberts先生認為投資者對於Anderson項目的可行性失誤了。

(A) accused
(B) regarded
(C) involved
(D) mistaken

注意空格的主語是investors(投資者)和viability of the Anderson project(Anderson項目的實現可能性)的意義上考慮正確答案。選項中與這兩種意義可以搭配使用的是(D)的mistaken(失誤的)。

詞彙 investor 投資者　viability 實現可能性　accuse 指控，控告　regard 看作，認為　involve 使捲入，干預

129.

那小冊子包含著很多資訊，因此得到賣場許多顧客的高度評價。

(A) informed
(B) information
(C) informative
(D) informs

想一想小冊子要如何才能獲得很高的評價，不難發現答案是(C)的informative(提供資訊的，有益的)。

詞彙 extremely 非常，極度　informative 給予情報的，有益的　praise 稱讚　inform 告知，給予情報

130.

儘管那件家具需要組裝，卻也不需要多少時間和精力。

(A) assembly
(B) purchase
(C) connection
(D) placement

關於furniture(家具)可能會需要時間或精力的工作應該是(A)的assembly(組裝)。

詞彙 even though 即使　assembly 組裝　effort 精力　connection 連接　placement 配置

PART 6

[131-134]

11月12日

致親愛的Sullivan先生，

通知您 **131.** 尚未收到10月3日的帳單款項。
明細單上的金額為894.23美元，每月的最低償還金額為75.00美元，結帳日期是10月31日，因此我們將會向您的帳戶收取30美元的 **132.** 滯納金，並以17.9%的利率向您收取全部欠款。我們建議您立即付款。如果您目前 **133.** 遇到財務困難，請致電1-800-945-9484與我們聯繫。**134.** 您將會與我們的職員商談及制定還款計劃。如果您對帳單有任何疑問，可以致電1-800-847-1739與我們聯繫。

Desmond Watts敬上
客戶服務主管
Silvan卡

詞彙 inform 通知　payment 支付，結帳　bill 帳單　monthly payment 分期，每月償還金額　due 應得；會費　as such 因此，因而　balance owed 欠款　interest 利息　encourage 鼓勵，激勵　hardship 困難，困境　work out a plan 制定計畫　repayment 情況

131.

(A) been received
(B) will receive
(C) be receiving
(D) to be received

這是一封催繳信用卡款項的信件。如果留意到空格前的has的話，就可以知道能完整表達出「應要繳納」意義的(D)為正確答案。

132.

(A) fee
(B) rate
(C) salary
(D) refund

滯納金是以late fee來表示的，因此(A)是正確答案。

詞彙 rate 比例；費用 salary 薪資，工資

133.

(A) experience
(B) experiencing
(C) have experienced
(D) be experienced

空格中應該要包括一個可以完成條件句動詞的單字，考慮到空格前面有are的話，正確答案是具有現在進行時態的(B)。

134.

(A) 因此您的信用卡將於本月底停止使用。
(B) 支付信用卡款項的地址在頁面下端。
(C) 與工作人員商談，以便制定還款計劃。
(D) 告知您如何來我們總店。

要在前面的句子中找到正確答案的線索。思考一下在遇到財政困難的情況下，打電話能獲得什麼樣的服務，選項中能夠最自然地延續文章脈絡的句子是「可以幫助解決問題」的(C)。

詞彙 instruction 說明 main office 總公司，總店

[135-138]

收信者：<undisclosed-recipients@ferris.com>
寄件者：<johnharper@ferris.com>
主旨：加班
日期：4月19日

致全體職員，

我們好不容易得到了幾份新合約，這將會使我們在接下來的2個月中工廠每天至少要開工20個小時。這次我們**135.**無意僱用新員工，取而代之的**136.**是我們希望現有的員工能夠加班。

如果您對加班有興趣，特別是在夜班或是週末，請立即與您的主管聯繫。**137.**或者您也可以回覆此電子郵件。**138.**每週最多可以加班15個小時，將會獲得正常工資的1.5倍的報酬。主管將按照先到先得的原則分配時間。

John Harper Dream
廠長
Ferris股份有限公司

詞彙 secure 獲得，得到 at least 最少的 intention 意圖，意向 particularly 特別地 night shift 夜班 immediate supervisor 直屬長官，直屬上司 up to 到~為止 compensate 報酬 allot 分配 first-come, first-served basis 先到先得方式

135.

(A) reasons
(B) announcements
(C) intentions
(D) plans

首先從內容上判斷，空格中可以填入表示「意向、意圖」意義的(C)或表示「計劃」含義的(D)，但如果有注意到之後的of，就能知道正確答案是(C)的intentions。have an intention of意思為「有意向去做」。

詞彙 reason 理由；理性 plan 計畫

136.

(A) that
(B) how
(C) why
(D) which

prefer之後可以接名詞、動名詞、to不定詞，以及that。在這裡空格之後可以找到「主語+動詞」的形態，所以正確答案是引領名詞的(A) that。

137.

(A) 或是回覆該電子郵件。
(B) 那樣的話，就會接受申請。
(C) 這樣工作時間會減少。
(D) 這樣做的話將會啟動調動申請程序。

因為前文談到了申請加班的方法，所以在空格中必須加入另一種申請方法，即提及電子郵件回覆的(A)，才能完成最自然的文章脈絡。

138.

(A) few
(B) many
(C) some
(D) each

正在說明每週最多可以加班的時數，所以正確答案是可以和week一起完整表達「每週」意思的(D)each。

[139-142]

Fullerton 圖書館維修工程

Fullerton (3月18日)--昨晚市議會投票**139.**贊成提供足夠的資金來修復Fullerton圖書館的停車場。多年來，圖書館的使用者都反映過那裡的坑洞及其他問題。**140.**不過該市一直聲稱缺乏維修所需的資金。

但該市最近從州政府那裡獲得了100萬美元的補助金，這筆錢預計用於改善該市的**141.**基礎設施。圖書館要求60,000美元的補助請求以4票對1票獲得了批准。這項工程計劃於3月23日開始，預計將在5天內結束。停車場也將在**142.**整個期間內關閉。

詞彙 city council 市議會　vote in favor of 通過投票批准，贊成　library patron 圖書館使用者　pothole 凹陷，坑洞　grant 補助金，援助金　conclude 作為結論，結束

139.

(A) lieu
(B) favor
(C) appearance
(D) state

in favor of意思為「贊成」，如果與vote一起使用則表示「(通過投票)批准~」。因此正確答案是(B)。

詞彙 lieu 場所

140.

(A) 該市經常做出增加圖書館藏書的承諾。
(B) 這樣將會為圖書館的使用者提供更多的服務。
(C) 但是該市總是聲稱維修工程所需資金不足。
(D) 因此今年圖書館利用率比以往任何時候都高。

空格之後要注意後面句子的however來找正確答案。因為下文中提到「但是(現在)已經得到了補助金」，所以空格中必須加入意思為「(之前)資金不足」的(C)，才能完成最自然的文章脈絡。

詞彙 frequently 常常，經常　usage使用

141.

(A) infrastructure
(B) budget
(C) schools
(D) roads

要在空格之後的句子中尋找正確答案的線索，即政府的補助金將用於圖書館設施的改善，因此空格中應該要填入有包含圖書館的概念(A)的infrastructure。

142.

(A) within
(B) during
(C) about
(D) since

要表明施工期間停車場將要關閉，因此(B)的during才是正確答案。

[143-146]

> 收信者：全體管理人員
> 寄件者：Jessica Blanco
> 主旨：培訓
> 日期：8月6日
>
> ¹⁴³·原定於明天進行的培訓延期，改為8月9日進行，並且¹⁴⁴·時間也變更了，預計於上午10點開始12點結束。最後，講師不為Timothy Warden先生，而是會變更成Simon Palmer先生。Warden先生因為一個重要項目，本周需要一直拜訪總部，這也是培訓延期的¹⁴⁵·原因。
>
> 請告知預計要參加培訓的職員。如若¹⁴⁶·不知道參加對象是誰的情況，請撥打電話內線號碼46給我，我將會通知您。

詞彙 postpone 延期　instructor 講師　not A but B 不是A而是B　home office 總部，總店　extension 內線號碼

143.

(A) 我們很高興地告知大家，Palmer先生將會負責各位的培訓。
(B) 再次告知培訓將在今天下午進行。
(C) 原定於明天進行的培訓延期。
(D) 全體職員從現在起3天後都需要報告自己的培訓情況。

是個應該加入通知主題的位置。透過內文的全部內容可以知道通知變更培訓時間為其目的，因此填入空格最恰當的句子是(C)。

詞彙 reminder 令人回憶的事物，提醒　report for 報告，申報

144.

(A) day
(B) instructor
(C) room
(D) time

在空格之後的句子中告知了變更的培訓時間，因此選項中可以填入空格的單字是(D)。

145.

(A) how
(B) why
(C) where
(D) what

因為是說明因果關係的句子，所以填入空格的單字是表示理由意思的關係副詞(B)的why。

146.

(A) unsure
(B) pleased
(C) reported
(D) aware

在傳達著「不清楚參加對象是誰」的情況下要求聯絡，因此(A)的unsure才是正確答案。

PART 7

[147-148]

> 12月16號
>
> 致負責人，
>
> 昨晚我為了即將到來的假日來到了位於Cloverdale購物中心的Deacon's服裝賣場，但我才知道原來我想要購買的幾款產品是買不到的，在收銀台排隊等候的人真的太多了。
>
> 我知道最近有比平時更多的顧客光顧您的賣場，儘管排隊的人有20人以上，但是收銀台卻只開放了一個，而且我看到了至少2名在那時候無所事事的員工。

我很想知道他們為什麼沒有開放第二個收銀台。另外我因為沒有時間,所以我什麼都沒有買就離開了賣場,取而代之的是我去了位於購物中心對面、您的競爭企業之一購物了。

Cynthia Harris 敬上

詞彙 acquire 獲得,得到 checkout counter 收銀台 stand in line 排隊 cash register 收銀機,收銀台 in a hurry 匆忙地,倉促地 competitor 競爭者,競爭企業

147.

Harris小姐提到了什麼問題?
(A) 無法購買某些產品。
(B) 有一位職員對她很無禮。
(C) 她不能試穿衣服。
(D) 等待的時間太長。

在第一段中Harris小姐指出了「在等待收銀台的人太多(just too many people waiting in line at the checkout counter)」的問題並對其抱怨。正確答案是(D)。

詞彙 rude 無禮的,粗魯的 try on 試穿

148.

Harris小姐離開Deacon's服裝賣場後做了什麼?
(A) 去了其他賣場。
(B) 前往其他購物中心。
(C) 在網上訂購產品。
(D) 打電話到賣場表示不滿。

從最後一個部分的"instead shopped at one of your competitors on the other side of the mall"中可以看出她離開賣場後所做的事情。她是在購物中心內的另一個賣場購物的,所以正確答案是(A)。

[149-150]

| Lisa Watson | 11:09 A.M. |
你好,Carl,請問你現在在辦公室嗎?

| Carl Venarde | 11:11 A.M. |
我正在樓下的販賣部喝咖啡,但5分鐘後就會回到位置上。有什麼事情嗎?

| Lisa Watson | 11:12 A.M. |
宅配人員打電話過來了,聽說有我的包裹,但我在市區的另一邊。可以幫我代收嗎?

| Carl Venarde | 11:13 A.M. |
當然可以,簽名後要放在哪裡呢?

| Lisa Watson | 11:14 A.M. |
因為內容物需要放在冰箱裡保存,所以得要開封。

| Carl Venarde | 11:15 A.M. |
交給我吧。

詞彙 deliveryman 送貨人員,外送人員 content 內容物 refrigerate 冷藏

149.

Watson為何聯繫Venarde?
(A) 為了讓他聯絡宅配人員。
(B) 為了請求幫忙。

(C) 為了詢問他訂購的產品。
(D) 為了要求他去郵局寄包裹。

當Venarde先生問到聯繫的原因時,Watson小姐說宅配人員會過來,然後問到能否代替自己收件,因此她傳訊息的理由可視為(B)。

詞彙 do a favor 接受請求,幫忙

150.

上午11點15分當Venarde先生傳了"Consider it done"時,他是在指什麼?
(A) 他已經簽完名拿到包裹了。
(B) 剛剛回到辦公室。
(C) 會將內容物放入冰箱。
(D) 將會支付運費。

給定的句子是「交給我」或「不要擔心」的意思,是在欣然接受對方請求時所使用的表達。此處是受託放入冰箱而說的話,因此句子的具體意義可以看作是(C)。

[151-152]

Medford Deli
42 Anchor 街42號
梅德福,伊利諾州

品目	數量	價格
火腿&起士三明治	1	$ 5.99
義大利麵沙拉	2	$13.98
火雞胸肉	1	$ 7.99
帕瑪森起士焗烤茄子	1	$ 8.49
	小計	$ 36.45
	稅金	$ 1.82
	外送費	$ 7.00
	合計	$ 45.27

您的訂單是以8944為結尾的信用卡結帳。謝謝您的使用。

151.

從發票上可以知道什麼?
(A) 顧客以現金結帳。
(B) 顧客購買每一種商品都各買了一個。
(C) 顧客有優惠。
(D) 顧客支付了外送費用。

發票下端標明7美元的外送費用,因此(D)為正確答案。由於從圖表下的文句中可以看出是用信用卡結帳的,所以(A)是錯誤的,從圖表的數量項目來看,義大利麵沙拉購買了2個,因此(B)也是錯誤的。(C)中關於打折的說法並沒有在發票中出現。

152.

根據發票,哪些餐點最貴?
(A) 帕瑪森起士焗烤茄子。
(B) 義大利麵沙拉。
(C) 火腿&起士三明治。
(D) 火雞胸肉。

仔細觀察每道菜的一人份價格,不難發現(A)的帕瑪森起士焗烤茄子是最貴的餐點,價格為8.49美元。

[153-154]

書籍免費贈送活動

本週六8月10日，Midtown圖書館將舉辦每年一次的圖書贈送活動。圖書館為了給新書留出空間，將會分發許多許久沒有被閱讀過的書籍。此次活動將於下午12點到3點在圖書館的主大廳舉行。數量有限，每人最多可拿到5本書。這次活動將包括所有年齡層的書籍，將會贈送大量科幻小說、幻想小說和浪漫小說，特別是要處理的兒童書籍相當地多。雖然不需要預約，但這次的活動只有中城的居民才能參加。

詞彙 giveaway 贈品 annual 每年的，年度的 give away 分給 make room for 空出空間給～ new arrival 新生兒，新產品 as long as 只要 science-fiction 科幻小說 dispose of 處理

153.

活動沒有提到的是什麼？
(A) 對人們可能擁有的書籍數有限制。
(B) 只有特定地區的人才能獲得書籍。
(C) 將包括不同類型的圖書。
(D) 計畫將於整個週末進行。

由於每人有五本的數量限制，所以(A)是有提到的內容，只有中城居民才可以參與，因此(B)也是符合的內容。科幻、幻想、浪漫小說等等是參與活動的書籍，所以(C)也是事實。在第一句中，由於通知活動日期是8月10日星期六一天，因此與事實不符的內容是(D)。

154.

對活動的書籍暗示了什麼？
(A) 可以以低廉的價格購買一些書籍。
(B) 來訪者如不交納滯納金的話，則不得領取書籍。
(C) 與其他類型的書籍相比，兒童圖書更多。
(D) 多數的書籍可能會是最近上市的書籍。

公告後半部分的"there are an especially large number of children's books"中可以推測出兒童圖書比其它種類的圖書更多，因此正確答案是(C)。因為沒有可以付費購買書籍或是接受以支付滯納金為條件拿到書籍的內容，因此(A)和(B)都是錯誤的。因為參與活動對象的書籍都是很久沒有被人查找的書籍，所以(D)也是錯誤的。

詞彙 library fine 圖書館滯納金 genre 類型

[155-157]

收信者：customerservice@kerrigans.com
寄件者：geraldlong@mymail.com
主旨：Easy Reader
日期：4月21日

致負責人，

我是Gerald Long，會員編號為3840-939348。我是您店裡的長期顧客，我購買的東西也從來沒有遇到過問題，但是在4月10日，我在您的網站上購買了Easy Reader，我一想到能讀到電子書就很興奮，於是第二天Easy Reader一到，我就訂購了5本電子書。但遺憾的是，我的Easy Reader昨晚突然關機，並且無法重新開機。在使用之前有充電過了，所以我認為不是電池的問題。

我今天早上打算再開機一次，但還是無法正常開啟，現在不知道該要做什麼了。我希望我的Easy Reader能修好，而不是得郵寄退貨。我可以在附近的Kerrigan's賣場修理嗎？

希望能盡快答覆我的提問。

Gerald Long 敬上

詞彙 longtime 長時間的 e-book 電子書 recharge 充電 operate 啟動，運轉 properly 恰當地，正常地 prompt 迅速的 inquiry 詢問，質疑

155.

4月10日發生了什麼事？
(A) 收到訂購的商品。
(B) 產品停止運作。
(C) 購買完成。
(D) 電池故障。

問題的關鍵語句4月10日可以在"However, on April 10, I bought an Easy Reader from your Web site."中找到。 當天是撰寫電子郵件者購買名為Easy Reader機器的日子，所以(C)是正確答案。

詞彙 malfunction 故障

156.

Long先生想做什麼？
(A) 在賣場維修Easy Reader。
(B) 對Easy Reader進行退款。
(C) 請教維修Easy Reader的方法。
(D) 請修理技師來訪。

在電子郵件的後半部分，Long先生表示想接受修理而不是退貨，然後詢問"Is it possible for me to have it fixed at my local Kerrigan's?"也就是說，他想要的是在附近賣場接受維修，所以(A)才是正確答案。

157.

在[1]，[2]，[3]，[4]中下列句子填入最合適的地方是哪裡？
「現在我都不知道該做什麼了。」
(A) [1]
(B) [2]
(C) [3]
(D) [4]

給予的句子應該是在撰寫電子郵件者嘗試了所有的解決方法之後接續的，這種嘗試涉及[4]的前一部分，因此應填入的位置是(D)。

[158-161]

MEMO

收件者：全體員工

寄件者：人事部Nancy Clark

主旨：內部網路系統

日期：10月9日

剛才IT部門通知我們新安裝了整個公司的內部網路系統。在得到ID和密碼之前，需要先接受有關如何正確利用系統的培訓。

預計從今晚開始在一週內每天晚上進行培訓。培訓將從下午6點開始一直持續到晚上8點，並預計在304號室及305號室同時進行培訓。一次最多20名可以進行培訓，而所有員工至少得要接受一次培訓。

部門主管們會通知日程的，分配的日期與本人行程不符時，可自行與其他員工交換，但是兩位員工要互相交換日期必須向管理人確認。本週不能接受培訓的情況，請立即向管理人員說明。

培訓將在正規工作時間之後進行，因此將會支付兩小時的加班費，而這將會反映在下一次的工資中。

詞彙 intranet 內部網路，內聯網 installation 安裝 companywide 公司全體的 utilize 利用 simultaneous 同時發生的 maximum 最大 at the same time 同時 undergo 經歷 at least 至少 switch 改變 fit 適合的，恰當的 reflect 反映 paycheck 薪水

158.

為什麼會發送通知？

(A) 為了要通知有關培訓的資訊。

(B) 為了要求提供關於培訓的反饋意見。

(C) 鼓勵管理人員與工作人員交談。

(D) 為了確保向工作人員支付培訓津貼。

通知的原因可以在第一段中確認。通知者告知設置了新的內部網路的消息之後，在發放ID前傳達了「應要接受內部網路培訓(you must take a training course to learn to how utilize the system properly)」的內容，所以通知的理由是(A)。並不確定與(D)的培訓津貼的相關內容，因此它難以成為此則通知的目的。

159.

各個員工在完成培訓之後將會得到什麼？

(A) 晉升。

(B) 證書。

(C) 用戶ID和密碼。

(D) 內部網路使用說明書。

透過"Before you will be given an ID and a password, you must take a training course to learn to how utilize the system properly. "這句子可以知道員工們在接受完培訓之後將會得到(C)的ID和密碼。

詞彙 certificate 證書，執照 manual 使用說明書，手冊

160.

關於培訓，那一個不是事實？

(A) 將會一直持續到週末。

(B) 課程將歷時兩個小時。

(C) 每天將會有兩堂課。

(D) 每堂課必須至少要有20名學生。

這週每天晚上的時間(each evening for the rest of the week)將會進行培訓，因此(A)的內容是正確的，培訓時間是從6點到8點，所以(B)也是事實。在304號和305號將會分別進行培訓這一點，因此(C)也是事實，但課程人員是最多20名(a maximum of 20 individuals)的關係，所以(D)與事實不符。

161.

想要更改日程的員工應該要做什麼？

(A) 聯絡講師。

(B) 跟上司說。

(C) 書面許可。

(D) 確認日程。

在第3段中提到想要更改聽課日期的員工「應該要讓管理者確認過(must confirm this with their managers)」，因此(B)為正確答案。

[162-164]

介紹一款全新的Waycool冰箱

Belmont公司自豪地為您介紹符合21世紀的完美冰箱：Waycool。它具備冰箱需要的一切以及更多，包含冷凍室在內的這台冰箱具有充足的空間可以放置新鮮水果及蔬菜，肉類，飲料以及冷凍食品。為了整理好冰箱，您也會喜歡上能夠區分不同食物的各個隔間。

Waycool擁有世界上填滿速度最快的製冰機，這個製冰機每5分鐘就能製成1公升的冰塊。冰箱門上的飲水機及製冰機可方便飲水，並配有兒童保護鎖防止發生危險事故，水在內部進入飲水機之前經過過濾，確保可以獲得最乾淨、最新鮮的水。Waycool的內部可以利用數位控制來調節溫度，也可以下載語音控制應用程序。該應用程序還可以啟動兒童保護鎖和製冰飲水機。

Waycool推出三種顏色四款不同的型號，售價為899美元起。到www.belmont.com/waycool可進一步瞭解Waycool。

詞彙 refrigerator 冰箱 refrigerator-freezer 附有冷凍室的冰箱 space 空間 compartment 隔間，客房 organize 組織，整理 ice maker 製冰機 be capable of 能夠 ice cube 冰塊 dispenser 自動發放機 (按下按鈕就可將內容物拿出來使用的裝置) child lock 兒童保護鎖 nasty 壞的，危險的 mishap 不幸，事故 filter 過濾

162.

根據廣告，顧客們會喜歡Waycool的哪一點？

(A) 獨特的設計。

(B) 各種顏色。

(C) 各種空間。

(D) 大尺寸。

第一段廣告裡聲稱消費者會喜歡「可以隔開食物的個別空間 (individual compartments that permit you to separate foods)」，因此(C)是正確答案。

詞彙 unique 獨特的 section 部分，劃分

163.

關於Waycool的特點，沒有提到什麼？
(A) 可以鎖住一部分。
(B) 內部照明。
(C) 速度很快的製冰機。
(D) 溫度調節。

Waycool的特點在第二段有詳細的介紹。(A)是child lock，(C)為the world's fastest-filling ice maker，(D)為digital control，但沒有提有關的(B)的相關功能。

164.

關於Waycool，可以知道什麼事？
(A) 銷售數年。
(B) 冰箱以四種顏色上市。
(C) 最新型號中沒有冷凍庫。
(D) 有些型號的價格可能會超過899美元。

從廣告標題中可以看出Waycool是新上市的冰箱，因此(A)不是正確答案。顏色不是四種而是有四種型號(four separate models)，所以(B)也是錯誤的。該冰箱是「附有冰凍室的冰箱(refrigerator-freezer)」，因此(C)也是錯誤答案。透過有提及最低價格是899美元這一點可以知道正確答案是(D)。

詞彙 on the market 已上市的，銷售中的

[165-168]

PRW Manufacturing 的健康
Oriana Verducci 撰寫

去年比以往任何時候有更多的員工請病假，也有員工報告健康問題導致生產效率低下，因此公司決定在今後12個月內把員工健康作為首要課題。

昨天人事部次長Daniel Herbst宣佈公司將採取若干措施來增進員工的健康。他從討論員工餐廳供餐開始，為了提供更多的蔬菜給員工，本週末員工餐廳將設置沙拉吧。同時員工餐廳的油炸食品將會減少，取而代之的是一些對健康有益，營養價值更高的餐點，而且餐點價格不會有太大的差異。自動販賣機上將不再販售巧克力、洋芋片和其他垃圾食品，取而代之的將是一些新鮮水果，例如柳橙，蘋果和香蕉。

公司還會為全體員工辦理離正門步行僅2分鐘、位在Hampton路129號Silver Star健身俱樂部的團體會員。員工只要出示工作證就可以在那裡免費運動。

最後公司將於4月對全體員工進行健康檢查。透過檢查來檢視員工的健康狀況，確認是否存在主要疾病或健康問題。Herbst說日程將會在3月中旬公佈。

詞彙 sickness 疼痛，疾病 result in 導致 productivity 生產率 primary 主要的 focus 集中，焦點 step 階段，措施 cafeteria 員工餐廳，自助餐廳 provide A for B 向B提供A nutritious 營養成分高的 vending machine 自動販賣機 contain 包含 mere 只是，僅僅 front gate 正門 work out 運動 health screening 健康檢查 checkup 檢查 post 公告

165.

關於PRW Manufacturing，暗示了什麼？
(A) 提高員工的健康保險費負擔金額。
(B) 去年受到生病員工的消極影響。
(C) 將獎勵健康良好的員工。
(D) 在設施內設立診所。

第一段指出去年請病假的員工很多，由於健康問題而「生產效率低下(resulted in lower productivity)」，因此(B)是正確答案。

詞彙 negatively 消極地 get in good shape 維持健康 health clinic 診所，私人診所

166.

沒有提到的飲食服務變化是什麼？
(A) 不再提供特定食物。
(B) 新的許多食物可能是營養豐富的食物。
(C) 將不再販售油炸食品。
(D) 員工可能會吃沙拉。

在自動販賣機中，現有的食品將不會再提供，因此(A)的內容是正確的，而且會提供有利於健康，營養豐富的食物，(B)也是正確的。從設置沙拉吧這一點來看，(D)有提及相關內容，但是只有說「在員工餐廳的油炸食品將會減少(the cafeteria will serve fewer fried foods)」，並沒有說到會完全消失，因此(C)為錯誤的描述。

167.

員工要如何使用Silver Star健身俱樂部？
(A) 透過網路登記。
(B) 透過每月繳納會費。
(C) 透過連絡管理人員。
(D) 攜帶工作證前往。

健身俱樂部的使用方法在第三段中可以找到，這裡有介紹說只要出示員工證(show their company ID)就可以使用健身俱樂部。正確答案是把company ID換成work ID的(D)。

168.

[1]，[2]，[3]，[4]中下列句子填入最為合適的地方是哪裡？
「另外，餐點價格不會有太大的差異。」
(A) [1]
(B) [2]
(C) [3]
(D) [4]

注意給予的句子中的the dishes就能知道這篇句子要寫進有提到飲食話題的句子後面。選項中位於飲食話題部分的是(B)的[2]。

[169-171]

收件者：Wayne Frasier <waynef@cranson.com>
寄件者：Ted Sutherland <tedsutherland@limnos.com>
主旨：新聞
日期：5月18日

親愛的Frasier，

我需要通知您剛才發生的事情。我很期待能夠參加5天後在達拉斯舉行的研討會，但我想我必須得要改變計劃。我公司在柏林的工廠發生了重大問題，代表決定派我去那裡處理問題，所以我打算今晚搭乘飛機過去那邊。

我不知道我什麼時候能夠回國，但聽說我至少會在那裡待上一個星期，因此我可能無法參加研討會。

我很遺憾我原作為一主講人卻發生這樣的事情。幸運的是，我知道一位可以替代我的完美人選，他叫Fred Peterson，是我實驗室的研究員。他對機器人技術非常瞭解，並且也是一位出色的演講者。他說他願意代替我演講，也不介意我已經準備好的演講。我告訴他您的電子郵件以便你們兩位可以討論這次的問題，希望這件事能往有利於您的方向發展。

Ted Sutherland 敬上

詞彙 inform A of B 向A介紹B　come up 發生，出現　alter 替換，變更　as though 就像～一樣　keynote speaker 主講人　replacement 代替，取代　accomplished 有能力的，有才能的　in one's place 代替　so that～can 為了可以～　work out to one's advantage 對～有利

169.

電子郵件的目的是什麼？
(A) 為了預約。
(B) 為了確定合約。
(C) 為了討論即將舉行的演講。
(D) 為了取消預定的出席。

電子郵件撰寫者Sutherland先生告知由於工廠發生的問題，原定的「參加研討會有困難(it appears as though I will not be able to attend the conference)」。正確答案是(D)。

170.

Sutherland先生為什麼要去柏林？
(A) 為了發表演說。
(B) 為了參加會議。
(C) 為了拜訪公司設施。
(D) 為了參加就業面試。

從第一段中的"my firm's factory in Berlin"中可以看出柏林是Sutherland先生公司工廠所在地，因此正確答案是(C)。作為參考，(A)和(B)是要前往研討會的預定地點達拉斯的理由。

171.

關於Peterson先生，Sutherland先生暗示了什麼？
(A) 他打算寫自己的演講稿。
(B) 他不久之後將會聯繫Frasier先生。
(C) 他將晉升為管理人。
(D) 他已經登記研討會了。

在電子郵件最後的部分，Sutherland先生為了讓代替自己的Peterson先生和電子郵件的收件者Frasier先生能夠互相討論，「將Frasier先生的聯繫方式給了Peterson先生(I have given him your e-mail address)」。因為Peterson先生不介意已經準備好的演講稿，因此(A)是與事實不符的內容，(C)和(D)則是從未提及的事項。

[172-175]

Brenda Long	1:11 P.M.
上季度業績會議的日程不久前定下了。預定在本週五上午週間會議結束後舉行。	
Harold Pruitt	**1:13 P.M.**
我們團隊誰要來發表？我還沒有看到詳細的數據。	
Brenda Long	**1:15 P.M.**
我也是。Frederick，你有銷售額及其他需要的資料嗎？	
Frederick Patton	**1:16 P.M.**
有的，我在10分鐘前全部都收到了。現在發給你們兩個。	
Harold Pruitt	**1:17 P.M.**
怎麼樣？業績和我們預期的一樣好嗎？	
Frederick Patton	**1:19 P.M.**
請打開電子郵件直接確認，然後請告訴我你們有什麼想法。	
Brenda Long	**1:23 P.M.**
哇，我們有可能會拿到獎金。	
Harold Pruitt	**1:24 P.M.**
真的是那樣啊，那我們之中應該由誰來發表呢？	
Frederick Patton	**1:25 P.M.**
Brenda，你在這裡待得最久。我覺得應該由你來發表。	
Brenda Long	**1:26 P.M.**
有道理。	

詞彙 detail 細節　be set to 預計　sales figure 銷售額　performance 成果，業績　in line for 有可能　reasonable 合理的

172.

星期五預定會有什麼事？
(A) 將會發放獎金。
(B) 將會公佈案件。
(C) 將會練習演講。
(D) 舉行業績會議。

在開始的部分，「上一季度業績會議日程(the meeting regarding sales last quarter)」預定在星期五上午舉行(set to take place this Friday morning)，因此正確答案是(D)。

詞彙 award 授獎；獎勵 agenda 議題，案件 rehearse 彩排，練習

173.

Patton先生是如何將議程交給Pruitt先生和Long小姐的？
(A) 直接展示。
(B) 透過傳真。
(C) 透過電子郵件發送。
(D) 透過實習員工拿來。

Pruitt先生表現出對於業績資料的好奇，Patton先生回答說"Open your e-mail and take a look for yourself."。 由此可知，相關資料是(C)「透過電子郵件轉達」。

174.

下午1點23分Long小姐說"It looks like we're in line for bonuses"的時候，她暗示的是什麼？
(A) 她期待比去年得到更多的錢。
(B) 她對獎金感到滿意。
(C) 她剛才看到銷售額了。
(D) 她已經超過自己的銷售目標量。

in line for是「有可能有~」的意思，給予的句子是對於要她確認銷售額的反應。也就是說，確認銷售額後暗示了銷售額高到可以拿到獎金的程度，因此(C)才是正確答案。不知道她去年拿了多少，所以不能選(A)為正確答案。

詞彙 be satisfied with 對～感到滿意 quota 配額

175.

Long小姐同意做什麼？
(A) 在即將舉行的會議上演講。
(B) 進行說明。
(C) 向Pruitt先生提出建議。
(D) 與議程相關而協助Patton先生。

由於在聊天室後半部有待的時間最長的理由，Long小姐被指定為發表者，她答說"That sounds reasonable."， 這是一種表示接受的意思，所以正確答案是(A)。

[176-180]

PTR 股份有限公司招聘公告

PTR 股份公司是一家生產高級電子產品的企業，目前正在招募新建成工廠的裝配線管理人員。應聘者至少要有7年的管理經驗，大學學位不為必須的而是優待事項。被聘用到該職位的人需要具備與其他人相配的能力，同時需要具備出色的時間管理及溝通能力。雖然是正式員工，但有時可能會需要加班，加班時會支付加班費。起薪為62000美元，並會提供福利，其中包括退休金和醫療保險。請在8月10日前，透過 henry_c@ptr.com向Henry Coburn發送簡歷。只有符合資格條件的人才會得到回覆，獲得面試機會的人才能接受有關業務能力的測試。

詞彙 manufacturer 製造企業，製造業者 high-end 高級的 college degree 大學學位 desire 期望，希望 get along well with 與～合適 possess 擁有 full-time position 正職 on occasion 有時候 overtime rates 加班費，加班津貼 pension 退休金 medical insurance 醫療保險

收件者：henry_c@ptr.com
寄件者：mauricedavidson@mymail.com
主旨：空缺職位
日期：8月4日

親愛的Coburn先生，

我的名字叫Maurice Davidson，我對貴公司的裝配線管理人員職位有興趣，附件有我的簡歷以及申請書，以便您瞭解我的資格條件。

我現在在Kendrick Motors工作，在這裡我負責管理Scottsdale工廠的裝配線。我過去五年一直在這裡工作，與公司所有高級主管及員工相處融洽。在我的工作期間內，工廠裡不曾發生過任何事故。我非常喜歡我的工作，並一直想繼續留在這個地方，但由於妻子在裡奇蒙找工作，所以我才會搬到裡奇蒙。

我可以透過電話或是直接過去面試，但過去那裡面試的話得需要安排旅行，所以可能需要一些時間。有什麼問題的話請聯絡我。希望能早日收到您的回覆。

Maurice Davidson 敬上

詞彙 attach 附加，附上 qualification 資格，資質 presently 目前 both A and B A及B全部 injury 受傷，傷害 in person 親身，親自 make travel arrangements 安排旅行

176.

關於裝配線管理員一職，沒有提及的是？
(A) 可能需要長時間工作的人。
(B) 從事該工作的人必須有資歷。
(C) 大學學位是必須的。
(D) 與他人好好交談的能力至關重要。

可通過第一段引文招聘公告裡確認正確答案。提到也許會需要偶爾加班(working overtime on occasion)，因此(A)是正確的，要求「至少有7年的管理經歷(a minimum of seven years of management experience)」，所以(B)也是有提及的事項，另外，作為資格條件強調了「與人相處的能力(ability to get along well with others)」，所以(D)也是事實，但是大學學位「不是必要的(not required)」 而是作為優待事項被寫上去的，正確答案是(C)。

177.

根據廣告，面試的人應該要做什麼？
(A) 證明知識。
(B) 會見代表理事。
(C) 進行年薪協商。
(D) 展現領導能力。

在廣告的最後一句中面試的人會「接受業務能力測試(will be required to complete a test of their skills and abilities)」。因此他們要做的將是(A)。

詞彙 leadership 指導能力，領導能力

178.

Davidson先生為什麼會發電子郵件？
(A) 為了接受入職提議。
(B) 為了確定面試日程。
(C) 為了詢問資格條件。
(D) 為了表示對職位的關注。

在電子郵件的第一句"I am interested in the assembly line manager position at your company"中可以知道Davison先生寫電子郵件的理由。他對於空缺的管理人員職位表示其意願，因此正確答案是(D)。

179.

關於Kendrick Motors的工作，Davidson先生提到了什麼？
(A) 他在那裡待超過10年。
(B) 與高級主管工作。
(C) 結果導致效率增加。
(D) 他負責工作人員的安全。

Davidson說自己在Kendrick Motors工作期間「工廠裡沒有事故(there have never been any injuries in the factory)」，選項中有提到的是(D)。提到工作了5年，所以(A)是錯誤的內容，(B)和(C)是完全沒有提到過的事項。

詞彙 decade 10年 involve 陪同，包含 efficiency 效率

180.

關於PTL股份有限公司，暗示了什麼？
(A) 正在向海外市場擴展業務。
(B) 在裡奇蒙開放了新的設施。
(C) 預期今年會有收益。
(D) 有幾個空缺職位。

PTR股份有限公司發佈招募公告的理由是要招聘最新設施(its newest facility)的裝配線管理人員。另外，在第二段引文的電子郵件中，Davidson先生說因為在裡奇蒙求職的妻子，所以要搬到那裡(I will be moving to Richmond)說明其離職理由，由此兩個事實綜合起來的話可以想像到PTR股份有限公司的最新設施將位在裡奇蒙，因此(B)為正確答案。

詞彙 make a profit 獲利

[181-185]

Florence 餐飲服務
1010 Lincoln 街1010號
塔爾薩,奧克拉荷馬市74108
(539) 830-9101

顧客名	Tom Snyder	公司名稱	Harrison Manufacturing
電話號碼	(539) 239-8347	電子郵件	t_snyder@hm.com
地址	74111奧克拉荷馬市塔爾薩Main街483號		
配送地點	74109奧克拉荷馬市塔爾薩Forest公園正門9		
訂購日期	6月28日	訂購日期	7月15日

商品編號	內容	數量	價格
4830	三明治拼盤（大）	3	$210.00
1012	沙拉拼盤（大）	2	$ 80.00
3829	義大利採樣拼盤（中）	2	$130.00
8393	甜品盤（大）	3	$120.00
7331	各式飲品（大）	4	$200.00
		小計	$ 740.00
		外送費	$ 0.00
		稅金	$ 37.00
		合計	$ 777.00

謝謝您的訂單。 訂單是用以7484結束的信用卡結帳的。如有疑問或是其他要求事項，請聯繫orders@florencecatering.com，我們將盡力幫助您。

詞彙 do one's best 盡最大的努力 accommodate 容納；協助，符合

收件者：t_snyder@hm.com
寄件者：orders@florencecatering.com
主旨：訂購
日期：6月30日

致親愛的Snyder先生，

您昨天提交的網路訂單以及詢問內容都已經收到了。想先跟您確認一下訂購明細。Florence餐飲服務的員工將於7月15日上午11點帶着產品抵達，以助於您準備食物。

將回答您最擔心的部分，其中一種甜點中含有花生，但由於有使用標籤明確標示，對花生過敏的員工可以不用擔心。另外，令人遺憾的是，我們一年中的這時候不出售鮭魚，但是我們可以輕鬆地為您提供大量漢堡肉、熱狗、小圓麵包方便讓您可以舉辦戶外野餐派對。如若有興趣的話，我們還可以帶幾個烤架。烤架出租時將會產生租借費用，並且對於所使用的瓦斯也將會收取費用。

除此之外，如果有需要提供幫助的地方，告訴我。

Melanie Jackson 敬上
Florence 餐飲服務

詞彙 representative 代表，代理；職員 assist 幫助 inquiry 疑問 be concerned about 對～感到憂慮 peanut allergy 花生過敏 salmon 鮭魚 plenty of 許多，大量的 have a cookout 戶外野餐 grill 烤架 rent 租借 propane gas 丙烷氣

181.

未列入訂單的資訊是什麼？
(A) 幾人份的食物。
(B) 誰訂購的。
(C) 總價多少。
(D) 產品將配送到那裡。

(B)、(C)、(D)分別可在訂單的"Customer Name"、"Total"以及"Deliver To"項目中確認。訂單中不能確認的事項是(A)。

182.

和訂單中第一段第三行"accommodate"單字最相似的是？
(A) 接受。
(B) 幫助。
(C) 借。
(D) 更新。

accommodate既可以用作「收容(人員等)」的意思,也可以用於「滿足(請求)」或是「幫助」的意思。此處在文章脈絡上被用作於後者的意思，因此正確答案是(B)的assist。

詞彙 house 房子；收容 assist 幫助

183.

根據Jackson小姐說的話，7月15日將會有什麼事？

(A) 食物將會送達。
(B) 將會付款。
(C) 將會確認訂購明細。
(D) 新的食物將會到達。

July 15這個日期可以在電子郵件的第一段中找到，在這裡Jackson小姐7月15日公司員工(a representative from Florence)會帶食物去幫忙準備，所以正確答案是(A)。

184.

哪些產品含有Snyder先生的員工不能食用的成分？

(A) 產品編號4830。
(B) 產品編號1012。
(C) 產品編號3829。
(D) 產品編號8393。

在電子郵件第二段中"one of the dessert items has peanuts in it"的語句中可以找到正確答案的線索。含有花生的食品是甜點之一，所以在訂購目錄中找到甜點商品，正確答案是Dessert Tray的產品編號(D)。

185.

Jackson小姐為什麼提議Snyder先生開一個戶外派對？

(A) 為了對Snyder先生提出的問題做出積極答覆。
(B) 為了提出可替代的食物。
(C) 為了勸說Snyder先生租用烤架。
(D) 為了提及可以利用的特價商品。

電子郵件中提到戶外派對的句子是"However, we could easily provide you with plenty of hamburger patties, hotdogs, and buns to have a cookout. "Jackson小姐說儘管沒有鮭魚，但他介紹了有許多其他食品可以舉辦戶外派對，因此她提到戶外派對的理由可以看作是(B)。

詞彙 alternative 替代的

[186-190]

www.westendstyle.com

顧客姓名：Heidi Mann
電子郵件地址：hmann@homemail.com
地址：483 Beaumont Avenue, Las Alamos, NM
會員編號：859403
訂購數量：9
訂購日期：5月12日

產品編號	內容	數量	價格
340834	高跟鞋(黑色皮革)	1	$120.00
923409	襯衫(S,藍)	2	$ 40.00
812374	毛衣(S,白)	1	$ 35.00
238433	T恤(S,紅)	1	$ 25.00
	小計		$220.00
	運費		$ 00.00
	合計		$220.00

* 您的訂單是用以8433結尾的信用卡結帳。
* 總金額為200美元以上時，可免費使用翌日特快快遞服務。
* 點擊此處，即可瞭解本月的特價促銷。

感謝您在**West End Style**購物。

收件者：hmann@homemail.com
寄件人：customerservice@westendstyle.com
主旨：訂購
日期：5月12日

致親愛的Mann小姐，

昨晚接到您的訂單，現在正在處理中。很高興地告訴您，您訂購的產品中有三件是可以購買的，但您要求購買的毛衣目前沒有庫存。根據我們的記錄，在今年秋天這件毛衣開始販售之前，該產品是不能購買的。 對於該產品，我們可以對於已經結帳的金額進行退款，也可以換成其他產品。在此期間，為了能讓您在明天可以收到，我們已經寄出其餘訂購的商品。追加訂購其他產品時，訂購產品無需另外費用，並將用普通郵件方式寄送。

Russell Washington 敬上
West End Style

詞彙 process 過程；處理 out of stock 無庫存的 either A or B A 或B其中之一 in the meantime 這段期間，那期間

收件者：hmann@homemail.com
寄件者：customerservice@westendstyle.com
主旨：訂購
日期：5月13日

致親愛的Mann小姐，

通知您，您所訂購的替代商品已經處理完畢，即將進行配送。由於您所購買的產品的價格是30美元，所以將會匯入5美元差額到您的帳戶。另外對於沒能購買初次訂購的產品表示歉意，請下載附件的優惠券，在下次訂購時使用的話，可選擇一款產品享受5折優惠。 此優惠券無有效期限。您在下次訂購時將立即成為West End Style的VIP會員，並將伴隨著多項優惠。 如有疑問，請撥打免付費電話1-888-394-8333。

Ashley Harper 敬上
West End Style顧客服務代表

詞彙 notification 通報，通知 replacement 替換，替代 credit 存款 initially 最初 attach 附加，附上 expiration date 有效期限 a variety of 多樣的 privilege 特權 toll-free hotline 免付費電話

186.

Mann小姐為什麼會有免費配送優惠？

(A) 她是VIP會員。
(B) 她結帳金額超過200美元。
(C) 她屬於購物俱樂部。
(D) 她使用優惠券。

第一個引文的表格下顯示「結帳金額在200美元以上(totaling $200 or more)可以免費配送」，因此Mann小姐獲得免費配送服務的理由為(B)。

187.

現在不能購買什麼產品？
(A) 產品編號340834。
(B) 產品編號923409。
(C) 產品編號812374。
(D) 產品編號238433。

透過第二段引文電子郵件中"the sweater which you requested is currently out of stock"的句子可以知道現在毛衣(sweater)是無法購買的商品。在第一段引文中找到毛衣的產品編號，正確答案為(C)。

188.

關於Mann小姐的訂單，Washington小姐提到了什麼？
(A) 有一部分正在配送。
(B) 大量採購時可享受折扣。
(C) 有一個商品的價格下降。
(D) 藉由電話訂購的。

在第二封電子郵件中Washington小姐對Mann小姐說「已經寄送出其餘的商品，為了能讓您在明天收到(we have mailed the other items you ordered so that you can receive them by tomorrow)」告知這一件事，所以在選項中提到的事實是(A)。

詞彙 be eligible for 有資格 bulk discount 大量訂購優惠

189.

Harper小姐要給Mann小姐什麼？
(A) 全額退款。
(B) 新的密碼。
(C) 1+1優惠券。
(D) 賣場中可使用的點數。

在最後的引文中，Harper小姐提及附上的優惠券，並告知使用該優惠券可以「享受50%的優惠(get 50% off any one item of your choice)」。因此選項中與折扣優惠有關的(D)才是正確答案。

190.

關於West End Style的VIP顧客，暗示了什麼？
(A) 每筆訂單平均花費100美元。
(B) 至少要訂購10次。
(C) 每月要訂購一次。
(D) 最高箱有折扣50%。

在最後的引文中，Harper小姐告訴Mann小姐「下次訂購時，您將成為West End Style的VIP顧客(upon making your next order, you will become a VIP shopper at West End Style)」，因此可以猜測出VIP優惠為可能需要訂購10次，因此(B)才是正確答案。

[191-195]

ISA

2月26日

致親愛的Sullivan小姐，

國際建築師協會(ISA)將於今年夏天7月9日至12日在英國倫敦舉行聚會。邀請身為ISA會員的您前來。

今年活動的主題是【建築設計新科技】。主演講人是世界著名建築師兼Croswell Architecture的所有人William Forsythe先生。不僅將會舉行多次研討會，還將進行演說，會議以及專題討論。各日期的主題如下：

7月9日	建築的現有科技
7月10日	建築的未來科技
7月11日	建築的國際趨勢
7月12日	建築的總體情況

隨函附上申請書。如欲出席，請填寫申請表，並於6月30日前寄出。也可以在網路上登記。會員的登記費用是90美元。

國際建築師協會副會長
Cindy Nguyen 敬上

詞彙 architectural 建築的 numerous 許多的 international 國際的 overall 全體的，全體性的 enclose 附上，附寄

收件者：Tracy Perry, Gordon Scott, Alexis Montgomery, Sabrina Murray
寄件者：Cynthia Sullivan
日期：3月10日
主旨：ISA活動

我知道你們有資格參加ISA倫敦的活動。有興趣參加的話，公司將會提供倫敦經濟艙往返機票、酒店住宿費和登記費用。預算上的關係，只能預訂兩間飯店的客房，所以客房需要共同使用，另外，一天的伙食費為60美元。如果預定要參加的話，請在本月末之前告訴我，那麼我會請旅行社做好必要的準備。為了能夠一起過去，會盡力和Forsythe老闆搭乘同一航班。

詞彙 be eligible for 有資格 round-trip 往返，來回 accommodations 住宿 share 共有 instruct 指示 make the arrangements 準備

收件者：Cindy Nguyen
寄件者：Cynthia Sullivan
主旨：登記
日期：6月29日

致Nguyen先生，

您好，我叫Cynthia Sullivan。我是ISA的會員(會員編號1934129)。我已經把我公司的4名員工登記在3月的會議上，現在打算再增加一名。但遺憾的是，我試圖在ISA的網站上登記，但是卻沒辦法完成手續。3月分做同樣事情的時候是完全沒有問題的，但這次網站卻無法正常運作。

寄送書面申請書的話，時間似乎會不夠。想知道能不能幫幫我，告訴我我該怎麼做嗎？

Cynthia Sullivan 敬上

詞彙 additional 額外的，追加的 be unable to 無法

191.

關於ISA會議，事實是什麼？
(A) 可能每天都會有主講人。
(B) 對非會員徵收更高的參加費用。
(C) 只在週末舉行。
(D) 需要事先登記。

第一段引文最後的部分要求「請在6月30日之前填寫並發送申請書(please complete it and return it by June 30)」，並說明活動開始的日期是7月9日。因此關於ISA會議屬於事實的是(D)。有提到主講人每天都會變更，而並沒有提及關於非會員的參加費用，因此(A)和(B)是無法確認的事項，活動連續進行4天，從這一點來看(C)是錯誤的內容。

詞彙 advance registration 事先登記，事先申請

192.

參加者什麼時候能夠學習不同國家的建築？
(A) 7月9日。
(B) 7月10日。
(C) 7月11日。
(D) 7月12日。

只要在第一段引文的圖表中找到與問題的核心語句"architecture in different countries"有關的主題即可。International Trends in Architecture(建築的國際傾向)就是那樣的主題，如果找到涉及這些主題的日期，答案就會是(C)的7月11日。

193.

關於Sullivan小姐，可以知道什麼？
(A) 在Croswell Architecture工作。
(B) 經常去倫敦。
(C) 將會參加在倫敦舉行的會議。
(D) 不屬於ISA。

關於Sullivan小姐，可以在第一段引文及第二段引文最後一句話得知，她是主講人(keynote speaker)、世界著名建築師(world-famous architect)以及Croswell Architecture公司的所有者(owner) William Forsythe先生的下屬，因此可以知道她是Croswell Architecture公司的員工，(A)選項符合事實。(B) (C)選項為引文中沒提到的部分，故不可選。另外，信件中有說明Sullivan小姐為ISA會員，因此(D)為錯誤選項。

詞彙 belong to 屬於

194.

Sullivan小姐在3月份為Scott先生做了什麼？
(A) 登記讓他參加會議。
(B) 預訂了他的機票。
(C) 把他介紹給Forsythe先生。
(D) 允許他參加特別活動。

Gordon Scott的名字可以在第二段引文的通知收件人名單中找到，在這裡Sullivan小姐要求收信人告知是否要參加ISA活動。在第三個引文電子郵件中，Sullivan小姐對ISA關係者說她本人在3月的會議上登記了4名員工。綜上所述，我們可以看出Sullivan小姐為Scott先生所做的事情是(A)。

195.

Sullivan小姐請Nguyen小姐做什麼？
(A) 打電話到自己的辦公室。
(B) 協助同事的登記。
(C) 取消登記。
(D) 協助訂房。

在最後一個引文電子郵件中，Sullivan小姐說「雖然想追加登記(I would like to sign up an additional person)」，但因為在ISA網站上沒辦法做到這一點，正在向收件者Nguyen求助，因此她請求的是(B)。

[196-200]

```
特別活動

Erica Yang要結束其32年的工作，準備離開Cross航空公司與家人一起度過。為了紀念她的辛勞，11月6日星期五在Madison酒店的大宴會廳將會為Erica舉辦一場晚會。晚會將於晚上6:30開始，預計9點左右結束。邀請所有職員，如果您打算前來，請在11月2日星期一之前通知人事部的Kelly Arbor。計劃會為Erica購買禮物，請提供您負擔的金額給Kelly。
```

詞彙 resign 辭職，退休 honor 禮遇，尊敬 ballroom 宴會場，宴會室 feel free to 隨意

Madison 酒店
特別活動預約申請書

公司名稱	Cross 航空
地址	伊利諾伊州史普林菲爾德Airport路829號
負責人	Kelly Arbor
電話號碼	854-3029
電子郵件地址	karbor@crossair.com
預約室	大宴會廳
日期	11月7日 星期六
時間	6:30 P.M. – 9:00 P.M.
預計參加人數	120
提供飲食	[✓] Yes　　[ ] No
用餐人數	120

特別要求: 宴會廳應要備有麥克風和音響設備的舞臺。需要爲素食主義者準備20人份的食物。其餘100人份的食物將會在一般菜單上點餐。

客戶簽名: Kelly Arbor	經理人簽名: Dave Fleming
日期: 10月31日	**日期:** 10月31日

詞彙 microphone 麥克風 a/v equipment 音響設備 vegetarian 素食主義者；素食主義者的

收件者：Teresa St. Clair
寄件者：Brian Crosby
主旨：為Erica舉辦的派對
日期：11月3日

致Teresa，

我想知道您是否能夠幫我個忙。我看起來似乎能夠參加為了Erica舉辦的派對，出差的工作進行得很順利，我原本以為會在布宜諾斯艾利斯待到週末，看來我們明天就會簽約。那樣的話，代表著兩天之後我就會回國。但因為我不知道負責人的電子郵件地址和電話號碼，所以希望您告知一下我打算參加，以及如果您願意替我支付30美元禮物費用的話，就更好了。我回辦公室之後會還給您的。

真的很感謝。

Brian

詞彙 give a hand 幫助，幫忙　after all 結果，總之　extremely 極度地，非常　contribute 貢獻，捐贈　pay back 還錢

196.

為什麼要舉行派對？
(A) 紀念退休。
(B) 為了頒發獎項。
(C) 為了介紹新進員工。
(D) 向代表理事致敬。

在第一段引文的開頭部分，公告通知是為了即將退休的Erica Yang舉辦派對。正確答案是(A)。

詞彙 celebrate 慶祝，紀念　hand out 分發

197.

根據申請表，公告的哪些資訊有誤？
(A) 參加活動的人員。
(B) 活動日期。
(C) 活動時間。
(D) 活動地點。

應該將第二段引文申請表各個項目的內容和引文上的內容進行比對找出正確答案。別的選項內容都一致，但(B)活動日期，申請表上標註的是Saturday, November 7，但公告上標註的卻是Friday, November 6。

198.

申請表中沒有要求的是什麼？
(A) 不加入肉類的食物。
(B) 麥克風。
(C) 花朵裝飾。
(D) 舞臺。

申請表上的要求可以在Special Requests項目中找到。為素食主義者準備的食物，麥克風，還有關於舞臺的事項都可以找到，但並未提及(C)的花朵裝飾。

詞彙 floral arrangement 花朵裝飾，插花

199.

Crosby先生請St. Clair小姐做什麼？
(A) 在自己傳真過去的合約上簽字。
(B) 向Arbor小姐說關於自己的事情。
(C) 為自己預購回國機票。
(D) 為Yang小姐購買禮物。

在最後一段引文的電子郵件中，Crosby先生向St. Clair小姐表示自己不知道活動負責人的聯繫方式，「如果能告訴負責人自己要參加派對，我會非常感謝(I'd appreciate your letting her know I'm planning to be there)」，因此他請求的事項可視為(B)。雖然委託她代付禮物費用，但並不是直接委託她買禮物轉送，因此不能選擇(D)為正確答案。

200.

與電子郵件中第一段第四行"contribute"一詞意義最相近的是？
(A) 提議。
(B) 提出。
(C) 捐款。
(D) 借。

這裡的contribute是「捐贈(錢)」的意思，所以正確答案是(C)的donate(捐獻，捐贈)。

PART 5   p.42

101. (C)	**102.** (D)	**103.** (A)	**104.** (D)	**105.** (B)
106. (C)	**107.** (A)	**108.** (D)	**109.** (A)	**110.** (C)
111. (C)	**112.** (A)	**113.** (B)	**114.** (C)	**115.** (A)
116. (C)	**117.** (C)	**118.** (B)	**119.** (C)	**120.** (D)
121. (C)	**122.** (D)	**123.** (A)	**124.** (B)	**125.** (C)
126. (A)	**127.** (D)	**128.** (C)	**129.** (B)	**130.** (B)

PART 6   p.45

131. (B)	**132.** (A)	**133.** (A)	**134.** (C)	**135.** (C)
136. (D)	**137.** (B)	**138.** (D)	**139.** (C)	**140.** (A)
141. (C)	**142.** (B)	**143.** (C)	**144.** (A)	**145.** (B)
146. (A)				

PART 7   p.49

147. (D)	**148.** (A)	**149.** (B)	**150.** (A)	**151.** (C)
152. (A)	**153.** (B)	**154.** (C)	**155.** (B)	**156.** (C)
157. (A)	**158.** (B)	**159.** (D)	**160.** (A)	**161.** (D)
162. (A)	**163.** (B)	**164.** (B)	**165.** (C)	**166.** (B)
167. (C)	**168.** (D)	**169.** (B)	**170.** (D)	**171.** (B)
172. (D)	**173.** (A)	**174.** (D)	**175.** (A)	**176.** (C)
177. (B)	**178.** (A)	**179.** (B)	**180.** (D)	**181.** (A)
182. (C)	**183.** (A)	**184.** (C)	**185.** (B)	**186.** (D)
187. (B)	**188.** (D)	**189.** (B)	**190.** (D)	**191.** (C)
192. (C)	**193.** (A)	**194.** (C)	**195.** (A)	**196.** (B)
197. (D)	**198.** (D)	**199.** (C)	**200.** (B)	

PART 5

101.

Shaw小姐因她善於交際的性格而成為許多年輕員工的理想導師。

(A) approaching
(B) approached
(C) approachable
(D) approachably

選項中最自然地修飾personality(性格)的單字是(C)的approachable(易交談的，易親近的)。

詞彙 approachable 易交談的，易親近的 personality 性格，人格 mentor 導師 approach 接近，靠近

102.

下午4點之後網站沒有接到任何訂單。

(A) because
(B) when
(C) even
(D) since

如果注意到時態是現在完成式，那麼就不難發現空格中需要加入

的是(D)since。

103.

顧客主張自己即使沒有發票也有權利可以退貨。

(A) insisted
(B) criticized
(C) talked
(D) resorted

如果在選項中找到以that句子作為賓語來表達「主張」之意的單字，正確答案就是(A)的insisted。(C)中的talked不接受that句子作為賓語使用，(D)使用resorted作為動詞「訴諸」使用時，需要有介系詞to。

詞彙 lack 沒有，缺少 insist 主張，固執 criticize 批判，批評 resort to 訴諸於～

104.

Flanders先生決定要投資原料市場。

(A) his
(B) him
(C) himself
(D) his own

如果沒看到空格前面的介系詞on，就有可能會選擇錯誤答案(C)。「一個人」或「單獨」是以on one's own一詞來表示。正確答案是(D)。

詞彙 commodities market 原料市場，生活必需品市場

105.

有幾位知名人士已經同意參加為了募捐100萬美元的慈善活動。

(A) are agreed
(B) have agreed
(C) were agreed
(D) have been agreed

由於主語是指人的several celebrities(幾位知名人士)，所以這篇文章應該成為主動語態的句子。選項中能完成主動語態句子的只有(B)。

詞彙 celebrity 知名的 benefit 好處；慈善活動 in an attempt to 試圖 charity 慈善

106.

隨著新筆記型電腦的上市，上一季度的收益有了令人印象深刻的增長。

(A) impressed
(B) impression
(C) impressive
(D) impresser

空格上應該有能修飾名詞amount(數量)的形容詞。正確答案是表示印象深刻的(C)的impressive。

詞彙 impressive 印象深刻的 thanks to 由於、感謝 impress 使銘記，給予深刻印象 impression 印象

107.

已撥款200多萬美元用來建造新倉庫。

(A) allocated

(B) determined

(C) restored

(D) purchased

「分配、抽出(錢或工作等)」的意思可以用allocate來形容。正確答案是(A)。

詞彙 **allocate** 分配，抽出 **warehouse** 倉庫 **determine** 決定；打聽 **restore** 復原，修復

108.

在過去三個月中，約有2,500名消費者參與了Max Performance的線上問卷調查。

(A) approximative

(B) approximation

(C) approximated

(D) approximately

表示「大概」、能修飾數字的單字是(D)的approximately。作為參考，roughly, around, about等副詞也表達了同樣的意思。

詞彙 **approximately** 大略，約 **approximative** 粗略的 **approximation** 近似值

109.

Lawrence Gardening 中心在每年春季和夏季提供各種免費課程。

(A) offers

(B) is offered

(C) has offered

(D) will offer

主語是一個名為Lawrence Gardening Center的機關，受詞是a variety of free instructional classes(多種免費課程)，因此動詞offer需轉變為被動式，同時為了要與during the spring and summer months each year副詞句相互協調，需要變成現在進行式時態，因此正確答案是滿足這兩個條件的(A)。

詞彙 **a variety of** 多樣的 **instructional class** 課程，培訓

110.

Lambert博士答應他將會搭乘最早的火車，以便準時到達並發表主題演講。

(A) early

(B) earlier

(C) earliest

(D) earlies

內容上要完成「最快出發的火車」的意義，所以空格中要加入(C)的earliest。透過空格前面有定冠詞the這一點可以看出空格應該包含最高級的表達。

111.

依靠天氣發展業務的公司，往往在冬季期間銷售都會下降。

(A) resilient

(B) considerate

(C) dependent

(D) apparent

「依靠、依存」的意思在句中以"be dependent on/upon"來表示。

(C)為正確答案。

詞彙 **be dependent on [upon]** 依靠 **slowdown** 減少，減產 **resilient** 有復原力的 **considerate** 考慮周到的 **apparent** 明白的，分明的

112.

對這個職位感興趣的人需要有卓越的領導能力和經歷。

(A) both

(B) some

(C) much

(D) none

在討論outstanding leadership skills(卓越的領導能力)和prior experience(經歷)這兩個條件，因此空格上要填入可以意指這兩個的(A)both。

詞彙 **prior experience** 經歷

113.

只有在國外的Cathy Vanderbilt可以不出席明天預定的會議。

(A) exemption

(B) exempt

(C) exempting

(D) exemptible

「免除」的意思以be exempt from來表示，因此正確答案是(B)。作爲參考，exempt的形容詞形態和動詞形態相同。

詞彙 **be exempt from** 免除 **exemption** 免除 **exempt** 免除的；免除，豁免 **exemptible** 可免除的

114.

Golden旅行社同意對West先生更改的航班不收其他費用。

(A) considering

(B) approving

(C) charging

(D) verifying

填入空格的單字應以a fee為受詞，完整表達出「不要求額外費用」的意思。正確答案是表示「收取(費用等)」的(C)charging。

詞彙 **charge** 收取，徵收(費用等) **verify** 證明

115.

儘管在三週前就訂購了產品，但Roswell先生還沒有收到任何東西。

(A) Despite

(B) However

(C) Since

(D) Moreover

透過之前訂購了和還沒有收到等內容以讓步的句子來連接是最自然的。在選項中，有讓步的含義為despite，因此正確答案是(A)。作為參考，(B)的However是連接副詞，而不是連接詞或介系詞。

詞彙 **moreover** 更加，再加上

116.

全世界的書迷都熱切地盼望着Martin Stewart的下一部小說出版。

(A) eager
(B) eagerness
(C) eagerly
(D) eagers

句型組成上沒有遺漏的地方,所以空格中應該填入可以修飾anticipating的副詞。正確答案是(C)。

詞彙 **eagerly** 熱切地,渴望地 **anticipate** 預想、期待 **eager** 熱切的 **eagerness** 熱誠,熱心

117.

顧客們可以在一年之中每月分期付款。

(A) issues
(B) units
(C) installments
(D) appropriations

必須要完整表達「可以每月分期付款來結帳」,因此正確答案是有「分期付款」意義的(C)installments。

詞彙 **installment** 分期付款 **issue** 話題,問題 **appropriation** 撥款(金額)

118.

按照公司的方針,員工們在2點到6點之間要休息一次。

(A) what
(B) that
(C) how
(D) when

如果知道it是虛主詞,就可以知道空格中需要填入能夠帶動作為主詞的名詞子句的連接詞that。正確答案是(B)。

詞彙 **guideline** 指南,方針

119.

經常需要護送設施內的訪客們,以確保他們不會進入禁止出入的區域。

(A) required
(B) are required
(C) require
(D) will be required

主語是指人的guests at the facility,受詞是an escort,因此需要被動語態的動詞,(A)和(C)都可以成為正確答案,但如果注意到at all times(經常)這一副詞句,正確答案應該要為現在式的(C)。

詞彙 **escort** 護送,護衛,陪同 **at all times** 經常 **off-limits area** 禁止出入區域

120.

在所有的銷售報告提交之前不得做出任何與公司財政有關的決定。

(A) financial
(B) financed
(C) financeable
(D) finances

空格中應該要填入能夠修飾所有格company's的名詞。正確答案是(D)的finances(財政,金融)。

詞彙 **finance** 財政,金融;供給資金 **financial** 財政的,金融的

121.

那位患者因為拿到了醫療保險的保障,所以只報銷了最低限度的費用。

(A) covers
(B) will be covering
(C) was covered
(D) has covered

Since句子的主語是the patient,而且因為有副詞句by health insurance,因此空格中應該填入cover的被動語態(C)。這時候cover代表的意思是「透過~保證」。

詞彙 **cover** 遮蓋,覆蓋;(透過保險等)保障 **healthy insurance** 健康保險,醫療保險 **minimal** 最小的

122.

招聘委員會正在考慮是向Medina小姐提出聘用提案,還是向Schultz先生提出聘用提案。

(A) if
(B) what
(C) which
(D) whether

如果留意到空格後面有接續to不定詞的事實和句子後半部分的or,就能知道正確答案是(D)的whether。(A)的if之後不會直接接上to不定詞,而(B)的what或(C)的which不會和or一起使用。

詞彙 **hiring committee** 招聘委員會

123.

由於律師們對幾個案件的意見不同,所以兩集團之間的合併尚未定案。

(A) pending
(B) considering
(C) negotiating
(D) discussing

應該要完整表達「雙方意見不一致,合併未確定」的意思,因此空格中應該要加入表示「未定的」或「保留中」意義的(A)pending。

詞彙 **merger** 合併 **pending** 未定的,保留中的 **lawyer** 律師,法學家 **negotiate** 協商

124.

應聘該職位的應徵者最遲將於本週五之前面試。

(A) have interviewed
(B) will be interviewed
(C) are interviewed
(D) have been interviewed

應徵者是面試的對象,空格應該要使用被動語態,如果考慮到副詞句no later than this Friday的話,時態應該要是未來式。正確答案是同時滿足這兩個條件的(B)。

125.

購物俱樂部的會員在網路上購買的物品無需額外費用即可獲得禮品包裝服務。

(A) nothing
(B) not
(C) no
(D) none

正在談論購物俱樂部會員可以得到的優惠，因此空格中應該要填入既可以表示否定意義的同時又可以修飾名詞charge (C)的no。

詞彙 **shoppers' club** 購物俱樂部(賣場向加入的會員提供多項優惠的項目) **gift-wrap** 禮品包裝

126.

在新聞發布會上發言人聲稱近期將會收購一間建築公司。

(A) statement
(B) release
(C) contract
(D) promise

「發表聲明」的意思是以issue a statement來表示。正確答案是(A)。

詞彙 **press conference** 新聞發布會 **issue a statement** 發表聲明 **acquisition** 接管

127.

請確認附件，查看顧客想要的家具規格。

(A) specific
(B) specifically
(C) specified
(D) specifications

空格中應該加入與冠詞the合適並能夠修飾之後for the furniture介系詞的名詞。選項中的名詞只有(D)的specifications(規格)。

詞彙 **attached file** 附件 **specification** 規格 **desire** 期望，希望 **specific** 特定的 **specifically** 特別地 **specify** 明確指出

128.

根據合約條件，之後的2個月內必須全額付款。

(A) for
(B) during
(C) within
(D) since

正在談論有關付款時間的合約規定。空格中要填入意義為「～之內」的介系詞(C)within，才能完整表達出最自然的句子。

詞彙 **term** 期間；條件 **call for** 要求

129.

Grande小姐知道在要報告中說什麼才能得到最積極的反應。

(A) considered
(B) positive
(C) convinced
(D) alert

在內容上應該要尋找能夠最自然地修飾response的形容詞。正確答案是(B)positive。

詞彙 **be aware of** 知道 **convince** 說服 **alert** 警惕；拉警報。

130.

Richardson先生寫了一份綜合報告是關於在墨西哥新設立分行時預期會產生的效果。

(A) comprehended
(B) comprehensive
(C) comprehension
(D) comprehensively

空格中應該加入能夠最自然地修飾report的形容詞。正確答案是(B)的comprehensive(大範圍的，全面的)。

詞彙 **comprehensive** 大範圍的，整體的 **benefit** 利益，好處 **comprehend** 理解 **comprehension** 理解，理解力

PART 6

[131-134]

收件者：jnightingale@homecafe.com
寄件者：sdavidson@andersonfestival.org
主旨：Anderson 慶典
日期：8月28日

致親愛的Nightingale，

恭喜您，您被選為Anderson慶典的**131.**攤商。9月12日至15日，在慶典期間每天都可以停放餐車。**132.**請參閱該電子郵件附件，有准許餐車停放的場所。

通知您每天至少要在活動開始前一小時抵達活動地點。另外，保持餐車周圍的清潔也是本人的**133.**責任。如不遵守，將會在第一次違規時受到警告。在第二次違規時，您的權限將會**134.**被終止。

如有問題請聯繫我。

Sam Davidson 敬上
Anderson慶典組織委員會

詞彙 **select** 選定 **vendor** 攤販，攤商 **set up** 建起，安裝 **food truck** 食物餐車 **from A to B** 從A到B **be responsible for** 對～有責任 **failure** 失敗 **result in** 導致 **warning** 警告 **violation** 違反 **privilege** 優惠，特權 **suspend** 猶豫，中斷 **organizer** 組織者，企劃者

131.

(A) organizers

(B) vendors

(C) sponsors

(D) guests

這是發給可以參加慶典的食物餐車業主的電子郵件。選項中可以指稱食物餐車的單字是(B)的vendors(攤商)。

詞彙 sponsor 贊助者

132.

(A) 請參閱本電子郵件附件。

(B) 請在9月4日之前寄出支票以作為保證金。

(C) 今年的慶典將比以往任何時候的規模都要大,且更有趣。

(D) 其他幾輛食物餐車將會在您周邊。

填入空格的句子中應該要提及後面句子主語it所指稱的事物。正確答案是(A),在這裡可以知道it指的是the file attached with this e-mail。

詞彙 check 支票 deposit 保證金,訂金 be located 位在～

133.

(A) responsible

(B) necessary

(C) considerable

(D) accurate

如果知道be responsible for(對～有責任)的意義,就可以很容易地找到正確答案。(A)為正確答案。

詞彙 considerable 相當大的,巨大的 accurate 正確的

134.

(A) suspension

(B) suspense

(C) suspended

(D) suspensive

考慮到空格前面有being,則空格中應該要填入能夠完成表達被動意義的過去分詞。正確答案是(C)。

詞彙 suspension 終止,休學 suspense 緊張感,掛慮 suspensive 終止的;充滿懸念的

[135-138]

論文徵集

國際地質學家協會(IAG)將於3月10日至12日舉行第15屆會議,此次活動將在英國倫敦的Hampton會議中心舉行。欲要在活動中提交論文的人**135.**最晚要在1月10日之前提交,提交**136.**論文時請通過網路submissions@iag.org進行,如成功**137.**寄出,將會在1月31日之前收到通知。每位發表者都必須由本人負擔交通費以及住宿費用,但是**138.**將會免去參加費用。IAG會員需要支付60英鎊,而非會員則需要支付85英鎊。

詞彙 papers 論文 take place 發生 individual 個人 submit 提交;順從 submission 提交;服從;應用 notify 通知 transportation 交通,運輸 accommodations 住宿 waive 除去,放棄

135.

(A) when

(B) for

(C) than

(D) as

如果知道no later than(最晚到~)一詞的意義,就能輕易地知道正確答案是(C)。或是注意到空格前面有比較級later,也可以知道正確答案是than。

136.

(A) it

(B) him

(C) her

(D) them

空格中應該要填入能接上既是事物又是複數papers的代名詞。正確答案是(D)。

137.

(A) are accepting

(B) have been accepted

(C) will be accepting

(D) being accepted

條件句的主詞是事物的submissions(提交),因此為了能與動詞accept一起使用,空格中必須要填入被動語態。選項中,可以以被動語態完成動詞句型的只有(B)。

138.

(A) 目前不再考慮申請。

(B) 提交論文的篇幅應至少在10頁以上。

(C) 如需補助金,可申請小額補助金。

(D) 但將會免除參加費用。

空格前文提到發表者的經費負擔,後文則是有關於登記費用的說明,因此考慮到這兩點,空格中應填入提及發言者免除參加費用內容的(D)。

詞彙 apply for 申請 grant 補助金,支援金

[139-142]

10月3號

致親愛的Lambert,

您要求更改12月11日和家人一起乘坐的航班日期。遺憾的是,該航空公司沒有在您要求變更的日期飛往開羅的航班。**139.**12月9日或12日前往的話如何呢?兩天都還有下午3點30分的座位。如果**140.**兩個日期都不符合您的行程,您可以取消整個旅遊團,但是會產生相當於團體旅遊價格15%的**141.**取消費用。請在工作時間撥打803-8547與我聯繫以便更詳細地討論**142.**問題。

David Smiley 敬上

Papyrus旅行社

詞彙 alter 變更 airline 航空公司 fit 合適,符合 cancelation fee 取消費用 value 價值,價格 regular business hours 工作時間,營業時間

139.

(A) 是否在考慮前往其他城市度假？
(B) 您想透過其它航空公司前往嗎？
(C) 12月9日或12日前往如何呢？
(D) 需要我一起更改您的酒店嗎？

留意空格後面句子的"on both days"來找正確答案。由於顧客要求變更的日期沒有機位，所以正在誘導變更為其他日期，所以推薦其他天的(C)是正確答案。

140.

(A) neither
(B) both
(C) each
(D) some

在內容上需要完整表達「如果兩個日期都不符合行程可以取消旅行」。在選項中可以同時體現兩個的概念和否定意義的單字是(A)的neither。

141.

(A) canceled
(B) canceling
(C) cancelation
(D) cancels

cancelation fee是複合名詞，表示取消費用。正確答案是(C)。

142.

(A) refund
(B) matter
(C) offer
(D) response

在文章脈絡上尋找最適合成為discuss的受詞單字。正確答案是(B)的matter(問題)。

[143-146]

值得一看的新場所
Elena Carter 記者

奧古斯塔(10月11日)--**143.**大範圍的裝修完畢後，近期Alderson酒店將會重新開業。諸多變化的其中之一就是增加了自助餐廳，酒店方面**144.**宣傳該餐廳是市區內最好的。本記者將會確認其主張是否正確。

自助餐包括牛肉、豬肉、雞肉、羊肉、魚以及海鮮，另外，配菜菜單、沙拉還有甜點也很多。食物很新鮮，而且食物會不斷地被填滿，**145.**所以不管想要什麼食物都無需等待。**146.**價格為每人95美元，稍微貴了一點，但由於食物的品質，還是值得這個費用的。推薦您先預約，尤其是到了週末更需如此。

詞彙 undergo 經歷，經驗 numerous 許多的 addition 追加 buffet 自助餐 assure 確認，保證 plate 盤子，碟子 refill 再裝滿 desire 希望，盼望 steep 陡的，貴的 worth 值得的 due to 因為 reservation 預約

143.

(A) extent
(B) extending
(C) extensive
(D) extendable

空格上應該要填入能夠修飾名詞renovations(維修，修理)的形容詞。(B)的extending是「正在擴大、正在延展」的意思，而(D)的extendable意思是「可延伸的」，因此文章脈絡上空格應該要填入的單字是含有「大範圍的」(C)。

詞彙 extent 程度，規模 extendable 可伸展的，可延伸的

144.

(A) promoting
(B) requesting
(C) sponsoring
(D) considering

必須找到與as the best(作為最好的餐廳)相符合的表達方式。正確答案是含有宣傳意義的(A)。

145.

(A) fairly
(B) continually
(C) exclusively
(D) variously

想一想在什麼情況下不用等自助餐就能很快地找到正確答案。正確答案是有「持續不斷地」或「繼續」意思的(B)continually。

詞彙 fairly 相當地，頗 exclusively 專門地，僅僅 variously 多樣地

146.

(A) 價格是人均95美元，稍微偏高。
(B) 三處宴會廳也可出租。
(C) 也可以要求廚師長如何烹煮肉。
(D) 工作人員非常親切且具有專業意識。

空格後面的句子中有"it's worth the cost"，所以空格應該要提到價格，而選項中提及價格的句子僅有(A)。

詞彙 banquet room 宴會廳 waitstaff 工作人員，服務員 attentive 傾聽的，體貼的 professional 專門的，專業的

PART 7

[147-148]

夏季郊遊

Harris Manufacturing將再次舉辦夏季郊遊，這是今年最受歡迎的活動，且今年的活動規模有望比去年更大、更有趣。該活動將於7月28日星期六中午至晚上四點在Forest公園舉行，將會邀請所有員工及其直系親屬參加。今年我們提供的食物將會與去年相同，但是為了慶祝我們最近在財務方面的成長，我們還會準備燒烤牛排以及鮭魚，也將會玩各種遊戲，所以這將是一個充滿歡樂的下午。請讓人事部的Tom Snyder（內線號碼91）知道您是否要參加以及同行的人數。我們期待著您的光臨。

詞彙 promise 約定，承諾 immediate family member 直屬親屬 celebrate 祝賀，慶祝 grill (用烤架)烤 accompany 陪伴，同行

147.

關於夏季野餐不屬實的是什麼？
(A) 提供的食物中可能會有牛排和鮭魚。
(B) 預定將於週末進行。
(C) 將會準備參加者可以玩的遊戲。
(D) 今年是首次舉辦。

第一句中提到是再次(once again)舉辦郊遊，因此(D)是錯誤的內容。其餘選項的飲食菜單、活動場所及時間，遊戲等所有內容都可以在引文中找到。

148.

公司員工被勸說要做什麼？
(A) 向同事說明是否要參加活動。
(B) 提前購買郊遊門票。
(C) 告知Snyder先生前往活動地點需要的交通方式。
(D) 告知將會帶那些食物。

最後一個部分是要求將是否出席(if you intend to be there)和出席人數(how many people will be accompanying you)告知人事部的Tom Snyder先生，因此正確答案是(A)。

[149-150]

Steve Lewis	2:25 P.M.
你好，Jennifer。辦公室裡有一個叫Percy Sinclair的人在找你。	

Jennifer Kelvin	2:26 P.M.
他已經到了嗎？會議在一個小時後。	

Steve Lewis	2:28 P.M.
他說道路比平常還要空，所以他沒有塞車。	

Jennifer Kelvin	2:30 P.M.
原來如此。你何不請他去樓下的咖啡廳？告訴他我會盡快到那裡的。	

Steve Lewis	2:31 P.M.
他說當妳到達的時候，他將在那裡等您。	

149.

下午2點26分，Kelvin小姐為什麼說"He's already here"？
(A) 為了再次確認自己說過的話。
(B) 為了表達驚訝。
(C) 為了徵求意見。
(D) 為了回答問題。

就在下一句中就說明了會議是一小時後(Our meeting isn't until an hour from now.)，所以給定的句子是對於早來的一種驚訝，因此(B)是正確答案。

150.

關於Kelvin小姐，暗示了什麼？
(A) 她將在去辦公室之前前往一家咖啡廳。
(B) 她常常因為工作而離開辦公室。
(C) 她以前從未親眼見過Sinclair先生。
(D) 她告訴Sinclair先生怎麼來辦公室。

透過前半部分的聊天內容可以看出Sinclair先生來到辦公室，而後半部分Kelvin小姐請求傳達要Sinclair先生去咖啡廳，然後說自己也會盡快過去那裡(I'll be there as soon as I can)。透過這些可以知道她現在在在辦公室外面，並會馬上過去咖啡廳，所以(A)是正確答案。

[151-152]

Stetson's可以幫助您改建您的房屋或辦公室。我們將幫助您充分利用現有空間來創建理想的居住空間或辦公室空間。

我們將與您聯繫，確定您想要什麼，然後我們將會以您的喜好來設計一切。我們是直接從主要的家具經銷商那裡購買的，因此您永遠可以以最低價格購買。

我們也會為您提供所需的配件，包括燈具，地毯和藝術品。我們也將會為您提供百葉窗、窗簾、壁紙和油漆。

現在就撥打980-1823享有免費估價。

詞彙 remodel 改建 make the most out of 充分利用 dealer 仲介，商人 accessory 附屬物品，配件 estimate 估價，預估

151.

Stetson's是什麼？
(A) 家具店。
(B) 建築辦事處。
(C) 室內設計公司。
(D) 造景公司。

選項中進行住宅及辦公室改建(remodel your home or office)工作，以及能夠提供家具(furniture)及燈具、地毯等等，因此Stetson's是(C)的室內設計公司。

152.

關於Stetson's，提及到的是什麼？
(A) 在居住設施和商業設施內工作。
(B) 為工作提供退款保證服務。
(C) 向客戶索取報價的費用。
(D) 有一個專為顧客準備的裝滿配件的倉庫。

因為廣告中說明為住宅或辦公室(home or office)的改造工作，所以將其改為"residences and businesses"的(A)就是正確答案。(B)和(D)為沒有提到的內容，而且估價是可以免費享有的，而(C)是與事實相反的內容。

[153-154]

★★★★☆

對於Pacific公司生產的Burger Master燒烤架，不管我怎麼說都不為過。Burger Master易於使用，可均勻烹飪食物而不會讓任何東西烤焦，它使用丙烷氣來烹煮並且可以輕鬆控制食物烹飪的溫度。每年春季及夏季，我每周至少要用這個做燒烤三次，由於烤架的爐柵上有不沾塗層使食物不易沾黏，因此烤架也方便清潔。我唯一的不滿是車輪並不能很好地轉動，這使得有時候在搬動Burger Master很難掌握。我希望能改善這一點。儘管如此，這燒烤爐非常出色，而且價格無與倫比。

David Carter

詞彙 cannot say enough about 對於～不管怎麼說都不為過 burn 燃燒，燒焦 propane gas 丙烷氣 barbecue 燒烤 thanks to 由於、感謝 grate 爐柵 no-stick 不沾的 rotate 旋轉 aspect 方面 cannot be beat 打敗不了

153.

關於Carter先生，暗示了什麼？
(A) 他使用燒烤架烹調肉類和蔬菜。
(B) 他喜歡在戶外做飯。
(C) 他最近購買了Burger Master燒烤架。
(D) 他是專業廚師。

透過"Every spring and summer, I barbecue food with it at least three times a week."這句子可以推測撰寫評論的Carter先生會喜歡在戶外做菜。正確答案是(B)。

154.

Carter先生希望要怎麼改進Burger Master燒烤架？
(A) 增加輪子。
(B) 改變設計。
(C) 使其更容易移動。
(D) 降低價格。

對燒烤架的輪子不好轉動，因此很難移動(makes moving the Burger Master difficult)表示不滿，因此他希望的改善點可以看作是(C)。

詞彙 mobile 移動的，移動式的

[155-157]

4月28號

致親愛的Spencer先生，

相信您正在熱切地等待申請結果。很高興通知您，您已獲准成為Center City Business協會的成員。對這結果表示祝賀，我們很期待您會對我們組織做出積極的貢獻。

在拿到會員卡自由利用之前，有幾件事情要先完成。首先，您需要繳納300美元的年會費及加入費用，之後每年只需繳納100美元的會費即可，因此請您在協會下一次會議開始之前繳納400美元。第二件事為您應該要出席下次會議，預定於5月6日星期六舉行，也將會見到其他新會員，這之後會在協會正式註冊。

如果需要幫助請撥打908-3842與我聯繫。

Stanley Harper 敬上
Center City Business協會會長

詞彙 eagerly 熱切地，懇切地 contribution 捐獻，貢獻 organization 組織，機關 gain access to 接近，得到 one-time fee 只需支付一次的費用 in addition to 除了～ annual membership fee 年會費 due 會費，費用 on an annual basis 以年為單位的，每年 officially 正式的 enroll 登記

155.

Harper先生為什麼會寄信？
(A) 為了請求Spencer先生繳納拖欠款項。
(B) 為了告知申請情況。

(C) 為了表示已提交所有需要的資料。
(D) 為了批准Spencer先生的提案。

在信件的開頭部分Harper先生通知Spencer先生他的申請結果(results of your application)，因此寫信的目的可視為(B)。

詞彙 late fee 滯納金 status report 現況報告

156.

Spencer先生在5月6日之前應該要做什麼？
(A) 跟協會的其他成員見面。
(B) 拿到會員卡。
(C) 繳納400美元。
(D) 直接與Harper先生見面並交談。

問題的核心語句May 6在"Second, you must attend that meeting, which will be held on Saturday, May 6."中找的到，從這裡可以知道下次會議的召開日是5月6日，因此在前文所述的下次會議之前(before the association's next meeting)應要繳納400美元就是Spencer先生在5月6日前要做的事情。

157.

[1]，[2]，[3]，[4]中最合適下列句子的地方是哪裡？
「我們對這樣的結果表示祝賀。」
(A) [1]
(B) [2]
(C) [3]
(D) [4]

文章脈絡上所指的句子的this achievement所指的可能是申請會員加入的結果，因此最好的是放在傳達已批准加入會員消息的後面[1]位置。正確答案是(A)。

[158-161]

Cardiff 滑雪度假村將會重新開放
Roger McCabe

佛羅倫斯（11月10日）--佛羅倫斯唯一的滑雪場Cardiff滑雪度假村計劃於今年12月1日重新開放。對於許多曾擔心過可能要到一月才能開放的滑雪者來說，這應該會是一個令人驚喜又開心的消息。

Janet Marston在過去五個月中一直監督該渡假村的裝修。業主命令進行的改建包括擴大主滑雪道，架設新的滑雪纜車以及新建兩個滑雪道。在主滑雪道新建了一個廚房和十個臥室，因此現在有三十間客房可供出租，另外，為了能讓滑雪者們從滑雪道回來後能夠聚集在一起取暖，還設有一個具有巨大壁爐的新休息室。標榜其整體內部都重整過，並採用飾有野生圖案的木板。

Marston女士說：「我決定要改善度假村的型態，並且對結果感到非常滿意。」說到滑雪纜車，它使用了最新技術，為搭乘者提供一個平穩，安全，快速，可以輕鬆抵達Cardiff山頂上的滑雪道。這兩個新滑雪道包括一個專門為單板滑雪者準備的滑雪道，單板滑雪者如今佔滑雪勝地遊客總數的30%左右。

26

詞彙 eager 熱心的，熱情的 oversee 監督，監視 renovate 翻新，改造 ski lodge 滑雪小屋(為了滑雪者的住宿設施) slope傾斜 fireplace 壁爐 gather around 聚集 redo 再做 panel 板，鑲板；用鑲板鑲嵌 motif 設計；主題，裝飾圖案 swift 迅速的 exclusively 專門地，獨佔地 comprise 構成

158.

報導主要是關於什麼？
(A) Cardiff 山的冬季運動。
(B) 滑雪度假村的變化。
(C) 在佛羅倫斯附近可以做的活動。
(D) 滑雪人氣的上升。

整篇報導都在說Cardiff滑雪度假村的開業消息以及度假村設施的變化，因此報導的主題是(B)。

159.

關於Cardiff滑雪度假村的暗示是什麼？
(A) 數十年前開始營業。
(B) 建在Cardiff山的半山腰。
(C) 有為了團體的特別收費。
(D) 位於佛羅倫斯附近。

在報導的第一部分介紹Cardiff Ski Resort為Florence's only place for skiing(在佛羅倫斯唯一能滑雪的地方)，所以正確答案為(D)。

160.

Marston小姐是誰？
(A) 度假村的所有者。
(B) 滑雪導師。
(C) 佛羅倫居民。
(D) 度假村工作人員。

在第2段中Janet Marston被介紹為是「監督維修工程的人(overseeing the renovating of the place)」，第3段則是透過採訪說明她是計畫了工程並對此感到滿意的人。選項中可能屬於這種人物的只有(A)的度假村所有者。

161.

關於Cardiff山的新滑雪道，提到的是什麼？
(A) 兩個都是專為單板滑雪者的。
(B) 被認為是上級路線。
(C) 尚未為滑雪者們作好準備。
(D) 位於離滑雪纜車較近的地方。

在第三段關於纜車的介紹中，有說明纜車會一直延伸到Cardiff山頂，「所有滑雪道都可以輕鬆地到達(where they can easily reach all of the slopes on the mountain)」，因此可以認為滑雪到和纜車就在附近，(D)為正確答案。由於專為單板滑雪者設計的滑雪道只有一個，所以(A)不能成為正確答案，(B)和(C)是報導中找不到的內容。

詞彙 consider 考慮，認為，視為

[162-164]

收件者：全體部門主管,Susan Rogers, Joseph Roth, Erica Dane
寄件者：Aaron Hoyle副總裁
主旨：會議
日期：9月21日

在有幾個部門出現超出其一年預算跡象的情況下，有三個部門則是已經使用了其所有的年度預算。這些超額支出已無法控制，但必須要停止才可以。

財務總監David Winter先生對於目前的支出額度感到不滿並打算要立刻處理這些問題。明天一點董事將會在五樓的大會議室主持會議，全體部門經理和會計部管理人員都要參加。本次會議將會持續一整個下午，因此請取消預定的其他日程，除非是已經外出的情況之外，不允許不參加。

請攜帶該部門的一年預算案和今年該部門所有與支出相關的資料過來。請準備好這些資料以便與同事共享。我們將討論透過減少支出可能會產生的收益，並討論是否實施與支出程序相關的的各種方針。

每位與會者可以帶一位部下來幫助處理文件和做筆記。

詞彙 be pace on to 將要～ allotment 分配額 get out of control 變得無法控制 halt 停止，使其中斷 CFO 財務總監 address 地址；辦理，處理 upper-level 上位的 absence 缺席 documentation 文件 share 分享，共有 potential 潛在的 implementation 履行，實施 assistant 助手，協助 notetaking 筆記

162.

Hoyle先生提到什麼問題？
(A) 部門支出過多。
(B) 公司預算將削減。
(C) 支出程序令人費解。
(D) 部門有不良記錄。

預算的超支使用，即過度支出(this type of overspending)是問題所在，因此正確答案是(A)。

163.

沒有要參加會議的是誰？
(A) 會計部員工。
(B) 公司代表董事。
(C) Winter先生。
(D) 所有部門主管。

會議的出席對象可在文章的第二段中確認，CFO David Winter、全體部門主管(all department heads)，以及會計部管理人員(upper-level accountants)為出席對象，選項中不屬於這些的人是(B)。

27

164.

與會者被要求帶什麼來開會？
(A) 為了增加個別預算的提案。
(B) 關於今年支出的資訊。
(C) 與過去三年的支出有關的文件。
(D) 明年預算案的副本。

與會者應攜帶的東西是部門的一年預算(your department's annual budget)和與所屬部門支出有關的文件(documentation of all the spending done in your department for the entire year)。正確答案是這兩種中後者的(B)。

[165-168]

収件者：undisclosed_recipients
寄件者：tinakline@museumofscience.org
主旨：新展覽
日期：9月10日

各位您好，

很高興地通知大家，曾經廣泛宣傳的今年秋季展覽的公開籌備工作已經基本就緒。以【19世紀的科學】為主題的新展覽預計將於10月第一天向公眾開放。

展館位於一樓西館，參觀者訪問的話將有機會參觀1800年代最重要的發明。請觀賞愛迪生燈泡的初創形態，也將會展出貝爾最初的一部電話。不僅僅只是電報機，就連早期的內燃機也有機會參觀，更好的是，因為這次的展覽會是體驗型展覽，您將可以知道機器實際上怎麼運作的，還有機會親自操作部分機器。

相信大家會好奇為了看展覽要怎麼等到10月開始的那一天。由於各位現在作為博物館的資金贊助人，在人滿為患前的9月29日和30日，可以到博物館參觀入場。兩天中任一天參觀時只需攜帶博物館發放的卡片。博物館將在正式開館期間開放，但這兩天內只有持卡人才能入場。

館長Tina Kline 敬上

詞彙 be about ready to 準備好要～ unveil 除去面紗，公開 much-hyped 廣泛宣傳的 entitle 題名 wing 翅膀，附屬建築 opportunity 機會 prototype 原型 internal combustion engine 內燃機 telegraph 電信，電報機 interactive 相互作用的，互相的 backer 贊助人，支援者

165.

收件者是誰？
(A) 附近學校的學生。
(B) 收集特殊物品的人。
(C) 博物館的贊助人。
(D) 以前訪問過博物館的人。

在電子郵件最後的段落中，電子郵件收件者被稱為current financial backers of the museum(現在作為博物館的贊助人)，透過這些可以推測出收件者可能是向博物館資助捐款的人，因此正確答案是(C)。

詞彙 donor 捐贈者，捐獻者

166.

關於展覽，可以知道什麼？
(A) 將在今年年底之前展出。
(B) 訪客可以使用展示中的物品。
(C) 展覽物品是出租給博物館的。
(D) 為了參觀需支付額外費用。

在第三段中介紹了本次展覽是「體驗型展覽(an interactive exhibit)」，所以可以親自操作機器(you will have the opportunity to handle some machines)，因此選項中提及的事項是(B)。

167.

展覽什麼時候會向一般大眾開放？
(A) 9月29日。
(B) 9月30日。
(C) 10月1日。
(D) 10月2日。

在第一段中提到，展覽的開館日期是10月第一天(the first day of October)。正確答案是(C)。作為參考，(A)和(B)是特別為博物館贊助人開放展覽的日子。

168.

[1]，[2]，[3]，[4]中下列句子最適合的地方是哪裡？
「兩天中任一天參觀時只需攜帶博物館發放的卡片。」
(A) [1]
(B) [2]
(C) [3]
(D) [4]

注意到either day一詞的話，所給定的句子應要放在提到9月29日和30日的後面，因此正確答案是(D)。透過下一句的「只有持卡人才能入場」也可以確認句子的位置。

[169-171]

第五大道大橋相關公告

特此通知，自5月15日開始，所有自用車輛在第五大道大橋的收費將從八十美分增加到一美元。該漲幅由市交通委員會在上次5月4日的會議上以3比2的投票通過。從通行費中收取的額外收入將用於協助城市發展自行車基礎設施，並將於6月10日開始在該城市一些最繁忙的街道上開始建設自行車道，比起自用車或是貨車，這是為了促進利用自行車而實施的，還有助於減少市區的交通壅塞並減少城市的空氣污染量。

詞彙 hereby 特此 toll 通行費 noncommercial 非商業的 commission 委員會 collect 收集，徵收 infrastructure 基礎建設 bicycle lane 自行車道 promote 促進；晉升 usage 使用 serve 提供；有幫助，貢獻 congestion 壅塞 pollution 汙染

169.

這是為了誰的公告？
(A) 市政府員工。
(B) 當地居民。
(C) 建設公司。
(D) 市委員會。

向通行第五大道大橋的所有自用車輛(all noncommercial vehicles)通知要提高通行費的訊息，因此使用該大橋的車輛司機將成為公告的對象，正確答案是(B)。

170.

5月4日會發生什麼事？
(A) 自行車道開始通行。
(B) 橋墩建設完成。
(C) 城市大眾交通設施獲得改善。
(D) 價格上漲獲得批准。

找到有May 4的問題核心句子的話，不難發現當天市委員會以3比2的投票表決(by a vote of 3-2)通過價格上調，因此5月4日發生的事情是(D)。

詞彙 vote on 表決通過

171.

關於自行車道的暗示是什麼？
(A) 將建設在城市大部分的道路。
(B) 有助於使城市更加乾淨。
(C) 由當地居民要求。
(D) 已經在建設中。

在公告最後的部分可以確認到自行車道的效果，也就是說，自行車道是用來緩解市中心交通壅塞，減少市內大氣污染量(to reduce the amount of air pollution in the city)，所以(B)是正確答案。因為說要在城市內建設大部分道路，所以(A)是錯誤的內容，自行車道的建設將從6月10日開始，所以(D)也不符合事實。

[172-175]

Greg Thompson	9:10 A.M.
剛才接到兩個心情很不好的顧客的電話，對於某些產品價格表示不滿。有沒有人知道發生了什麼事？	
Mia Carter	9:11 A.M.
我沒聽說過，Dave？	
Dave Washington	9:12 A.M.
稍等，我來確認一下。	
Dave Washington	9:15 A.M.
我和Marcus聊過了。他說因為午夜把最新軟體的價格提高了，聽說收到了很多電子郵件。	
Greg Thompson	9:16 A.M.
而且今天可以通話了，所以顧客們就換成打電話了。	
Deana Wilson	9:17 A.M.
那麼我們應該對人們說什麼？	
Dave Washington	9:19 A.M.
跟他們說我們理解他們的感受，並說最晚在今天中午之前會在網站上公布新的定價。	
Mia Carter	9:20 A.M.
哇，主管們非常迅速地做出了決定。	

Greg Thompson	9:21 A.M.
那麼以高價購買的人要怎麼辦？	
Dave Washington	9:22 A.M.
如果有這種人打來的話，跟他們說我們將會退還他們支付的多餘金額。	

詞彙 go on 發生(事情或是情況等等) apparently 看起來，聽說 line 線；電話線 error 錯誤，失誤 regular price 定價 swift 迅速地 inflated 暴漲的

172.

線上聊天室主要是關於什麼？
(A) 應退還的金額。
(B) 公司最新軟體的使用。
(C) 公司產品價格。
(D) 公司最近做出的決定。

正在討論因產品價格上漲而引起顧客不滿的問題。即在說軟體漲價(we raised the price of our newest software)而引起了顧客們的抗議電子郵件和抗議電話，因此討論的主題是(D)。

173.

上午9點15分，Washington先生說"We've been getting lots of e-mails."的時候，他指的是什麼？
(A) 有許多顧客提出不滿。
(B) 他最近確認了電子郵件信箱。
(C) 使用者告知了軟體的缺陷。
(D) 有一些顧客正在退貨購買的產品。

正因為前文提到漲價決定，所以可以推測出句子中的電子郵件是抗議性電子郵件，因此所給定的句子含義應要視為(A)。

詞彙 e-mail inbox 電子郵件收件箱 bug 蟲子；(電腦的)缺陷

174.

關於軟體，暗示了什麼？
(A) 發現了一些問題。
(B) 有一些電腦不能使用。
(C) 最初販售的時間是昨天晚上。
(D) 公司將其價格下調。

當問及如何應對顧客的不滿時，Washington先生說「會在網絡上再次公告定價(the new regular price will be listed on the Website)」。Carter聽了之後說「主管們迅速地做出了決定(swift decision by management)」，因此認為最終公司可能會調降軟體的價格，因此正確答案是(D)。

詞彙 be compatible with 與～共存

175.

Thompson先生在詢問什麼？
(A) 要如何應對顧客。
(B) 價格為什麼要變更。
(C) 什麼時候會接到更多電話。
(D) 應將錯誤歸咎於誰。

在聊天室後半部分Thompson先生說"What about the people who purchased it at the inflated price?"，在詢問該要如何回應以高價

購買產品的人，因此他詢問的事情可視為(A)。

[176-180]

新休假規定

Azuma公司將要引入新的休假規定。員工必須得要在休假離開前一周申請休假，例外僅適用於疾病和緊急家庭問題，此外員工必須獲得書面許可方可休假，經理可准許員工為期一至五天的假期，對於六天或更長時間的假期，必須要經由部門主管授予許可。休假超過五天的員工還必須要以書面形式說明他們需要這麼多時間的原因。主管將會在收到請求後的二十四小時內批准或拒絕請求。該規定將於6月1日生效。

詞彙 institute 引入(制度等等) time off 休假 exception 例外 family emergency 家庭緊急情況 permission 允許，許可 grant 給予，授予；許可 indicate 指出，顯露 deny 拒絕 go into effect 生效

收件者：a_yeager@azumacorp.com
寄件者：peter-matthews@azumacorp.com
主旨：休假
日期：6月20日

親愛的Yeager小姐，

謹通知您我現在負責的兩個項目將會在6月28日之前完成。請查看這封電子郵件的附件，該附件顯示出這兩項業務中我已完成的部分以及尚未完成的部分。

從6月29日起我將不會有重要業務，所以我想正式申請休假。我將於6月30日至7月14日休假，共11天不上班。如果您有疑問，我妻子和我將會在這段時間去澳洲旅遊，相信您知道我們每年夏天都會去長途旅行。去年去了義大利，在那之前也去過俄羅斯旅行，也去過南非的狩獵旅行。

今年我妻子發現了一件驚人的特價商品，於是我們購買了飛往雪梨的機票。另外，因為有親戚在墨爾本，所以我打算去那邊看看。我不在的期間會讓Phil Jenkins和Denise Kennedy做好準備，以便接待我的顧客們。請您批准我的休假申請。

Peter Matthews 敬上

詞彙 presently 現在 describe 描寫，說明 assignment 作業，工作 task 工作，業務 formally 正式地 workday 工作日 in case 假如，萬一 curious 愛探究的，好奇的 take advantage of 利用 relative 親戚 see fit 決定

176.

要怎麼申請三天的假期？
(A) 透過在網路上填寫表格。
(B) 透過聯絡部門主管。
(C) 透過向管理者交談。
(D) 透過聯繫人事部。

在第一段引文上寫著一至五天的休假(vacations lasting between one and five days)是由supervisors(管理者)許可的。

177.

根據公告，管理者們在請假方面應該要做什麼？
(A) 與申請的員工直接交談。
(B) 迅速做出答覆。
(C) 以書面形式批准所有申請。
(D) 用電子郵件回覆。

在公告的後半部分中，管理人員要在收到申請後的24小時內(within twenty-four hours of receiving them)予以批准或拒絕，所以正確答案是(B)。(A)和(D)是未提及的事項，因為管理人員可能會拒絕請假，(C)也不能成為正確答案。

178.

Matthews先生用電子郵件發了什麼？
(A) 工作報告。
(B) 旅遊行程副本。
(C) 她必須簽字的表格。
(D) 費用帳單。

Matthews先生附加的東西在電子郵件的第一段"a file describing the work I have completed and which is yet to be on"有提到，也就是說，因為附上說明自己完成的工作和尚未完成的工作的文件，所以用update on his work(工作報告)來表達的(A)就是正確答案。

詞彙 update 更新；最新情報 itinerary 旅遊日程 reimbursement 償還，退款

179.

關於Yeager小姐，暗示了什麼？
(A) 她現在在國外。
(B) 她是一部門的主管。
(C) 她擁有多位私人客戶。
(D) 她將會很快地將新項目交給Matthews先生。

透過第二段引文的電子郵件，可得知Matthews先生將要離開共十一天(a total of 11 workdays)的休假。在第一個公告中說明了5天以內的休假申請是由管理人同意，而六天以上的假期(for vacations of six days or longer)是由部門主管批准的，因此可以推測出電子郵件的收件人Yeager小姐是部門主管，正確答案是(B)。(A)和(D)是與引文完全無關的內容，(C)不是與Yeager小姐有關，而是與Matthews先生有關的事項。

180.

關於門票，Matthews先生暗示了什麼？
(A) 不能退款。
(B) 通過旅行社預訂的。
(C) 不可更改。
(D) 以低廉的價格購買的。

電子郵件最後一段的"my wife took advantage of an outstanding offer"是正確答案的線索，因為可以得知他的妻子購買了特價商品的機票，所以正確答案是(D)。

[181-185]

Rockport音樂節將於一周後開始

Kendra Ellington 記者

羅克波特(5月21日)--每年舉行的Rockport春季慶典將於下週二開始。它將在5月29日開始,並在6月3日結束。這次春季慶典的規模已經擴大,將在兩個地方進行。第一個地方是傳統慶典場所Liberty公園,第二個地方則是Shell海灘。

策劃人Donovan West說:「我們預計本次慶典將會有超過35,000人來參加,將會舉行各種活動,包括音樂表演、農貿市場、世界美食博覽會,還會準備遊樂設施。」另外也將舉行釣魚比賽,釣魚比賽將會與每晚的煙火表演一同在海邊舉辦。

該項目前正在尋找慶典的志願者,以確保一切能夠順利進行。有興趣的人請致電849-9382與市政府聯繫。

詞彙 be set to 預定 conclude 終了,結束 expand 擴大 take place 出現,發生 venue 場所 farmers' market 農貿市場 along with 和~一起 fireworks show 煙火表演 smoothly 順利地 urge 催促

Rockport慶典華麗落幕

Craig Sinclair 記者

羅克波特(6月4日)--Rockport春季慶典於昨晚結束。最後一天有20,000人參加,主辦方估計慶典期間有超過70,000人參加。George Allard市長說「志願者們都很優秀,得益於此,本次的慶典達到了歷屆之最。」

有許多慶典參與者說他們是來看Shell海灘的,這個海灘已被污染多年,但在冬季期間歷時兩個月的垃圾清理,海灘已經復原了。目前該海灘是州中最美麗的地方之一。

Julie Smith說「我打算夏末要再來一次」,而這位哈維佛德居民說「簡直不敢相信海邊會有這麼漂亮,回家後我會告訴所有我認識的人關於海灘的一切。」

詞彙 end on a high note 華麗落幕,完美結尾 come to a conclusion 結束 in attendance 參與的 estimate 估算,估計 remark 提及 pollute 汙染 garbage 垃圾 restore 恢復,復原

181.

關於釣魚比賽,暗示了什麼?

(A) 首次舉行。
(B) 在Liberty公園舉行。
(C) 有數百名參加。
(D) 有參加費。

有關釣魚大會的內容可在第一篇報導的第二段中找到,這裡介紹到的是「釣魚大會將會在海邊舉行(which will be held at the beach)」。另外,在第一段中提到這次慶典將在原來曾舉行過慶典的公園和此次成為慶典場所的海邊舉行。因此綜合以上這些內容,可以得知釣魚大會是首次舉行的,因此正確答案是(A)。

詞彙 participate in 參與,參加 entry fee 報名費

182.

為什麼要給市政府打電話?

(A) 為了要預購慶典門票。
(B) 為了要申請參加慶典活動。
(C) 為了要幫助慶典。
(D) 為了要捐款給慶典。

在第一篇報導的最後一段中有一句"Interested individuals are urged to contact city hall at 849-9382."可以找到市政府的電話號碼。文章脈絡上interested individuals是指對志願服務感興趣的人,因此需要撥打市政府電話的理由可以看作是(C)。

詞彙 make a donation 捐款

183.

關於Rockport春季慶典可以知道什麼?

(A) 參加人數超出預期。
(B) 大部分活動都受到與會者的歡迎。
(C) 平均每天有20,000人來訪。
(D) 預定的遊行應要取消。

在第一篇報導中預計參加慶典的人數會達到35,000人以上(more than 35,000 people),而第二篇報導的實際參加人數可能達到70,000人以上(more than 70,000 people),因此參加慶典的人可能比預想的多兩倍左右,所以正確答案是(A)。

詞彙 attendee 參與者 average 平均;平均為~

184.

提到與Shell海灘有關的是什麼?

(A) 有來自其他州的訪客。
(B) 6月重新向大眾開放。
(C) 景觀變好。
(D) 設施仍在維修。

關於Shell海灘的內容可以在第二篇報導的中半部分之後確認。在這裡介紹了Shell海灘雖然被污染了很多年(had been polluted for years),但透過復原工作,現在成為了州中最漂亮的地方之一(among the most beautiful ones in the state),因此關於Shell海灘的事項是(C)。

185.

Smith小姐是誰?

(A) 慶典的策劃者。
(B) 慶典的參加者。
(C) 慶典的志願者。
(D) 慶典的攤販。

Julie Smith這個名字在第二篇文章的最後一個段落中可以找到,這裡她作為哈維佛德居民(the resident of Haverford)對慶典表示滿意。因此她的身份是(B)。(A)的「慶典策劃人」名字在第一篇報導中以Donovan West出現,而(C)和(D)的名字從未提及過。

[186-190]

3月11號

致親愛的Andre先生，

招聘委員會在3月8日的會議上對您印象深刻。我們很喜歡您的社交性格、以前的經歷，以及流暢的英語、法語和西班牙語運用能力。因此為了能讓您在我們公司的法國南特分公司工作，我們想向您提供工作機會。您作為銷售經理，不僅會負責整個西班牙地區，還將負責法國以西地區的銷售，因此您將會不斷地奔波。

該職位的年薪起薪為95,000美元，您可以按照營業額領取季度獎金。現在因為您在希臘雅典，您的搬家費用將會由我們負擔，並會提供南特中心區三間臥室的公寓。最後，您將獲得兩週的帶薪休假，也會享有包括醫療保險和退休金在內的所有福利。

請致電749-3844通知我您的決定。

Javier Solas 敬上
Hardaway International

詞彙 outgoing 外向的，社交的 attitude 態度 fluent command 流暢的口才 extend an offer 提議 be responsible for 負責 on the road 移動中的 quarterly 按季度 based on 根據 pension 退休金

收件者：Lucia Bouchard
寄件者：Javier Solas
主旨：David Andre
日期：3月18日

我從Andre先生那裡得到了關於我們提議的確定答覆了。他不僅會得到每年110,000美元，還會獲得我們以前討論過的福利待遇。Andre先生開始工作的日期是4月10日。我告訴他你的電話號碼了，所以他會打電話給你。另外，因為在法國生活需要幫助，所以我也告訴他Rene Faucher的電子郵件地址了，請跟Rene說他在第二天左右就會收到Andre的來信。

詞彙 confirmation 確認 previously 之前地 transition 過渡，轉換

---

http://www.hardawayinternational.com/newsletter

David Andre給人留下積極的印象
Kate Jung

(7月11日)--David Andre與我們一起工作才3個月，但他已經給我們留下了深刻的印象。得益於此，4月以後法國及西班牙國內的交易數量增加了兩倍，達到38件。Andre先生說「在這裡工作真好。我童年時期一直是在法國度過的，因為工作的緣故，我在法國各地到處奔波。能夠一邊工作一邊體驗過去是一件令人高興的事情。」

Andre先生4月開始工作，並在短時間內獲得總經理Lucia Bouchard的信任。她說「我知道他會成為一位優秀的員工，但我沒想到會有這種事。我會繼續給他更多的工作來看看他會怎麼處理。」

詞彙 impression 印象 customer 顧客，商業夥伴 youth 青春時期 relive 再次體驗 delightful 令人高興的 confidence 信賴，信任

186.

信中沒有提到Andre先生的是什麼？
(A) 他將負責銷售業務。
(B) 他目前在其他國家。
(C) 他具有友善的性格。
(D) 他以前在西班牙工作過。

Andre先生作為銷售經理，將負責銷售(you'll be responsible for sales)，因此(A)是提到過的事項。透過「他現在在希臘的雅典，公司會負擔搬家費用(we'll pay for you to move)」可以得知(B)也是事實。(C)的friendly personality與outgoing attitude意思相同，這種性格也是有提到的事項，但因為沒有提到有關於在西班牙工作的經驗，所以(D)為正確答案。

187.

擔任銷售經理的條件是什麼？
(A) 必須要具有市場營銷學歷。
(B) 必須要跑外勤。
(C) 必須要講外語。
(D) 必須要讓顧客高興。

在第一篇引文的信中句子"As a sales manager, you'll be responsible for sales in the western region of France as well as all of Spain, so you'll be on the road constantly."中可以找到正確答案的線索。說明他作為銷售經理經常會要跑來跑去，因此在選項中他擔任銷售經理的條件可視為是(B)。(C)雖然是Andre先生具有的能力，但並不是作為銷售經理的條件被提及的。

188.

通知的目的是什麼？
(A) 為了要求提供有關員工的資訊。
(B) 為了確定面試日程。
(C) 為了告知聯繫方式。
(D) 為了告知新徵聘的員工。

通知是告知有關接受入職提議的Andre先生相關資訊，即薪資、開始工作日期等等，因此通知的目的可視為(D)。

189.

Andre先生似乎做了什麼？
(A) 調任巴黎分公司。
(B) 拒絕了最初的年薪提議。
(C) 3月直接與Faucher先生見過面。
(D) 在雅典有房子。

在第一篇引文的信件中，向Andre先生提議的年薪為95,000美元，從第二篇引文通知中可以看出，他的實際年薪為110,000美元。綜合以上這兩個事實，可以推斷出他拒絕了第一個年薪提議，因此(B)是正確答案。

190.

關於Bouchard小姐的暗示是什麼？
(A) 即將調往西班牙。
(B) 為社報寫了文章。
(C) 出差是與Andre先生同行。
(D) 增加Andre先生的工作。

Ms. Bouchard這個名字可以在第三篇引文的最後一段落中找到，在這裡她評價Andre先生時說"I'm going to keep giving him more assign"。由此可以看出她是指派給Andre先生很多工作的人，正確答案是(D)。

詞彙 company newsletter 社報 responsibility 責任，職務

[191-195]

Barton's 辦公用品

需要辦公用品嗎？在每次物品用完的時候請打電話給Barton's。我們擁有市內最好的產品，並且提供最低價格。

本週將進行特價促銷：
原子筆與鉛筆：七折
事務用家具：八折
白色影印紙和彩色影印紙：六五折
影印機墨水：九折

請到我們網站www.bartons.com或致電749-0493訂購。

結帳超過80美元以上的話，在市內我們將提供免費配送服務。

詞彙 run out of 用完，耗盡　city limits 城市範圍

Barton's 辦公用品
Broadway 街 384號
阿什蘭,維吉尼亞州
749-0493

顧客名：Leslie Devers
公司：Parker International
地址：Cumberland 路48號, 阿什蘭,維吉尼亞州
電話號碼：473-2984
電子郵件地址：lesliedevers@parkerint.com
客戶帳號：3847302
訂購日：8月18日
配送日：8月18日

商品編號	內容	數量	價格
584-393	影印紙 (白色)	5箱 (每箱1,500張)	$48.75
202-192	原子筆 (黑色)	3箱 (每箱20袋)	$11.50
943-293	影印機墨水 (藍色)	2個墨盒	$28.80
331-004	春季筆記本	10 (100頁)	$20.00
		小計	$109.05
		運費	$5.45
		總計	$114.50

您的訂單是以4980為結尾的信用卡結帳的。謝謝您使用我們的Barton's辦公用品。

收件者：customerservice@bartons.com
寄件者：lesliedevers@parkerint.com
主旨：訂購
日期：8月19日

致負責人，

我是Parker International的Leslie Devers。我們公司昨天從貴公司網上購買了辦公用品，產品在今天一早就送到了，這一點令我們印象深刻，與提供如此快速的配送服務的賣場交易還是第一次。

但我查看了和產品一起送來的發票，發現我們購買的墨水盒根本就沒有折扣。我確信貴方存在一些單純錯誤，如果您能將錢匯入我們的公司帳戶，我們將不勝感激。

希望今後能夠繼續與貴公司交易。

Leslie Devers 敬上
Parker International

191.
根據廣告，促銷將會持續多久？
(A) 一天。
(B) 兩天。
(C) 一週。
(D) 一個月。

從句子"This week, we're having a special sale."可以得知折扣期間是(C)。

192.
關於Parker International的訂單可以知道什麼？
(A) 訂貨後過了一天才發貨。
(B) 寄出了兩個箱子。
(C) 並非為免費配送。
(D) 透過配送員送達的。

從第二段引文可以得知，訂單中收取了$5.45元的運費，並非為免費配送的服務，因此(C)為正確答案。訂購後第二天早上收到的，因此配送時間花費一天以上的(A)不能成為正確答案，而且沒有提到箱子數量及配送方法，因此(B)和(D)也是錯誤的。

193.
與電子郵件中第一段第二行"deal with"的意義最接近的是？
(A) 交易。
(B) 談判。
(C) 認可。
(D) 報告。

deal with一詞的意思是「處理」，但也可以像這裡一樣用於表達「與~進行交易」的意思，因此正確答案是(A)。

詞彙 approve of 認可

194.

關於Parker International的暗示是什麼？
(A) 在全國多個城市設立分公司。
(B) 位於Barton's的對面。
(C) 於Barton's首次採購。
(D) 接待出版行業的客戶。

電子郵件寄件人Devers小姐提到「如此快速的配送還是第一次。(This is the first time for us to deal with a store that provides such quick delivery service before.)」可以推測出這是Parker International和Barton's之間的第一次交易，因此(C)為正確答案。

195.

Devers小姐想得到多少折扣？
(A) 10%
(B) 20%
(C) 30%
(D) 35%

在最後一段引文的電子郵件中，Devers小姐寫說「墨盒沒有折扣(no discount had been applied to the ink cartridges)」，從第一段引文的廣告中查找墨盒的折扣額度，就可以輕易知道正確答案是(A)的九折。

[196-200]

軟體培訓研討會

10月8日星期六上午9點至下午5點將在Delta諮詢舉行有關於軟體培訓的每日研討會。將會舉辦以下課程：

★ 9 A.M. – 11 A.M. 物聯網和軟體的發展 (Rohit Patel)

★ 11 A.M. – 12 P.M. 人工智能對於軟體的影響(Igor Rachmaninov)

★ 1 P.M. – 3 P.M. 軟體設計的問題們 (George Arnold)

★ 3 P.M. – 5 P.M. 新編碼語言及其用途(Hans Dietrich)

講師都是各自領域的專家。如果是個人要預訂座位為每人250美元，但五人以上的團體可享有折扣。請致電384-0938進行預約。如果仍有位置的話，當天也可以申請。

詞彙 expert 專家 consist of 由～組成 make the arrangements 準備 same-day registration 當天申請

收件者：sbrandt@deltaconsulting.com
寄件者：awells@kaysoftware.com
主旨：請求
日期：10月10日

致親愛的Brandt小姐，

我代表Kay Software出席了週六在貴公司舉行的培訓研討會，我認為研討會相當有幫助。由於我們公司目前遇到與演講主題有關的問題，因此我對Rachmaninov先生的演講很感興趣。我很想知道他是否能夠訪問我們公司，為我們軟體工程師們演講。他們一定能夠從他的經驗中學到很多東西的。

對於我們來說，最好的日期與時間是：10月19日下午3點、10月21日下午1點、11月3日上午9點，以及11月5日下午3點。三個小時的演講和Q&A環節應該就很充足了。

期待您的答覆。

Alicia Wells 敬上
Kay Software

詞彙 represent 代表，代替 educational 教育的 sufficient 充分的 response 回答，答覆

收件者：awells@kaysoftware.com
寄件者：sbrandt@deltaconsulting.com
主旨：[Re]請求
日期：10月16日

您好，Wells小姐。

很抱歉沒能儘快回覆您的請求，我直到15日為止一直都在巴西，所以今天才聯絡上Rachmaninov先生。實際上，我剛和他通完電話。

他說到十二月為止日程大都是滿的，但您提到的第二個日期可以去拜訪貴公司，另外Rachmaninov先生對於貴公司的訪問要求每小時1,000美元的演講費用，他住在市內，所以不會要求出差旅費。

如果您能接受這些條件，請致電584-3822與我聯繫，以便我們能夠確認詳細內容。

Stacia Brandt 敬上
Destin 諮詢

詞彙 get off the phone 掛斷 travel expense 旅行經費，差旅費 acceptable 可接受的，可忍受的 finalize 結束，確定

196.

根據傳單，關於研討會的什麼為事實？
(A) 每月進行一次。
(B) 對團體可適用於較低的價格。
(C) 門票可在網上購買。
(D) 參加者會領取結業證書。

在"discounts will be given to groups consisting of 5 or more people"中，5人以上的團體將適用折扣費用，因此正確答案是(B)。

197.

Wells小姐對研討會有什麼看法？
(A) 認為太貴。
(B) 覺得蠻有趣的。
(C) 沒能度過愉快的時光。
(D) 學到了很多東西。

在第二封電子郵件的開頭部分，Wells小姐認為研討會十分有益(quite educational)，因此(D)是正確答案。

198.

Kay Software的軟體工程師們需要什麼方面的幫助？

(A) 編碼語言。

(B) 物聯網。

(C) 軟體設計。

(D) 人工智能。

在第二封電子郵件中，Wells小姐表示自己的公司正在經歷「與Rachmaninov先生演講主題有關的問題(problems regarding the topic of his talk)」，邀請Rachmaninov先生為公司內的軟體工程師演講，因此在第一段引文的傳單上找到Rachmaninov先生的演講主題的話，他們需要幫助的領域就是(D)的人工智能。

199.

Brandt小姐為什麼要道歉？

(A) 忘記必須要答覆請求。

(B) 錯過了Wells小姐提到的截止日期。

(C) 有好幾天沒有發送電子郵件。

(D) 找不到Wells小姐的講師。

在最後一段引文電子郵件的開頭部分，Brandt小姐對於未能儘快回覆(not responding to your request faster)在道歉，因此(C)是正確答案。

200.

Rachmaninov先生什麼時候能訪問Wells小姐的公司？

(A) 10月19日。

(B) 10月21日。

(C) 11月3日。

(D) 11月5日。

第二封電子郵件中，"he can visit your firm on the second date you mentioned"是正確答案的線索。也就是說，在Wells小姐提到的第二個日期中Rachmaninov先生表示他可以拜訪，因此在第一封電子郵件中選擇符合這些日期的話，正確答案就會是(B)的10月21日。

PART 5

101.
建築工人們將會加強建築物的基礎，以防建築物倒塌。
(A) strong
(B) stronger
(C) strength
(D) strengthen

如果留意到助動詞will，就可以知道空格應該要填入動詞原型。正確答案是(D)的strengthen。

詞彙 strengthen 強化，加強 foundation 基礎 collapse 倒塌，崩潰 strength 力量，強度

102.
根據報導，Randolph先生正在考慮提案，他將會在3天之內做出相關決定。
(A) will considered
(B) is considering
(C) has been considered
(D) considers

注意and以後的時態，尋找適當的時態動詞。因為主語是人，所以被動式型態的(B)和(C)其中之一是正確答案，從意義上看，如果要在10天之內做出決定，必須是「現在正在考慮」的狀態，所以空格中應該填入現在進行式，因此正確答案是(B)。

詞彙 consider 考慮 make a decision 決定

103.
有些類型的運動鞋已經沒有庫存了，必須要從倉庫運到商場。
(A) shelf
(B) amount
(C) stock
(D) order

如果注意到so之後的內容的話，就必須要完整表達出「沒有庫存」的意思。「有庫存的」一詞以in stock來表示，因此正確答案是(C)。

詞彙 sneakers 運動鞋 no longer 不再 in stock 有庫存的 warehouse 倉庫 shelf 架子

104.
Robinson先生一向有決斷力，這是員工們由衷讚賞的地方。
(A) decision
(B) decisive
(C) deciding
(D) decided

考慮到關係代名詞句型的內容，空格中應該填入與獲得高度評價的品性或人格等相關的單字。正確答案是「具有決斷力」意義的(B)decisive。

詞彙 decisive 有決斷力的 truly 真心地，由衷地 appreciate 感激；欣賞

105.
總公司建築物竣工後，Delmont分公司的大部分員工都轉移到那裡了。
(A) most
(B) much
(C) every
(D) somebody

要找到既是可數名詞又能夠修飾複數型employees的形容詞。選項中只有(A)的most能夠滿足上述兩個條件。

詞彙 headquarters 總部，總公司

106.
該設備如果不按照手冊的指示事項進行適當管理的話，很有可能會發生週期性的故障。
(A) regular
(B) regularity
(C) regulation
(D) regulatory

「週期性」或是「正確無誤地」的意思是以with regularity來表達。正確答案是(B)。

詞彙 properly 合適地，恰當地 maintain 維持，管理 be liable to 易於 with regularity 有規則地；正確無誤地 regulation 規定 regulatory 有控制能力的，管理的

107.

Sheldon先生請求幫助的話，有些人會很樂意幫忙的。

(A) asks
(B) is asking
(C) will ask
(D) had asked

主句的過去式為「would have p.p.」形態的假設語氣過去完成式，因此條件句的時態也應該要是過去式，所以正確答案是(D)。

詞彙 be willing to 願意 provide 給予，提供

108.

訂購該公司產品最簡單的方法是到線上購物中心。

(A) ordering
(B) ordered
(C) to order
(D) have ordered

空格中應該要填入可以將something作為受詞，修飾way的形容詞，因此現在分詞(A)和to不定詞(C)中有一個將會是正確答案，如果考慮到the easiest way和order之間的關係，就可以知道(C)的to order為正確答案。如果將(A)填入空格，將其換成關係代名詞的話，就會形成"the easiest way which is ordering something"的尷尬主語。

109.

我們對於決定要投資海外資源市場感到非常驚訝。

(A) high
(B) highness
(C) higher
(D) highly

空格中應該要有能夠修飾surprised的副詞，正確答案是表示「非常」意思的(D)highly。作為參考，high作為形容詞時表示「高的」，作為副詞時則為「高高地」的意思。

詞彙 highly 非常 commodities market 資源市場，原料市場 highly 高的；高度地

110.

Breckinridge小姐說她以前來這城市時，已經去過博物館了。

(A) previous
(B) probable
(C) practical
(D) positive

如果注意到had already visited一詞的話，空格中應該填入表示「以前的」之意的(A)。

詞彙 remark 提及 previous 以前的 probable 有可能的 practical 實用的 positive 積極的；確信的

111.

研究員們習慣做實驗並編寫其相關報告。

(A) accustomed
(B) utilized
(C) comfortable
(D) approved

如果知道be accustomed to(對～熟悉)一詞的意思，就可以很容易地找到正確答案，正確答案是(A)。作為參考，be used to也表達了同樣的意思。

詞彙 researcher 研究員，調查員 be accustomed to 對～熟悉 conduct 實行，實施 utilize 充分利用

112.

如果不擴大港口的寬度和深度，大型船隻將無法進入港口，因此它們將會前往其他地方。

(A) at
(B) over
(C) to
(D) in

因為要完整表達出「要去別的地方」而不是港口的意義，所以空格中要填入表示方向的介系詞(C)的to比較合適。

詞彙 port 港口 deepen 變身 dock 入港，入塢 sail 航行

113.

根據租約，租戶可以透過在一個月前以書面通知，搬出公寓。

(A) written
(B) writer
(C) write
(D) writing

「以書面形式」是以in writing來表達，因此正確答案是(D)。透過空格前面有介系詞這一點也可以知道正確答案是動名詞writing。

詞彙 lease 出租，租約 tenant 承租人 unit 組成單位；單位，部件 notice 通報，通知 in writing 以書面形式

114.

休假回來的Hollister小姐發現有許多工作需要處理。

(A) Be returned
(B) Returning
(C) Have returned
(D) Returns

這題是分詞構句的問題。主語是人Ms. Hollister，所以空格中應該填入現在分詞的形態。正確答案是(B)。

詞彙 a large amount of 許多的，大量的

115.

有些顧客為了在乘坐飛機時得到更好的服務和座位，願意支付附加費用。

(A) scale
(B) discount
(C) premium
(D) wage

為了在飛機上獲得更好的服務和座位(better service and seats)，需要支付的可能是(C)的premium(附加費用)。

詞彙 premium 附加費用，津貼；高級的 obtain 得到，獲得 scale 規模；天平 wage 薪水

116.

雖然演奏會比預想的還要久，但卻並不像觀眾所期待的那樣精彩。

(A) good
(B) well
(C) better
(D) best

只有知道「as + 形容詞/副詞 + as」的句型才找得到正確答案。這時形容詞或副詞的位置必須要填入原型，所以正確答案是(A)。

詞彙 as ~ as 和～一樣 audience 觀眾

117.

要求所有來賓遵守所有規則及規定，否則將會被要求離開。
(A) obey
(B) follow
(C) comply
(D) observe

因為選項都帶有遵照或遵守的意思，所以要找到能與空格之後的介系詞with搭配使用的動詞。正確答案是(C)，comply with表示「順從、遵守」的意思。

詞彙 comply with 順從，遵守 premise 用地，區域 obey 服從 observe 遵照，遵守；觀察

118.

必須提前支付訂單費用才能開始運輸程序。
(A) through what
(B) so that
(C) as such
(D) until then

只有瞭解表示其目的意義的「so that~can」句型才能找到正確答案。正確答案是(B)。

詞彙 in advance 預先，首先 so that ~ can為了～ initiate 開始

119.

市場調查企業要整理最近實施的問卷調查結果需要一週左右的時間。
(A) compile
(B) compiled
(C) compilation
(D) compiler

如果掌握了整體句型架構的話，就可以很容易地找到正確答案。因爲句子開頭的it是虛主詞，而真主詞為to不定詞句型，因此正確答案是動詞原型(A)。作為參考，這個句子中to不定詞其意義上的主詞是"the market research firm"。

詞彙 market research 市場調查 compile 編輯，整理

120.

這些訂單大部分都是來自常客的，都在早上裝箱並發貨了。
(A) by what
(B) of whom
(C) in that
(D) of which

空格中應該要填入與most相配又能夠意指出先行詞the orders的關係代名詞，因此正確答案是(D)。在句子中"The orders were boxed and shipped out in the morning."以及"Most of them were from regular clients."是透過which來連接的。

詞彙 regular client 常客 box 裝進箱子裡，打包

121.

鼓勵具有碩士學位或更高學歷的人申請應聘主管職位。
(A) have encouraged
(B) will encourage
(C) are encouraging
(D) are encouraged

encourage A to B意為「鼓勵A做B」，如果被用作被動型態，則通常會帶有be encouraged to的形態。正確答案是(D)。

詞彙 encourage 鼓勵，激勵 master's degree 碩士學位

122.

與Reynolds先生和Venters小姐超額完成了這個月的目標量。相反地，Stark先生沒能做到。
(A) exceeded
(B) prepared
(C) indicated
(D) supported

如果留意到連接詞while，就會發現空格中應該填入與fail相反的單字，在選項中，表達出這種意思的同時又能夠將their quotas(配額，目標量)作為受詞的動詞是(A)的exceeded(超過)。

詞彙 exceed 超過 quota 配額 indicate 指出，表明

123.

Thompson小姐要求提供幾份文件為了她本人的介紹。
(A) she
(B) her
(C) hers
(D) herself

空格中應該填入意指Ms. Thompson又能夠修飾名詞presentation的所有格代名詞，因此正確答案是(B)。作為參考，be前面省略了助動詞should。

124.

到了下週末，Rogers先生就在Stevens諮詢工作15年了。

(A) was employed

(B) is being employed

(C) will have been employed

(D) has been employed

注意"by the end of next week"來尋找正確答案。這句子傳達了「到下週末工作將滿15年」的意思，所以空格中應該填入同時體現未來和完成意義的時態，因此表示未來完成式時態的(C)為正確答案。

125.

車輛的所有功能應在上市前得到確認。

(A) capacities

(B) capabilities

(C) capably

(D) capable

空格中必須要填入能夠修飾full和of引領的介系詞句型的名詞，因此(A)和(B)其中一個會是正確答案，但是這兩個單字拼寫也很相似，也都帶有「能力」的意思，所以要特別注意每個意思的差異。capacity通常表現為潛在的能力，事物的容量和生產力，而capability通常是指具體能力或者是事物的功能等居多，因此在這個問題上，與vehicle更合適的是(B)capabilities為正確答案。

詞彙 capability 能力，(機械的)功能 determine 了解，決定 capacity 能力，生產力 capably 能幹地

126.

未經經理的書面許可，不可購買辦公用品。

(A) through

(B) among

(C) around

(D) without

如果知道may not表示禁止的意思，這樣就可以輕鬆解決問題。為了完整表達「未經書面許可就不得購買」的意義，需要在空格中填入(D)的without。

詞彙 permission 准許，許可

127.

只要將收據提交給人事部的話，將會全額資助搬家費用。

(A) mover

(B) moved

(C) moving

(D) movable

搬家費用一詞以moving expense來表示，因此正確答案是(C)。作為參考，這裡的moving是動名詞。

詞彙 expense 經費，費用 in full 全部 so long as 只要 movable 可移動的

128.

由於新上市的化妝品徹底失敗，所以公司代表董事辭職了。

(A) transition

(B) resignation

(C) retraction

(D) improvement

想想新產品的徹底失敗(the complete failure)會給代理董事的去留帶來什麼樣的結果，就可以很容易地找到正確答案。正確答案是表示「卸任」之意的(B)resignation。

詞彙 cosmetic 化妝品 result in (結果)導致～ resignation 卸任，辭職 transition 過度 retraction 撤回，取消

129.

希望到國外工作的人必須要為公司工作3年。

(A) committing

(B) committee

(C) committed

(D) commitment

從空格前面的冠詞和形容詞來推斷的時候，空格裡應該要填入名詞。因此正確答案是表示「獻身」之意的(D)commitment。作為參考，獻身一詞的意思是以make a commitment來表達的。

詞彙 commitment 獻身；承諾 commit 犯罪，犯錯 committee 委員會

130.

沒有討論到議程上的所有內容，因此另外安排了一次會議來討論這些主題。

(A) everything

(B) anyone

(C) another

(D) one

如果注意到so以後的內容的話，需要表達出「沒有討論到所有主題」的意思，整體上才能夠成為一個自然的句子。正確答案是(A)。

詞彙 agenda 議案，議題 cover 蓋；處理 topic 主題

PART 6

[131-134]

居民須知

每年春季，Bayside公寓都會派遣管理人員去檢查每件家具。檢查將於4月2日至12日**131·**實施。檢查一般需要30~45分鐘左右即可完成。請至www.baysideapartment.com/inspections**132·**申請檢查時間。**133·**進行檢查時，您必須要待在家裡。

我們的工作人員將會查看設備故障，管道問題以及諸如褪色或破爛的地毯及油漆等問題。**134·**如若需要更換或修理的情況，工作人員將會約定好時間進行工作。在過去4年內未曾得到油漆服務的住戶可以申請其相關服務。

詞彙 tenant 居住者，承租人 maintenance office 管理處 unit 組成單位；單位，部件 inspection 檢查，視察 such as 和～一樣 faulty 錯誤的 appliance 器具，家用電器 plumbing 配管 faded 褪色 schedule a time 約定時間

131.

(A) replacing
(B) approving
(C) considering
(D) conducting

在選項中以inspection(檢查)作為受詞，並有「實施、實行」之意的單字是(D)的conducting。

詞彙 approve 批准 consider 考慮

132.

(A) registering
(B) be registered
(C) to register
(D) have registered

在文章脈絡上，空格中應要加入表示其目的或結果的to不定詞才能形成最通順的句子。正確答案是(C)。

133.

(A) 希望您對檢查結果感到滿意。
(B) 謝謝您讓我們知道您什麼時候有空。
(C) 登記時請務必填寫問卷調查，以便評估檢查人員。
(D) 在檢查過程中，您必須待在家裡。

在上一句中要求申請檢查時間，因此空格中應要填入有關其說明和注意事項才是最自然的。在選項中滿足此條件的句子是(D)。

134.

(A) Because
(B) However
(C) If
(D) Moreover

在選項中既可以引導從屬子句，又能夠表達出條件「如果有需要更換或修理的」意義的連接詞是(C)的if。

[135-138]

> 12月11日
>
> 致編輯們，
>
> 昨天在*Daily Times*上Peter Chase撰寫的《Mulberry股份有限公司下個月將關閉工廠》的新聞中包含著幾個**135.**錯誤的內容。首先，該工廠並不會關閉，實際上第三裝配線和第四裝配線將會引進尖端機器，因此工廠設施將會變得更好。**136.**且公司不會解僱員工，**137.**我們打算在2月份新僱用最多30名員工。最後，我們公司沒有遇到任何財政問題，實際上，在今年第二季度和第三季度，我們取得了創紀錄的收益，我們也預期本季度還會發生同樣的事情。請貴公司在報紙上刊登**138.**更正報導。
>
> Dean Morris 敬上
> Mulberry股份有限公司代表董事

詞彙 factual 根據事實的　error 錯誤，失誤　in question 有問題的，有爭議的　in actuality 事實上，實際上　state-of-the-art 最新的　machinery 機械　assembly line 裝配線　lay off 解僱　anticipate 預期，期望　correction 更正，修正

135.

(A) appearances
(B) data
(C) statements
(D) errors

有一封主張其報紙的報導與事實不符，即說其刊登錯誤報導的信件，因此有錯誤或失誤之意的(D)errors是正確答案。

詞彙 statement 陳述，主張

136.

(A) So
(B) But
(C) Nor
(D) And

通過空格前後的內容可以看出目前討論的公司正在促進設備投資以及招募員工，因此為了將該句子與上下文自然地連貫起來，應要填入空格的為包括否定意義(C)的Nor。

137.

(A) 我們打算在2月份新聘請最多30名員工。
(B) 在幾個月以後，會有幾位員工可能會晉升。
(C) 由於取得結出的成果，他們的工資提高了。
(D) 這就是我們不再僱用的理由。

有人指出「將要解僱」是與事實不符的內容，所以空格中應該要是與此相反的內容，即「將會再招聘」，因此(A)為正確答案。

138.

(A) correctives
(B) corrections
(C) correctible
(D) correctly

空格中應該要填入能夠讓appreciate成為受詞的名詞。 選項中是名詞只有(B)。

詞彙 corrective 修正的，校正的　correctible 可修正的

[139-142]

> **本季度優秀員工獎**
>
> 很高興公布本季度Drummond Technology的優秀員工。今年第二季度的獲獎者是營業部的Derrick Hutchinson。Derrick是達成4月、5月和6月**139.**合計達到270萬美元以上價值合約的主角。**140.**他還在北京分公司進行了幾次研討會及專題討論會，以便提高員工的營業**141.**能力。Derrick**142.**在六年的期間一直在Drummond Technology工作，這次是第三次獲獎。看到他的話，請不要忘記祝賀他的驚人成就。

詞彙 be responsible for 對～負責 combine 結合 value 價值 skill 技術，手藝，能力

139.

(A) combination
(B) combined
(C) combining
(D) combinate

空格中必須要填入能夠修飾名詞value(價值)的形容詞，因此從形態上來看，(B)和(C)都可成為正確答案。另一方面，在文章脈絡上應該要包含合在一起的價值即總價值的意思，兩者中具有這種意味的是過去分詞形的(B) combined。

詞彙 combination 組合，結合 combinate 結合

140.

(A) 他們會和兩家新公司一起。
(B) 他還在北京分公司。
(C) 關於這一點，代表理事親自表達了祝賀。
(D) 這是三個月來誰也沒有達到的業績。

注意到空格後面句子的there並尋找正確答案。換句話說，它提到在某些地點舉行了研討會和專題討論會，因此在前面空格處應填入提及Beijing office的(B)。

141.

(A) contracts
(B) lessons
(C) skills
(D) deals

要找尋能夠跟sales(營業)相符合又能夠讓improve(提高)受詞的單字。正確答案是表示「技術」或「能力」之意的(C)。

142.

(A) for
(B) since
(C) during
(D) after

for和during都表示「～期間」的意思，但兩者中能與six years此具體時間一起使用的是(A) for。

[143-146]

Cumberland 遊行取消

坎伯蘭(5月11日)--原定於5月12日星期六舉行的年度活動Cumberland遊行被取消。該**143.**決定是在昨天晚上市長和市議會參加的緊急會議上做出的。David Cord市長表示「遊行是維持了52年的傳統，所以並不想取消，但是**144.**由於位於城市附近的樹林中野火蔓延，因此認為並不適合舉行慶典。**145.**總而言之，有許多人正從他們的家中撤離。」Cord市長表示他希望遊行日程能夠重新安排在夏季中旬。但他說最**146.**緊急的事情是撲滅大火。

詞彙 emergency meeting 緊急會議 mayor 市長 tradition 傳統 on account of 因為 wildfire 野火，山火 rage 盛怒；迅速擴散的 festive 慶典的 appropriate 恰當的 remark 提及 urgent 緊急的 put out 撲滅

143.

(A) election
(B) result
(C) promise
(D) decision

如果在選項中找到會在emergency meeting(緊急會議)發生的事物，正確答案就會是(D)的decision。

詞彙 election 選舉 result 結果

144.

(A) in addition to
(B) on account of
(C) in spite of
(D) instead of

為了表示因為大火活動不得不取消的意思，空格中應該要填入表達其原因及理由的敘述，因此正確答案是(B)。作為參考，"because of"、"due to"、"owing to"等表述也可以成為正確答案。

詞彙 in addition to 除此之外 in spite of 儘管 instead of 代替

145.

(A) 因此遊行將會按照原定計劃進行。
(B) 因此它將會延期到下星期六。
(C) 野火已被撲滅，因此有很多需要做的事情。
(D) 總而言之，有許多人正從他們的家中撤離。

空格中需要填入不得不取消慶典的理由，才能完成最自然的文章脈絡，選項中能夠成為那樣的理由只有(D)。

詞彙 initially 最初 now that 因為 extinguish 熄滅

146.

(A) urgent
(B) urgently
(C) urgency
(D) urgencies

空格中應該要填入能夠被most修飾，又能夠修飾名詞thing的形容詞。正確答案是(A)的urgent。

詞彙 urgency 緊急，急迫

PART 7

[147-148]

MEMO

收件者：全體員工
寄件者：Kimberly Wingard
日期：10月22日

儘管我們春天進行了維修工程，但食品店的銷售額在過去的幾個月裡一直在減少。8月份下降了11%，上個月下降了17%。

若是這種情況一直持續下去，有可能會關閉賣場。我希望大家都能考慮一下方案，找到一些您認為能夠改善財務狀況的方法，請思考如何才能說服客戶來這裡花更多的錢。明天，在開始工作之前，希望各位能與直屬上司交流自己的想法，不要羞於分享自己的想法，沒有想法的話就太傻了。我們正面臨著嚴重的問題，需要立刻改善。

詞彙 undergo 經歷 decline 減少，衰退 drop 掉落 trend 傾向，趨勢 brainstorming 集體研討 financial 金融的，財政的 convince 說服，使信服 shift 轉移；輪班 share 共有 shy 害羞的，羞澀的 silly 糊塗的

147.

問題是什麼？
(A) 工作人員人數不夠。
(B) 需要進行維修工程。
(C) 附近有類似的賣場開業。
(D) 銷量減少。

通過第一個段落可以知道賣場的銷售額在過去幾個月間持續減少，接著為了解決這種情況，正在討論方案，因此正確答案是(D)。

148.

Wingard小姐請員工做什麼？
(A) 改變工作日程。
(B) 拿著同樣的薪水並工作更長的時間。
(C) 想出吸引更多消費者的方法。
(D) 擬訂可實行的特別宣傳活動。

在第二段中Wingard小姐請員工想出可以吸引顧客過來，讓他們花更多的錢(to convince customers to come and spend more money here)的方法，因此她要求的是(C)。

[149-150]

```
╔══════════════════════════════════════╗
        Wallace百貨公司免費贈送活動

  Wallace百貨公司為了顧客進行的特別促銷。活動將從7月1日
  開始至8月10日結束。

  顧客可享有以下優惠：

  購買50美元時免費贈送Watson護手霜
  購買100美元時免費贈送Stetson太陽眼鏡
  購買200美元時免費贈送Verducci T恤
  購買400美元時贈送免費電影票

  贈品可在顧客服務中心領取，只需攜帶發票。此次活動除
  費爾維尤與威爾明頓賣場以外，適用於Wallace百貨公司所
  有分店。
╚══════════════════════════════════════╝
```

詞彙 offer 提案，提議；優惠 valid 有效的

149.

廣告中沒有提到的是什麼？
(A) 宣傳活動為期兩個月。
(B) 要獲得贈品需要發票。

(C) 一部分賣場將不會參加活動。
(D) 顧客可以免費獲得多種贈品。

宣傳活動的期間寫著"from July 1 to August 10"，因此(A)的內容與事實不符。只需要收據就可以得到贈品，因此(B)的內容是正確的，而且有兩家賣場沒有參加活動，因此(C)也是有提及的事項。根據金額準備了多樣的贈品，所以(D)也是事實。

詞彙 complimentary 免費的

150.

消費者要如何獲得免費服裝商品？
(A) 透過消費50美元以上。
(B) 透過消費100美元以上。
(C) 透過消費200美元以上。
(D) 透過消費400美元以上。

中半部分介紹了按照消費金額來分的贈品，因此仔細查看就可以找到正確答案。符合clothing item的贈品只有Verducci T恤，因此拿到的條件(C)為正確答案。

[151-152]

```
┌────────────────────────────────────────────┐
│ Robert Harkness                  11:25 A.M.  │
│ 您好，和Stephanie Grimes老闆的工作處理完了嗎？ │
│                                              │
│ Stephanie Lowe                   11:27 A.M.  │
│ 對不起，Robert。我整個上午都在辦公室裡開會，所以到現在 │
│ 為止我都還沒有機會和大家說話。                  │
│                                              │
│ Robert Harkness                  11:30 A.M.  │
│ 請跟秘書聯絡，讓她知道今天之內要結束協商是多麼重要的事 │
│ 情，老闆如果不在合約上簽字的話，我們就會失去客戶的。 │
│                                              │
│ Stephanie Lowe                   11:31 A.M.  │
│ 知道了，我打電話給Tina。                       │
│                                              │
│ Robert Harkness                  11:33 A.M.  │
│ 好的，我中午之後再過來。如果到時候還沒談妥，我會直接過 │
│ 去老闆辦公室。                                 │
│                                              │
│ Stephanie Lowe                   11:35 A.M.  │
│ 好的，待會見。                                 │
└────────────────────────────────────────────┘
```

詞彙 progress 進展，發展 secretary 秘書

151.

提到了哪些問題？
(A) 會失去客戶。
(B) Grimes先生不在辦公室。
(C) 沒有在文件上簽名。
(D) 午餐聚會被取消了。

Harkness主張協商應該要在當天之內結束，並擔心Grimes先生如果沒有在合約上簽字(if he won't sign the contract)將會失去客戶，因此問題的部分可視為(C)。由於尚未失去客戶，所以(A)不能成為正確答案，Grimes先生正在辦公室開會，因此(B)也不是正確答案。

152.

上午11點31分,當Lowe小姐說"I'll give Tina a call"時,她在暗示什麼?

(A) 她將與客戶交談。
(B) 她會給自己的主管打電話。
(C) 她將會聯絡她的客戶。
(D) 她將會聯絡Grimes先生的祕書。

給定的句子中Tina是誰可以透過前文來確認,也就是說可以推測Tina是Grimes先生的秘書(secretary),因此透過給定的句子可以將Lowe小姐的意圖看作是(D)。

[153-154]

需要推薦

推薦年度員工獎候選人的時間到了。所有正式員工都有推薦同事的資格。想要推薦人的話,請至www.fostertech.com/awards填寫表格。請不要忘記寫下員工的名字及部門,然後用簡短的文字說明為什麼認為他應該要獲得年度員工獎。推薦信必須要在12月15日之前繳交。獲獎者將於12月29日在年終聚會中揭曉。今年的獲獎者將獲得現金2,500美元的獎金,並享有一週的特別休假和晉升獎賞。

詞彙 nomination 提名,推薦 be eligible to 有資格 fellow 同事

153.

要怎麼繳交推薦信?

(A) 透過發送電子郵件。
(B) 透過在網路上填寫表格。
(C) 透過與主管交談。
(D) 透過提交手寫表格。

"visit www.fostertech.com/awards and complete the form"是正確答案的線索。為了要推薦需要到網路上填寫表格,所以(B)為正確答案。

154.

獲獎者得不到什麼?

(A) 休假。
(B) 獎金。
(C) 免費旅行券。
(D) 更高的職位。

在最後一句中,獲獎者將會獲得2,500美元的現金($2,500 cash bonus)、一週的特別休假(one extra week of vacation),以及晉升獎賞(promotion)。選項中不包含在內的是(C)的免費旅行券。

詞彙 monetary 貨幣的

[155-157]

觀光博覽會

每年舉行的觀光博覽會今年計劃在佛羅里達奧蘭多舉行。會議將於10月10日星期五開始至10月14日星期一在Radcliffe酒店的會議中心舉行,雖然會像平時一樣設置博覽會的展位,但也會討論有關國內及國外旅行的各種問題,還將會有幾位世界知名的演講人。特別值得一提的是,有許多旅行社及航空公司考慮引進的關於新旅行服務電腦軟體的研討會,強烈推薦您提前預訂。全部的日程請在會議的網站上(www.travelindustrytradeshow.org)確認。有意參加者需在10月5日前繳納75美元的參加費用。此次會議將不會為參加者預約酒店客房,因此請提前預訂。

詞彙 booth 展位 domestic 家庭的;國內的 international 國際的,國外的 be responsible for 負責 book 預訂 in advance 事先,預先

155.

關於博覽會,屬於事實的是什麼?

(A) 主講人是電腦程式設計師。
(B) 首次舉行。
(C) 需要事先登記。
(D) 重點為國外旅行。

在引文最後的部分,有意參加的人在(開幕日之前)10月5日之前必須支付75美元(Those wish to attend should pay the required fee of $75 before October 5.),所以(C)為正確答案。(A)是從未提及的事項,透過annual一詞可知(B)也並非事實,因為會討論國內旅行、海外旅行、旅遊相關軟體等等,所以(D)也是錯誤的。

156.

關於電腦系統的研討會有什麼樣的暗示?

(A) 由設計它的人進行。
(B) 為了參加需要另外支付費用。
(C) 只能使用75個座位。
(D) 許多人將有興趣參加。

關於研討會,因為強烈推薦advance reservations(提前預約),因此(D)才是正確答案。其餘的選項中提及的講師,費用,座位數等相關資訊都是在引文中找不到的。

詞彙 spot 場所,地方

157.

參加者被建議要做什麼?

(A) 親自預訂住宿。
(B) 成為協會的成員。
(C) 提前參加一些活動。
(D) 到10月10日前繳納參加費用。

在最後一句中,主辦方不會預訂客房,提醒參加者要提前預訂酒店(please make sure you do so in advance),因此(A)是正確答案。

詞彙 organization 組織,機關 show up 露面,出現

[158-161]

收件者：	Wendy Carson <wcarson@wilsonlab.com>
寄件者：	Dwight Henderson <dwight_h@mayfair.com>
主旨：	問候
日期：	3月21日

親愛的Carson小姐，

您好，我是位於多倫多Mayfair公司的Dwight Henderson。在奧爾巴尼舉行的網絡設計會議上，很榮幸能與您交談。也許您會記得，上週我們聊了一下本公司的產品，在當時，您似乎對我們的新產品無線路由器有興趣。但可惜的是，那時候我還要跟其他客戶見面，所以沒辦法和你聊很久。

幸運的是，我下週在去巴黎的途中將會在倫敦短暫停留一下。我想在您的辦公室跟您見面，向您演示幾個本公司的新產品。3月27日星期二我一整天都會在那裡，如果日程上28日更適合的話，我可以在28日前往您的辦公室。

我們公司開發了一種新型的無線網路系統，可以在不降速或網路中斷的情況下使用。這不但比市面上的任何東西都還要優秀，而且其價格更是便宜了20%。請接受我的建議以讓我展示高科技的最新產品。

期待著您的答覆。

Dwight Henderson 敬上
Mayfair公司

詞彙 recall 回想，回憶　wireless 無線的　router 路由器　stopover 暫時停留，滯留　on one's way to 去往～的途中　lag time 延遲時間　interruption 妨礙　take up on 接受　cutting-edge 尖端的

158.

根據電子郵件，Henderson先生是怎麼認識Carson小姐的？
(A) 在同一間公司工作。
(B) 她在網路上聯絡了他。
(C) 他在專業會議上見到她。
(D) 他們讀的是同一所大學。

透過在電子郵件第一段的"It was a real pleasure to talk to you at the Internet Designer Conference in Albany."中，可以得知他們是在網路設計師會議上見過面的，因此正確答案是將會議改寫成professional meeting的(C)。

159.

Henderson先生提議要在哪裡跟Carson小姐見面？
(A) 倫敦。
(B) 奧爾巴尼。
(C) 巴黎。
(D) 多倫多。

在第2段中，Henderson先生提議前往Carson小姐的倫敦辦公室，因此(A)為正確答案。順帶一提，(B)是他們曾經見過面的會議舉辦地點，(C)是Henderson先生的出差地區，(D)是Henderson先生的公司所在地。

160.

Henderson先生想為Carson小姐做什麼？
(A) 安裝無線路由器。
(B) 贈送小冊子。
(C) 進行產品演示。
(D) 重新談判合約。

在第二段的"I would love to visit you in your office to demonstrate some of my firm's newest products."句子中，可以知道Henderson先生想做的是(C)產品演示。

詞彙 renegotiate 重新談判

161.

關於Mayfair公司的網絡系統，提到了什麼？
(A) 尚未開始販賣。
(B) 價格低於其他類似產品。
(C) 以折扣價格提供。
(D) 應要由技術人員安裝。

在第三段中，Mayfair公司的網絡系統不會降速或中斷(with no lag time or interruptions)、比市面產品還要優秀(better than anything else available on the market)，且價格便宜20%(20% cheaper)。選項中有提到與這些相關的只有(B)。

[162-164]

6月11號

致親愛的Robinson先生，

想通知您Whitson股份有限公司將要發生的一個變化。人事部制定了新的方針，比起將各項工作交給跟您一樣的自由業者，我們更希望我們的員工全心全意致力於我們的公司和願景。

根據這項新準則，我們將不再委託勵志演講者為我們的員工演講，但是我們將會為了勵志演講家而創造出一正式職位。這將會是一個高級管理職位。

多年來，您令人印象深刻的演講，對於Whitson的成功貢獻很大，我們希望您能夠應徵這個職位。我們現在正接受申請，並將會一直持續直到填滿職位。應聘者將根據其演講及其成果進行評價，而我們相信您是最佳人選。

期待您的答覆。

Jason Daniels 敬上
Whitson股份有限公司

詞彙 institute 採用，開始　policy 政策，方針　outsourcing 委託(外部企業等)，委任　freelancer 自由職業者　commit 承諾　motivational speaker 勵志演說家　specialist 專家　contributor 捐贈者，有功勞的人　effective 有效果的；印象深刻的　see fit to 決定　evaluate 評價　influential 有影響力的　prime 主要的，最好的

162.

Daniels先生為什麼要寫信給Robinson先生？
(A) 為了請求他在公司進行演講。
(B) 為了證實他被聘用了。

(C) 為了告知可應徵的職位。

(D) 為了告訴大家即將到來的面試。

在第三段的"We hope you see fit to apply for the position."句子中，可以知道寫信的目的。電子郵件撰寫者Daniels先生向作為外部人士進行演講的Robinson先生提出了作為正式講師的工作，因此正確答案是(C)。從這引文可以看出，要注意信件的目的有可能會出現在信件的後半部分。

163.

關於Robinson先生，新工作中提到了什麼？

(A) 需要大學學位。

(B) 將隸屬於人事部。

(C) 出差會很多。

(D) 將成爲正式員工。

在第二段中，新職位被介紹為「勵志講師專家的正式職位(a full-time job for an employee motivation specialist)」，因此選項是有提到事實的為(D)。

164.

[1]，[2]，[3]，[4]中下列句子填入最為合適的地方是哪裡？

「這將會是一個高級管理職位。」

(A) [1]

(B) [2]

(C) [3]

(D) [4]

需要掌握給定的句子其所指的"this"是指什麼，才能找到正確答案。透過upper-management position這句來推測出this所指的是工作職位，即是[2]的a full-time job，因此正確答案是(B)。

[165-168]

Delvin Patterson	10:35 A.M.
大家都看到了我們曾經做過的問卷調查結果嗎？	

Melanie Smith	10:37 A.M.
和我預想的不一樣。	

Ralph Taylor	10:38 A.M.
你說的對。關於顧客服務的評價怎麼會那麼低？	

Delvin Patterson	10:39 A.M.
看了下問卷調查中人們留下的意見。看來我們員工對於銷售的產品並不是很瞭解，有幾名員工告訴顧客錯誤的資訊。	

Amy Chou	10:41 A.M.
另一個不滿的是，他們有時會忽略顧客。	

Melanie Smith	10:42 A.M.
我建議對所有員工進行再培訓。不能放任這樣的問題繼續下去。	

Amy Chou	10:43 A.M.
為了實施再培訓，我們已經做好了準備。	

Ralph Taylor	10:44 A.M.
太好了，預計什麼時候開始培訓？	

Delvin Patterson	10:46 A.M.
明天早上。而且從代表理事到最近進來的實習員工，公司裡的所有人都要參加。午休時間過後日程表出來的話，我會發電子郵件給你。	

詞彙 survey 問券調查 comment 評論，註解 apparently 看起來，顯然地 staffer 員工 be familiar with 對～熟悉 retrain 再教育 from A to B 從A到B

165.

問題是什麼？

(A) 公司收益減少。

(B) 員工工作不力。

(C) 太多員工請病假。

(D) 最近物價快速上漲。

根據問卷調查結果，正在討論關於顧客服務的評價不好(perform so poorly on customer service)的問題，因此(B)是正確答案。

詞彙 revenue 收益 call in sick 請病假 prices 價格 lately 最近的

166.

傳訊息的人是在哪種領域工作？

(A) 零售業。

(B) 諮詢。

(C) 製造業。

(D) 旅遊業。

透過「職員們對於銷售的產品不太瞭解(our staffers aren't always familiar with the products we sell)」等句子可以推測出傳訊息的人們工作的領域是與販售有關的，因此(A)是正確答案。

167.

上午10點43分，當Chou小姐寫下"We've already arranged for that to happen"的時候，她是指什麼？

(A) 有幾位員工將被解僱。

(B) 將會張貼招聘廣告。

(C) 將要道歉。

(D) 將要實施培訓。

從前後文脈看，所給文章的that指的是再教育(retraining session)。因此，所給文章中所指的可視爲(D)。

詞彙 fire 解雇 job advertisement 招聘廣告 apology 道歉

168.

Patterson先生下午要做什麼？

(A) 用電子郵件告知資訊。

(B) 參加管理層會議。

(C) 確定研討會的議程。

(D) 與銷售人員交談。

在最後一個句子"I'll send you the schedule by e-mail when it comes out after lunch."中，可以知道他中午後會透過電子郵件發送培訓日程，因此將schedule改寫為information的(A)為正確答案。

[169-171]

http://www.fairfaxmuseum.org

| 首頁 | 營業時間 | 特別活動 | 新聞 | 所在位置 |

很高興為您介紹，Fairfax博物館是以恐龍化石為主題的一個有趣、全新的展覽。將要展示的化石中包括幾乎為完整形態的霸王龍化石和迅猛龍化石，預計將展出三十兩種恐龍化石。從小雞蛋到成為巨大的雷龍的局部骨骼，化石的大小也各式各樣。這些化石不僅來自Central大學，而且還來自Jarod Watson及Melanie Zhong各自的私人收藏品。

展覽定於6月10日開始至6月30日舉行。博物館將按照正常參觀時間開放，正式參觀時間為星期二至星期五，上午9點到下午6點。您需要支付不同的費用才能觀看展覽，十幾歲及成人需要繳交七美元的費用，六十歲以上的老年人需繳交五美元，12歲以下的兒童可以免費入場。團體費用(10人以上)請諮詢584-7212。博物館會員可以免費參觀展覽。

想要獲得有關展覽會照片或是恐龍的更多資訊，請點此處。

詞彙 featuring 以～為特徵 dinosaur 恐龍 fossil 化石 range A from B 範圍從A到B partial 部分的，局部的 skeleton 骨骼，骨頭 enormous 巨大的 on loan 租借的 private collection 私人收藏品 separate 分離的 regular hours of operation 正常營業時間 senior citizen 老人，高齡者 group rate 團體費用

169.
這個資訊會在哪裡？
(A) 首頁。
(B) 特別活動。
(C) 新聞。
(D) 所在位置。

介紹即將開始的恐龍展示會，因此很有可能張貼在(C)的新聞。

170.
關於化石的暗示是什麼？
(A) 在鄰近地區發現。
(B) 非博物館所有。
(C) 大多數情況都不好。
(D) 被同一人發現。

在第一段中，恐龍化石是向Central大學及Jarod Watson以及一個叫Melanie Zhong的人租借的(on loan)，因此(B)為正確答案。

171.
關於展覽會，沒有提到什麼？
(A) 兒童不用付錢就可以參觀。
(B) 星期一不能參觀。
(C) 將在不到一個月的時間內開放。
(D) 團體可享受10%的優惠。

因為兒童可以免費入場，所以(A)的內容是正確的，而正常參觀時間是星期二到星期五，所以(B)也是事實。展覽時間為6月10日至6月30日，因此(C)也是有提到的內容，沒有提到有關團體參觀的具體費用，因此正確答案為(D)。

[172-175]

預定工作

通知各位住戶，Harbor View公寓管理處下週將進行幾項維修工作。請仔細觀察以下內容，必要時請調整日程。

5月12日星期二： 從上午10點至中午，整個社區將會斷電。在這段時間內，整個社區的電器系統將會安裝新的主控板。這代表所有建築物的電梯都將不會啟動。電腦和電視也不會運行，冷藏室、冷凍室或是洗衣機也都是如此。

5月13日星期三： 下午2點至下午5點，將會切斷101號樓和105號樓的瓦斯。在這段期間內，將會更換一部分的管道，維修期間建築物也不會有熱水。另外，瓦斯爐及烤箱也不能使用。

5月14日星期四： 為了要清掃106號樓和109號樓之間的游泳池，預計將會關閉游泳池。游泳池全天不開放。

5月15日星期五： 預計要修剪雜草及維修草坪。請過敏者注意。

請注意工作時間僅為預期時間。如果工作時間比預期的長，各種服務將在較長時間內不可使用。隨著工作的進行，我們將隨時為各位提供最新情報。

詞彙 tenant 承租人 take note of 注意 adjustment 調節，調整 daily schedule 每日日程 nonoperational 無法運作的 washing machine 洗衣機 gas stove 瓦斯爐 lawn 草坪 maintenance 維持，維修 take precautions 注意 unavailable 無法使用

172.
公告的目的是什麼？
(A) 為了向住戶告知要檢查。
(B) 為了讓人們瞭解即將進行的維修工程。
(C) 為了尋求住戶對社區管理的幫助。
(D) 為了告知社區的一些問題。

從第一句中就可以找到公告的目的，因為通知的是「預計於下週進行的維修工作(some repair work to be done in the coming week)」，所以正確答案是(B)。

詞彙 advise A of B 向A通知B

173.
根據公告，5月12日不會發生什麼？
(A) 每棟公寓將接受檢查。
(B) 電子設備暫時不能運作。
(C) 將會進行有關電氣系統的工作。
(D) 在兩個小時內不會通電。

查看May 12項目中將要進行的事情。因為作業時間是上午10點到中午(from 10 A.M. to noon)，所以(D)是事實。社區內的電氣系統(the complex's entire electric system)要安裝新零件，電腦、電視、冰箱等電子產品不能運作，所以(B)和(C)也是有提到的內容。但找不到要檢查家家戶戶的內容，所以(A)才是正確答案。

174.

社區內的草坪美化工程什麼時候完成？
(A) 5月12日。
(B) 5月13日。
(C) 5月14日。
(D) 5月15日。

如果知道問題的landscaping work代表著美化工作，就能輕易地找到正確答案。正確答案是進行草坪相關工作的(D)5月15日。

175.

[1]，[2]，[3]，[4]中下列句子填入最為合適的地方是哪裡？
「請注意工作時間僅為預期時間。」
(A) [1]
(B) [2]
(C) [3]
(D) [4]

注意到"the times"的話，給定的句子應要填入有提及工作時間的部分。[4]後面正在談論工作時間變長的情況，因此正確答案是(D)。

[176-180]

收件者：Angela Carpenter <angela_c@performancemail.com>

寄件者：Robert Harper <robert@tourpro.com>

主旨：旅遊行程

日期：5月12日

附件：Carpenter_itinerary

親愛的Carpenter小姐，

感謝您為即將到來的歐洲旅行費用進行結帳，通知您，您的機票、火車票以及酒店都已經預訂完成了。

請查看附件的完整旅遊日程表。您將於6月20日從波士頓的Logan機場出發，在同日抵達意大利羅馬的Fiumicino機場，在那裡可以租車。6月26日將搭乘飛機前往希臘雅典，6月30日將會前往德國慕尼黑。在7月5日旅行結束時，您將從瑞士蘇黎世的Kloten機場出發返回波士頓。

如需更改旅遊行程，最晚請於5月31日前告訴我，在此之前進行的更改將不會收取任何費用，但隨後的每次更改都將收取50美元的費用。

Robert Harper 敬上
Tour Pro

詞彙 itinerary 旅遊行程表 make the payment for 支付～費用 depart 離開 rental car 租車 conclusion 結論，結尾 prior to ～以前 alternation 變更

收件者：Robert Harper <robert@tourpro.com>

寄件者：Angela Carpenter <angela_c@performancemail.com>

主旨：旅行

日期：7月6日

致親愛的Harper先生，

我丈夫和我剛從歐洲旅行回來。我想讓您知道我們經歷了一生一次的旅行，並且感謝您為實現這一目標所做的一切。

我們兩個人，對於您說我們去的所有地方都住在四星級酒店的說法感到有些懷疑，但是這句話真的很對。我對雅典的Pallas酒店印象特別深刻。所有地區的導遊們不僅擁有淵博的知識，而且英語也很流利，對我們幫助很大。唯一遺憾的是，從羅馬到威尼斯的火車晚了兩三個小時，但這只是小小的差錯而已。

貴方旅行社以及您提供的高水平旅遊，我一定轉告各位朋友。下次去旅行時，我還會再聯繫您的。

Angela Carpenter 敬上

詞彙 of one's lifetime 一生一次的 skeptical 懷疑的，有疑心的 claim 主張，要求 be the case 的確如此 memorable 值得懷念的 knowledgeable 博學的 fluent 流利的 merely 只是 setback 差錯；逆行

176.

Harper先生沒有提到的交通方式是什麼？
(A) 飛機。
(B) 火車。
(C) 汽車。
(D) 計程車。

看一下Harper先生撰寫的第一封電子郵件的內容。透過第一段中的"your airline, railroad, and hotel reservations have all been made"提到了飛機和火車，第二段的"You can pick up your rental car there."提到了租車，因此在選項中沒有提到的交通方式是(D)的計程車。

177.

根據Harper先生說的話，3月31日以後會發生什麼事？
(A) 將不會退款。
(B) 更改需要支付費用。
(C) 無法取消門票。
(D) 酒店住宿費將會提高。

問題的關鍵語句"May 31"可在第一封電子郵件的最後的段落中找到。Harper先生說對於在3月31日之前完成的變更將不會收取費用，但對於在那之後的變更事項表示每件會有50美元附加費用(a charge of $50 for each)，因此正確答案是(B)。

178.

Carpenter小姐為什麼要發電子郵件？
(A) 為了要表示感謝。
(B) 為了要求澄清。
(C) 為了進行新的預約。
(D) 為了批評服務。

可透過Carpenter先生撰寫的第二封電子郵件第一段確認答案。

對於旅行表示感謝是撰寫電子郵件的直接原因，因此正確答案是(A)。

詞彙　clarification 說明，解釋　criticize 批判，批評

179.

Carpenter小姐什麼時候候入住Pallas酒店？
(A) 6月20日。
(B) 6月26日。
(C) 6月30日。
(D) 7月5日。

從第二封電子郵件的"The Pallas Hotel in Athens was particularly memorable."中可以得知Pallas酒店位於雅典。另外，在第一封電子郵件中寫著抵達雅典的日期是June 26，綜合上述兩項內容，最終Carpenter小姐入住Palls酒店的日期是(B)的6月26日。

180.

與第二封電子郵件中第二段第六行"setback"一詞最接近的是？
(A) 後退。
(B) 延遲。
(C) 處罰。
(D) 取消。

setback的意思是「差錯」和「逆行」，如果注意到前面句子的"depart late"一詞，就會知道這裡會是(B)。

詞彙　retreat 後退，撤退　penalty 處罰　cancelation 取消

[181-185]

Edward Halpern	9:32 A.M.
你好，Carla，下週二我們預計將會為了產品演示開會，不是嗎？	
Carla Welch	9:34 A.M.
是的，Ed。你什麼時候會過來這裡？你已經準備好出差了嗎？	
Edward Halpern	9:35 A.M.
剛才才從旅行社那收到了旅遊行程表。下週一晚上會搭飛機過去。RE232次航班將會在晚上10點45分抵達。	
Carla Welch	9:36 A.M.
需要去機場接你嗎？我可以在那裡找個人送你去酒店。	
Edward Halpern	9:37 A.M.
真的很感謝你，但我這次決定要租車。如果有空閒時間的話，我想去觀光一下。	
Carla Welch	9:38 A.M.
太好了，我可以告訴你幾個一定要去的地方，下週見。	

詞彙　arrange 準備，籌備　take A to B 將A帶去B　do sightseeing 觀光　point out 指出，提出

Schloss 旅行社
蘇黎世，瑞士
Edward Halpern 先生的旅遊行程表

電話號碼：493-1933

電子郵箱地：edhalpern@mmc.com

負責人：Edith Mann

日期	航班	出發時間	出發地點	抵達地點
4月12日	RE232	9:25 P.M.	蘇黎世	柏林
4月15日	RE11	10:30 A.M.	柏林	華沙
4月17日	NM490	2:05 P.M.	華沙	雅典
4月21日	RE98	12:15 P.M.	雅典	蘇黎世

所有座位均為商務艙。出發前，所有機場都備有VIP休息室。您可以攜帶兩件合計不超過40公斤的行李。請至少在起飛前兩小時抵達機場。

詞彙　check 檢查，查驗　weigh 稱重　combine 合計　take off 起飛，脫

181.

Halpern先生為什麼會傳訊息給Welch小姐？
(A) 為了討論演示會。
(B) 為了告知抵達日期。
(C) 為了確認會議。
(D) 為了合約進行協商。

聊天室的第一句"We're still planning to meet for the product demonstration next Tuesday, aren't we? "中 Halpern先生在詢問為了產品演示的會議是否按照預定的進行，因此他開始傳訊息的理由是(C)。

182.

Welch小姐提議要做什麼？
(A) 調整與Halpern先生的會議議程。
(B) 為Halpern先生安排市內旅遊。
(C) 為Halpern先生租車。
(D) Halpern 先生到達後與某人見面。

Welch小姐詢問Halpern先生是否需要去機場迎接的人(someone to pick you up at the airport)，然後提議「在機場接到他帶他到酒店的人(a driver to meet you there to take you to your hotel)」，因此她提議的是(D)。

183.

根據旅遊行程表，那些不是事實？
(A) Halpern先生將於4月17日訪問雅典。
(B) Halpern先生的手提行李有重量限制。
(C) Halpern 先生將坐在頭等艙。
(D) Halpern先生將於4月15日搭乘RE11航班。

旅遊行程表的下面寫著"All of your seats are confirmed for business class."，因此Halpern先生將會乘坐商務艙，與事實不符的內容是(C)。

184.

Halpern先生將會在哪裡與Welch小姐見面？
(A) 蘇黎世。

(B) 柏林。

(C) 華沙。

(D) 雅典。

在聊天室Halpern說"I'll be arriving at 10:45 P.M. on Flight RE232."，所以他為了要和Welch小姐見面所搭乘的航班是RE232，如果從日程表上尋找的話，就會知道RE232的目的地是柏林，因此兩人最終見面的場所會是(B)。

185.

Mann小姐似乎是誰？

(A) 航空公司工作人員。

(B) Halpern先生的同事。

(C) 旅行社工作人員。

(D) Welch 小姐的司機。

Mann這個名字可以在第二張日程表中"Prepared By"一欄中找到。透過這些可以推測出Mann小姐可能是撰寫Halpern先生旅行日程表的Schloss旅行社工作人員，因此(C)是正確答案。

[186-190]

> **收件者**：Cranston Burgers 加盟店主全員
> **寄件者**：David Cotton
> **主旨**：收益
> **日期**：4月4日
>
> 我們計算了一下今年第一季度的收益，結果大部分都是正面的。與去年同期相比，全體收益增加了。但是有一個賣場比其他賣場還要落後。Tom Reynolds，為了幫助您改善加盟店的情形，我需要親自檢查您的店面，看看是否有任何我能夠發現的明顯問題存在。另外收益比平時還要高很多，看得出來三月的特別活動非常成功。為了能讓顧客能夠持續來我們的店，我們再多想想像是Edith Thompson建議的那些想法。
>
> 我調查完Tom的店之後將會在我的辦公室召開會議。我打算在4月16日那一周召開，之後再通知你們。

詞彙 revenue 收益，收入 calculate 改善 lag behind 落在～後面 inspect 調查 establishment 設立 in person 直接，親自 obvious 明顯的 detect 發現，查出 call a meeting 召開會議 be in touch 聯絡

Cranston Burgers 收益

加盟店位置	1月收益	2月收益	3月收益
華登湖	$220,000	$240,000	$280,000
愛丁堡	$310,000	$315,000	$350,000
漢普頓	$175,000	$160,000	$180,000
溫莎	$255,000	$270,000	$305,000

> **收件者**：David Cotton
> **寄件者**：Tom Reynolds
> **主旨**：收益
> **日期**：6月3日
>
> 致親愛的Cotton先生，

自從您4月初訪問我們飯店以後，員工們和我忙於履行您的建議，剛開始，對於一些事項是否能夠產生效果，我承認我多少有些懷疑，但其他方法都沒有什麼效果，所以我決定試一試。

所有東西都需要花費兩週才能夠發揮效果，因此4月份的收益只得到了一定程度的改善，改變的效果在5月份顯現出來了。收益增長到了相當程度的水平，雖然我還沒有看到確切的數據，但大致上，我們取得了與2月份Windows店所記錄的差不多程度的收益，到目前為止，這是在我餐廳裡不曾見過的最高收益。期待之後會有更成功的月份。

Tom Reynolds 敬上

詞彙 attempt 試圖 implement 實踐，履行 admit 承認 somewhat 稍微的，有點 skeptical 懷疑的 give a try 試試看，試圖 go into effect 發揮效果 moderately 恰當地 reveal 展現，揭露 considerable 龐大的，可觀的 bring in 帶來～ by far 到目前為止

186.

關於Thompson小姐，Cotton先生提到了什麼？

(A) 3月份顧客減少。

(B) 計算了所有收益。

(C) 在自己的賣場進行促銷。

(D) 想出了最近的宣傳活動。

Ms. Thompson這個名字可以在第一個引文的最後一部分找到，通知的撰寫者Cotton先生提到3月活動的成功之後，提議說要多想想和Edith Thompson所提議過的相似點子(some more ideas like the one Edith Thompson suggested)，透過這個可以推測出Thompson先生是提出有關活動想法的人，所以(D)才是正確答案。

詞彙 think of 思考，想到

187.

關於Reynolds先生的暗示是什麼？

(A) 有漢普頓的賣場。

(B) 最近成為所有者。

(C) 最近跟Cotton先生見面了。

(D) 經營餐廳的經驗。

在第一個引文中，Reynolds先生知道比其他賣場更加落後的賣場(one store is lagging behind the others)的加盟店主任，因此如果從第二段引文的表格中找到收益最低的賣場，Reynolds先生的賣場應該就會是漢普頓賣場，因此正確答案是(A)。

188.

那個加盟店整體收益最高？

(A) 華登湖。

(B) 愛丁堡。

(C) 漢普頓。

(D) 溫莎。

如果將月收入合計的話，就可以知道加盟店第一季度的總收益。正確答案是(B)，愛丁堡總收益是最高的，為975,000美元。

189.

Reynolds先生為什麼發電子郵件？

(A) 為了請求許可。

(B) 為了傳達最新資訊。

(C) 為了報告失敗。

(D) 為了提出提案。

Reynolds先生在整個電子郵件中都談到了執行Cotton先生建議的結果，因此正確答案是(B)。出現了正面的結果，所以(C)不能成為正確答案。

190.

根據Reynolds先生的話，他的店面5月份收入大概在多少？

(A) 240,000美元。

(B) 255,000美元。

(C) 270,000美元。

(D) 280,000美元。

在最後一段引文的第二段中，Reynolds先生談到5月份的收益時說2月份我們取得了與溫莎專賣店創下的相當水準的收益(we brought in somewhere around the amount the Windsor franchise recorded in February)。從第二段引文中找2月溫莎店的收益的話，5月Reynolds先生的店面收益將會是(C)的270,000美元。

[191-195]

徵求插畫家

Samson Publishing出版社在招募專職插畫家為薩拉托加公司工作。理想的候選人應要具有插畫家的專業經歷，並且優先考慮出版社、報紙或雜誌的經歷，不需要大學學位，但需要高中畢業文憑。被選定的人必須要能夠處理多個項目，按時完成任務並熟悉快速的工作環境。申請人應精通Art Decorator和Graphic Illustrator等軟件程序。薪水和津貼將取決於您的職業。有興趣的申請人應將簡歷，求職信和作品發送至illustratorjob@samsonpublishing.com。申請截止日期為8月1日。面試將在8月中旬進行。

詞彙 illustrator 插圖畫家 preferably 偏好，盡可能地 college degree 大學學位 diploma 畢業證書，學位證書 multiple 多數的 be good at 擅長～，熟練 meet a deadline 遵守截止日期 fast-paced 快速進行的 proficient 熟練的 cover letter 求職信

插畫家的面試日程已經確定了。請關注以下內容：

應徵者	面試日期	面試時間	地點	面試官
Josh Sheldon	8月14日	10:30 A.M.	103號	Eric Martel
Rosie Rodriguez	8月14日	1:00 P.M.	102號	Jane Garbo
Lawrence Smith	8月15日	1:00 P.M.	105號	Ken Murray
Adison Mattayakhun	8月16日	9:00 A.M.	108號	Eric Martel
Lily Ngoc	8月17日	2:30 P.M.	102號	Tim Watson

面試官應要全面記錄，請將所有相關訊息以及面試官推薦與否一起透過suegrossman@samsonpublishing.com發送給Sue Grossman。第二次面試預定於8月下旬進行。

詞彙 take note of 注意 take notes 記筆記，做紀錄 comprehensive 全面的，綜合的 relevant 有關的 along with 與～一起 forward 轉交

收件者：amattayakhun@wondermail.com

寄件者：suegrossman@samsonpublishing.com

主旨：插畫家職位

日期：8月19日

致親愛的Mattayakhun先生，

我的名字叫Sue Grossman。我是Samson出版社的員工，在公司負責招聘工作。您的面試官對於您、特別是您靈活運用多種電腦程序的能力感到印象深刻，因此推薦您進行第二次面試。

我們已安排您在8月25日星期六上午9點到這裡。面試將會持續好幾個小時，請做好一整天都會待在這裡的準備。那時候您將會與大家見面，並且為了親自確認您的能力，我們將會要求您畫幾幅插圖。與您見面的人之中會有一部分人要查看您的作品集，因此當您過來的時候，請勿忘記攜帶您的作品集。

期待著您的到來。

Sue Grossman 敬上
Samson出版社

詞彙 in charge of 擔任～，負責 particularly 特別是 call in 打電話，撥叫 get a first-hand look at 直接查看～ skill 技術，手藝 portfolio 作品集，文件夾

191.

關於職位，提到了什麼？

(A) 要求有大學學位。

(B) 8月1日開始工作。

(C) 要求使用電腦。

(D) 有關報紙的工作。

在第一個引文的招聘廣告中可以找到正確答案。不需要大學學位，因此(A)不是事實，(B)的8月1日不是開始工作的日期，而是應徵截止日，因為是出版社的招聘廣告，所以(D)也是錯誤的內容。正確答案為(C)，招聘廣告中提出應聘者必須要精通指定軟體(applicants must be proficient in software programs)的條件。

192.

廣告中無法知道的是什麼？

(A) 薪水隨聘用的人而有差異。

(B) 有興趣的人應以訪問受理的方式應徵。

(C) 偏愛有經驗的人。

(D) 報名截止日期為8月1日。

廣告後半段寫著應聘者應將相關資料發送至 illustratorjob@samsonpublishing.com，因此應徵方法不是透過(B)的訪問受理，而是通過電子郵件應徵。

193.

關於Rodriguez小姐的暗示是什麼？

(A) 能夠與其他人相處融洽地工作。

(B) 可以同時做好幾種工作。

(C) 主修電腦工程。

(D) 有管理經驗。

Ms. Rodriguez這名字可以在面試者名單上看到，所以可以知道她是一個滿足招聘廣告資格條件的應聘者，也就是說，她是具有廣告中提到的資格條件，即可以推測出她具備能夠處理多樣項目的能力(be able to handle multiple projects)遵守截止日期和迅速處理工作的能力(be good at meeting deadlines and working in a fast-paced environment)，因此正確答案為在這兩項條件中敘述前者的(B)。

194.

誰推薦了Mattayakhun先生再次進行面試？

(A) Eric Martel

(B) Jane Garbo

(C) Ken Murray

(D) Tim Watson

從第二段引文的表格中查看Mattayakhun先生的Interviewer欄位，就可以找到推薦他的面試官名字。正確答案是(A)。

195.

Grossman小姐向Mattayakhun先生要求做什麼？

(A) 面試時要穿著正式服裝。

(B) 打電話給她以確認他的臉。

(C) 帶他的作品集過來。

(D) 把他的簡歷副本以電子郵件形式發送。

在最後一段引文電子郵件中Grossman小姐正在叮囑Mattayakhun先生帶作品集過來 (make sure you have your portfolio)，因此正確答案是將portfolio改寫為a collection of his work的(C)。

詞彙 formal clothes 正式服裝 appearance 外貌，長相

[196-200]

```
年度拍賣

位於西徹斯特郡的慈善機構Paulson集團將於12月18日星期六在Regina酒店的黃金間舉辦拍賣會。該活動將於晚上六點從提供五道菜餚的晚餐開始，Paulson集團董事長兼創始人Laurie Mitchell將在晚上七點三十分發表簡短的演講，之後在八點將會進行無聲拍賣。拍賣商品包括當地居民Ken Dellwood的藝術作品以及簽名電影紀念品和兩人夏威夷旅行券。當晚將以當地最受歡迎的汽車經銷商Varnum所捐贈的Sidewinder跑車競標作為結尾。Paulson集團希望能夠籌集到200,000美元。活動的所有收益將用於支援城市的服務團體。若是想要購買晚餐及參加拍賣的門票，請撥打383-9487。
```

詞彙 auction 拍賣 charity 慈善，慈善團體 festivity 慶祝活動 autograph (親筆)簽名 silent auction 無聲拍賣 memorabilia 紀念物，紀念品 bid 投標 proceeds 收益，錢 good cause 慈善團體，服務團體

```
難忘的夜晚
Anna Belinda 記者

西徹斯特郡(12月19日)--昨晚顯然是一個令主辦年度籌集活動的Paulson集團印象深刻的夜晚。超過450人參加了在Regina酒店舉行的晚宴活動及隨後進行的無聲拍賣。

活動的精彩之處是跑車以50,000美元售出，這超出了預期售價的38,000美元。其餘拍賣品也都以高價售出，最終結果是當晚籌集了超過370,000美元以上。Paulson集團的董事長Laurie Mitchell說「我簡直不敢相信這次活動會有這麼成功，去年只籌集到150,000美元。我想感謝西徹斯特郡居民讓這次的活動圓滿成功。如果沒有他們，就不會有這種事情了。」
```

詞彙 definitely 明確地 fundraiser 資金籌集活動 fetch 拿來；(拍賣)賣出 end result 最終結果

```
12月23日

致親愛的Anderson先生，

謹在此通知您，您在星期六晚上出價的50,000美元尚未匯款。一般規定要在拍賣成立當天晚上就要支付出價價格，但您出價的價格過高，所以多給了您一些時間。

但是過了好幾天，在拍賣成立當晚之後，我們未曾從您那邊聽到任何消息。是否能請您撥打754-3722告訴我您打算怎麼付款嗎？希望能夠盡快收到您的消息。

Laurie Mitchell 敬上
Paulson集團董事長
```

詞彙 transfer 轉移；轉帳 bid 出價價格，喊價；投標

196.

Dellwood先生是誰？

(A) 拍賣人。

(B) 捐贈者。

(C) 畫家。

(D) Paulson集團員工。

Mr. Dellwood的名字可以在第一個公告中說明拍賣物品的部分，即"some artwork by local resident Ken Dellwood"中找到，因此Dellwood先生是畫美術作品的畫家。

197.

參加星期六活動的人該要做什麼？

(A) 小額捐款。

(B) 發送電子郵件。

(C) 購買門票。

(D) 預約。

在公告的最後一句"Call 383-9487 to purchase tickets for the dinner and auction."中，可以知道想要參加活動的人需要購買門票，(C)為正確答案。

198.

關於拍賣可以知道的是什麼？

(A) 開始的時間比預期的晚。

(B) 超過了團體的目標金額。

(C) 參加人數創歷屆之最。

(D) 可以免費參加。

從第一段引文中可以知道拍賣活動的目標金額為200,000美元，透過第二段引文的報導，可得知籌集了270,000美元以上(more than $270,000 was raised)這一事實，因此綜合以上兩個事實，關於拍賣提及的事項是(B)。

199.

Mitchell小姐為什麼會寫信給Anderson先生？

(A) 為慶祝他得標。

(B) 確認他是否收到物品。

(C) 為了請求付款。

(D) 為了表示感謝他參加拍賣。

從信件的開頭部分可以知道信件的目的是催繳欠繳的得標價格，因此正確答案是(C)。

200.

Anderson先生投標了什麼東西？

(A) 車輛。

(B) 畫。

(C) 旅行。

(D) 有簽名的物品。

透過信件的開頭部分"you have not yet transferred the $50,000 you bid"的敘述中可以看出Anderson先生的得標價格為50,000美元。另外在第二段引文中，有介紹到得標價為50,000美元的拍賣物品是sports car，因此正確答案是將跑車改寫成vehicle(車輛)的(A)。

PART 5

101.

調動費用的一半將由公司支付，但其餘部分將由Rosemont先生負擔。

(A) rest
(B) amount
(C) salary
(D) lease

如果注意到half of一詞，空格中應該包含調動費用「剩餘的一半」的意思，因此正確答案是(A)的rest。

詞彙 relocation cost 調動費用　handle 對待，處理　lease 租約

102.

在發生交貨延誤及其他問題時，LRW Manufacturing將對供應商提出不滿。

(A) another
(B) each other
(C) any other
(D) others

為了表示「(除了延誤之外)其他問題」，空格中就必須填入(C)的any other。作為參考，句子開頭的should前面省略了if，(A)的another是由a(n)和other合併而成的，表示「另一個」的意思，而(B)中的each other則是表示「彼此」的意思，(D)中的others是表示「其他人」或「其他東西」意思的代名詞。

詞彙 file a complaint 提出不滿　each other 彼此

103.

總裁預計要參加，所以要求員工開會不要遲到。

(A) late
(B) lately
(C) lateness
(D) latest

late可以表示形容詞「遲的」的意義和副詞「遲到」的意思。空格中填入的單字是副詞(A)的late。需注意(B)的lately為表示「最近的」意義。

詞彙 request 要求，請求　in attendance 出席的　late 遲的；遲到　lately 最近的　latest 最新的

104.

Chen先生在審查過企劃書之後，主張需要考慮對企劃書的幾個部分進行修改。

(A) revised
(B) revision
(C) revisor
(D) revisable

空格前面有介系詞for，空格裡應該要填入名詞。選項中為名詞的是(B)和(C)兩個，考慮到沒有冠詞等等，以及句子的整體意義，帶有「修改」之意的(B)的revision是正確答案。

詞彙 proposal 提案，計劃書　revision 修正，訂正　revise 修訂　revisor 校訂者

105.

由於Wilson先生辭職了，因此將由Cartwright小姐負責項目。

(A) has overseen
(B) overseeing
(C) will oversee
(D) was overseen

只有知道now that的正確用法才能找到正確答案。now that雖然就像表示理由或原因的連接詞一樣來使用，但根據now這個單字的特性，主句不會使用現在完成式，而是現在或未來時態，如果在選項中找到符合上述條件的動詞的話，就能知道正確答案為(C)。

詞彙 oversee 監督　resign 辭職，辭去

106.

Davidson先生在網路上看到招聘廣告後知道了那份工作。

(A) when
(B) therefore
(C) so
(D) but

由於(B)的therefore是連接副詞，所以是錯誤的，而空格連接的兩個句子也並非因果或是轉折的關係，因此(C)的so和(D)的but也不是正確答案。正確答案是表示時間意義的連接詞(A)的when。

107.

修理故障設備的所有努力都失敗了，所以訂購了新設備。

(A) failed
(B) resisted
(C) attempted
(D) considered

以連接詞so為基準，前面的內容是原因，後面的內容是結果，可以推測出會購買新設備是因為無法立即修理，因此正確答案是表示「失敗」意思的(A)failed。

詞彙 effort 努力 resist 抵抗 attempt 試圖

108.

因為違反保安系統，特定個人無法使用電腦文件。

(A) access
(B) accession
(C) accessible
(D) accessing

能夠修飾to the computer files這個介系詞句型，又能夠成為動詞has been denied主詞的是(A)的access(接近，進入)。在所給予的文句中，沒有必要特地加入「動作」的語意，所以動名詞(D)不能成為正確答案。

詞彙 security 保安，安全 breach 違反 access 接近，進入 deny 拒絕 accession 就職，登基 accessible 可以接近的，可以使用的

109.

Cranston先生將會接任Daniel Kim的職務，他結束了在研發部十年的工作決定辭職。

(A) because
(B) which
(C) after
(D) thereby

若是將將空格之後的句子視為動名詞子句，則可以填入介系詞，若是看作是分詞子句，則可以填入連接詞，從句子的意義來判斷的話，無論是在哪種情況下都應要加入與時間相關的單字。在選項中只有(C)的after符合這些條件。

詞彙 replace 代替，取代 depart 離開，出發 thereby 因此

110.

嘗試招募新訂閱者，結果導致超過550人在網路上申請訂閱。

(A) purchase
(B) recruit
(C) announce
(D) suspend

要找到能讓new subscribers(新訂閱者)作為受詞的動詞，正確答案是(B)的recruit(招募；聘用)。

詞彙 recruit 招募；聘用 subscriber 訂閱者 result in 導致 announce 通知，發表 suspend 推遲，保留

111.

博物館館長宣佈以文藝復興美術為主題的新展覽即將開始。

(A) features
(B) will feature
(C) to be featured
(D) featuring

因為沒有遺漏的句子組成部分，空格中應該要填入能夠修飾a new exhibit的形容詞或是能夠引導的單字或是句子。因此從形態上判斷的話，(C)和(D)其中一個為正確答案，因為必須要讓art能夠作為受詞，正確答案為(D)的featuring。

詞彙 curator 館長 feature 特徵；以～為特徵

112.

有些人抱怨高級工程師分配工作項目不公平。

(A) distributor
(B) distribution
(C) distributed
(D) distributive

空格需要能夠修飾形容詞unfair，並能夠被of引導的介系詞句修飾的名詞。在名詞(A)和(B)中，更符合句子內容的單字是(B)的distribution(分配)。

詞彙 unfair 不公正的，不公平的 distribution 分配，分布 distributor 批發商，經銷商 distributive 流通的

113.

Culberson International的律師們一提高報價，協商就結束了。

(A) if
(B) on
(C) as
(D) for

若是知道as soon as的意思為「一～就～」的話，就可以很輕易知道(C)是正確答案。

詞彙 come to an end 完結，結束

114.

由於春季促銷的人氣，決定在一個月後再進行一次促銷。

(A) popular
(B) popularly
(C) popularity
(D) popularities

留意冠詞the就能知道空格中必須要有名詞，因此(C)和(D)中有一個是正確答案，但沒有特殊理由一定要使用複數型，所以正確答案是(C)的popularity。

115.

重要的是增加公司銷售的高利潤的產品數量。

(A) involve
(B) produce
(C) maneuver
(D) increase

應該要找到能夠讓the number of profitable items成為受詞的動詞，選項中唯一能與「數值」配合使用的動詞是(D)的increase。

詞彙 vital 必要的，非常重要的　profitable 有利潤的　involve 干涉，連累　maneuver (軍隊等的)調動；機動演習

116.

明天早上開盤的話，該公司的股價預計將會上漲。

(A) value
(B) asset
(C) sale
(D) movement

股價寫作value of a stock，正確答案是(A)的value。

詞彙 value 價值，價格　stock 股份　asset 財產

117.

Sullivan先生對於研究人員開發的藥品效果提出了幾個問題。

(A) on account of
(B) in response to
(C) with regard to
(D) on top of

從內容上來看的話，空格中應該要填入表示「關於」的意思。正確答案是(C)的with regard to。

詞彙 with regard to 關於　effectiveness 效果　on account of 因為　in response to 作為對～的答覆　on top of 除此之外

118.

如果您想了解如何登記該項目，請留下聯絡方式給Winger小姐。

(A) leave
(B) be leaving
(C) will leave
(D) have left

空格應該要有能夠引導祈使句的動詞原型，因此正確答案是(A)的leave。

詞彙 contact information 聯絡方式

119.

在所有申請調動的人中，只有Appleton小姐的被批准了。

(A) transfers
(B) raises
(C) promotions
(D) positions

在內容上要與move elsewhere意思相通的表達才能填入空格，正確答案是「移動」或「調動」(A)的transfers。

120.

Richards先生很少參加會議，而是更偏好派自己部門內的其他員工代替自己去。

(A) always
(B) appropriately
(C) seldom
(D) eventually

如果注意到instead(代替)的話，前面部分的內容應該為「Richards先生本人不喜歡去」或「本人不去」，因此正確答案是具有否定意義的(C)的seldom。

詞彙 appropriately 適當地　seldom 不常　eventually 最終，終於

121.

自己的項目即將要結束的工程師們將會星期四從Ross小姐那裡分配到新的工作。

(A) whom
(B) whose
(C) which
(D) who

需要連接先行詞engineers和projects的關係代名詞。因此正確答案是關係代名詞的所有格形態的(B)whose。作為參考，如果改寫成完整的關係代名詞句型的話，就會變成"Their (Engineers') projects are about to conclude."。

122.

博物館將舉辦招待會以紀念新展覽的開始。

(A) receiver
(B) receptor
(C) reception
(D) receiving

在選項中能夠成為動詞host(主辦，舉辦)的受詞只有(C)的reception(招待會)。

詞彙 host 主辦，舉辦　reception 宴會，招待會　celebrate 祝賀，慶祝　receptor 感覺接受器，感覺器官

123.

若要全額退款，產品需要以原包裝狀態退貨。

(A) origin
(B) original
(C) originally
(D) originality

空格應該要填入有能夠修飾動名詞packaging的形容詞。正確答案是(B)的original。

詞彙 original 原本的，獨創的　qualify for 有資格～

124.

所有要參加會議的人都需要告知主辦方預定到達的時間。

(A) Any
(B) Each
(C) All
(D) Much

由於給定的句子是敘述句，因此(A)不能成為正確答案，(B)與their estimated times的複數敘述不相符，(D)是與不可數名詞一起使用的，也是錯誤的，因此正確答案是(C)的All。

詞彙 estimate 估算，估計 organizer 策劃人，組織者

125.

Focus Machinery的實習員工通常會負責一個能給自己帶來實踐經驗的項目。

(A) provide
(B) provision
(C) provisional
(D) provided

空格中應該填入能夠讓先行詞that作為主詞的同時又可以將them作為受詞的動詞，因此(A)和(D)其中有一個是正確答案，因為主要子句的時態是現在式，所以正確答案是provide的現在時態(A)。

詞彙 practical experience 實踐經驗 provision 供應 provisional 臨時的，暫時性的

126.

房地產企業同意展示設施以努力找尋承租人。

(A) with
(B) for
(C) by
(D) in

如果掌握it所指的是facility(設施)這一點，就可以知道在選項中，最適合填入空格的介系詞是表示其目的或對象意義的(B) for。

詞彙 real estate agency 房地產仲介 give a tour of 讓~參觀，介紹 in an effort to 為了~而努力 renter 出租人，承租人

127.

White先生為了讓團體遊客避開市區交通堵塞推薦繞路。

(A) form
(B) transportation
(C) concept
(D) detour

注意to avoid the heavy traffic downtown的意義並找出正確答案。為了避免交通堵塞，選項中值得推薦的只有(D)的detour(繞道)。

詞彙 detour 繞道 transportation 交通 concept 概念

128.

在結帳的期間，顧客需要等待一段時間。

(A) puts
(B) will put
(C) was put
(D) is putting

put~on hold表示「等待、保留」，因此正確答案是將此改為被動態形式的(C)。

詞彙 payment 支付，結帳 put~on hold 等待，保留

129.

新公寓建築物裡面有娛樂室、洗衣間和其他設施。

(A) facilities
(B) accommodations
(C) utilities
(D) functions

空格中應該要填入與a recreation room和a laundry room概念相符合的單字。正確答案是意指「設施」的(A) facilities。

詞彙 accommodations 宿舍，住所 utility (如水，電等)公用事業 function功能

130.

經理們預計至少每一季度都會跟員工見一次面，以便追蹤進度。

(A) some
(B) once
(C) few
(D) any

留意at least的意義並找到正確答案。必須要完整表達出「一季度至少要見一次面」，所以正確答案是表示次數意義的(B)once。

PART 6

[131-134]

收件者：Sandra Carter
寄件者：Melissa Sanchez
日期：5月27日
主旨：新員工

131.通知您從明天起將會有三位新員工在你的部門開始工作。他們的名字叫Cleo White, Marcia Strong還有Xavier Thompson。White先生將會在Roland Porter的小組工作，Strong小姐和Thompson先生將會隸屬於Kendra Murray的小組。上午三人都會參加在講堂舉辦的說明會，**132.**之後12點將會在員工餐廳與總裁及部長們一起吃午餐，**133.**在這時候有機會可以見到他們，午餐時間結束後，你將**134.**帶領他們回到部門，然後介紹給那裡的每一個人。請盡最大的努力讓他們能夠在這裡舒服地度過第一周。

詞彙 auditorium 講堂 escort 護衛，護送 comfortable 舒服的，安逸的

131.

(A) advice
(B) advisory
(C) advised
(D) advisor

「通知您~」的意思經常用"Please be advised that ~"來表示，正確答案是(C)，即使不知道，只要把握住空格前面有be動詞這一點，就能知道空格中應該要填入被動語態。

132.

(A) Afterward

(B) However

(C) Beforehand

(D) Occasionally

觀察前後的文章脈絡，不難發現寄件者正在按照時間順序談論行程，正確答案是表示「之後」意義的(A)。

詞彙 beforehand 預先，事先 occasionally 偶爾，有時候

133.

(A) 不需要你出席一整天。

(B) 在這時候有機會可以見到他們。

(C) 在整個過程中，人事部員工將會引導他們。

(D) 說明會將會在那時候進行。

前一句正在說明總裁及部長們和新進員工將在員工餐廳一起用餐，另一方面，從第一句及引文後半部分的內容推測出通知的收件人應該會是部門主管，因此空格中必須填入(B)才能完成最自然的文章脈絡。

134.

(A) approach

(B) instruct

(C) leave

(D) escort

內容上傳達要把新員工帶到部門介紹的意思，所以空格中應該填入表示「護衛、護送」意義的(D)。

詞彙 approach 接近 instruct 指示，教授

[135-138]

3月8日

致親愛的Grimes先生，

135.已經找到新房客要租您想搬離的房屋了。她預計將於4月3日搬入公寓，因此您必須最晚於4月2日之前**136.**搬離。在**137.**離開之前，請聯絡大樓管理員George Shultz，他將會在最後一天檢查房屋的狀況，如果公寓完好無損，則押金將會**138.**全額退還，如果發現有問題的話，則可能需要支付維修費用。請務必要告知他什麼時候要搬家。在過去五年期間，我們很高興能邀請您成為Griswold Apartments的住戶。

Karen Lawson 敬上

Griswold公寓業主

詞彙 tenant 承租人 take possession of 拿到，得到 premise 前提；用地 security deposit 押金 in full 全額 detect 察覺，查明

135.

(A) 您所詢問的公寓決定要租給其他人了。

(B) 您的貸款已獲得批准，您可以入住公寓。

(C) 已經找到新房客要租您想搬離的房屋了。

(D) 公寓每月租金50美元。

這是給從公寓裡搬出去的人的通知。空格中應該要填入後面句子中主詞she所指對象在的句子，正確答案是(C)，she所指的是a replacement tenant。

詞彙 mortgage 貸款，融資 rent 租金，月租 raise 提高；徵收

136.

(A) attempt

(B) move

(C) terminate

(D) vacate

前文提到出現了新搬來的人，所以空格中應該填入將premise作為受詞，同時帶有「空出(空間等)」意思的(D) vacate。

詞彙 terminate 結束，終止

137.

(A) left

(B) leave

(C) to leaving

(D) will leave

prior to意思為「～以前」，在這裡to是介系詞，因此正確答案要填入和to一起成為動名詞的(C)。

138.

(A) full

(B) complete

(C) amount

(D) entire

「全部」或「全額」的意思以in full來表達。正確答案是(A)。

[139-142]

Munford 隧道即將重新開放

139.貫穿Sidewinder山的Munford隧道預計於4月21日重新開放。為了修理通風系統，該隧道處於關閉的狀態，**140.**因為空調不好，空氣無法循環到隧道內外，之後這些問題將會解決，隧道會再次成為安全通過的地方。 隧道重新開通後，附近地區的交通將會變得**141.**順暢，**142.**而且通勤時間也會大大減少。如欲進一步瞭解隧道及隧道水利工程相關資訊，請撥打580-2948市政府專線。

詞彙 go through 通過 directly 筆直地，直接 ventilation 換氣 air conditioning 空調 cycle 循環 ease 減輕，緩和 commuting time 通勤時間 by a significant amount 相當大地程度 mayor's office 市政府

139.

(A) direction

(B) directive

(C) directly

(D) directed

空格前面的goes是作為不及物動詞來使用，空格中應該要填入可以修飾它的副詞(C)directly。

140.
(A) In spite of
(B) In return for
(C) Due to
(D) Instead of

空調不好和空氣循環不好是因果關係，因此空格中應該填入表示原因的(D)Due to。

詞彙 in spite of 不管，無論　in return for 補償，報答

141.
(A) ease
(B) approve
(C) involve
(D) remove

如果思考過隧道開通後會對traffic conditions(交通狀況)產生什麼樣的影響，就能輕易找到正確答案。正確答案是表示「減輕、緩和」的(A)ease。

詞彙 involve 介入，使～關聯　remove 去除

142.
(A) 為了完成必要的工作，需要更多的資金。
(B) 隧道終於建成，社區居民很高興。
(C) 車輛可能要到5月份才能通過隧道。
(D) 而且通勤時間也會大大減少。

前文中提到了隧道開通的效果或是影響，所以空格中也要填入與此相關的句子才能完成最自然的文章脈絡。正確答案是(D)，這裡it指的是the reopening of the tunnel。

[143-146]

介紹 Chamberlain 咖啡廳

Chamberlain咖啡廳預定將於11月1日 **143·**首次營業。位於Duncan街和Lucent街之間Maple大廈的一樓。咖啡廳將會販賣所有種類的熱飲和冷飲，顧客們還可以購買糕點、三明治和沙拉。咖啡廳開幕當天所有食物及飲料都將會以半價販賣。若是購買飲料即可免費 **144·**使用WiFi。還可以外帶及提供五個街區內的 **145·**配送服務，**146·**總價將會包含少許配送費用。請到我們的網站www.chamberlaincafe.com瞭解詳細內容。

詞彙 for the first time 第一次，最初　beverage 飲料　delivery 運送，遞送　location 位置

143.
(A) at
(B) for
(C) on
(D) in

for the first time是「第一次、最初」的意思，正確答案是(B)。

144.
(A) available
(B) installed
(C) applied
(D) considered

需要完整表達購買飲料時可以免費使用wifi的意義，因此正確答案是表示「可利用的」之意的(A)available。

145.
(A) delivery
(B) deliverance
(C) deliveries
(D) delivered

配送可以用make a delivery來表達，另外在這句中與and連接的takeout services是複數型，因此空格中也應該填入複數形態，正確答案是(C)。

詞彙 deliverance 解救，救援

146.
(A) 關於我們販賣的飲料種類，請詢問工作人員。
(B) 此類優惠僅適用於位在市區的賣場。
(C) 我們的顧客們可能無法停止談論我們的服務。
(D) 總價將會包含少許配送費用。

正因為前文介紹了配送服務，所以正確答案是提到配送費用的(D)。

詞彙 server 員工，服務生　city limits 城市範圍

PART 7
[147-148]

Grayson 體育館正在進行改建工程

Grayson體育館因為改建工程的關係，預計將於4月10日至4月16日關閉。在此期間體育館面積將會增加近70%，如此一來體育館會員們鍛鍊的空間將會變得更大。改建工程完成之後，還將會提供額外空間給舉重訓練、瑜伽以及有氧運動。男性及女性更衣室也將會擴大，並增加兩室壁球場，大部分的設備也將換成更新、更現代化的機器。但很遺憾的是，在改建工程期間體育館將不會營業。

詞彙 renovation 維修，改建　additional 額外的　space 空間
　weightlifting 舉重；舉重訓練　aerobics 有氧運動　locker
　room 更衣室　enlarge 擴大　squash 壁球　modern 現代化的

147.
根據公告，對於改建工程那一項是不符合事實的？
(A) 做有氧運動的空間將會擴大。
(B) 將會建造壁球場和三溫暖。
(C) 增加新設備。
(D) 體育館將會更寬敞。

雖然有新設壁球場的內容，但是找不到提及三溫暖的內容，所以(B)是正確答案。

148.

對體育場館會員暗示了什麼？
(A) 4月份的會費將會提高。
(B) 要求實施翻修工程。
(C) 課程時間表將因營運團隊而改變。
(D) **4月10日至16日期間將無法運動。**

在公告的第一句中寫著「4月10日至16日因為維修工程將會關閉體育館(will be closed for renovations from April 10 to April 16)」，在最後一部分寫了在施工期間(during the renovation period)將會關閉而感到遺憾， 因此施工期間不可能使用體育館，正確答案是(D)。

[149-150]

收件者：brycewatson@quantummail.com
寄件者：grace_peters@mallardelectronics.com
主旨：好消息
日期：4月25日

致親愛的Watson先生，

我是Grace Peters。在一個小時前，我和您通了話，很高興能夠向您傳達好消息。工程師發現了您寄給我們的Tristan 300的問題，配線有輕微的缺陷，這就是使拍攝的照片看起來模糊的原因。已經修理完畢，預定於今日下午將Tristan 300寄送給您，因為是以隔夜即達郵件寄送的，所以您將會在明天上午收到。很抱歉造成您的不便，已經在您的Mallard Electronics帳號中增加了50美元的積點，您可以在我們網路賣場上購買想要的商品時使用。如有疑問請回覆此電子郵件。祝您與Tristan 300一起度過愉快的時光。

Grace Peters 敬上
Mallard Electronics 顧客服務代表

詞彙 **minor** 較小的，細微的 **fault** 錯誤 **wiring** 配線 **blurry** 模糊的，灰濛濛的 **overnight mail** 隔夜即達郵寄，速達郵寄 **inconvenience** 不便 **credit** 信用；學分；(賣場等)積點 **enjoyment** 享受

149.

Tristan 300是什麼？
(A) 筆記型電腦。
(B) **數位相機。**
(C) 雷射列印機。
(D) 傳真機。

"causing it to make the pictures it took look blurry"是正確答案的線索。在選項中，能夠拍照的機器只有(B)的數位相機。

150.

Peters先生給了Watson先生什麼？
(A) **賣場中可以使用的積點。**
(B) 優惠券。
(C) 免費使用手冊。
(D) 免費配飾。

Peters先生為不便道歉，同時向Watson先生贈與Mallard Electronics帳號50美元的積點(a credit of $50 to your Mallard Electronics account)，因此(A)為正確答案。

[151-152]

Susan Watts	2:38 P.M.
您好，Duncan先生，您訂購的產品到店裡了。	

Jeff Duncan	2:41 P.M.
好消息啊，謝謝。7點之後我會過去的。	

Susan Watts	2:42 P.M.
可惜我們今晚6點關門。如果到那時候還不能來的話，明天9點到5點之間可以拿到小說。	

Jeff Duncan	2:43 P.M.
明天為什麼那麼早關門？	

Susan Watts	2:44 P.M.
因為週六營業時間更短。有需要的話，也可以像之前一樣用郵寄的。	

Jeff Duncan	2:46 P.M.
沒關係，我明天2點到3點之間會過去。	

151.

Watts先生應該是在哪裡工作？
(A) 電子產品賣場。
(B) 服裝賣場。
(C) 鞋店。
(D) **書店。**

從"If you can't make it by then, you can pick up your novels tomorrow between nine and five."可以看出顧客訂購的商品是novels(小說)，因此Watts先生工作的地方應該是(D)的書店。

152.

下午2點46分，Duncan先生為什麼會寫"That's all right"？
(A) 為了感謝Watts先生的幫助。
(B) 為了告知自己將於明天過去。
(C) 為了表達喜悅。
(D) **為了拒絕提議。**

給予的句子是對於"I could always mail your items to you if you'd like."的反應，在給予的句子之後Duncan先生回答說明天自己要親自去取，間接暗示了不要郵寄，因此(D)是正確答案。

詞彙 **turn down** 拒絕

[153-154]

Westside 飯店

持有此優惠券的人
可以享受Westside飯店的青少年套房
一周的免費住宿優惠。

● 此優惠在全球153家Westside飯店皆有效。
● 優惠券持有人至少要提前兩周預約。

59

- 此優惠券無使用期限，全年皆可隨時使用。
- 欲要預約或詢問可撥打1-888-403-3039。
- 飯店沒有可入住客房時，預約申請可能會被拒絕。

153.

關於Westside飯店，暗示了什麼？
(A) 最好的客房是青少年套房。
(B) 可以在許多國家找到。
(C) 平均住宿費用超過一晚250美元。
(D) 向所有再入住飯店的客人發放優惠券。

在底下第一項說明中說可以在全世界153家飯店(all 153 Westside Hotel locations around the world)使用，因此(B)是正確答案。

154.

關於優惠券可以知道什麼？
(A) 不得在特定月份使用。
(B) 可以升級更好的客房。
(C) 可以住7天。
(D) 僅一年有效。

透過"a free stay in a junior suite for one week" (在青少年套房中免費住宿一週)可以知道(C)是正確的答案。第三項說沒有特定的有效期限，一整年任何時候都可以使用，因此(A)和(D)是錯誤的，(B)是優惠券無法找到的優惠。

[155-157]

新的開始
Rachel Weiss

庫珀斯敦(3月27日)--近年來，庫珀斯敦經歷了一段艱難的時期。人口減少，一些主要企業離開了這裡，有許多當地居民認為城市將面臨滅亡的危險。

幸運的是，有一位來自庫珀斯敦的人還記得自己的根。 Harold Williams在18歲的時候離開了庫珀斯敦，但他並沒有忘記自己曾經成長過的地方。Williams先生成為了一個成功的企業家，在全國擁有多個鋸木廠。上個月，Williams先生賣掉了自己的資產準備退休。

他迅速聯絡了庫珀斯敦市議會，詢問該市需要自己做什麼。昨晚，記者瞭解到市區兩所學校將要完全改建，以及聘用更多教師，Williams先生將承擔一切事情的費用。Williams先生說「我希望這裡的孩子能夠受到良好的教育，為了這城市，我確信在不久的將來，我還會做其他的事情。我不知道會是什麼事情，但我準備好接受提議了。」

詞彙 as if 像～一樣 in danger of 面臨～的危險 native son 當地出生的人 root 根，根源 sawmill 鋸木廠 property 資產 promptly 迅速地 open to 願意

155.

報導的目的是什麼？
(A) 為了對當地居民進行評價。
(B) 為了說明正在進行的改建工程。

(C) 為教師職缺的招聘廣告。
(D) 為了報導對市鎮的捐贈。

報導為一個名叫Harold Williams的退休企業家捐款給庫珀斯敦的內容，因此(D)是正確答案。這不是人物本身，而是涉及到一個人物的捐贈行為，因此不應選擇(A)作為正確答案。

詞彙 profile 側面；對人物評論 ongoing 進行中的 donation 捐獻，捐贈

156.

從報導中可以知道Williams先生的什麼？
(A) 不再工作。
(B) 重新搬回Cooperstown。
(C) 將成為教師。
(D) 在Cooperstown出售財產。

在"Last month, Mr. Williams sold his properties so that he could retire."這句可以看出他在上個月退休的事實，因此在選項中可得知的事實是(A)。

157.

[1]，[2]，[3]，[4]中最適合填入下列句子的地方是哪裡？
「我不知道會是什麼事情。」
(A) [1]
(B) [2]
(C) [3]
(D) [4]

思考一下句子中的代名詞I和that所指的是什麼，就能輕易找到正確答案。I是指Williams先生，that是指something else for the town，因此要填入句子的位置是(D)的[4]。

[158-160]

MEMO

收件者： 全體主管
寄件者： David Bowman
主旨： 員工名單
日期： 12月18日

人事部將更新員工名單，因此需要公司內部所有主管們的近期照片。可以直接繳交照片，也可以在12月20日下午1點到4點之間到182號室拍照。

繳交本人照片時，照片穿著需為正式服裝，背景是白色的才可以。如果您決定在這裡拍照，請不要忘記穿著適合星期五的服裝。照片應於12月23日星期一繳交。

由於公司近年來不斷發展壯大，員工名單將不會再印發，取而代之的是會網路上公布。各位主管們的簡歷也將會公布在其中，請用150字寫一篇關於本人的文章，內容應該要包含學歷、經歷及關心領域。

詞彙 employee directory 員工名單 formal wear 正式服裝 elect 選出，選擇 accordingly 相應地 biography 傳記 include 包含

158.

通知說明了什麼東西？
(A) 員工可以上傳名單的位置。
(B) 名單更新的理由。
(C) 負責編制名單的人。
(D) 應列入名單的東西。

要更新員工名單(employee directory)而要求所需要的公司內部主管們的最新照片(recent pictures of every manager at the firm)，因此(D)是正確答案。

159.

關於照片提到了什麼？
(A) 應以黑白照拍攝。
(B) 可以在公司拍攝。
(C) 應穿著休閒裝拍攝。
(D) 應於12月23日拍攝。

有關照片的事項為可以提交原有照片，也可以於12月20日在公司重新拍攝，照片中的服裝必須是正式服裝，以及照片背景必須是白色。如果在選項中找到符合這些內容的事實，(B)就是正確答案。

160.

關於員工名單，暗示了什麼？
(A) 員工應為其支付費用。
(B) 因為太多，所以無法印刷。
(C) 已經公布了。
(D) 需要編輯。

在通知最後的段落中，可以知道由於公司的發展「名單現在不會印製，將在網路發布(the directory will no longer be printed but will instead be posted online)」，也就是說，由於人數增加而認為印製可能會有困難，因此(B)是正確答案。

[161-164]

收件者：Rachel Bellinger <rachelb@condortech.com>

寄件者：Gerald Storm <g_storm@condortech.com>

主旨：本週五

日期：9月8日

親愛的Bellinger小姐，

本週五是Pike工作的最後一天，我收到了一封有關於Pike送別會通知的電子郵件。我很高興過去六年能和Pike先生一起工作，他成了我的導師，我從他那裡學到了許多有關技術方面的東西。

經過漫長歲月，我聽到他將要退休離開這裡感到很傷心，但我很遺憾地要通知妳我不能參加送別會，我那天預定要在達拉斯主持研討會，所以沒有辦法給研討會的主辦方添麻煩更改日程。

我想知道我是否可以在送別會上為Pike先生發一段語音訊息，我想那將能夠表達我的感激並告訴大家我是有多麼想念他的一種好方法。另外為了要增添一筆錢購買禮物給Pike先生，我會在午餐時間過後到妳的辦公室去。

Gerald Storm 敬上

詞彙 farewell party 送別會　alongside 和～一起　mentor 導師　after all these year 經過漫長歲月　recorded message 語音訊息　express 表達，表現　drop by 順便拜訪　contribute 捐獻，貢獻

161.

無法得知Pike先生的什麼？
(A) 他將要辭職。
(B) 他的導師是Storm先生。
(C) 他將於本週五辭職。
(D) 他將在其他城市生活。

在"his last day of work this coming Friday"這一句中可得知(C)，透過"he is retiring and moving away"這句可以得知(A)及(D)都是事實。正確答案是(B)，只有Pike先生和Storm先生的立場相互調換，(B)才會符合內容。

162.

Storm先生預定在星期五做什麼？
(A) 進行與工作有關的活動。
(B) 去國外出差。
(C) 與研討會主辦方見面。
(D) 面試應聘者。

透過"I'm scheduled to lead a seminar in Dallas on that day"的部分可以得知Storm先生週五要做的事情是主持研討會，所以將seminar改寫為professional event的(A)為正確答案。

163.

Storm先生請求讓他可以做什麼？
(A) 購買屬於自己的餞別禮物。
(B) 晚一點到Pike先生的送別會。
(C) 為了要讓Pike先生能聽得到，要把告別錄下來。
(D) 對所有參加活動的人表示感謝。

Storm先生在第三段中為了表達感謝及遺憾提議要為Pike先生準備語音訊息(a recorded message that you could play for Mr. Pike the)，因此他請求的是(C)。

詞彙 going-away present 餞別禮物　show up 露面，出現

164.

Storm先生下午會做什麼？
(A) 拜訪Pike先生。
(B) 打電話給Bellinger小姐。
(C) 發送電子郵件。
(D) 捐款。

在電子郵件最後的部分，Storm先生說它會在午餐時間後去找Bellinger小姐加錢購買餞別禮物(to contribute to the fund to purchase a gift for Mr.Pike)，因此他下午要做的事情是(D)。

---

http://www.hartautomobiles.com

| 首頁 | 車輛 | 公司介紹 | HART代理商 |

Hart汽車從來不是家喻戶曉的名字，但我們影響了這國家。本公司由7名投資者幫助的John Hart於1911年創立，最早的Hart汽車，理所當然地被稱為Hart。它的技術能力得到了很高的評價。

1914年我們自發性地把員工的工資從每天平均2.30美元提高到4.00美元，上調近一倍，是為數不多的幾家公司之一。這雖無助於擴大利潤，卻提升了數十名Hart員工的生活品質。

前幾十年我們專注於生產平價汽車，John Hart說「我們的目標是為普通工人提供無負擔購買的平價汽車」，他的兒子Tim Hart在創立者去世的1933年繼承了公司。

1970年代發生石油危機時，Hart為了提高燃料效能，是國內第一家將方向轉向了製造更小更輕的汽車。近年來，公司成為了太陽能汽車及自動駕駛汽車部門的創新企業，我們的目標是製造不會危害環境的車輛。明年新車將會成為比之前生產的任何一款還能夠更高效率使用能量的汽車。雖然我們不是規模最大或收益最高的汽車製造企業，但我們為它對員工及環境的影響感到驕傲。

詞彙 household name 家喻戶曉的名字　found 建立，創立
investor 投資者　appropriately 適當地　voluntarily 自發地
wage 薪水　double 變成兩倍　profit margin 利潤率　dozens
of 數十個的　objective 目的　take over 接管　pass away 去世
oil crisis 石油危機　domestic 國內的，家庭的　switch 改變，
轉換　efficiency 效率性　innovator 創新者　self-driven car 自
動駕駛汽車　environment 環境　profitable 有利的

165.

根據資訊，關於Hart汽車，什麼是事實？
(A) 銷售太陽能汽車。
(B) 由Tim Hart設立。
(C) 全國規模最大的汽車製造企業。
(D) 製造了一輛消耗燃料量更少的車輛。

不知道太陽能汽車是否已經開發完成，因此(A)不能成為正確答案，(B)的Tim Hart是創始人John Hart的兒子，最後一句中說不是規模最大的汽車企業，所以(C)也是錯誤的內容。正確答案是(D)，最後一段中寫到1970年代的Hart汽車是燃料效率優秀的小巧輕便汽車(smaller and lighter cars to increase their fuel efficiency)。

166.

Hart汽車是什麼時候提高員工工資的？
(A) 1911年。
(B) 1914年。
(C) 1933年。
(D) 1970年。

在第二段的第一句中，介紹到Hart汽車在1914年主動提高員工工資(voluntarily increase our employees)，為數不多的幾間公司之一。正確答案是(B)。

167.

Hart汽車現在的目標是什麼？
(A) 製造市場上最廉價的汽車。
(B) 以車輛來保護環境。
(C) 向工作人員提供有競爭力的薪水。
(D) 增加每年獲得的收益。

現在的目標是在第3段中段的"Our objective is to manufacture vehicles which won't harm the environment"句子中可以找到，現在的目標是製造不危害環境的汽車，所以正確答案是(B)。

168.

[1]，[2]，[3]，[4]中最適合填入下列句子的地方是那裡？
「它的技術能力得到了很高的評價。」
(A) [1]
(B) [2]
(C) [3]
(D) [4]

技術能力得到認可的「它(it)」所指的對象應該要在前面句子中提及，正確答案是(A)的[1]，it所指的是Hart公司的首輛汽車the Hart。

詞彙 workmanship 手藝，技術

[169-171]

11月8日

親愛的Bell先生，

感謝您持續使用Whistler健身俱樂部。您過去三年是我們的寶貴顧客。

此通知是為了告知您，如若想使用我們的服務，需要定期繳納使用費用。根據我們的記錄，您決定每月繳納30美元，可能您上個月過於繁忙導致您忘記了，我們還尚未收到10月份的使用費用，繳費期限是到10月31日。從您之前的繳納紀錄中推測出您一般會在每月25日至29日之間繳納月費。

能夠請您儘快繳納10月份的使用費用嗎？您可以到體育館以現金繳納，也可以簽發支票寄送到下列地址給Whistler健身俱樂部：威斯康辛麥迪遜Grant街4938號，也可以設定網路銀行自動轉帳方式，自動轉帳方式請至www.whistlerhealthclub.com/payment確認。

期待很快就能收到您的積極答覆。

Jeremy Gill 敬上
Whistler健身俱樂部

詞彙 patronage 資助，贊助　valued 珍貴的　remind 提醒，使想起
utilize 使用，利用　opt 選擇　check 支票　automatic 自動的

169.

Gill先生為什麼寄信？

(A) 為了要求更新會員資格。

(B) 為了提供相關服務的資訊。

(C) 為了詢問未繳納款項。

(D) 為了中止客戶的權限。

在第二段中，Gill先生告知收信人Bell先生"we have not yet received the payment for October"，可以得知10月的學費尚未繳納，因此寄信的理由可視為(C)。

詞彙 renewal 更新　provide an update 提供情報，告知消息
suspend 保留；中止

170.

關於Bell先生的暗示是什麼？

(A) 以前都是按時繳納。

(B) 每天都在體育館運動。

(C) 他的家位於體育館附近。

(D) 他工作的地方會替他繳納會費。

透過在第二段最後一句"you normally take care of your monthly bill between the 25th and 29th of each month"的部分，可以知道Bell先生平時都是在固定的時間繳納使用費用，因此(A)是正確答案。

171.

根據信件，顧客不能使用的結帳方式是什麼？

(A) 支票。

(B) 轉帳。

(C) 現金。

(D) 信用卡。

最後一段寫到繳款可以以現金，也可以使用支票，也可以透過自動轉帳(automatic payments)，因此在選項中未提及的方式是(D)的信用卡結帳。

[172-175]

Elaine Halpern	1:23 P.M.
陳列室看起來怎麼樣？半小時後有一位重要客戶要來，狀態必須要保持完美才行。	
Mark Stromberg	1:24 P.M.
剛才用拖把清掃過整個空間了，等一下地板就會乾了。	
Darlene Maples	1:25 P.M.
Craig和我按照指示設置了梳妝臺和桌子。陳列了最漂亮的古董家具。	
Elaine Halpern	1:26 P.M.
妳還記得用木材做的都要拋光嗎？	
Mart Stromberg	1:27 P.M.
Russell 先生說不要那樣做。他說買家不喜歡這種外觀。	
Elaine Halpern	1:29 P.M.
哦，我不知道這一點，能這麼說真是萬幸。	
Darlene Maples	1:30 P.M.
預計什麼時候到達？	

Elaine Halpern	1:32 P.M.
我現在在計程車上，10分鐘內會到那邊。到達後會仔細查看整個賣場，看看有沒有我錯過的部分。	
Darlene Maples	1:33 P.M.
好的，為了留下良好的印象，我們會確保一切都正常的。	

詞彙 showroom 展示廳，陳列室　potential 潛在的　mop 拖把；用拖把清掃　dresser 梳妝臺　instruct 指示　antique 古董　polish 拋光，擦亮　check over 檢查，仔細查看　impression 印象

172.

Halpern小姐應該會是在哪裡工作？

(A) 家具店。

(B) 電子產品賣場。

(C) 汽車代理商。

(D) 食品店。

透過從設置梳妝台和桌子(dressers and tables)和「應該讓木製成的一切變得有光澤(polith everything made of wood)」的表達可以推測出話者工作的地方是(A)的家具店。

詞彙 car dealership 汽車銷售處，汽車經銷代理商

173.

根據訊息，他們沒有做的事情是什麼？

(A) 布置商品。

(B) 拖地。

(C) 除去價格標籤。

(D) 陳列商品。

(A)和(D)從1點25分Maples小姐的話中可以得知，(B)是從1點24分Stromberg小姐說的話中可得知的行動，因此選項中話者沒有做的是(C)。

174.

下午1點27分，Stromberg先生說"Mr. Russell instructed us not to"的時候，他暗示的是什麼？

(A) 他沒有與客戶聯繫。

(B) 他今天不上班。

(C) 他正在等待其他指示。

(D) 他什麼都沒拋光。

給定句子的to是to polish anything made of wood的縮寫，因此給定的句子是「被指示不要拋光」，所以說最後Stromberg先生說的意思可以看作是(D)。

175.

Maples小姐接下來要做什麼？

(A) 為Halpern先生叫計程車。

(B) 與客戶交談。

(C) 查看賣場。

(D) 清理陳列室。

在聊天室最後的部分，Maples小姐為了留下好印象說會確認一切(we'll make sure everything looks fine)，她要做的事情是(C)。

[176-180]

> ### Hampton 路工程
>
> 6月10日星期一至6月12日星期三，施工人員將會在Hampton路施工，每天早上6點開始至晚上9點結束，受工程影響的五個地區在Jackson路和Carpenter街之間。上個月的暴風雨導致洪水暴漲，給街道造成了相當大的損失，因此為了維修這些設施將會施工。這期間司機們要避免使用Hampton路，施工期間只會開放各方向的一條車道。如需確認工程的準確位置和可替代使用的道路，請至網站www.oxford.gov/construction。

詞彙 crew 空勤人員；團隊，小組 affect 造成影響 a large amount of 許多的，大量的 flashflood 突然的水災 thunderstorm 雷雨 lane 車道，線道 precise 準確的 alternative 替代的

> ### 市政府對於長期的工程道歉
> Christine Lee 記者
>
> 牛津(6月17日)--Hampton路的工程於6月15日星期六完工5天以來，市區的司機們經歷了嚴重的塞車現象。牛津居民Dean Reynolds抱怨說「平時上班只花35分鐘，但是這周上班前每天都要花兩個小時。」
>
> 其他許多通勤人士也都表達了類似的不滿。昨天晚上，Melissa Carmichael市長在記者會上對於此問題道歉。「對於工程時間延長感到遺憾，但道路受損程度比開工前預想的還要嚴重，幸好現在一切都變好了。」
>
> 根據市長說的話，Hampton路所有車道都重新開放，本週交通狀況將有所改善。否則市政府肯定會接到許多憤怒市民的電話。

詞彙 commute 通勤 press conference 記者會 lengthy 長的 severely 嚴重地 anticipate 預期 now that 由於 mayor's office 市政府

176.

根據公告，關於Hampton 路的工程不符合事實的是？
(A) 整條道路被關閉。
(B) 從早到晚持續進行。
(C) 會顯示在市網站的地圖上。
(D) 在多數地點進行。

在第一段引文公告的後半部分，說明只開放一條車道(only one lane will be open)，因此(A)的內容與事實不符。因為作業時間是上午6點到晚上9點，所以說(B)為事實，施工位置可以在市網站上確認，所以(C)也是事實。 透過five affected areas一詞可以得知有多個地方受到工程影響，因此(D)的內容也是正確的。

詞彙 shut down 關門，關閉 map 地圖 multiple 多數的

177.

Hampton路發生災害的原因是什麼？
(A) 暴雪。
(B) 交通事故。
(C) 水位上升。
(D) 瓦斯爆炸。

"flashflood that happened during last month's thunderstorms"是災害的原因，因此將flashflood(水災，洪水)改寫成Rising water levels的(C)才是正確答案。

詞彙 explosion 爆炸

178.

關於Hampton 路的道路工程，提到的是什麼？
(A) 由兩間不同的公司負責。
(B) 交通沒有受到阻礙。
(C) 尚未支付工程款。
(D) 時間比預期長。

第一段引文公告上寫著工期為6月10日至12日，但第二段引文報導上寫著工程已於6月15日結束。另外在報導中，市長說他對漫長的施工時間(lengthy construction period)表示遺憾，因此在選項中提及道路施工的事實是(D)。

詞彙 interfere 妨礙

179.

6月16日發生了什麼事？
(A) 道路工程完工。
(B) 舉行了記者會。
(C) 禁止道路通行。
(D) 街道被檢查。

第二篇報導是6月17日撰寫的，考慮到報導中提到的"Mayor Melisa Carmichael apologized for the problems at a press conference last night."的話，就可以得知6月16日有記者會，因此(B)是正確答案。

180.

關於牛津居民，暗示了什麼？
(A) 對道路工程不滿。
(B) 其中多數表示對市長感到不滿。
(C) 反對道路工程。
(D) 其中一部分由市政府籌備會議。

從報導的第二段"Many other commuters made similar complaints."中可以看出答案是(A)。由於居民並非直接對市長表示不滿，因此(B)不能成為正確答案，而將表達不滿解釋為「反對」是提高一個層面的，所以(C)也是錯誤的。

詞彙 object to 反對

[181-185]

> ### Benjamin's
> ### 今日的精選菜單
>
> 點主菜的話可以選擇湯或沙拉。另外，客人還可以免費挑選冷飲。今日的精選菜單每天都會變更，所有可選擇的開胃菜和主菜都可以在一般菜單上找到。
>
> | 開胃菜 | 價格 | 主菜 | 價格 |
> |---|---|---|---|
> | 炸魷魚 | $4.99 | 海鮮燉飯 | $18.99 |
> | 酸橘汁醃魚 | $6.99 | 牛肉千層麵 | $15.99 |
> | 烤茄子 | $5.99 | 沙威瑪 | $19.99 |
> | 鮪魚沙拉 | $6.99 | 鮮蝦義大利寬麵 | $17.99 |
>
> 持有 Benjamin's會員卡的顧客不適用於上述菜單的優惠。

詞彙 entrée 主菜 beverage 飲料 on a daily basis 每一天，每日

收件者：benjamin@benjamins.com
寄件者：lisajacobs@thismail.com
主旨：午餐
日期：10月11日
附件：receipt.jpg

親愛的Morris先生，

我的名字是Lisa Jacobs。昨天10月10日，我在貴餐廳和我職場的一位同事一起吃了午飯。我真的很喜歡為我準備的餐點，開胃菜和主菜令人印象深刻，女服務員推薦的甜點巧克力慕斯是我吃過有史以來最棒的，以後一定會再去您的餐廳。

但是從我附在電子郵件中的收據照片可以知道這費用太高了。本應該只要付18.99美元的，但我卻付了28.99美元的餐費，我相信這次是單純的失誤，請退還10美元的差額至我的信用卡。

謝謝。

Lisa Jacobs

詞彙 thoroughly 徹底地，完全地 chocolate mousse 巧克力慕斯
receipt 收據 extra 多餘的，額外的

181.

點主菜的人會免費得到什麼？
(A) 配菜。
(B) 沙拉和咖啡。
(C) 冷飲。
(D) 甜點。

在第一段引文的開頭部分，點主菜的人可以免費獲得湯或沙拉(soup or salad)及冷飲(cold beverage)。正確答案是(C)。

182.

可以知道關於Benjamin's的什麼？
(A) 每週提供5天的精選菜餚。
(B) 每個季節都會更改菜單。
(C) 位於購物中心內。
(D) 有些顧客適用於折扣價格。

菜單下面的"Customers with a Benjamin's Membership Card will not have any discounts applied to the above menu items. "，將其逆向推想的話，點的餐點不為今日精選料理的會員卡持有者將會得到折扣優惠，因此(D)才是正確答案。

183.

Jacobs小姐提到關於自己吃的甜點的事情是什麼？
(A) 很好吃。
(B) 以前過來時曾點過的。
(C) 詢問其料理方法。
(D) 認為它與飲食很相配。

Jacobs小姐吃到的甜點是巧克力慕斯，她說這是有史以來最好吃的(the best I've ever had)，對它的評價很高，因此選項中關於甜點的事項可視為(A)。

184.

Jacobs小姐為什麼發電子郵件？
(A) 為了預約。
(B) 為了稱讚女服務員。
(C) 為了退還部分款項。
(D) 為了詢問下一次的精選菜單。

在電子郵件的第二段中，Jacobs小姐告知自己被要求支付太多餐費之後表示"I would like to have the extra $10.00 refunded to"說明自己的要求，也就是說，Jacobs小姐是為了退款而發送電子郵件的，因此撰寫電子郵件的理由就是(C)。

185.

Jacobs小姐主菜吃了什麼？
(A) 海鮮燉飯。
(B) 牛肉千層麵。
(C) 沙威瑪。
(D) 鮮蝦義大利寬麵。

從電子郵件中"I should have been charged only $18.99"的部分可以知道她吃的餐點價格原本是18.99美元。如果在菜單上找到相同價格的餐點的話，(A)的海鮮燉飯就是正確答案。

[186-190]

Cumberland Clothes 問卷調查

我們Cumberland Clothes很珍惜顧客。填寫這份問卷調查之後，交給店內工作人員，您將會獲得價值5美元的優惠券。如果您留下姓名和聯繫方式時，則將參加抽獎活動，會給予10位中獎者特別的禮物。

下列項目會給我打幾分？

	非常好	好	普通	糟糕	非常糟糕
商品挑選			✓		
商品價格		✓			
商品品質				✓	
商品款式					✓

想說的話：以前我在這裡每個月都會去購物，但以後再也不會來了，衣服老氣又很容易破裂，如果在這裡購物感覺就像在浪費錢一樣，所以我不會再來了。
姓名：Wilma Hamilton
聯繫方式：whamilton@personalmail.com

詞彙 value 珍惜，重視 drawing 抽獎 old fashioned 老式的 get
worn out 破爛，磨損 waste 浪費

收件者：Daniel Marbut, Raisa Andropov, Jordan West, Elaine Nash
寄件者：Craig Murphy
主旨：問卷調查結果
日期：8月21日

在過去六個禮拜，透過線上和線下問卷調查共收到了1,700個回覆，總體上結果令人失望，但是這樣的反應可以明確地說明為什麼我們會失去這麼多顧客。基本上顧客都不喜歡我們服裝的設計，都會使用比如「不漂亮」、「老氣」、「退流行」等等話語。也有很多顧客認為我們的服裝做得不好，他們抱怨會有破掉、撕裂的以及褪色的商品，同樣也是不滿意我們提供的服務。

我冒昧地和所有在問卷上留下聯繫方式的人交談過，並得到了其中多數人的詳細答覆。我們要做的就是改變我們銷售的商品品牌，否則我們馬上就要破產了。

詞彙 overall 總體上 disappointing 令人失望的 basically 基本上 refer to 指出，指稱 out of style 退流行的 rip 撕破 tear 扯破，撕裂 fade 褪色 take the liberty of 冒昧地，擅自 in-depth 深刻的，詳細的 go out of business 破產，歇業

大降價

Cumberland Clothes
全部分店
於10月1日至31日折扣優惠。

新品服裝即將亮相。
銷售的服裝品牌如下：
Urias, Marconi, Andretti, Christopher's.

您將會愛上這些服裝的品質和設計，
是最新流行的時裝，
且我們所引以為傲的價格會維持不變，
請不要擔心。
請到全新的Cumberland Clothes，
我們販賣顧客們想要的服飾。

186.
關於Hamilton小姐，能知道的是什麼？
(A) 因為品質而從Cumberland Clothes購買商品。
(B) 認為Cumberland Clothes的商品價格過高。
(C) 屬於Cumberland 購物俱樂部。
(D) 收到Cumberland Clothes的優惠券。

Ms. Hamilton這個名字可以在第一段引文調查問卷的填寫者欄中發現。在調查問卷一開始的部分，填寫調查問卷後，如果交給Cumberland Clothes賣場員工，將會獲得5美元優惠券(a coupon for $5)，因此(D)為正確答案。

詞彙 belong to 屬於

187.
Hamilton小姐是如何看待Cumberland Clothes的產品？
(A) 認為它退流行了。
(B) 認為它價格過高。
(C) 認為它做得非常好。
(D) 覺得它色彩很華麗。

在第一段引文調查問卷的Comment項目中，她評論說Cumberland Clothes的服裝太老氣(too old fashioned)，容易破損(get worn out quickly)，因此將old fashioned改寫為out of style的(A)就是正確答案。

188.
關於Murphy先生的暗示是什麼？
(A) 他是Cumberland Clothes的所有人。

(B) 他向Hamilton小姐發送電子郵件。
(C) 他在市場調查企業工作。
(D) 他不喜歡Cumberland Clothes的產品。

Murphy先生是第二個引文中寄郵件的人，在最後一個段落中，可以知道他聯繫過所有在問券調查留下聯絡方式的人(I took the liberty of speaking with every individual who left contact information on the survey)，另外第一個引文的Hamilton小姐在問卷調查上留下了自己的電子郵件地址，因此可以推測出Murphy先生可能試圖透過電子郵件與她聯繫，因此(B)是正確答案。

189.
Murphy先生提議要做什麼？
(A) 販賣新品牌的產品。
(B) 更好地培訓工作人員。
(C) 降價。
(D) 進行新的問卷調查。

在通知的最後部分，Murphy先生提出了應該要更換銷售產品的品牌(change the brands of the items we sell)的主張，因此(A)是正確的答案。

190.
客戶的不滿事項中廣告中未提及的是什麼？
(A) 服裝的款式。
(B) 顧客服務。
(C) 擁有的產品。
(D) 服裝的設計。

透過廣告中介紹的新服飾品牌的名稱和"the quality and the look of these clothes, the most fashionable on the market"等類似表述可以確認到選項中的內容，但(B)顧客服務的內容在廣告中找不到。

[191-195]

2月15日

致親愛的Swanson先生，

恭喜您被Greenbrier飯店錄用了。您的入職日期是3月10日，您將隸屬於客房服務部，有時會像您現在的工作一樣忙著準備食物，或者是可能要幫客房裡的客人送食物，也有可能會在三樓的高級餐廳Crawford's當服務員。

客房服務部的員工經常得要穿著制服，在廚房或是送食物時則要穿白色褲子和白色襯衫，在Crawford's工作時，則需要穿著黑色褲子和帶有紐扣的白色襯衫。 請填寫隨信附上的訂單，並希望您能夠立即回覆。上面提到的每件衣服，其中各兩件的價錢將由Greenbrier飯店支付，其餘的商品則需由您負擔。

Tabitha Lang 敬上
Greenbrier飯店客房服務部主管

詞彙 at times 有時候 wait staff 服務員 dining establishment 餐廳，飲食店 button-down shirt 帶有鈕扣的襯衫

Imperial Fashions

Crossway 路874號
英國，倫敦
WP36 7TR

訂單

顧客姓名：Allan Swanson
地址：英國倫敦Baker街39號, OL432SE
電話號碼：954-3922
電子郵件 地址：allanswanson@thamesmail.com

商品	數量	單價	合計
褲子,黑色(L)	2	£20	£40
襯衫,白色(L)	1	£17	£17
鈕扣襯衫,白色(L)	3	£25	£75
褲子,白色(L)	2	£22	£44
		總計	£176

付款人 Greenbrier 飯店客房服務部
顧客編號 9404392

客房服務部日程

4月1日 – 7日

員工 Allan Swanson

日期	時間	場所	備註
4月1日	9 A.M. – 6 P.M.	廚房	送貨+準備食物
4月2日	9 A.M. – 6 P.M.	廚房	送貨
4月3日	1 P.M. – 9 P.M.	Crawford's	服務
4月4日	1 P.M. – 9 P.M.	Crawford's	服務+準備食物
4月5日	6 P.M. – 2 A.M.	廚房	送貨

參考
4月6日和7日沒有工作，但若是其他員工兩天中申請一天的休假時，此日程表可能會更動。若是需要您上班時，最晚會在4月4日下午6點之前通知您。

詞彙 **day off** 休息日　**be subject to** 可能

191.

信件的目的是什麼？
(A) 為了說明過程。
(B) 為了告知議程。
(C) 為了提出請求。
(D) 為了說明。

在告知入職通知的同時還對工作需要的各種事項進行說明，例如工作內容及服裝規定等等，因此信件的目的可視為(D)。

192.

Crawford's是什麼？
(A) 便利商店。
(B) 餐廳。
(C) 咖啡廳。
(D) 麵包店。

在第一段引文信件中，Crawford's被介紹為our fine-dining establishment(高級餐廳)，因此(B)是正確答案。

193.

關於Swanson先生，可以知道什麼？
(A) 預計將會在飯店的前臺工作。
(B) 2月將會開始做新工作。
(C) 具有在飲食行業的經歷。
(D) 他將會領到時薪。

查看信件中的內容，Swanson先生要做的工作是準備食物，送貨，服務等等，因此(A)是錯誤的內容，開始工作的日期是March 10，所以(B)也與事實不符。正確答案是(C)，透過"you will assist with food preparation like the type you're doing at your current job" 這句可以知道他現在的職場也在做與準備食物相關的工作，關於工資，因為是完全沒有提到的內容，所以(D)也是錯誤的。

194.

Swanson先生該還給飯店多少錢？
(A) 17英鎊。
(B) 20英鎊。
(C) 22英鎊。
(D) 25英鎊。

信件最後的部分說明每件衣服各兩件(two of each clothing item)的價錢將會由飯店方面負擔，其餘部分應由本人負擔。另一方面，查看第二個引文訂單，購買超過兩件的只有Button-Down Shirt，因為其價格是25英鎊，最後他要還給飯店的金額是(D)25英鎊。

195.

根據日程表，關於Swanson先生的哪一項為事實？
(A) 4月3日應該要穿黑色褲子。
(B) 4月1日至7日間休息3天。
(C) 4月2日將會上夜班。
(D) 4月5日將會料理食物。

第三段引文的日程表和各段引文的內容要互相比較。從日程表上來看，4月3日是要到Crawford's當服務員的日子，因為在第二段引文中提到在餐廳工作時要穿黑色褲子和帶紐扣的白色襯衫，所以(A)為正確答案。休息日為4月6日和7日，因此(B)並非為事實。(C)4月2日的工作是從上午9點到下午6點，所以這也是錯誤的內容。從日程表上來看，4月5日不是要準備食物，而是要進行送貨工作，因此(D)也是錯誤的。

[196-200]

Archer 食品店來到紐黑文

Nabil Apu

紐黑文(1月4日)--擁有全國連鎖店的Archer食品店的總裁表示希望今年能在紐黑文開店。David Leatherwood提到「紐黑文市內沒有超市」，他補充「如果能在那裡開店的話，當地居民將會得到優惠。」

Archer以其販賣的多種價格低廉的新鮮食品而受到高度評價。為了方便購物者，所有Archer賣場都設有熟食店及麵店，每週7天全天24小時營業。大部分的Archer賣場都位在被稱為食品沙漠的地方，這代表著是相對來說難以買到新鮮食品的地方，因此聽到Archer可能要到這裡來的消息之後，當地居民都積極響應。

詞彙 lack 沒有，缺少 be highly regarded for 以～獲得高度評價 deli 熟食店 convenience 便利，方便 feature 以～為特徵 food desert 食物沙漠(很難找到新鮮食物的地方) relative 相對的 react 反應

收件者：Francis Zuniga <fzuniga@valiantmail.com>
寄件者：David Leatherwood <david@archer.com>
主旨：紐黑文賣場
日期：1月11日

致親愛的Zuniga小姐，

恭喜您被選為預計在紐黑本開業的Archer食品店所有人。您的提案不僅僅是最為突出的，而且我們也贊成您振興紐黑文市中心的企劃。

首先第一件要做的事就是選定位置。賣場應位於25,000平方英尺和35,000平方英尺之間的面積，並位在單層建築物裡，且應該要位於主要街道沿線的地鐵站步行範圍之內，並且擁有足夠大小的停車場。

您可能很清楚該城市不允許市中心的商店在凌晨2點到凌晨6點之間營業，我正在進行遊說以改變這些規定，但並沒有成功。

當您找到可以接受的地點，請告訴我。

David Leatherwood 敬上

詞彙 select 選定，選擇 approve of 批准，贊成 order of business 要做的事，課題 single-story building 單層建築 ample 充分的 lobby 大廳；遊說 meet with a success 成功

詞彙 property 財產 foot traffic 流動人口 retail store 零售店

196.

Leatherwood先生是誰？
(A) 紐黑文居民。
(B) 調查員。
(C) 消費者。
(D) 公司總裁。

在第一段引文報導的開頭部分，名叫David Leatherwood的人物被介紹為"CEO of Archer Grocery Store"。正確答案是把CEO(總裁，社長)改寫為company president的(D)。

197.

與報導中第二段第九行的"relative"一詞最相似的是？
(A) 家庭。
(B) 過度的。
(C) 不幸的。
(D) 相對的。

relative表示「比較」或「相對」的意思，因此(D)的comparative為正確答案。

詞彙 familial 家庭的 excessive 過度的 comparative 比較的，相對的

198.

Leatherwood先生為什麼會發電子郵件？
(A) 為了說明限制條件。
(B) 為了提出合約。
(C) 為了促成交易。
(D) 為了答覆提案。

在第二段引文電子郵件中，Leatherwood先生向即將成為新店主的Zuniga小姐說明了加入賣場所必須滿足的條件，即佔地面積、建築物層數、位置等相關事項，因此發送電子郵件的目的可視為(A)。

詞彙 restriction 限制，限制條件

199.

紐黑文Archer食品店與其他Archer食品店有什麼不同？
(A) 不會有麵包店。
(B) 將位於二樓。
(C) 每天晚上會關門。
(D) 販售進口食品。

在第二段引文電子郵件中"I'm sure you're aware that the city requires stores downtown to shut their doors from 2:00 to 6:00 in the morning."可以找到正確答案的線索。第一段引文報導中介紹Archer賣場是24小時營業，從電子郵件中可以知道紐黑文市政府規定從凌晨2點至6點禁止營業，因此紐黑文的Archer食品店可能凌晨不能營業，因此(C)才是正確答案。

200.

Zuniga小姐可以向Leatherwood先生推薦的位置在哪裡？
(A) Main 街743號。
(B) Maynard 街58號。
(C) Avery 路912號。
(D) White Horse 路44號。

房地產可在第三段引文圖表中找到符合電子郵件中所提及的條件。由於賣場面積應要在25,000到35,000平方英尺之間，因此(C)不包括在候選裡，而且不為單層建築的(A)和(D)也不能成為推薦對象，因此滿足所有條件的房地產(B)才是正確答案。

Actual Test 5

PART 5				p.132
101. (C)	**102.** (C)	**103.** (A)	**104.** (B)	**105.** (D)
106. (A)	**107.** (B)	**108.** (B)	**109.** (D)	**110.** (B)
111. (B)	**112.** (A)	**113.** (D)	**114.** (D)	**115.** (A)
116. (C)	**117.** (C)	**118.** (C)	**119.** (B)	**120.** (C)
121. (A)	**122.** (B)	**123.** (C)	**124.** (B)	**125.** (C)
126. (D)	**127.** (A)	**128.** (B)	**129.** (C)	**130.** (A)

PART 6				p.135
131. (C)	**132.** (D)	**133.** (A)	**134.** (B)	**135.** (B)
136. (C)	**137.** (B)	**138.** (D)	**139.** (A)	**140.** (C)
141. (D)	**142.** (A)	**143.** (C)	**144.** (B)	**145.** (B)
146. (A)				

PART 7				p.139
147. (C)	**148.** (B)	**149.** (C)	**150.** (A)	**151.** (B)
152. (C)	**153.** (D)	**154.** (A)	**155.** (A)	**156.** (C)
157. (C)	**158.** (D)	**159.** (D)	**160.** (C)	**161.** (A)
162. (C)	**163.** (B)	**164.** (C)	**165.** (D)	**166.** (A)
167. (A)	**168.** (D)	**169.** (C)	**170.** (D)	**171.** (A)
172. (D)	**173.** (A)	**174.** (D)	**175.** (A)	**176.** (D)
177. (A)	**178.** (B)	**179.** (C)	**180.** (B)	**181.** (A)
182. (D)	**183.** (C)	**184.** (A)	**185.** (B)	**186.** (D)
187. (D)	**188.** (A)	**189.** (B)	**190.** (B)	**191.** (A)
192. (D)	**193.** (C)	**194.** (B)	**195.** (D)	**196.** (D)
197. (C)	**198.** (A)	**199.** (C)	**200.** (B)	

PART 5

101.

Collins小姐在會議時談到與Delmont Shipping簽訂合約的若干好處。

(A) reasons
(B) opinions
(C) advantages
(D) considerations

需要找到一個名詞能夠最自然地修飾of所引導的介系詞句型。正確答案是其意義為「優點」的(C) advantages。

詞彙 cite 引用，提及 advantage 優點 reason 理由，理性 consideration 考慮

102.

為了提高工作現場工人們的效率，安裝了新的切割機。

(A) effective
(B) effecting
(C) effectiveness
(D) effectively

作為increase的受詞最恰當的是表示「效率」意義的(C) effectiveness。

詞彙 cutting machine 切割機 effectiveness 效率 factory floor 工廠，工作現場

103.

對於變更加入會員條款有興趣的人們有幾種選擇。

(A) Several
(B) All
(C) Much
(D) Little

內容上必須要完整表達「部分用戶有幾個條件」的意思，正確答案是(A)的Several。(B)與空格後面的句子句意不符，空格後面接options複數型，因此與不可數名詞一起使用的(C)和(D)不會是正確答案。

詞彙 option 選擇 exist 存在 terms 條件

104.

簽書會的門票將在一周內按照先後順序發放。

(A) are giving
(B) are being given
(C) have been giving
(D) will give

因為主詞是事物的"tickets for the book signing"，give的形態應該要是被動型，因此(B)和(C)其中之一為正確答案，又與現在完成式all week long(整整一周)的副詞句型不相符，所以(B)是正確答案。

詞彙 book signing 簽書會 first-come, first-served basis 先到先得原則 all week long 整整一周

105.

市長希望在六月初實施改善城市基礎設施的計劃。

(A) attract
(B) report
(C) approach
(D) implement

需要找到一個能夠讓the plan作為受詞，又能夠與"at the beginning of June"副詞句型相匹配的動詞。正確答案是表示「實施」意義的(D)implement。

詞彙 implement 實施 infrastructure 基礎設施 attract 引起，吸引

106.

自從本地幾家製造商開始僱用更多的員工以來，大幅改善了當地的失業率。

(A) tremendously
(B) eventually
(C) responsibly
(D) quietly

要找到能夠自然地修飾數值失業率(unemployment rate)的副詞。正確答案是(A)的tremendously。

詞彙 unemployment rate 失業率 tremendously 巨大地，極大地 manufacturer 製造企業，製造業者 eventually 最終，終於 responsibly 有責任感地

69

107.

主管們正在調查如何預防類似昨天發生的事故。

(A) incidental

(B) incidents

(C) incidentally

(D) incident

空格中應該要填入與happened yesterday及can be avoided相符合的單字，因此正確答案是指事故的(B)和(D)之一，但因為空格前面沒有不定冠詞，所以應該要填入複數型的(B)。

詞彙　investigate 調查　incident 事故　avoid 避開　incidental 偶然的　incidentally 偶然地

108.

想要在冬天休假的人需要先得到主管的許可。

(A) for

(B) with

(C) by

(D) on

clear A with B是「B允許A」的意思。正確答案是(B)的with。

詞彙　take time off 請假　clear A with B B允許 A

109.

一般來說，選擇新供應商時，公司會選擇價格最低廉的地方。

(A) afford

(B) afforded

(C) affording

(D) affordable

選項中能夠最自然地修飾option的形容詞是(D)的affordable(價格適中的)。

詞彙　as a general rule 一般來說，通常　affordable 適中的，負擔得起的　afford 有餘裕去～

110.

那位員工為了表示他預約失誤的歉意，將Carpenter小姐的房間升級成了套房。

(A) awarded

(B) upgraded

(C) announced

(D) paid

思考一下飯店員工作為道歉的方法能為a suite(套房)提供什麼樣的服務，就可以馬上找到正確答案。正確答案是(B)的upgraded(升級)。

詞彙　suite 套房　as a way of 為了～以此方法

111.

雖然僅有三人應聘了該職位，但他們都具備有充分的資格，很難選出理想的候選。

(A) each

(B) all

(C) both

(D) none

注意連接詞while的意義並留意關係代名詞之後的內容來找正確答案。由於應徵者有三人，因此(C)不能成為正確答案，(D)與句子的整體含義不符，所以(A)和(B)中有一個為正確答案，動詞是were所以正確答案是表示複數意義的(B)。

詞彙　highly qualified 具備充分資格的　candidate 候補，候選人

112.

由於突然宣布新項目的關係，有一些人變更了自己的行程。

(A) changed

(B) been changing

(C) will change

(D) are changed

have被用作使役動詞時，如果事物在受詞位置上的話，受詞補語就應要變成過去分詞，因此過去分詞的(A)就是正確答案。

詞彙　time off work 休假　grant 同意，授予

113.

如果在合約上簽名的話，在48小時之內必須匯款支付原料款項的資金。

(A) accounts

(B) intentions

(C) matter

(D) funds

要找到能夠最自然地修飾形容詞句型"to pay for the raw materials"的名詞。正確答案是(D)的funds(資金，金錢)。

詞彙　raw material 原料，原材料　account 帳號，帳戶　intention 意圖，意向

114.

實習員工們在Ampere公司開始工作的第一天就和總裁一起吃了午餐。

(A) him

(B) his own

(C) he

(D) himself

因為沒有缺漏的句子組成部分，空格中應該填入強調用的反身代名詞。正確答案是(D)。

115.

Kennedy小姐最多將會批准6名員工參加本週末在狄蒙因舉行的研討會。

(A) permit

(B) credit

(C) remit

(D) submit

如果知道permit A to B表示「允許A做B」，就可以很容易地找到正確答案。正確答案是(A)的permit。

詞彙　credit 相信，信任；信用　remit 匯款

116.

那位畫家打算在Furman美術館即將舉辦的展覽上展出30幅以上最新作品。

(A) has been intended
(B) will have been intended
(C) intends
(D) is intended

主詞是表現人的the artist，因此intend(意圖)的形態應要是主動語態。選項中的主動語態只有(C)。

詞彙 intend to 意圖，打算 upcoming 即將到來的

117.

所有應聘者在參加公司的工作能力測試前都要面試。

(A) applications
(B) applies
(C) applicants
(D) applicable

參加工作能力測驗(firm's competency test)跟必須面試(must be interviewed)的人是(C)應徵者。

詞彙 competency test 能力測驗，資格測驗 application 志願，申請 applicable 適用的

118.

Thompson小姐與Roberts先生的會議一結束就聯絡顧客。

(A) instead of
(B) as a result of
(C) as soon as
(D) in spite of

空格之後會延續句子，因此空格中應該要填入能夠起到連接詞作用的表達。在選項中，能夠起到連接詞作用的只有(C)的as soon as(一～就)，其餘都是像介系詞一樣使用的詞句。

詞彙 get in touch with 聯絡 conclude 下結論，結束 as a result of 結果是～ in spite of 不管，無論

119.

當時的值班主管Hoskins小姐批准了承包公司的倉庫出入許可。

(A) Clear
(B) Clearance
(C) Clearly
(D) Cleared

為了讓空格後的介系詞句子可以修飾就必須要填入名詞(B)的clearance。作為參考，clearance既可以用來表示「整理」，也可以表示「准許」，這個問題中為後者的意思。

詞彙 clearance 整理；准許，許可 contractor 契約人，承包商，承包公司 on duty 值班

120.

Fulton 研究從去年11月開始聘用了在幾家實驗室工作的科學家。

(A) will hire
(B) will be hiring
(C) has been hiring
(D) was hired

如果留意到"ever since last November"這一副詞子句的話，就會發現空格上應該要填入現在完成型。正確答案是使用現在完成進行時態的(C)。

詞彙 laboratory 實驗室

121.

有許多當地媒體的記者們參加了RC Technology的產品展示會。

(A) members
(B) performers
(C) editors
(D) reporters

「新聞媒體人們」或「記者們」的表述可以以"members of the media"來表達。如果留意到問題的修飾子句"of the local media"，就會知道(A)是正確答案。

詞彙 demonstration 示範，示威 a large number of 許多的 editor 編輯

122.

公司的新商標贏得了顧客們和業界人士的廣泛好評。

(A) insides
(B) insiders
(C) inside
(D) insider

如果掌握了both A and B的並列結構的話，就能夠輕易找到正確答案。找到能夠和Customers處於對等關係的事物，就會知道正確答案就是表示人的複數名詞(B)insiders。

詞彙 logo 商標 widespread 廣泛的 praise 稱讚，讚美 industry insider 業內人士，業界關係者

123.

要求提出建議時，有幾位員工提出了個有趣的建議。

(A) admission
(B) submission
(C) request
(D) approval

為了要員工們提出提議，可以推測出得要先有「要求」，因此正確答案是(C)的request(要求)。

詞彙 proposal 提議 deem 認為是～ admission 許可 submission 提交；屈服 approval 批准

124.

在交叉路口進行道路施工期間，車輛得繞道。

(A) intersect
(B) intersection
(C) intersective
(D) intersected

思考一下在什麼場合施工才能讓車輛繞道的話，很快就能找到正確答案。正確答案是表示「交叉路口」的(B)intersection。即使考慮到空格前面有冠詞，正確答案也應當為名詞。

詞彙 divert 繞道 construction work 施工工程 intersection 交叉路口 intersect 交叉

125.

Lincoln Interior在開始工作之前總是會先發報價單給顧客。

(A) endorsement
(B) warranty
(C) estimate
(D) support

思考一下在開始裝修之前能提供什麼。正確答案是(C)的estimate，以price estimate表示「報價單」的意思。

詞彙 price estimate 報價單　endorsement 支持；背書　warranty 保證

126.

即使報導遭到編輯拒絕，其他雜誌社也可能會也有興趣刊登報導。

(A) Since
(B) However
(C) In addition
(D) Even if

報導被拒絕和報導可能會被刊登含有相反的意義，因此空格中應該填入表示讓步的(D)Even if。

詞彙 even if 雖然　reject 否決，拒絕　publish 發表，發行　in addition 此外

127.

由於雪下得太大，所以在鏟雪車過來之前市中心大部分的車輛都無法動彈。

(A) so
(B) very
(C) too
(D) most

只有知道表示「太～所以～」意思的so~that~句型才能找到正確答案。正確答案是(A)。

詞彙 snowfall 降雪　snowplow 除雪機，鏟雪車

128.

檢查員想確認是否有遵守安全規定。

(A) arrange
(B) determine
(C) clear
(D) approve

讓我們想想檢查員(inspector)在是否遵守安全規定方面會希望什麼。正確答案是有「查明」之意的(B) determine。

詞彙 inspector 調查員　determine 決定；查明　safety regulation 安全規定　approve 准許

129.

如果身份證不能儘快修改好的話，身份證持有者將無法打開整個設施的任何一個門。

(A) fix
(B) will fix
(C) are fixed
(D) have fixed

條件句的主詞是the ID cards，因此此動詞位置應要用被動式型態。選項中，符合被動式型態的只有(C)的are fixed。

130.

合約必須要在星期五晚上之前簽訂，否則合約將被視為無效。

(A) by
(B) within
(C) about
(D) in

「到～為止」的時間意義可以以介系詞by來表示，因此(A)是正確答案。作為參考，by和表示特定時間的話一起使用，而(B)的within和within one week是與表示一段時間的句子一起使用。

詞彙 agreement 協議，協定　invalid 無效的，沒有效力的

PART 6

[131-134]

收件者: rclark@betaengineering.com
寄件者: lmarlowe@personalmail.com
主旨: 工程師職位
日期: 9月28日

親愛的Clark先生，

昨天我透過掛號信件收到您的招聘信，和家人 **131.** 討論之後，我決定接受你的建議，期待著不久後能在Beta Engineering工作。

在您的來信中，**132.** 您提到希望我從10月15日起開始工作，您是否能夠等到11月1日？我現在的僱主聲稱一定要在辭職前30天通知，而且我還要帶著家人一起搬到新城市，這會需要 **133.** 一些時間。

關於您提議的有關 **134.** 金錢方面的補償和福利待遇，我很滿意。我會在合約上簽名，明天就會寄給您。

Lewis Marlowe 敬上

詞彙 certified mail 掛號信　in the near future 不久的將來　current 現在的　employer 僱主　notice 通知　resign 簽名　financial 金融的，財政的　benefits package 福利待遇

131.

(A) discussed
(B) discussion
(C) discussing
(D) discusses

空格前面有介系詞after，空格中可以放入名詞或動名詞，如果考慮到空格後面的the matter，應該要填入可以將此作為受詞的動名詞，因此(C)的discussing是正確答案。

132.

(A) 如果把我的年薪提高10,000美元左右，可能會更理想。
(B) 我想儘快在我的公司開始工作。
(C) 我再考慮一下這個問題對我來說重要。
(D) 在您的來信中，您提到希望我從10月15日起開始工作。

在空格之後的文章中在請求諒解推遲工作開始日期，因此空格中

要填入提及對方要求開始工作日期的(D)，才能完整表達出最自然的文章脈絡。

詞彙 ideal 理想的 tenure 任期 firm 公司 consideration 考慮

133.

(A) some
(B) few
(C) many
(D) any

為了要完整表達出「搬家需要一些時間」的意義，必須要填入(A)的some。從語法上來看，與可數名詞一起使用的(B)和(C)不會是正確答案，(D)的any主要是使用於否定句或是疑問句。

134.

(A) compensate
(B) compensation
(C) compensated
(D) compensatory

能夠讓形容詞financial修飾，並且完整表達出「金錢上的補償」含義的是(B)的compensation。作為參考，這裡所謂的金錢補償，歸根究底就是指薪水。

詞彙 compensate 補償 compensatory 補償的，賠償的

[135-138]

收件者: 全體部門經理
寄件者: Jason Cheswick
主旨: 資金
日期: 3月25日

就如同你們所知道的，部門資金是按季度發放。**135.**今年第一季度的最後一天是3月31日，直到那時候尚未使用的資金，要以書面說明應該要留存預算的**136.**理由，否則將會轉為公司的一般資金，同時，沒有使用到全部金額時，**137.**在下一季度的預算將會減少。已超支使用季度預算時，最晚要在4月4日之前需要一份說明其理由的**138.**文件，超出預算所使用的金額，除非我另有決定，否則將會從第二季度預算中提取。

詞彙 distribute 分配 on a quarterly 按季度 general fund 一般資金 budget 預算 decrease 減少，縮減 exceed 超過 documentation 文件；寫成文件 extract 抽出，提取

135.

(A) 我們正在考慮修改這項政策。
(B) 今年第一季度的最後一天是3月31日。
(C) 如果是急需的情況，可申請追加資金。
(D) 我不能使用給你的資金。

要注意在後面句子中的by that time的表達並找出正確答案。即空格中應包含表示具體期限的詞語，而這種敘述在(B)中以March 31來表達。

詞彙 have access to 接近，利用

136.

(A) where
(B) when
(C) why
(D) how

前後的文章脈絡上應該要完整表達出解釋資金要留在預算中的理由，因此(C)是正確答案。

137.

(A) has resulted
(B) may result
(C) will have resulted
(D) is resulting

名詞子句failure to spend all of the money代替了條件句。也就是說，這個名詞子句表達的是如果失敗的條件意義，因此空格中應該要填入單純使用假設語氣的時態(B)。

138.

(A) document
(B) documented
(C) documentable
(D) documentation

如果考慮到動詞need，空格中可能會填入成為need受詞的(A)document(文件，文檔)或(D)documentation(文件；寫成文件)，但是為了要加入可數名詞document，則前面需要有冠詞或所有格等，但是因為沒有這些東西，所以正確答案是不可數名詞(D)。

[139-142]

本森住宅價格繼續攀升

本森(8月19日)--根據最新統計顯示，本森個別住宅區價格在過去14個月裡連續上漲。7月，市區3間臥室的住宅平均價格為147,400美元，**139.**這比6月份的平均價格還要上漲了1.2%。

隨著**140.**人口的急劇增加，本森目前面臨住宅短缺的現象。會發生這樣的事情是由於附近幾家企業擴張事業，僱用了相當多的員工的關係。

在本森的建築公司正忙於建設新住宅，**141.**但第一棟住宅預計要到11月份才會完工，如此一來預計房價將會在一定程度上**142.**穩定下來。

詞彙 latest 最新的，最近的 statistics 統計，統計學 in a row 成一排，持續 shortage 不足 dramatically 戲劇性地 be busying 忙於～ stabilize 使穩定 to some extent 一定程度上

139.

(A) 這比6月份的平均價格還要上漲了1.2%。
(B) 居民可透過多間房地產企業出售住房。
(C) 7月份房屋價格小幅下滑。
(D) 有一些居民認為公寓更方便。

前文介紹了有關現在房價的資訊，因此在空格中也要填入與住宅價格相關的內容，才能形成自然的文章脈絡。正確答案是通過具體數據表明住房價格漲幅的(A)。

詞彙 real estate agency 房地產仲介 by a slight amount 稍微
convenient 便利的

140.

(A) unemployment
(B) income
(C) population
(D) taxation

如果從邏輯上思考是什麼導致住宅價格上漲的話，就能輕易找到
正確答案。正確答案是(C)的population(人口)。

詞彙 income 收入 taxation 課稅，稅制

141.

(A) or
(B) when
(C) before
(D) but

要找到能夠將建設公司正在建設住宅的事實以及住宅不會馬上
完工的內容自然連接起來的連接詞。正確答案是表示轉折的(B)
but。

142.

(A) stabilize
(B) appear
(C) increase
(D) advertise

住房供應順利的話，就會知道將會使住房價格趨於穩定，因此(A)
是正確答案。

[143-146]

3月4日

致親愛的Merriweather先生，

寫這封信的目的是想通知您，**143.**您申請加入Salem社區游泳池
會員的申請已獲得批准。您申請的是家庭會員卡，這已獲得批
准，**144.**一年會費總共750美元。但是其中有150美元的登記費
145.適用於今年的會費，其餘的600美元，最晚請於3月31日前
繳納，否則我們將會假定您對於加入游泳館會員不再感興趣。
如欲進一步瞭解游泳館、**146.**營業時間、游泳課程以及游泳隊相
關資訊，請於營業時間內撥打電話843-9283。

Steve Atkins 敬上
Salem 社區游泳池

詞彙 grant 批准 application fee 加入費用 apply to 適用於～，
相當於～ assume 假定，推測 no longer 不再 regular
business hours 工作時間，營業時間

143.

(A) my
(B) his
(C) their
(D) your

空格中應該要填入指收件者Merriweather先生的代名詞的所有格。
正確答案是(D)。

144.

(A) 在採訪中，我很高興能見到您的家人。
(B) 一年會費總共750美元。
(C) 祝您在游泳池裡游得愉快。
(D) 現在隨時都可以自由地使用游泳池。

在空格之後的內容是延續關於會費或使用費用的說明，因此要在
空格中填入告知每年會費金額的(B)，才能完成最自然的文章脈
絡。

詞彙 be welcome to 歡迎

145.

(A) deducted
(B) applied
(C) reduced
(D) observed

已繳納的150美元入會費適用於750美元的會費內，根據介紹只需
要繳納剩下的600美元即可，因此正確答案是具有「適用」意義
的(B)，而apply經常會與to相互搭配使用。

詞彙 deduct 扣除，減去 observe 觀察；遵守

146.

(A) regular
(B) regulated
(C) regulation
(D) regulatory

營業時間或是工作時間以regular business hours來表達。正確答案
是(A)。

詞彙 regulated 管制的，控制的 regulation 規定 regulatory 管制
的，控制的

PART 7

[147-148]

員工福利

如同先前所宣布過的，我們將會變更醫療保險及牙齒保險公
司，新公司可以提供更便宜的保險產品。這些變化不僅會保證
大家的薪水將會變得更高，而且還會為大家提供更全面的醫療
保險待遇。依照法律，新的保險公司要使用各位的個人資訊需
要各位的准許，請登入電腦系統更新並確認姓名及生日等家族
紀錄後。另外，為了確保實施過程順利，請勾選畫面下方的
「同意」方格。期限到本週五下午6點為止。

詞彙 previously 之前的 switch 改變，轉換 provider 供應商，
供應業者 affordable 低廉的 not only A but also B不僅
是A，B也～ guarantee 保證 monthly paycheck 薪水
comprehensive 廣泛的，綜合的 family record 家族事項
transition 轉移，轉換 smoothly 順利地 deadline 期限，結
束

147.

公告了什麼？
(A) 提高健康保險費用。

(B) 繳納保險費的新方式。

(C) 員工福利的變更事項。

(D) 每年進行的員工健康檢查日期。

在公告的第一句中通知將要變更保險公司(we are switching medical and dental insurance providers)的事實，並對於變更需要的程序進行說明。正確答案是(C)。

148.

員工被要求做什麼？

(A) 填寫表格。

(B) 確認資訊。

(C) 繳費。

(D) 選擇新的供應商。

員工們為了要同意收集個人資訊，被要求登入電腦確認家庭紀錄(log on to the computer system and update and confirm your family records)，因此正確答案是(B)。

[149-150]

收件者：Georgia Worthy

寄件者：David Schwartz

主旨：Martinez先生

日期：2月18日

致Worthy小姐，

Dresden Manufacturing的Martinez先生昨天下午來到我的辦公室，我們看過了妳的團隊正在執行的工廠設計。總體來說，他很滿意平面圖，但希望能修改兩處。首先，工廠說需要第三條裝配線，這樣的話工廠面積將會擴大40%左右。另外，他希望屋頂能夠安裝太陽能板。

你今天可以到我辦公室來仔細檢查一下嗎？我2點到3點半之間有時間可以跟妳見面，如果能和Peter Verma一起來的話，可以跟兩位一次討論完，希望你們能夠一起過來。

David Schwartz 敬上

詞彙 **look over** 查看，探討 **plan** 計劃；平面圖 **adjustment** 調整 **solar panel** 太陽能板 **go over** 察看 **in detail** 詳細地，仔細地 **at the same time** 同時

149.

Schwartz先生為什麼會發送電子郵件？

(A) 為了徵求意見。

(B) 為了請求建議。

(C) 為了傳遞最新訊息。

(D) 為了道歉。

Schwartz先生通知有關於Martinez先生的到訪結果需要對設計進行修改。正確答案是(C)。

150.

關於Verma先生，暗示了什麼？

(A) 與Martinez先生的項目有關聯。

(B) Dresden Manufacturing的員工。

(C) 沒有直接見過Schwartz小姐。

(D) 目前正在視察設施。

透過最後一句"Bring Peter Verma with you because I'd prefer to speak with both of you at the same time"可以推測出Verma先生是與收件者Worthy小姐一起進行Martinez先生委託的項目的人，因此(A)是正確答案。

[151-152]

Oceanside 度假村
96813夏威夷檀香山,Pacific街488號
電話: (808) 371-8473

發票

姓名：Caroline Mason

地址：90219加利福尼亞洛杉磯Liberty 路81號

電子郵件地址：carolinemason@privatemail.com

預約日期：5月3日

預約號碼：OR847-944

日期	內容	**Amount**
5月5日	雙人房	$75.00
5月6日	雙人房	$75.00
5月6日	客房服務	$22.00
5月7日	雙人房	$75.00
5月7日	迷你吧	$34.00
	小計	$281.00
	稅金	$16.86
	總計	$287.86

結帳日期：5月8日

信用卡持有人：Caroline Mason

簽名：Caroline Mason

151.

Mason 先生是什麼時候在Oceanside度假村辦理入住的？

(A) 5月3日。

(B) 5月5日。

(C) 5月6日。

(D) 5月7日。

從發票明細來看的話，第一次結帳的日子是5月5日(雙人房客房費用結帳)，因此認為有可能在這一天辦理了入住手續，所以(B)才是正確答案。

152.

關於Mason小姐，可以知道什麼？

(A) 在度假村住了四晚。

(B) 在網路上預訂了客房。

(C) 在客房裡用餐。

(D) 拿到費用折扣。

在發票明細中可以找到Room Service項目，因此可以知道Mason小姐是在客房內用餐的，因此提及的事項是(C)。從5月5日開始到7日，所以不是四晚，而是兩晚，所以(A)不是正確答案。

[153-154]

Sylvia Hasselhoff	10:11 A.M.
Cliff，我過幾分鐘之後要去Wilbur's，有需要我帶的嗎？	
Cliff Mellon	10:12 A.M.
謝謝你問我，我的清單很長。	
Sylvia Hasselhoff	10:13 A.M.
我不知道我一個人能不能全都帶來。	
Cliff Mellon	10:14 A.M.
那麼跟我一起去怎麼樣？能等半個小時嗎？我現在要和項目有關的Donovan先生見面。	
Sylvia Hasselhoff	10:15 A.M.
我沒關係。準備要去的時候請告訴我，我會在辦公室等你。	

詞彙 by oneself 獨自

153.

上午10點13分，Hasselhoff小姐說"I don't know if I can carry everything by myself"的時候，她是要表達什麼意思？
(A) 最近不能去體育館。
(B) 她決定改為開車到商店。
(C) 將會請其他工作人員一起前往。
(D) 不能購買Mellon先生想要的所有東西。

給定的句子是對於"I've got a long list."的回應，意思是說很難拿著所有拜託的商品回去，因此她的意思可以看作是(D)。

154.

Mellon 先生接下來會做什麼？
(A) 與Donovan先生交談。
(B) 到Hasselhoff小姐的辦公室。
(C) 駕車前往Wilbur's。
(D) 打電話。

在Mellon先生的最後一句話"I have to meet with Mr. Donovan about my project now."中可以看出他即將要與Donovan先生見面，正確答案是(A)。

[155-157]

收件者：customerservice@falconair.com	
寄件者：pedrodelgado@lombard.com	
主旨：FA34航班	
日期：8月18日	

致負責人，

我的名字是Pedro Delgado。我今天早上乘坐佛羅里達邁阿密Falcon FA34航班來到了巴拿馬的巴拿馬城，預約號碼是GT8594AR，我坐在經濟艙45B。

遺憾的是，我下飛機的時候，似乎沒有帶到所有隨身物品。我整段飛行時間都在工作，重要的文件都放在前排座位的收納袋裡面，到了下飛機的時候，我忘了要把那些文件拿下來，您能幫我打聽一下有誰找到它們了嗎？明天的會議上需要那些文件。

我住在巴拿馬城中心街的Excelsior飯店283號房，隨時都可以聯繫我的手機號碼(615) 398-9021。

謝謝。

Pedro Delgado

詞彙 as though 就像～一樣 possession 所有物，攜帶物品 get off 從～下來，下車 in front of 在～前面 recover 找回，恢復

155.

Delgado 先生提到了什麼問題？
(A) 在飛機上放了某個東西就下飛機了。
(B) 錯過了飛往巴拿馬的飛機。
(C) 會議會晚到。
(D) 未能預訂返程航班。

在第二段中告知下飛機時沒帶到隨身物品(I didn't take all of my possessions when I got off the plane)的問題，因此(A)為正確答案。

156.

關於Delgado先生的暗示是什麼？
(A) 他以前乘坐過FA34飛機。
(B) 他在佛羅里達邁阿密的辦公室工作。
(C) 他偏好電話聯絡。
(D) 他在飛機上換座位。

Delgado先生在第三段中請求說請用手機號碼與自己聯繫(can be reached anytime on my cellphone at (615) 398-9021.)，透過這些可以推測出的事項為(C)。

157.

[1]，[2]，[3]，[4]中下列句子最適合填入下列句子的地方是哪裡？
「您能幫我打聽一下有誰找到它們了嗎？」
(A) [1]
(B) [2]
(C) [3]
(D) [4]

要仔細想想them指的是什麼。從has found這個動詞子句推測出them所指的應該是話者落下的文件，因此給予的句子應填入(C)的[3]。

[158-161]

MPT 股份有限公司證照研討會

MPT股份有限公司將會在全國幾個城市為軟體資格證舉行研討會。
6月和7月時間表如下：

日期	時間(研討會限定)	場地	軟體	講師
6月14日	9 A.M.–12 P.M.	洛杉磯加利福尼亞	Art Pro	Darlene Campbell
6月28日	1 P.M.–4 P.M.	休斯頓德克薩斯	Omega	Sophia Beam
7月12日	11 A.M.–2 P.M.	芝加哥伊利諾斯州	Art Pro	Rudolph Mudd
7月19日	2 P.M.–5 P.M.	巴爾的摩馬里蘭州	Diamond	Martin Croft
7月26日	10 A.M.–1 P.M.	亞特蘭大喬治亞	Vox	Sophia Beam

各研討會由三次關於該軟體的演講所組成，然後經過一個小時的休息後，進行資格證書考試。考試時間根據軟體的不同而有所差異。

所有研討會的報名費用為250美元，登記時間從6月1日開始，各研討會的登記時間將在開始授課前一天結束。有意報考者需繳納150美元的報名費，想要同時申請兩種的顧客只需支付優惠價350美元即可。個人可以至www.mpt.com/seminarregistration登記。應試者在應考後24小時內會得到分數通知。

詞彙 certification 資格 consist of 由～組成 break 休息時間
depend upon 取決於～ registration 登記 testing fee 考試
費用，報名費 notify 告知，通知 score 分數

158.
關於Diamond的研討會在哪裡舉行？
(A) 芝加哥。
(B) 亞特蘭大。
(C) 洛杉磯。
(D) 巴爾的摩。

在Software項目中找到Diamond的話，就可以知道有關於它的研討會將會在(D)巴爾的摩進行。

159.
關於Beam小姐，可以知道的是什麼？
(A) 她在休斯頓分公司工作。
(B) 她偏愛下午的研討會。
(C) 她是Art Pro的專家。
(D) 她因為工作需要出差。

在Instructor項目中找到一個名為Beam的姓氏，你會發現她將在6月28日和7月26日分別在休斯敦和亞特蘭大演講，因此可以知道她為了演講而需要移動，因此(D)是正確答案。(B)的情況下，她的演講主題不是Art Pro而是Omega和Vox。

160.
想在休斯頓考試的人報名時間到什麼時候？
(A) 截至6月25日。
(B) 截至6月26日。
(C) 截至6月27日。
(D) 截至6月28日。

"Registration for each seminar will end the day before it is scheduled to take place."是正確答案的線索。也就是說，需要在研討會開始前一天登記才行，因此登記截止日期是在休斯頓的研討會開始日，即6月28日的前一天的(C)6月27日。

161.
對於7月19日參加考試的人有什麼暗示？
(A) 將於7月20日知道分數。
(B) 將會學習美術相關軟體。
(C) 上午將考試。
(D) 將支付400美元作為研討會的參加費及報考費。

因為考試成績是在考試後24小時內(within 24 hours of taking the exam)通知的，所以7月19日參加考試的人會在第二天20日知道考試成績，因此正確答案是(A)。(D)的情況，同時參加研討會和考試的人只需支付350美元。

[162-164]

在城市裡舉行慶典
Brad Thompson 記者

貝賽 (10月2日)--貝賽一直以來都是以美麗的海灘和出色的海鮮餐廳廣為人知，但城市裡的其他地區近年來卻一直被忽視，得益於這首次舉辦的貝賽慶典改變了這種情況。

慶典預計將在10月5日星期五至10月7日星期日舉行。慶典將重點放在城市的歷史方面，該城市建於1753年。慶典大部分將會在Harbor公園舉行，但也會在城市內各處安排遊客可以去的地方。城市內的43座歷史性房屋中有大多數都可以參觀，而Bayside博物館將會與慶典同時舉行特別活動。

還將會舉辦一些重現歷史事件的特別活動，在重現活動中將包括城市的創建，在這裡展開的戰鬥，再現建設城市的兩家族Burns家族及Watsons家族的競爭，這些演出可以在公園裡觀賞。

眾多的餐廳和賣場也將會參與慶典。若有興趣，相關活動及位置的詳細說明可至www.baysidefestival.org查詢。

詞彙 be known for 以～出名 ignore 無視 inaugural 就任的，
首次的 focus on 集中在～ majority 多數 host 主辦，舉辦
coincide with 同時發生～ reenactment 重新制訂 recreate
重現 rivalry 競爭 take part in 參與 description 描述，說明

162.
報導主要是關於什麼？
(A) 城市內活動的結果。
(B) 貝賽的地區歷史。
(C) 在即將舉行的慶典中進行的活動。
(D) 貝賽的創建。

在第一段中告知有關於這次首次舉行的慶典(inaugural Bayside Festival)之後，介紹在之後的慶典中計劃要進行的各項活動，因此報導的主題是(C)。

163.
關於活動，沒有提到的是什麼？
(A) 將在多個地點舉行。
(B) 將由眾多餐廳贊助。
(C) 為首次舉行。
(D) 將重點放在城市的歷史上。

將會有公演及在其他場所進行，所以(A)的內容是正確的，而且今年是第一次舉行的活動，因此(C)也是有提到的事項，找得到將重點放在城市歷史上的內容，所以(D)也是事實。正確答案是(B)，雖然有提及多家商家及餐廳將會參加慶典，但找不到餐廳會贊助活動的內容，所以(B)才是正確答案。

詞彙 sponsor 贊助 for the first time 第一次，最初

164.
想要觀看重現歷史活動的人應該去哪裡？
(A) Bayside博物館。
(B) 歷史性房屋。

(C) Harbor 公園。

(D) 碼頭。

重現歷史的活動在第三段有提到，這時「可以在公園裡觀賞到這些活動(These can be viewed at the park.)」，介紹了活動場地。在文章脈絡上，這裡所說的公園就是Harbor公園，所以正確答案是(C)。

詞彙 waterfront 海岸，碼頭

[165-168]

Eric Inness	9:34 A.M.
我們要舉辦的研討會就在兩星期後了。為了練習我們每個人將要演講的課程，好像應該要開一下會。星期三上午怎麼樣？	
Jasmine Park	9:36 A.M.
我那時打算為新進員工進行說明會。	
Peter Welch	9:37 A.M.
我也會和Jasmine一起進行。	
Henrietta Graves	9:39 A.M.
星期五下午怎麼樣？結束之後我們可以一起邊吃晚餐邊討論一些需要改進的地方。	
Eric Inness	9:41 A.M.
我那時候需要和Donald Radcliffe見面，但我會詢問一下他那天能不能早點見面。	
Peter Welch	9:42 A.M.
那天我一整天都沒有事情，我都可以。	
Jasmine Park	9:43 A.M.
我也會過去。	
Eric Inness	9:46 A.M.
好的，我會透過人事部的Landry小姐預約一下。會議大約會在大會議室其中的一個地方從2點開始到6點結束，我知道是幾號房之後會再跟你們說。如果有問題的話會馬上跟大家說的。	

詞彙 host 主辦 get together 聚集 count in 包含，把～算在內 handle 對待，處理 arrangement 準備 run into 偶遇，邂逅

165.

Inness 先生為什麼會開始線上聊天？
(A) 為了討論研討會的議程。
(B) 為了改變計劃。
(C) 為了確定會議議程。
(D) 為了徵求意見。

在聊天室的開頭部分，Inness先生談到了即將開始的研討會，然後提議為了練習將要進行的講座而見面(to get together to practice the individual)，因此在選項中開始聊天的理由可以看作是(C)。

166.

上午9點37分，當Welch先生說"I'll be working with Jasmine as well"的時候，他在暗示什麼？
(A) 他星期三上午很忙。
(B) 他與Park先生共用一間辦公室。

(C) 他最近被錄用。
(D) 他即將要出差。

如果留意到as well的話，就可以很容易地找到正確答案。 因為前文Park說要進行說明會，所以給定的句子的意思是「我也會和她一起進行說明會」，因此Welch先生也委婉地表明若要參加Inness先生提議的星期三上午的會議會有困難，因此(A)是正確答案。

167.

Graves 小姐提議要做什麼？
(A) 一起吃飯。
(B) 推遲研討會。
(C) 與Radcliffe先生見面。
(D) 在大會議室講話。

聊天室中間部分，從Graves小姐說「邊吃晚餐邊聊要改善的地方(we could go out to dinner and discuss what we ought to improve upon)」，就可以看出她提議的是(A)。

168.

Inness先生說自己要做什麼？
(A) 向Radcliffe先生發送電子郵件。
(B) 練習今天的課程。
(C) 邀請Landry先生參加聚會。
(D) 預訂場地。

在聊天室最後的部分，Inness說"I'll tell you the number once I find out."，透露出自己要打聽會議地點的意思。 因此他要做的是(D)。

詞彙 rehearse 排練，彩排

[169-171]

邀請大家參加全世界首次上演的戲劇*Daylight*
*Daylight*是Jodie Camargo的最新作品。這故事是有關於一個男人人生的最後一天和那天他所做的事情。
戲劇將於11月8日星期五晚上7時在春田市市中心的Humboldt劇院首次演出。演出後將會安排Camargo先生以及有獲獎經歷的導演Neil Peterson進行特別的Q&A時間。
戲劇票價為每人35美元。其中包含演出及Q&A時間。演出後，想到後臺參觀的觀眾需購買60美元的門票，這門票只會賣40張。
門票可在劇場網站www.humboldttheater.com購買，演出當天下午5點開始也可以在劇場售票處購買，價格較高的門票只能在網路上購買。有關演出的問題請撥打854-1732諮詢Darlene Mercy。

詞彙 premier 首演 play 戲劇，劇本 Q&A session 問答時間 award-winning 有得獎經歷的 director 導演 backstage 後臺 address 地址；表達

169.

在廣告什麼？
(A) 作家的簽名會。

(B) 劇院開幕。

(C) 戲劇的首演。

(D) 電影首映。

從第一句"the world premiere of the play *Daylight* "的句子中可以看出該廣告是為了宣傳戲劇*Daylight*，正確答案是(C)。

詞彙　autograph session 簽名會

170.

關於*Daylight*，提到了什麼？
(A) 只有一名演員會出現。
(B) 聽眾興致勃勃地觀看。
(C) 舞臺是春田市。
(D) 由Camargo先生撰寫。

沒有提到演員的數量，所以(A)是錯誤的，這次是首次演出，所以(B)與事實不符，將要首次上演的劇場所在地是春田市，但作品背景並不是春田市，因此(C)也是錯誤的內容。在引文的前半部分中介紹戲劇是Jodie Camargo最近的作品，因此在選項中提到的只有(D)。

171.

可以去後臺的門票要如何購買？
(A) 透過造訪網頁。
(B) 透過與黃牛接觸。
(C) 透過拜訪劇院。
(D) 透過電話。

最後一個段落介紹可以買到門票的地方是劇院的網站和售票處，其中說明價格更貴的門票(the more expensive tickets)只能在網路上購買。另一方面，在廣告的中半部分，雖然票價是35美元，但若是為了要造訪舞臺則需要支付60美元，因此最終只能在網路上購買能夠參觀看舞臺的門票，因此(A)是正確答案。

[172-175]

收件者：全體員工
<undisclosed_recipients@belmontindustries.com>
寄件人：Brian Lockwood <blockwood@belmontiindustries.com>
主旨：Trenton Fun Run
日期：4月18日

致全體員工，

Trenton Fun Run預定將於4月28日星期六舉行，而我們又將成為這次活動的贊助廠商之一。萬一您不知道我再告知您一遍，這項跑步比賽是為了幫助地區小學購買在課堂上所需教材的募捐活動。

我們鼓勵Belmont Industries全體員工參加比賽。主要項目是10公里賽跑，但也準備了5公里、3公里和6公里的步行項目。十公里的項目將於上午九點三十分開始，而其他項目則會在稍晚一點的上午開始。參加費用為15美元，報名時可以免費領取T恤及水壺。

對於自身不適合跑步的情況，主辦方希望各位能夠抽出時間參與志工服務。需要在報名過程中提供幫助的人、在比賽中向參賽選手分發水的人，以及在終點線提供幫助的人。關於這項問題可以向Jade Kennedy了解一下。

希望下週六能在那裡見面。Belmont Industries的員工們將會一起跑步，如有意參加，請告知Maynard Williams。不是為了贏得獎項，而是要專注於享受跑步比賽。

Brian Lockwood 敬上

詞彙　sponsor 贊助者　in case 萬一　material 材料，資料
　　　encourage 激勵，鼓勵　participate in 參加　entry fee 報名費
　　　devote 奉獻，犧牲　finish line 終點線

172.

電子郵件的目的是什麼？
(A) 為了慈善活動請求捐款。
(B) 為了公佈跑步比賽的獲獎者。
(C) 為了鼓勵人們參加郊遊活動。
(D) 為了宣傳體育活動。

介紹公司計劃贊助名為Trenton Fun Run的跑步比賽，並鼓勵員工參與活動，因此撰寫電子郵件的目的可視為(D)。

173.

要怎麼才可以得到T恤？
(A) 透過參加跑步比賽。
(B) 透過在一項競賽中獲獎。
(C) 透過志工服務。
(D) 透過捐錢。

在"you will receive a free T - shirt and water bottle upon registering"(報名時免費贈送T恤和水壺)的句子可以知道T恤是給參加比賽的人。(A)為正確答案。

174.

關於Trenton Fun Run，沒有提到的是什麼？
(A) 利用無償人員們的服務。
(B) 有步行比賽和跑步比賽。
(C) 將在上午開始。
(D) 所有年齡的人均可報名。

提到需要志工，可知(A)為事實，因為有10公里的跑步比賽和比它更短的步行比賽，所以(B)也是有提到的事項，提到跑步項目將在上午9點30分開始，其他項目將在此後的上午時間段開始，因此(C)的內容也是正確的，但是沒有提及有關於(D)對於參加者年齡限制的規定。

175.

根據電子郵件，Kennedy小姐負責什麼工作？
(A) 接待願意提供幫助的人。
(B) 組成跑步選手。
(C) 收集申請表。
(D) 安排志工們的交通。

Ms. Kennedy這個名字可以在"You can speak with Jade Kennedy regarding this."中找到，從前後文章脈絡上可以知道這句的this所指的是志願者的工作，因此她負責的工作是(A)。

[176-180]

Coldwater 學院
課程申請表

請完整填寫申請表，並在8月30日之前直接繳交到前台。秋季學期的課程預定於8月31日開始。課程費用是每學分200美元。

姓名	Roger Dare	地址	俄亥俄州米爾頓W. Davidson街930號
電話號碼	857-4093	電子郵件地址	roger_dare@homemail.com

課程編號	課程名稱	星期/時間	學分
RJ54	機器人學概論	一 9:00 A.M.–11:30 A.M.	3
AT22	機械工程學	四 1:00 P.M.–3:00 P.M.	4
MM98	高級微積分	三 9:00 A.M.–10:30 A.M.	2
XR31	有機物理實驗	五 2:00 P.M.–5:00 P.M.	3

是復學生嗎？	[✓] 是		[ ] 否
您正在接受經濟援助嗎？	[ ] 是		[✓] 否
付款方式	[✓] 信用卡	[ ] 現金	
	[ ] 支票	[ ] 銀行轉帳	

總金額：$2,400
簽名：Roger Dare
繳交日期：8月27日

詞彙 in its entirety 完整地，完全地 credit 信用；學分 calculus 微積分 returning student 復學生 bank transfer 傳達，轉讓，劃撥

收件者：roger_dare@homemail.com
寄件者：registration@coldwateracademy.edu
主旨：秋季學期
日期：8月29日

親愛的Dare先生，

我期待再次歡迎您成為Coldwater學院的學生。茲收到您的聽課申請，並告知您表中的三個課程已為您成功登記了。

但遺憾的是，原本打算要教授微積分的Wilcox教授，由於個人原因，今年秋天不會在這裡上課，因此他的課程已經關閉了。

我們新聘請了一位代替他的人。他的姓名是Andrea Wang，如若要向他學習的話，可以在星期一下午2點到3點半上課。請在學期開始的前一天，即明天下午6點之前告知您的意向為何。

希望您即將到來的學期會有好運。

Meredith Watson
教務處

詞彙 enroll 註冊 intention 意圖，意向

176.
8月31日會發生什麼事？
(A) 將會進行新生說明會。
(B) 將開始接受受理。
(C) 一名教授將會辭職。
(D) 將要開始上課。

問題的關鍵語句August 31可以從第一段引文的"Classes for the fall session will begin on August 31."中找到，可以得知8月31日是秋季課程開學的日期，因此(D)是正確答案。

177.
關於Dare先生，能知道的是什麼？
(A) 他於8月27日到過學院。
(B) 他將首次參加學院學習。
(C) 他主要對管理學方面有興趣。
(D) 他以轉帳匯款的方式繳納學費。

第一段引文中有寫到「必須要親自繳交至前台(submit it in person to the front office)」，引文最下面的繳交日期寫著8月27日，因此Dare先生可能於8月27日到學院繳交申請表，因此正確答案是(A)。申請表表格中將Dare先生紀錄為returning student，因此(B)不是事實，考慮到申請聽課的科目主要是理工大學的科目，所以(C)也是錯誤的內容，在申請表的表格，他付款的方式是信用卡，所以(D)也是錯誤的。

詞彙 primarily 主要地

178.
Dare 先生為哪一堂課程支付了最高昂的學費？
(A) 機器人學概論。
(B) 機械工程學。
(C) 高級微積分學。
(D) 有機物理實驗。

第一段引文中說明學費為$200 per credit(每學分200美元)，因此在表格中選擇學分最高的科目即可，正確答案是申請科目中為4學分、學分最高的(B)。

179.
那一堂課被停課了？
(A) RJ54
(B) AT22
(C) MM98
(D) XR31

電子郵件第二段中關於被停課的Wilcox教授的說明為"whom you were scheduled to learn calculus with"，也就是說，可以得知Wilcox教授的微積分課程已經被停講，此微積分課程的課程編號(C)就是正確答案。

180.
Watson 小姐要求Dare先生做什麼？
(A) 參加學期第一天的課程。
(B) 到隔天為止回答問題。
(C) 打電話討論課程。
(D) 繳納最終的學費。

在電子郵件最後的句子中，Watson小姐就是否接受更換微積分課程的講師一事囑咐說「請在明天下午6點之前告訴我Dare先生的想法(we would appreciate your informing us of your intentions before 6:00 P.M. tomorrow)」，因此在選項中她要求的是(B)。

詞彙 tuition payment 學費，聽課費

[181-185]

Deerfield 分公司搬遷

國內最大的製造高階電子產品的企業之一的Hobson股份有限公司旗下的Deerfield分公司將搬遷。Deerfield分公司有27名正式員工和12名非正式員工，將會搬到安多佛。新分公司將位於Fulton街982號，是Hobson股份有限公司名下的建築，也是為容納新分公司進駐而特別建造的建築。Deerfield分公司將於4月19日星期五關閉，在下星期一，也就是4月22日，Andover分公司將會開業。Andover分公司將會處理附近3個州的所有業務，因此將會聘用多名在那裡工作的新員工。Deerfield分公司及Andover分公司位置相關問題或其他問題請撥打897-1902詢問Melvin Sullivan。

詞彙 high-end 高檔的 relocate 搬遷，遷移 specifically 特別地 house 容納 tri-state area 橫跨3個州的地區 comment 註釋，評論

收件者：Ken Worthy, Sue Parker, Elliot Jung, Rosemary Kline
寄件者：Andrew Meade
主旨：調動
日期：4月4日

已經決定關於國內分公司的內部調動了。茲告知已批准調動的分公司總經理名單。在所有情況下，在新的分公司也將保持同樣的職位和業務。

分公司總經理	現位置	新位置	調動日期
Dina Smith	比洛克西	哈里斯堡	4月10日
Serina Chapman	斯威特沃	巴頓魯治特	4月17日
Lucas Bobo	傑克遜維爾	安多佛	4月22日
Tom Wright	安尼斯敦	雅典	4月29日
Peter Sullivan	哈里斯堡	蓋恩斯維爾	5月1日

預計調動的一般員工的名單太長了，中午以後再發電子郵件給您。隨時都可以用內線號碼58與我聯繫。

詞彙 internal transfer 內部調動 domestic 家庭的，國內的 retain 保留，保持 title 標題，職稱 duty 任務

181.

關於Deerfield分公司，提到了什麼？
(A) 將會被關閉。
(B) 由Sullivan先生運行。
(C) 將迎接新的主管。
(D) 最近解僱了一些員工。

第一段引文正在傳達Deerfield分公司將遷往其他地方的消息。該分公司將於4月19日關閉(will close on Friday, April 19)並遷往安多佛，因此在選項中提到的Deerfield分公司事項為(A)。

182.

與公告中第一段第九行中的"maters"一詞意思最相似的是？
(A) 協會。
(B) 評論。
(C) 建築物。
(D) 工作。
名詞matter原意義為「問題」或是「案件」，思考一下與該文章

中使用的branch(分公司)、handle(對待，處理)等詞語的關聯性的話，和選項中的(D)business(事業，工作)意思最為接近。

詞彙 association 關聯(性)，協會

183.

關於Sullivan先生的暗示是什麼？
(A) 請求調往雅典。
(B) 最近在Hobson股份有限公司開始工作。
(C) Smith小姐將會接替他。
(D) 將搬往其他州。

從第二段引文通知的名單上找到Sullivan這個名字的話，會發現他現在在哈里斯堡工作，很快就會調動到蓋恩斯維爾。另外，即將來到哈里斯堡的分公司總經理寫著Dina Smith，因此在選項中可以推測出的事項是(C)。

184.

關於Andover分公司，能知道的是什麼？
(A) Bobo 先生將擔任分公司總經理。
(B) 將位於建築物一樓。
(C) 在那裡將會有50名正式員工。
(D) 將會面對海外客戶。

在第二段引文的表格中，將調動至安多佛的人名為Lucas Bobo，因此(A)是正確答案。對於要搬遷的建築物層數，並沒有提到過，因此(B)不是正確答案，而且也找不到搬遷後的具體員工人數，所以(C)也是錯誤的，Andover分公司不是海外業務，而是處理鄰近三州(tri-state area)的業務，因此(D)也是錯誤的內容。

185.

Meade 先生下午可能會做什麼？
(A) 做出關於調動的決定。
(B) 以電子郵件的方式向同事發送名單。
(C) 諮詢員工們。
(D) 確定關於調動的會議議程。

Meade先生是撰寫通知的人，他在通知的最後部分寫了"The list of regular workers who are transferring is much longer, so it will be sent through e-mail sometime after lunch. "，從這裡可以得知他會在中午以後把普通員工的名單以電子郵件的形式發送出去，所以他下午要做的是(B)。

[186-190]

Calhoun 圖書館研討會

5月23日星期六在Calhoun圖書館將會為作家們舉行研討會。將舉行以下活動：

10:00 A.M. – 10:50 A.M.	塑造小說中的角色	Carlos Correia
11:00 A.M. – 11:50 A.M.	創造新的世界觀	Mei Johnson
1:00 P.M. – 2:50 P.M.	編輯	Xavier Mahler
3:00 P.M. – 3:50 P.M.	原稿出版	Belinda York

本次活動只要是里奇蒙居民均可免費參加，但座位有限。欲要預訂座位請撥打482-8274。

81

每個研討會的主持人都是活躍在附近地區的小說家,他們的作品將會在研討會當天在圖書館販賣。

研討會將會在圖書館二樓的Belmont室進行,將會以較低的價格提供小點心及冷飲。

詞彙 fictional 虛構的 manuscript 原稿 session 時間,期間 locally based 以當地區域作為基礎 fiction novel 小說 on sale 販售中的 beverage 飲料

對於Calhoun圖書館的建議

嘉賓: Carla Stewart
日期: 5月23日

建議: 我每年都會參加數場圖書館的研討會,這次是我參加過有史以來最好的一次。雖然我到11點之前還沒到,但我卻可以坐到結束,因為我現在正在寫小說,所以在研討會上聽到的建議非常寶貴。如果運氣好的話,我可能會在今年年底完成我的作品,正式成為作家。

詞彙 have been to 去過~ manage to 設法做到 invaluable 非常寶貴的 with luck 運氣好的話 published author 出書的作家

研討會很受歡迎

Jefferson Lee

自去年起,Calhoun圖書館開始舉辦研討會,研討會成為那裡最受歡迎的活動。上週末為作家舉行了研討會,座無虛席,由於索票的預備作家太多,因此圖書館計劃在下個月也要舉辦同樣的研討會。圖書管理員Beth Robinson承諾除了一名作家之外,所有作家都還會再來。Xavier Mahler預計將會宣傳最近發表的小說《月的黑暗面》,因此Melissa Gilbert將會代替他。

根據Robinson小姐的介紹,圖書館計劃每月舉辦兩次研討會直到今年結束。如果能夠獲得更多的資金,明年將會召開更多的研討會。

詞彙 aspiring 立志;有抱負的 commit 犯罪,約定 conclude 做結論;結束 funding 資金;提供資金

186.

關於Calhoun圖書館的暗示是什麼?
(A) 有三層樓。
(B) 對於拖欠圖書收取滯納金。
(C) 每週末舉行研討會。
(D) 位於里奇蒙。

在第一段引文中,因為里奇蒙居民可以免費參加活動(this event may be attended at no charge by all residents of Richmond),可以推測出Calhoun圖書館應是位於里奇蒙地區的。正確答案是(D)。

187.

關於研討會有哪一項不符合事實?
(A) 住在該區域的人可以參加。
(B) 可以購買小點心。
(C) 研討會期間販售小說。
(D) 有參加費用。

要在第一段引文公告中逐一確認每個選項的內容。里奇蒙的居民可以免費參加,因此(A)是事實,但(D)不為事實,所以(D)為正確答案。會準備小點心跟飲料,因此(B)是有提到的內容,研討會主持人的小說也將會販賣的關係,(C)也是事實。

詞彙 refreshment 點心

188.

Stewart小姐不能參加誰的研討會?
(A) Correia 先生的研討會。
(B) Johnson小姐的研討會。
(C) Mahler先生的研討會。
(D) York小姐的研討會。

Stewart小姐是填寫意見卡的人,在卡片上她提到"I didn't arrive until eleven but managed to stay until the end. ",因此從第一段引文的表格中找到11點以前進行的研討會,就可以知道她錯過的研討會是(A)。

189.

報導主要是關於什麼?
(A) 圖書館的擴展。
(B) 項目的成功。
(C) 今後圖書館的活動。
(D) 寫書的最佳方法。

從新聞標題中可以知道新聞報導了在Calhoun圖書館進行的活動獲得高人氣的消息,因此報導的主題可視為(B)。

190.

關於Gilbert小姐,可以知道什麼?
(A) 和Robinson小姐是朋友。
(B) 出版了小說。
(C) 在出版社工作。
(D) 認識Mahler先生。

在第三段引文新聞報導的第二段最後一句中,我們可以看到名為Melissa Gilbert的人將取代Xavier Mahler成為研討會主持人。另外,在第一段引文中,各研討會的主持人都是在附近地區活動的小說家(locally based writers of fiction novels),由此可以推測出Gilbert也是,因此(B)是正確答案。

[191-195]

Memories of Georgia
Richard Horner
Kirkwood 工作室

四年間沒有錄音和巡迴演出的Richard Horner回來了。作為銷售數百萬張唱片的民歌歌手和作詞家,他不久前發表了名為《Memories of Georgia》的新專輯。本張專輯收錄的歌曲是在出道專輯《My Life》和他的第二張專輯《Heading out West》之後最好的歌曲,超越上張專輯《What's Going On?》。若是知道Horner先生不僅僅是寫了這張專輯的所有歌詞,而且還演奏了所有樂器時,歌迷們一定會很高興。這張專輯無疑會得到出色的音樂性的認可,第一首歌曲〈Appalachian Home〉已經可以在全國播放的電臺上聽到。一定要購買這張專輯,等到他以後巡迴演出到你所在的城市去的時候,別忘了去看看Horner先生的演出。

詞彙 absence 缺席 entitle 命名，賦予權利 tremendous 巨大的
lyrics 歌詞 musical instrument 樂器 recognize 認識，認知
outstanding 出色的 airplay 電臺，電臺播放時間

Richard Horner

睽違四年，Richard Horner將重返路易維爾的Rosemont劇場。

Horner先生將在下列日期晚間進行現場表演：

9月28日 星期四
9月29日 星期五
9月30日 星期六
10月1日 星期日

所有演出將在下午七點開始。欲訂購請撥打849-2892或到
www.rosemonttheater.com購票。票價為每張30美元起。不要
錯過能夠在眼前看到活生生的傳說機會。

詞彙 legend 傳說 up close and personal 近距離，眼前

收件者：tickets@rosemonttheater.com
寄件者：lucypeters@homemail.com
主旨：Robert Horner
日期：9月22日

致負責人，

兩天前我為了觀看Robert Horner的演出，透過電話預訂了4張
門票。預訂了在您的劇場舉行的最後一晚演出的門票，雖然因
為能夠看到他的演出而興奮不已，但遺憾的是，由於個人原
因，我不得不與家人一起離開這城市而無法使用門票。我想知
道是否會退款。對於您的答覆，我將不勝感激。

Lucy Peters 敬上

191.

關於Horner先生，沒有提到的是什麼？

(A) 新專輯尚未發行。
(B) 可以演奏樂器。
(C) 作詞。
(D) 上一張專輯幾年前上市。

在第一段引文的開頭部分，傳達了Horner先生發表了名為
《Memories of Georgia》的專輯，因此(A)的內容與事實不符。透
過"Mr.Horner not only wrote all the lyrics to the songs on this album
but also played every single musical instrument"可以確認到(B)和
(C)，以及"after a four-year absence from recording and touring"可
以確認到(A)的內容。

192.

評論中與第一段第九行中的"recognized"一詞最相似的是？

(A) 授予。
(B) 問候。
(C) 理解。
(D) 承認。

recognize表示「認知」或「承認」，因此如果要在選項中找到與
此意思最為相似的單字的話，正確答案就會是(D)。

詞彙 greet 問候 appreciate 感謝，承認

193.

Horner先生最後來到路易維爾的時候，是發行了哪張專輯？

(A) *Heading out West*
(B) *Memories of Georgia*
(C) *What's Going On?*
(D) *My Life*

從第二段引文的第一句中可以知道Richard Horner是時隔4年(after
a four-year absence)再次造訪路易維爾。 另外，在第一段引文
中，透過"after a four-year absence from recording and touring"來
表示他四年沒有進行活動，以及透過"his last album What's Going
On? "可以確認到他空白期前的專輯名稱。綜合這些事實，我們可
以知道Horner在4年前造訪路易維爾之前發表的專輯名稱是What's
Going On?。

194.

Peters小姐為什麼會發電子郵件？

(A) 為了預購演出門票。
(B) 為了諮詢與退款有關的問題。
(C) 為了瞭解座位的位置。
(D) 為了詢問付款方式。

電子郵件後半部分的"I wonder if you are offering refunds on them."
中可以確認撰寫電子郵件的理由。發送電子郵件是為了要諮詢有
關退票的問題，所以正確答案是(B)。

195.

Peters小姐訂購了哪一場演出的門票？

(A) 9月28日。
(B) 9月29日。
(C) 9月30日。
(D) 10月1日。

從電子郵件中的"I booked tickets for the last night he'll be playing
at your theater."中可以知道她預訂了最後一天的演出。另外，在
第二段引文介紹中，最後的公演日期是10月1日，因此最終她預
訂的演出日期是(D)。

[196-200]

收件者：Susan Wallace <susanwallace@caravanhotel.com>
寄件者：Cathy Wilde <cathy_w@honoria.com>
主旨：提問
日期：3月14日

親愛的Wallace小姐，

我是Honoria股份有限公司的Cathy Wilde。我們準備為長期在
公司工作、將要離職的員工準備一頓特殊的晚餐，想要在您
的其中一間餐廳請他吃晚餐，這次的活動預定於3月29日星期
五，大約下午6點30分至9點舉行，活動將會有40人參加。

我們希望每人的餐費在60美元至75美元之間，此價格可不包含
飲料，但必須要包含開胃菜和甜點在內。雖然自助餐風格的晚
餐也很好，但海鮮餐廳或是牛排餐廳等風格也會令人滿意。我
們偏好包廂，上次在那裡舉辦活動的時候，得知每一間餐廳都
沒有包廂，但最近聽說重新裝潢了，所以這次期待能得到您的
好消息。

Cathy Wilde 敬上
Honoria股份有限公司

Caravan 飯店餐廳

公司名稱：Honoria 股份有限公司
負責人：Cathy Wilde
人數: 40人

餐廳	飲食	價格(每人/總價)	包廂
The Grill	牛排/燒烤	$62 / $2,480	有
Blue Rhapsody	海鮮	$85 / $3,400	無
The Washingtonian	西式/亞洲式自助餐	$80 / $3,200	有
Green Forest	素食	$50 / $2,000	有

須在用餐前至少三天支付總金額一半的訂金，訂金將不會退還，並且需在用餐前一天預訂餐點。

詞彙 nonrefundable 不退還 deposit 訂金，押金 prior to 在～之前

收件者：Cathy Wilde <cathy_w@honoria.com>
寄件者：Susan Wallace <susanwallace@caravanhotel.com>
主旨：[Re]預約
日期：3月25日

致親愛的Wilde小姐，

透過我的上司得知您為了晚餐聚會全額付清了3,400美元，謝謝您迅速處理。您的訂位將會於本週五晚上6點30分配合您們到達的時間準備好的。為了讓貴公司的活動變成更難忘的活動，若還要我做什麼的話，請不吝與我聯繫。

Susan Wallace 敬上
Caravan飯店

詞彙 promptness 迅速 memorable 難忘的 hesitate 猶豫

196.

根據第一封電子郵件，將會進行哪種類型的活動？
(A) 生日派對。
(B) 簽約儀式。
(C) 頒獎儀式。
(D) 送別會。

透過第一封電子郵件的開頭部分中提到"a special dinner for an employee who's leaving the firm after many years"可以得知是為了將要離開公司的員工舉辦的活動，因此將要舉辦的活動種類是(D)的送別會。

197.

Wilde小姐提到有關於Caravan飯店的什麼？
(A) 飯店費用漲價。
(B) 以前從未在那裡吃過飯。
(C) 最近裝修了。
(D) 不久前，在那裡開了一家新餐廳。

在第一封電子郵件的後半部分，Wilde小姐說「我知道最近那裡裝潢完成了(I believe you underwent some renovations recently)」，因此(C)為提到過的事項。她說以前曾在那裡舉辦過活動，因此(B)的內容與事實相反，(A)的飯店收費和(D)的新餐廳則是完全沒有提到過的事情。

198.

那間餐廳收費最符合Wilde小姐提到的預算？
(A) The Grill
(B) Blue Rhapsody
(C) The Washingtonian
(D) Green Forest

在第一封電子郵件中，Wilde小姐表示餐費希望落在每人60美元至75美元(between $60 and $75 per person)，因此在第二段引文尋找符合條件的餐廳，就會知道正確答案為餐費一人62美元的(A) The Grill。

199.

Wallace小姐為什麼會發送電子郵件給Wilde小姐？
(A) 為了詢問預約。
(B) 為了告知晚餐菜單。
(C) 為了確認付款。
(D) 為了改變晚餐時間。

在第二封電子郵件中，Wallace小姐告知Wilde小姐支付了晚餐聚會的3,400美元(full amount of $3,400 for your dinner party)，因此撰寫電子郵件的理由可視為(C)。

200.

將會向Honoria股份有限公司的人提供哪種食物？
(A) 牛排。
(B) 海鮮。
(C) 西餐和亞洲料理。
(D) 素食。

從最後一段引文電子郵件中，可得知Wilde小姐的公司支付了3,400美元，而在第二段引文中，總餐費為3,400美元的地方寫著Blue Rhapsody，也就是說，Honoria股份有限公司最終選擇的餐廳是Blue Rhapsody，而這裡的菜單是(B)的海鮮。

ANSWER SHEET

TOEIC TOEIC實戰測試

裁切線

確認

准考證號碼

姓名

LISTENING COMPREHENSION (Part 1-4)

No.	ANSWER	No.	ANSWER	No.	ANSWER	No.	ANSWER
1	Ⓐ Ⓑ Ⓒ Ⓓ	21	Ⓐ Ⓑ Ⓒ	41	Ⓐ Ⓑ Ⓒ Ⓓ	61	Ⓐ Ⓑ Ⓒ Ⓓ	81	Ⓐ Ⓑ Ⓒ Ⓓ
2	Ⓐ Ⓑ Ⓒ Ⓓ	22	Ⓐ Ⓑ Ⓒ	42	Ⓐ Ⓑ Ⓒ Ⓓ	62	Ⓐ Ⓑ Ⓒ Ⓓ	82	Ⓐ Ⓑ Ⓒ Ⓓ
3	Ⓐ Ⓑ Ⓒ Ⓓ	23	Ⓐ Ⓑ Ⓒ	43	Ⓐ Ⓑ Ⓒ Ⓓ	63	Ⓐ Ⓑ Ⓒ Ⓓ	83	Ⓐ Ⓑ Ⓒ Ⓓ
4	Ⓐ Ⓑ Ⓒ Ⓓ	24	Ⓐ Ⓑ Ⓒ	44	Ⓐ Ⓑ Ⓒ Ⓓ	64	Ⓐ Ⓑ Ⓒ Ⓓ	84	Ⓐ Ⓑ Ⓒ Ⓓ
5	Ⓐ Ⓑ Ⓒ Ⓓ	25	Ⓐ Ⓑ Ⓒ	45	Ⓐ Ⓑ Ⓒ Ⓓ	65	Ⓐ Ⓑ Ⓒ Ⓓ	85	Ⓐ Ⓑ Ⓒ Ⓓ
6	Ⓐ Ⓑ Ⓒ Ⓓ	26	Ⓐ Ⓑ Ⓒ	46	Ⓐ Ⓑ Ⓒ Ⓓ	66	Ⓐ Ⓑ Ⓒ Ⓓ	86	Ⓐ Ⓑ Ⓒ Ⓓ
7	Ⓐ Ⓑ Ⓒ Ⓓ	27	Ⓐ Ⓑ Ⓒ	47	Ⓐ Ⓑ Ⓒ Ⓓ	67	Ⓐ Ⓑ Ⓒ Ⓓ	87	Ⓐ Ⓑ Ⓒ Ⓓ
8	Ⓐ Ⓑ Ⓒ Ⓓ	28	Ⓐ Ⓑ Ⓒ	48	Ⓐ Ⓑ Ⓒ Ⓓ	68	Ⓐ Ⓑ Ⓒ Ⓓ	88	Ⓐ Ⓑ Ⓒ Ⓓ
9	Ⓐ Ⓑ Ⓒ Ⓓ	29	Ⓐ Ⓑ Ⓒ	49	Ⓐ Ⓑ Ⓒ Ⓓ	69	Ⓐ Ⓑ Ⓒ Ⓓ	89	Ⓐ Ⓑ Ⓒ Ⓓ
10	Ⓐ Ⓑ Ⓒ Ⓓ	30	Ⓐ Ⓑ Ⓒ	50	Ⓐ Ⓑ Ⓒ Ⓓ	70	Ⓐ Ⓑ Ⓒ Ⓓ	90	Ⓐ Ⓑ Ⓒ Ⓓ
11	Ⓐ Ⓑ Ⓒ Ⓓ	31	Ⓐ Ⓑ Ⓒ	51	Ⓐ Ⓑ Ⓒ Ⓓ	71	Ⓐ Ⓑ Ⓒ Ⓓ	91	Ⓐ Ⓑ Ⓒ Ⓓ
12	Ⓐ Ⓑ Ⓒ Ⓓ	32	Ⓐ Ⓑ Ⓒ	52	Ⓐ Ⓑ Ⓒ Ⓓ	72	Ⓐ Ⓑ Ⓒ Ⓓ	92	Ⓐ Ⓑ Ⓒ Ⓓ
13	Ⓐ Ⓑ Ⓒ Ⓓ	33	Ⓐ Ⓑ Ⓒ	53	Ⓐ Ⓑ Ⓒ Ⓓ	73	Ⓐ Ⓑ Ⓒ Ⓓ	93	Ⓐ Ⓑ Ⓒ Ⓓ
14	Ⓐ Ⓑ Ⓒ Ⓓ	34	Ⓐ Ⓑ Ⓒ	54	Ⓐ Ⓑ Ⓒ Ⓓ	74	Ⓐ Ⓑ Ⓒ Ⓓ	94	Ⓐ Ⓑ Ⓒ Ⓓ
15	Ⓐ Ⓑ Ⓒ Ⓓ	35	Ⓐ Ⓑ Ⓒ	55	Ⓐ Ⓑ Ⓒ Ⓓ	75	Ⓐ Ⓑ Ⓒ Ⓓ	95	Ⓐ Ⓑ Ⓒ Ⓓ
16	Ⓐ Ⓑ Ⓒ Ⓓ	36	Ⓐ Ⓑ Ⓒ	56	Ⓐ Ⓑ Ⓒ Ⓓ	76	Ⓐ Ⓑ Ⓒ Ⓓ	96	Ⓐ Ⓑ Ⓒ Ⓓ
17	Ⓐ Ⓑ Ⓒ Ⓓ	37	Ⓐ Ⓑ Ⓒ	57	Ⓐ Ⓑ Ⓒ Ⓓ	77	Ⓐ Ⓑ Ⓒ Ⓓ	97	Ⓐ Ⓑ Ⓒ Ⓓ
18	Ⓐ Ⓑ Ⓒ Ⓓ	38	Ⓐ Ⓑ Ⓒ	58	Ⓐ Ⓑ Ⓒ Ⓓ	78	Ⓐ Ⓑ Ⓒ Ⓓ	98	Ⓐ Ⓑ Ⓒ Ⓓ
19	Ⓐ Ⓑ Ⓒ Ⓓ	39	Ⓐ Ⓑ Ⓒ	59	Ⓐ Ⓑ Ⓒ Ⓓ	79	Ⓐ Ⓑ Ⓒ Ⓓ	99	Ⓐ Ⓑ Ⓒ Ⓓ
20	Ⓐ Ⓑ Ⓒ Ⓓ	40	Ⓐ Ⓑ Ⓒ	60	Ⓐ Ⓑ Ⓒ Ⓓ	80	Ⓐ Ⓑ Ⓒ Ⓓ	100	Ⓐ Ⓑ Ⓒ Ⓓ

READING COMPREHENSION (Part 5-7)

No.	ANSWER	No.	ANSWER	No.	ANSWER	No.	ANSWER	No.	ANSWER
101	Ⓐ Ⓑ Ⓒ Ⓓ	121	Ⓐ Ⓑ Ⓒ Ⓓ	141	Ⓐ Ⓑ Ⓒ Ⓓ	161	Ⓐ Ⓑ Ⓒ Ⓓ	181	Ⓐ Ⓑ Ⓒ Ⓓ
102	Ⓐ Ⓑ Ⓒ Ⓓ	122	Ⓐ Ⓑ Ⓒ Ⓓ	142	Ⓐ Ⓑ Ⓒ Ⓓ	162	Ⓐ Ⓑ Ⓒ Ⓓ	182	Ⓐ Ⓑ Ⓒ Ⓓ
103	Ⓐ Ⓑ Ⓒ Ⓓ	123	Ⓐ Ⓑ Ⓒ Ⓓ	143	Ⓐ Ⓑ Ⓒ Ⓓ	163	Ⓐ Ⓑ Ⓒ Ⓓ	183	Ⓐ Ⓑ Ⓒ Ⓓ
104	Ⓐ Ⓑ Ⓒ Ⓓ	124	Ⓐ Ⓑ Ⓒ Ⓓ	144	Ⓐ Ⓑ Ⓒ Ⓓ	164	Ⓐ Ⓑ Ⓒ Ⓓ	184	Ⓐ Ⓑ Ⓒ Ⓓ
105	Ⓐ Ⓑ Ⓒ Ⓓ	125	Ⓐ Ⓑ Ⓒ Ⓓ	145	Ⓐ Ⓑ Ⓒ Ⓓ	165	Ⓐ Ⓑ Ⓒ Ⓓ	185	Ⓐ Ⓑ Ⓒ Ⓓ
106	Ⓐ Ⓑ Ⓒ Ⓓ	126	Ⓐ Ⓑ Ⓒ Ⓓ	146	Ⓐ Ⓑ Ⓒ Ⓓ	166	Ⓐ Ⓑ Ⓒ Ⓓ	186	Ⓐ Ⓑ Ⓒ Ⓓ
107	Ⓐ Ⓑ Ⓒ Ⓓ	127	Ⓐ Ⓑ Ⓒ Ⓓ	147	Ⓐ Ⓑ Ⓒ Ⓓ	167	Ⓐ Ⓑ Ⓒ Ⓓ	187	Ⓐ Ⓑ Ⓒ Ⓓ
108	Ⓐ Ⓑ Ⓒ Ⓓ	128	Ⓐ Ⓑ Ⓒ Ⓓ	148	Ⓐ Ⓑ Ⓒ Ⓓ	168	Ⓐ Ⓑ Ⓒ Ⓓ	188	Ⓐ Ⓑ Ⓒ Ⓓ
109	Ⓐ Ⓑ Ⓒ Ⓓ	129	Ⓐ Ⓑ Ⓒ Ⓓ	149	Ⓐ Ⓑ Ⓒ Ⓓ	169	Ⓐ Ⓑ Ⓒ Ⓓ	189	Ⓐ Ⓑ Ⓒ Ⓓ
110	Ⓐ Ⓑ Ⓒ Ⓓ	130	Ⓐ Ⓑ Ⓒ Ⓓ	150	Ⓐ Ⓑ Ⓒ Ⓓ	170	Ⓐ Ⓑ Ⓒ Ⓓ	190	Ⓐ Ⓑ Ⓒ Ⓓ
111	Ⓐ Ⓑ Ⓒ Ⓓ	131	Ⓐ Ⓑ Ⓒ Ⓓ	151	Ⓐ Ⓑ Ⓒ Ⓓ	171	Ⓐ Ⓑ Ⓒ Ⓓ	191	Ⓐ Ⓑ Ⓒ Ⓓ
112	Ⓐ Ⓑ Ⓒ Ⓓ	132	Ⓐ Ⓑ Ⓒ Ⓓ	152	Ⓐ Ⓑ Ⓒ Ⓓ	172	Ⓐ Ⓑ Ⓒ Ⓓ	192	Ⓐ Ⓑ Ⓒ Ⓓ
113	Ⓐ Ⓑ Ⓒ Ⓓ	133	Ⓐ Ⓑ Ⓒ Ⓓ	153	Ⓐ Ⓑ Ⓒ Ⓓ	173	Ⓐ Ⓑ Ⓒ Ⓓ	193	Ⓐ Ⓑ Ⓒ Ⓓ
114	Ⓐ Ⓑ Ⓒ Ⓓ	134	Ⓐ Ⓑ Ⓒ Ⓓ	154	Ⓐ Ⓑ Ⓒ Ⓓ	174	Ⓐ Ⓑ Ⓒ Ⓓ	194	Ⓐ Ⓑ Ⓒ Ⓓ
115	Ⓐ Ⓑ Ⓒ Ⓓ	135	Ⓐ Ⓑ Ⓒ Ⓓ	155	Ⓐ Ⓑ Ⓒ Ⓓ	175	Ⓐ Ⓑ Ⓒ Ⓓ	195	Ⓐ Ⓑ Ⓒ Ⓓ
116	Ⓐ Ⓑ Ⓒ Ⓓ	136	Ⓐ Ⓑ Ⓒ Ⓓ	156	Ⓐ Ⓑ Ⓒ Ⓓ	176	Ⓐ Ⓑ Ⓒ Ⓓ	196	Ⓐ Ⓑ Ⓒ Ⓓ
117	Ⓐ Ⓑ Ⓒ Ⓓ	137	Ⓐ Ⓑ Ⓒ Ⓓ	157	Ⓐ Ⓑ Ⓒ Ⓓ	177	Ⓐ Ⓑ Ⓒ Ⓓ	197	Ⓐ Ⓑ Ⓒ Ⓓ
118	Ⓐ Ⓑ Ⓒ Ⓓ	138	Ⓐ Ⓑ Ⓒ Ⓓ	158	Ⓐ Ⓑ Ⓒ Ⓓ	178	Ⓐ Ⓑ Ⓒ Ⓓ	198	Ⓐ Ⓑ Ⓒ Ⓓ
119	Ⓐ Ⓑ Ⓒ Ⓓ	139	Ⓐ Ⓑ Ⓒ Ⓓ	159	Ⓐ Ⓑ Ⓒ Ⓓ	179	Ⓐ Ⓑ Ⓒ Ⓓ	199	Ⓐ Ⓑ Ⓒ Ⓓ
120	Ⓐ Ⓑ Ⓒ Ⓓ	140	Ⓐ Ⓑ Ⓒ Ⓓ	160	Ⓐ Ⓑ Ⓒ Ⓓ	180	Ⓐ Ⓑ Ⓒ Ⓓ	200	Ⓐ Ⓑ Ⓒ Ⓓ

ANSWER SHEET

TOEIC TOEIC實戰測試

准考證號碼

姓名

確認

LISTENING COMPREHENSION (Part 1-4)

No.	ANSWER	No.	ANSWER	No.	ANSWER	No.	ANSWER	No.	ANSWER
1	Ⓐ Ⓑ Ⓒ Ⓓ	21	Ⓐ Ⓑ Ⓒ	41	Ⓐ Ⓑ Ⓒ Ⓓ	61	Ⓐ Ⓑ Ⓒ Ⓓ	81	Ⓐ Ⓑ Ⓒ Ⓓ
2	Ⓐ Ⓑ Ⓒ Ⓓ	22	Ⓐ Ⓑ Ⓒ	42	Ⓐ Ⓑ Ⓒ Ⓓ	62	Ⓐ Ⓑ Ⓒ Ⓓ	82	Ⓐ Ⓑ Ⓒ Ⓓ
3	Ⓐ Ⓑ Ⓒ Ⓓ	23	Ⓐ Ⓑ Ⓒ	43	Ⓐ Ⓑ Ⓒ Ⓓ	63	Ⓐ Ⓑ Ⓒ Ⓓ	83	Ⓐ Ⓑ Ⓒ Ⓓ
4	Ⓐ Ⓑ Ⓒ Ⓓ	24	Ⓐ Ⓑ Ⓒ	44	Ⓐ Ⓑ Ⓒ Ⓓ	64	Ⓐ Ⓑ Ⓒ Ⓓ	84	Ⓐ Ⓑ Ⓒ Ⓓ
5	Ⓐ Ⓑ Ⓒ Ⓓ	25	Ⓐ Ⓑ Ⓒ	45	Ⓐ Ⓑ Ⓒ Ⓓ	65	Ⓐ Ⓑ Ⓒ Ⓓ	85	Ⓐ Ⓑ Ⓒ Ⓓ
6	Ⓐ Ⓑ Ⓒ Ⓓ	26	Ⓐ Ⓑ Ⓒ	46	Ⓐ Ⓑ Ⓒ Ⓓ	66	Ⓐ Ⓑ Ⓒ Ⓓ	86	Ⓐ Ⓑ Ⓒ Ⓓ
7	Ⓐ Ⓑ Ⓒ Ⓓ	27	Ⓐ Ⓑ Ⓒ	47	Ⓐ Ⓑ Ⓒ Ⓓ	67	Ⓐ Ⓑ Ⓒ Ⓓ	87	Ⓐ Ⓑ Ⓒ Ⓓ
8	Ⓐ Ⓑ Ⓒ Ⓓ	28	Ⓐ Ⓑ Ⓒ	48	Ⓐ Ⓑ Ⓒ Ⓓ	68	Ⓐ Ⓑ Ⓒ Ⓓ	88	Ⓐ Ⓑ Ⓒ Ⓓ
9	Ⓐ Ⓑ Ⓒ Ⓓ	29	Ⓐ Ⓑ Ⓒ	49	Ⓐ Ⓑ Ⓒ Ⓓ	69	Ⓐ Ⓑ Ⓒ Ⓓ	89	Ⓐ Ⓑ Ⓒ Ⓓ
10	Ⓐ Ⓑ Ⓒ Ⓓ	30	Ⓐ Ⓑ Ⓒ	50	Ⓐ Ⓑ Ⓒ Ⓓ	70	Ⓐ Ⓑ Ⓒ Ⓓ	90	Ⓐ Ⓑ Ⓒ Ⓓ
11	Ⓐ Ⓑ Ⓒ Ⓓ	31	Ⓐ Ⓑ Ⓒ Ⓓ	51	Ⓐ Ⓑ Ⓒ Ⓓ	71	Ⓐ Ⓑ Ⓒ Ⓓ	91	Ⓐ Ⓑ Ⓒ Ⓓ
12	Ⓐ Ⓑ Ⓒ Ⓓ	32	Ⓐ Ⓑ Ⓒ Ⓓ	52	Ⓐ Ⓑ Ⓒ Ⓓ	72	Ⓐ Ⓑ Ⓒ Ⓓ	92	Ⓐ Ⓑ Ⓒ Ⓓ
13	Ⓐ Ⓑ Ⓒ Ⓓ	33	Ⓐ Ⓑ Ⓒ Ⓓ	53	Ⓐ Ⓑ Ⓒ Ⓓ	73	Ⓐ Ⓑ Ⓒ Ⓓ	93	Ⓐ Ⓑ Ⓒ Ⓓ
14	Ⓐ Ⓑ Ⓒ Ⓓ	34	Ⓐ Ⓑ Ⓒ Ⓓ	54	Ⓐ Ⓑ Ⓒ Ⓓ	74	Ⓐ Ⓑ Ⓒ Ⓓ	94	Ⓐ Ⓑ Ⓒ Ⓓ
15	Ⓐ Ⓑ Ⓒ Ⓓ	35	Ⓐ Ⓑ Ⓒ Ⓓ	55	Ⓐ Ⓑ Ⓒ Ⓓ	75	Ⓐ Ⓑ Ⓒ Ⓓ	95	Ⓐ Ⓑ Ⓒ Ⓓ
16	Ⓐ Ⓑ Ⓒ Ⓓ	36	Ⓐ Ⓑ Ⓒ Ⓓ	56	Ⓐ Ⓑ Ⓒ Ⓓ	76	Ⓐ Ⓑ Ⓒ Ⓓ	96	Ⓐ Ⓑ Ⓒ Ⓓ
17	Ⓐ Ⓑ Ⓒ Ⓓ	37	Ⓐ Ⓑ Ⓒ Ⓓ	57	Ⓐ Ⓑ Ⓒ Ⓓ	77	Ⓐ Ⓑ Ⓒ Ⓓ	97	Ⓐ Ⓑ Ⓒ Ⓓ
18	Ⓐ Ⓑ Ⓒ Ⓓ	38	Ⓐ Ⓑ Ⓒ Ⓓ	58	Ⓐ Ⓑ Ⓒ Ⓓ	78	Ⓐ Ⓑ Ⓒ Ⓓ	98	Ⓐ Ⓑ Ⓒ Ⓓ
19	Ⓐ Ⓑ Ⓒ Ⓓ	39	Ⓐ Ⓑ Ⓒ Ⓓ	59	Ⓐ Ⓑ Ⓒ Ⓓ	79	Ⓐ Ⓑ Ⓒ Ⓓ	99	Ⓐ Ⓑ Ⓒ Ⓓ
20	Ⓐ Ⓑ Ⓒ Ⓓ	40	Ⓐ Ⓑ Ⓒ Ⓓ	60	Ⓐ Ⓑ Ⓒ Ⓓ	80	Ⓐ Ⓑ Ⓒ Ⓓ	100	Ⓐ Ⓑ Ⓒ Ⓓ

READING COMPREHENSION (Part 5-7)

No.	ANSWER	No.	ANSWER	No.	ANSWER	No.	ANSWER	No.	ANSWER
101	Ⓐ Ⓑ Ⓒ Ⓓ	121	Ⓐ Ⓑ Ⓒ Ⓓ	141	Ⓐ Ⓑ Ⓒ Ⓓ	161	Ⓐ Ⓑ Ⓒ Ⓓ	181	Ⓐ Ⓑ Ⓒ Ⓓ
102	Ⓐ Ⓑ Ⓒ Ⓓ	122	Ⓐ Ⓑ Ⓒ Ⓓ	142	Ⓐ Ⓑ Ⓒ Ⓓ	162	Ⓐ Ⓑ Ⓒ Ⓓ	182	Ⓐ Ⓑ Ⓒ Ⓓ
103	Ⓐ Ⓑ Ⓒ Ⓓ	123	Ⓐ Ⓑ Ⓒ Ⓓ	143	Ⓐ Ⓑ Ⓒ Ⓓ	163	Ⓐ Ⓑ Ⓒ Ⓓ	183	Ⓐ Ⓑ Ⓒ Ⓓ
104	Ⓐ Ⓑ Ⓒ Ⓓ	124	Ⓐ Ⓑ Ⓒ Ⓓ	144	Ⓐ Ⓑ Ⓒ Ⓓ	164	Ⓐ Ⓑ Ⓒ Ⓓ	184	Ⓐ Ⓑ Ⓒ Ⓓ
105	Ⓐ Ⓑ Ⓒ Ⓓ	125	Ⓐ Ⓑ Ⓒ Ⓓ	145	Ⓐ Ⓑ Ⓒ Ⓓ	165	Ⓐ Ⓑ Ⓒ Ⓓ	185	Ⓐ Ⓑ Ⓒ Ⓓ
106	Ⓐ Ⓑ Ⓒ Ⓓ	126	Ⓐ Ⓑ Ⓒ Ⓓ	146	Ⓐ Ⓑ Ⓒ Ⓓ	166	Ⓐ Ⓑ Ⓒ Ⓓ	186	Ⓐ Ⓑ Ⓒ Ⓓ
107	Ⓐ Ⓑ Ⓒ Ⓓ	127	Ⓐ Ⓑ Ⓒ Ⓓ	147	Ⓐ Ⓑ Ⓒ Ⓓ	167	Ⓐ Ⓑ Ⓒ Ⓓ	187	Ⓐ Ⓑ Ⓒ Ⓓ
108	Ⓐ Ⓑ Ⓒ Ⓓ	128	Ⓐ Ⓑ Ⓒ Ⓓ	148	Ⓐ Ⓑ Ⓒ Ⓓ	168	Ⓐ Ⓑ Ⓒ Ⓓ	188	Ⓐ Ⓑ Ⓒ Ⓓ
109	Ⓐ Ⓑ Ⓒ Ⓓ	129	Ⓐ Ⓑ Ⓒ Ⓓ	149	Ⓐ Ⓑ Ⓒ Ⓓ	169	Ⓐ Ⓑ Ⓒ Ⓓ	189	Ⓐ Ⓑ Ⓒ Ⓓ
110	Ⓐ Ⓑ Ⓒ Ⓓ	130	Ⓐ Ⓑ Ⓒ Ⓓ	150	Ⓐ Ⓑ Ⓒ Ⓓ	170	Ⓐ Ⓑ Ⓒ Ⓓ	190	Ⓐ Ⓑ Ⓒ Ⓓ
111	Ⓐ Ⓑ Ⓒ Ⓓ	131	Ⓐ Ⓑ Ⓒ Ⓓ	151	Ⓐ Ⓑ Ⓒ Ⓓ	171	Ⓐ Ⓑ Ⓒ Ⓓ	191	Ⓐ Ⓑ Ⓒ Ⓓ
112	Ⓐ Ⓑ Ⓒ Ⓓ	132	Ⓐ Ⓑ Ⓒ Ⓓ	152	Ⓐ Ⓑ Ⓒ Ⓓ	172	Ⓐ Ⓑ Ⓒ Ⓓ	192	Ⓐ Ⓑ Ⓒ Ⓓ
113	Ⓐ Ⓑ Ⓒ Ⓓ	133	Ⓐ Ⓑ Ⓒ Ⓓ	153	Ⓐ Ⓑ Ⓒ Ⓓ	173	Ⓐ Ⓑ Ⓒ Ⓓ	193	Ⓐ Ⓑ Ⓒ Ⓓ
114	Ⓐ Ⓑ Ⓒ Ⓓ	134	Ⓐ Ⓑ Ⓒ Ⓓ	154	Ⓐ Ⓑ Ⓒ Ⓓ	174	Ⓐ Ⓑ Ⓒ Ⓓ	194	Ⓐ Ⓑ Ⓒ Ⓓ
115	Ⓐ Ⓑ Ⓒ Ⓓ	135	Ⓐ Ⓑ Ⓒ Ⓓ	155	Ⓐ Ⓑ Ⓒ Ⓓ	175	Ⓐ Ⓑ Ⓒ Ⓓ	195	Ⓐ Ⓑ Ⓒ Ⓓ
116	Ⓐ Ⓑ Ⓒ Ⓓ	136	Ⓐ Ⓑ Ⓒ Ⓓ	156	Ⓐ Ⓑ Ⓒ Ⓓ	176	Ⓐ Ⓑ Ⓒ Ⓓ	196	Ⓐ Ⓑ Ⓒ Ⓓ
117	Ⓐ Ⓑ Ⓒ Ⓓ	137	Ⓐ Ⓑ Ⓒ Ⓓ	157	Ⓐ Ⓑ Ⓒ Ⓓ	177	Ⓐ Ⓑ Ⓒ Ⓓ	197	Ⓐ Ⓑ Ⓒ Ⓓ
118	Ⓐ Ⓑ Ⓒ Ⓓ	138	Ⓐ Ⓑ Ⓒ Ⓓ	158	Ⓐ Ⓑ Ⓒ Ⓓ	178	Ⓐ Ⓑ Ⓒ Ⓓ	198	Ⓐ Ⓑ Ⓒ Ⓓ
119	Ⓐ Ⓑ Ⓒ Ⓓ	139	Ⓐ Ⓑ Ⓒ Ⓓ	159	Ⓐ Ⓑ Ⓒ Ⓓ	179	Ⓐ Ⓑ Ⓒ Ⓓ	199	Ⓐ Ⓑ Ⓒ Ⓓ
120	Ⓐ Ⓑ Ⓒ Ⓓ	140	Ⓐ Ⓑ Ⓒ Ⓓ	160	Ⓐ Ⓑ Ⓒ Ⓓ	180	Ⓐ Ⓑ Ⓒ Ⓓ	200	Ⓐ Ⓑ Ⓒ Ⓓ

裁切線

ANSWER SHEET

TOEIC TOEIC實戰測試

裁切線

確認

准考證號碼

姓名

LISTENING COMPREHENSION (Part 1-4)

No.	ANSWER	No.	ANSWER	No.	ANSWER	No.	ANSWER	No.	ANSWER
1	(A) (B) (C) (D)	21	(A) (B) (C)	41	(A) (B) (C) (D)	61	(A) (B) (C) (D)	81	(A) (B) (C) (D)
2	(A) (B) (C) (D)	22	(A) (B) (C)	42	(A) (B) (C) (D)	62	(A) (B) (C) (D)	82	(A) (B) (C) (D)
3	(A) (B) (C) (D)	23	(A) (B) (C)	43	(A) (B) (C) (D)	63	(A) (B) (C) (D)	83	(A) (B) (C) (D)
4	(A) (B) (C) (D)	24	(A) (B) (C)	44	(A) (B) (C) (D)	64	(A) (B) (C) (D)	84	(A) (B) (C) (D)
5	(A) (B) (C) (D)	25	(A) (B) (C)	45	(A) (B) (C) (D)	65	(A) (B) (C) (D)	85	(A) (B) (C) (D)
6	(A) (B) (C) (D)	26	(A) (B) (C)	46	(A) (B) (C) (D)	66	(A) (B) (C) (D)	86	(A) (B) (C) (D)
7	(A) (B) (C) (D)	27	(A) (B) (C)	47	(A) (B) (C) (D)	67	(A) (B) (C) (D)	87	(A) (B) (C) (D)
8	(A) (B) (C) (D)	28	(A) (B) (C)	48	(A) (B) (C) (D)	68	(A) (B) (C) (D)	88	(A) (B) (C) (D)
9	(A) (B) (C) (D)	29	(A) (B) (C)	49	(A) (B) (C) (D)	69	(A) (B) (C) (D)	89	(A) (B) (C) (D)
10	(A) (B) (C) (D)	30	(A) (B) (C)	50	(A) (B) (C) (D)	70	(A) (B) (C) (D)	90	(A) (B) (C) (D)
11	(A) (B) (C) (D)	31	(A) (B) (C)	51	(A) (B) (C) (D)	71	(A) (B) (C) (D)	91	(A) (B) (C) (D)
12	(A) (B) (C) (D)	32	(A) (B) (C)	52	(A) (B) (C) (D)	72	(A) (B) (C) (D)	92	(A) (B) (C) (D)
13	(A) (B) (C) (D)	33	(A) (B) (C)	53	(A) (B) (C) (D)	73	(A) (B) (C) (D)	93	(A) (B) (C) (D)
14	(A) (B) (C) (D)	34	(A) (B) (C)	54	(A) (B) (C) (D)	74	(A) (B) (C) (D)	94	(A) (B) (C) (D)
15	(A) (B) (C) (D)	35	(A) (B) (C)	55	(A) (B) (C) (D)	75	(A) (B) (C) (D)	95	(A) (B) (C) (D)
16	(A) (B) (C) (D)	36	(A) (B) (C)	56	(A) (B) (C) (D)	76	(A) (B) (C) (D)	96	(A) (B) (C) (D)
17	(A) (B) (C) (D)	37	(A) (B) (C)	57	(A) (B) (C) (D)	77	(A) (B) (C) (D)	97	(A) (B) (C) (D)
18	(A) (B) (C) (D)	38	(A) (B) (C)	58	(A) (B) (C) (D)	78	(A) (B) (C) (D)	98	(A) (B) (C) (D)
19	(A) (B) (C) (D)	39	(A) (B) (C)	59	(A) (B) (C) (D)	79	(A) (B) (C) (D)	99	(A) (B) (C) (D)
20	(A) (B) (C) (D)	40	(A) (B) (C)	60	(A) (B) (C) (D)	80	(A) (B) (C) (D)	100	(A) (B) (C) (D)

READING COMPREHENSION (Part 5-7)

No.	ANSWER	No.	ANSWER	No.	ANSWER	No.	ANSWER	No.	ANSWER
101	(A) (B) (C) (D)	121	(A) (B) (C) (D)	141	(A) (B) (C) (D)	161	(A) (B) (C) (D)	181	(A) (B) (C) (D)
102	(A) (B) (C) (D)	122	(A) (B) (C) (D)	142	(A) (B) (C) (D)	162	(A) (B) (C) (D)	182	(A) (B) (C) (D)
103	(A) (B) (C) (D)	123	(A) (B) (C) (D)	143	(A) (B) (C) (D)	163	(A) (B) (C) (D)	183	(A) (B) (C) (D)
104	(A) (B) (C) (D)	124	(A) (B) (C) (D)	144	(A) (B) (C) (D)	164	(A) (B) (C) (D)	184	(A) (B) (C) (D)
105	(A) (B) (C) (D)	125	(A) (B) (C) (D)	145	(A) (B) (C) (D)	165	(A) (B) (C) (D)	185	(A) (B) (C) (D)
106	(A) (B) (C) (D)	126	(A) (B) (C) (D)	146	(A) (B) (C) (D)	166	(A) (B) (C) (D)	186	(A) (B) (C) (D)
107	(A) (B) (C) (D)	127	(A) (B) (C) (D)	147	(A) (B) (C) (D)	167	(A) (B) (C) (D)	187	(A) (B) (C) (D)
108	(A) (B) (C) (D)	128	(A) (B) (C) (D)	148	(A) (B) (C) (D)	168	(A) (B) (C) (D)	188	(A) (B) (C) (D)
109	(A) (B) (C) (D)	129	(A) (B) (C) (D)	149	(A) (B) (C) (D)	169	(A) (B) (C) (D)	189	(A) (B) (C) (D)
110	(A) (B) (C) (D)	130	(A) (B) (C) (D)	150	(A) (B) (C) (D)	170	(A) (B) (C) (D)	190	(A) (B) (C) (D)
111	(A) (B) (C) (D)	131	(A) (B) (C) (D)	151	(A) (B) (C) (D)	171	(A) (B) (C) (D)	191	(A) (B) (C) (D)
112	(A) (B) (C) (D)	132	(A) (B) (C) (D)	152	(A) (B) (C) (D)	172	(A) (B) (C) (D)	192	(A) (B) (C) (D)
113	(A) (B) (C) (D)	133	(A) (B) (C) (D)	153	(A) (B) (C) (D)	173	(A) (B) (C) (D)	193	(A) (B) (C) (D)
114	(A) (B) (C) (D)	134	(A) (B) (C) (D)	154	(A) (B) (C) (D)	174	(A) (B) (C) (D)	194	(A) (B) (C) (D)
115	(A) (B) (C) (D)	135	(A) (B) (C) (D)	155	(A) (B) (C) (D)	175	(A) (B) (C) (D)	195	(A) (B) (C) (D)
116	(A) (B) (C) (D)	136	(A) (B) (C) (D)	156	(A) (B) (C) (D)	176	(A) (B) (C) (D)	196	(A) (B) (C) (D)
117	(A) (B) (C) (D)	137	(A) (B) (C) (D)	157	(A) (B) (C) (D)	177	(A) (B) (C) (D)	197	(A) (B) (C) (D)
118	(A) (B) (C) (D)	138	(A) (B) (C) (D)	158	(A) (B) (C) (D)	178	(A) (B) (C) (D)	198	(A) (B) (C) (D)
119	(A) (B) (C) (D)	139	(A) (B) (C) (D)	159	(A) (B) (C) (D)	179	(A) (B) (C) (D)	199	(A) (B) (C) (D)
120	(A) (B) (C) (D)	140	(A) (B) (C) (D)	160	(A) (B) (C) (D)	180	(A) (B) (C) (D)	200	(A) (B) (C) (D)

ANSWER SHEET

確認

TOEIC TOEIC實戰測試

准考證號碼

姓名

確認

LISTENING COMPREHENSION (Part 1-4)

No.	ANSWER	No.	ANSWER	No.	ANSWER	No.	ANSWER	No.	ANSWER
1	Ⓐ Ⓑ Ⓒ Ⓓ	21	Ⓐ Ⓑ Ⓒ	41	Ⓐ Ⓑ Ⓒ Ⓓ	61	Ⓐ Ⓑ Ⓒ Ⓓ	81	Ⓐ Ⓑ Ⓒ Ⓓ
2	Ⓐ Ⓑ Ⓒ Ⓓ	22	Ⓐ Ⓑ Ⓒ	42	Ⓐ Ⓑ Ⓒ Ⓓ	62	Ⓐ Ⓑ Ⓒ Ⓓ	82	Ⓐ Ⓑ Ⓒ Ⓓ
3	Ⓐ Ⓑ Ⓒ Ⓓ	23	Ⓐ Ⓑ Ⓒ	43	Ⓐ Ⓑ Ⓒ Ⓓ	63	Ⓐ Ⓑ Ⓒ Ⓓ	83	Ⓐ Ⓑ Ⓒ Ⓓ
4	Ⓐ Ⓑ Ⓒ Ⓓ	24	Ⓐ Ⓑ Ⓒ	44	Ⓐ Ⓑ Ⓒ Ⓓ	64	Ⓐ Ⓑ Ⓒ Ⓓ	84	Ⓐ Ⓑ Ⓒ Ⓓ
5	Ⓐ Ⓑ Ⓒ Ⓓ	25	Ⓐ Ⓑ Ⓒ	45	Ⓐ Ⓑ Ⓒ Ⓓ	65	Ⓐ Ⓑ Ⓒ Ⓓ	85	Ⓐ Ⓑ Ⓒ Ⓓ
6	Ⓐ Ⓑ Ⓒ Ⓓ	26	Ⓐ Ⓑ Ⓒ	46	Ⓐ Ⓑ Ⓒ Ⓓ	66	Ⓐ Ⓑ Ⓒ Ⓓ	86	Ⓐ Ⓑ Ⓒ Ⓓ
7	Ⓐ Ⓑ Ⓒ	27	Ⓐ Ⓑ Ⓒ	47	Ⓐ Ⓑ Ⓒ Ⓓ	67	Ⓐ Ⓑ Ⓒ Ⓓ	87	Ⓐ Ⓑ Ⓒ Ⓓ
8	Ⓐ Ⓑ Ⓒ	28	Ⓐ Ⓑ Ⓒ	48	Ⓐ Ⓑ Ⓒ Ⓓ	68	Ⓐ Ⓑ Ⓒ Ⓓ	88	Ⓐ Ⓑ Ⓒ Ⓓ
9	Ⓐ Ⓑ Ⓒ	29	Ⓐ Ⓑ Ⓒ	49	Ⓐ Ⓑ Ⓒ Ⓓ	69	Ⓐ Ⓑ Ⓒ Ⓓ	89	Ⓐ Ⓑ Ⓒ Ⓓ
10	Ⓐ Ⓑ Ⓒ	30	Ⓐ Ⓑ Ⓒ	50	Ⓐ Ⓑ Ⓒ Ⓓ	70	Ⓐ Ⓑ Ⓒ Ⓓ	90	Ⓐ Ⓑ Ⓒ Ⓓ
11	Ⓐ Ⓑ Ⓒ	31	Ⓐ Ⓑ Ⓒ	51	Ⓐ Ⓑ Ⓒ Ⓓ	71	Ⓐ Ⓑ Ⓒ Ⓓ	91	Ⓐ Ⓑ Ⓒ Ⓓ
12	Ⓐ Ⓑ Ⓒ	32	Ⓐ Ⓑ Ⓒ Ⓓ	52	Ⓐ Ⓑ Ⓒ Ⓓ	72	Ⓐ Ⓑ Ⓒ Ⓓ	92	Ⓐ Ⓑ Ⓒ Ⓓ
13	Ⓐ Ⓑ Ⓒ	33	Ⓐ Ⓑ Ⓒ Ⓓ	53	Ⓐ Ⓑ Ⓒ Ⓓ	73	Ⓐ Ⓑ Ⓒ Ⓓ	93	Ⓐ Ⓑ Ⓒ Ⓓ
14	Ⓐ Ⓑ Ⓒ	34	Ⓐ Ⓑ Ⓒ Ⓓ	54	Ⓐ Ⓑ Ⓒ Ⓓ	74	Ⓐ Ⓑ Ⓒ Ⓓ	94	Ⓐ Ⓑ Ⓒ Ⓓ
15	Ⓐ Ⓑ Ⓒ	35	Ⓐ Ⓑ Ⓒ Ⓓ	55	Ⓐ Ⓑ Ⓒ Ⓓ	75	Ⓐ Ⓑ Ⓒ Ⓓ	95	Ⓐ Ⓑ Ⓒ Ⓓ
16	Ⓐ Ⓑ Ⓒ	36	Ⓐ Ⓑ Ⓒ Ⓓ	56	Ⓐ Ⓑ Ⓒ Ⓓ	76	Ⓐ Ⓑ Ⓒ Ⓓ	96	Ⓐ Ⓑ Ⓒ Ⓓ
17	Ⓐ Ⓑ Ⓒ	37	Ⓐ Ⓑ Ⓒ Ⓓ	57	Ⓐ Ⓑ Ⓒ Ⓓ	77	Ⓐ Ⓑ Ⓒ Ⓓ	97	Ⓐ Ⓑ Ⓒ Ⓓ
18	Ⓐ Ⓑ Ⓒ	38	Ⓐ Ⓑ Ⓒ Ⓓ	58	Ⓐ Ⓑ Ⓒ Ⓓ	78	Ⓐ Ⓑ Ⓒ Ⓓ	98	Ⓐ Ⓑ Ⓒ Ⓓ
19	Ⓐ Ⓑ Ⓒ	39	Ⓐ Ⓑ Ⓒ Ⓓ	59	Ⓐ Ⓑ Ⓒ Ⓓ	79	Ⓐ Ⓑ Ⓒ Ⓓ	99	Ⓐ Ⓑ Ⓒ Ⓓ
20	Ⓐ Ⓑ Ⓒ	40	Ⓐ Ⓑ Ⓒ Ⓓ	60	Ⓐ Ⓑ Ⓒ Ⓓ	80	Ⓐ Ⓑ Ⓒ Ⓓ	100	Ⓐ Ⓑ Ⓒ Ⓓ

READING COMPREHENSION (Part 5-7)

No.	ANSWER	No.	ANSWER	No.	ANSWER	No.	ANSWER	No.	ANSWER
101	Ⓐ Ⓑ Ⓒ Ⓓ	121	Ⓐ Ⓑ Ⓒ Ⓓ	141	Ⓐ Ⓑ Ⓒ Ⓓ	161	Ⓐ Ⓑ Ⓒ Ⓓ	181	Ⓐ Ⓑ Ⓒ Ⓓ
102	Ⓐ Ⓑ Ⓒ Ⓓ	122	Ⓐ Ⓑ Ⓒ Ⓓ	142	Ⓐ Ⓑ Ⓒ Ⓓ	162	Ⓐ Ⓑ Ⓒ Ⓓ	182	Ⓐ Ⓑ Ⓒ Ⓓ
103	Ⓐ Ⓑ Ⓒ Ⓓ	123	Ⓐ Ⓑ Ⓒ Ⓓ	143	Ⓐ Ⓑ Ⓒ Ⓓ	163	Ⓐ Ⓑ Ⓒ Ⓓ	183	Ⓐ Ⓑ Ⓒ Ⓓ
104	Ⓐ Ⓑ Ⓒ Ⓓ	124	Ⓐ Ⓑ Ⓒ Ⓓ	144	Ⓐ Ⓑ Ⓒ Ⓓ	164	Ⓐ Ⓑ Ⓒ Ⓓ	184	Ⓐ Ⓑ Ⓒ Ⓓ
105	Ⓐ Ⓑ Ⓒ Ⓓ	125	Ⓐ Ⓑ Ⓒ Ⓓ	145	Ⓐ Ⓑ Ⓒ Ⓓ	165	Ⓐ Ⓑ Ⓒ Ⓓ	185	Ⓐ Ⓑ Ⓒ Ⓓ
106	Ⓐ Ⓑ Ⓒ Ⓓ	126	Ⓐ Ⓑ Ⓒ Ⓓ	146	Ⓐ Ⓑ Ⓒ Ⓓ	166	Ⓐ Ⓑ Ⓒ Ⓓ	186	Ⓐ Ⓑ Ⓒ Ⓓ
107	Ⓐ Ⓑ Ⓒ Ⓓ	127	Ⓐ Ⓑ Ⓒ Ⓓ	147	Ⓐ Ⓑ Ⓒ Ⓓ	167	Ⓐ Ⓑ Ⓒ Ⓓ	187	Ⓐ Ⓑ Ⓒ Ⓓ
108	Ⓐ Ⓑ Ⓒ Ⓓ	128	Ⓐ Ⓑ Ⓒ Ⓓ	148	Ⓐ Ⓑ Ⓒ Ⓓ	168	Ⓐ Ⓑ Ⓒ Ⓓ	188	Ⓐ Ⓑ Ⓒ Ⓓ
109	Ⓐ Ⓑ Ⓒ Ⓓ	129	Ⓐ Ⓑ Ⓒ Ⓓ	149	Ⓐ Ⓑ Ⓒ Ⓓ	169	Ⓐ Ⓑ Ⓒ Ⓓ	189	Ⓐ Ⓑ Ⓒ Ⓓ
110	Ⓐ Ⓑ Ⓒ Ⓓ	130	Ⓐ Ⓑ Ⓒ Ⓓ	150	Ⓐ Ⓑ Ⓒ Ⓓ	170	Ⓐ Ⓑ Ⓒ Ⓓ	190	Ⓐ Ⓑ Ⓒ Ⓓ
111	Ⓐ Ⓑ Ⓒ Ⓓ	131	Ⓐ Ⓑ Ⓒ Ⓓ	151	Ⓐ Ⓑ Ⓒ Ⓓ	171	Ⓐ Ⓑ Ⓒ Ⓓ	191	Ⓐ Ⓑ Ⓒ Ⓓ
112	Ⓐ Ⓑ Ⓒ Ⓓ	132	Ⓐ Ⓑ Ⓒ Ⓓ	152	Ⓐ Ⓑ Ⓒ Ⓓ	172	Ⓐ Ⓑ Ⓒ Ⓓ	192	Ⓐ Ⓑ Ⓒ Ⓓ
113	Ⓐ Ⓑ Ⓒ Ⓓ	133	Ⓐ Ⓑ Ⓒ Ⓓ	153	Ⓐ Ⓑ Ⓒ Ⓓ	173	Ⓐ Ⓑ Ⓒ Ⓓ	193	Ⓐ Ⓑ Ⓒ Ⓓ
114	Ⓐ Ⓑ Ⓒ Ⓓ	134	Ⓐ Ⓑ Ⓒ Ⓓ	154	Ⓐ Ⓑ Ⓒ Ⓓ	174	Ⓐ Ⓑ Ⓒ Ⓓ	194	Ⓐ Ⓑ Ⓒ Ⓓ
115	Ⓐ Ⓑ Ⓒ Ⓓ	135	Ⓐ Ⓑ Ⓒ Ⓓ	155	Ⓐ Ⓑ Ⓒ Ⓓ	175	Ⓐ Ⓑ Ⓒ Ⓓ	195	Ⓐ Ⓑ Ⓒ Ⓓ
116	Ⓐ Ⓑ Ⓒ Ⓓ	136	Ⓐ Ⓑ Ⓒ Ⓓ	156	Ⓐ Ⓑ Ⓒ Ⓓ	176	Ⓐ Ⓑ Ⓒ Ⓓ	196	Ⓐ Ⓑ Ⓒ Ⓓ
117	Ⓐ Ⓑ Ⓒ Ⓓ	137	Ⓐ Ⓑ Ⓒ Ⓓ	157	Ⓐ Ⓑ Ⓒ Ⓓ	177	Ⓐ Ⓑ Ⓒ Ⓓ	197	Ⓐ Ⓑ Ⓒ Ⓓ
118	Ⓐ Ⓑ Ⓒ Ⓓ	138	Ⓐ Ⓑ Ⓒ Ⓓ	158	Ⓐ Ⓑ Ⓒ Ⓓ	178	Ⓐ Ⓑ Ⓒ Ⓓ	198	Ⓐ Ⓑ Ⓒ Ⓓ
119	Ⓐ Ⓑ Ⓒ Ⓓ	139	Ⓐ Ⓑ Ⓒ Ⓓ	159	Ⓐ Ⓑ Ⓒ Ⓓ	179	Ⓐ Ⓑ Ⓒ Ⓓ	199	Ⓐ Ⓑ Ⓒ Ⓓ
120	Ⓐ Ⓑ Ⓒ Ⓓ	140	Ⓐ Ⓑ Ⓒ Ⓓ	160	Ⓐ Ⓑ Ⓒ Ⓓ	180	Ⓐ Ⓑ Ⓒ Ⓓ	200	Ⓐ Ⓑ Ⓒ Ⓓ

NEW 新制多益

TOEIC

閱讀5回

全真模擬試題 ＋ 詳盡解析

★★★ 解析本 ★★★